THE ASCENSION TRILOGY

BOOK ONE:

CLOUDBUSTING

Enn Kae

ISBN: 978-90-833526-3-3

This book is dedicated to the two angels in my life:

my sister, with her violet-white light and my better half, who holds all the colors.

Chapter 1

Fata Morgana

Jan Lam always knew that nothing in this world was what it seemed. That was confirmed to her by accident. Until then, she was happy going through her life, living it unassumingly. But she always felt at odds with the world, as if it was a fabrication, as if she was watching a constructed version of someone else's reality. She always felt it but couldn't put her finger on it, like the time she spotted a glitch in the matrix whilst sipping tea from the porch of her first-floor apartment in Santa Clara, California.

Down the street from where she sat, on her porch, she saw the traffic lights turn, and the cars lined up, and a boy on his bike waited to cross. When she peered up from her cup of tea, the boy had crossed the street. But, not from the spot where he had originally approached the crossing, moments prior. The boy was returning to the place he originally stood, at the traffic lights. It was as if Jan was seeing him through a mirror, as if she was watching a movie that was rewinding the event.

Jan shook her head and didn't think too much of it, certain that she had herself confused because there was no other explanation for the boy on the bike - how he could have moved from one side of the street to the one opposite, in the blink of an eye, and then proceed to cross it back, to his original spot, as if he was walking back on himself, as if he had forgotten something, before crossing it in the first place. Jan shook her head and continued to drink her tea, forgetting all about the trick of the eye, and began to settle down for the weekend after a long week of work. The phone rang, breaking her train of thought:

"Hey, girl, what are you up to?" asked the caller. It was her bestie, Susan.

"Nothing. And you? What you got going on?" sounded Jan.

"Oh, nothing," said Susan.

"Same here..." echoed Jan: "you know - broke as! Saving up for my trip to Egypt," she continued, enthused about her imminent plans. Whilst she welcomed the telephone call, Jan didn't really have much to say. It annoyed her somewhat, to be reminded of the sacrifice she had to make, to have the holiday she wanted. It was for that reason, Jan resented knowing what would come next:

"Girl, do you want to go out tomorrow?" asked Susan.

"Well, as long as it doesn't cost more than 20 bucks!" explained Jan, hoping Susan would take the hint and hang up. Once Jan set her sights on something, nothing was going to stand in her way. She was determined not to dip into her savings, for the trip of a lifetime to Egypt, definitely not for a night out in the college-town where she lived, in Santa Clara.

"Girl, I gotchu!" reassured Susan. Susan was well aware of Jan's obsessive nature when it came to saving, or anything else she set her sights on, for that matter.

"Nah, don't worry. Imma stay in." said Jan, firmly.

"Okay, I'll tell you what. I'll come to you and we'll have a nice girly night in. I'll bring some goodies," suggested Susan, undeterred. Susan was known to be persistent, unlike her friend Jan, who just wanted to do her own thing at her own pace and in her own time. But Jan was always easily swayed by her good friends.

"Okay, girl, you're on," said Jan, happy at the possibility of a cheap Friday night, with her bestie.

Jan then hung up the phone in her apartment in Santa Clara, California, after a long week as an administrator at one of the town's university buildings. She led an innocuous life, in an innocuous town, surrounded by streets that were lined with sheltering trees that shaded the sidewalks and supplied the residents with respite from the summer heat. The center of Santa Clara housed boutiques and weekend farmer's markets that Jan often frequented just to get out of her tiny one-bedroom apartment.

Though Jan often looked around, she never bought any items from the boutiques. She did, however, indulge in other sensual pleasures. The supply of fresh goods from the farmer's markets was too good for Jan to pass and she proudly stuck to her monthly food budget, whilst frequenting the farmers' markets.

Jan breathed a sigh of relief that her week ended. When she entered her apartment, Jan readily kicked back into a carbohydrate-induced coma of loaded potato wedges and a burger, followed by spoonfuls of Ben and Jerry's. The day had been hard on Jan, and she waited for the sugars to kick in and the sleep to take over, sending her into a deep nap, before she would wake 30 minutes later, feeling sick from the nap, annoyed with herself for having eaten badly for her condition - type 2 diabetes.

It was a condition Jan hated since being diagnosed with it, but she did her best to not let it run or ruin her life. Despite the strict regime that she put herself through, with a restricted diet and 10,000 steps a day, there were moments when Jan Lam needed the comfort of sugars to envelop her, especially after a difficult week.

And it had been a difficult week. Her manager let her get on with her work but sometimes could be overbearing, sometimes piling on more work than was necessary or justified. It didn't sit well with Jan's amiable disposition. She was too polite to say anything, to fight back, or raise a query. It was a part of her that annoyed her but she knew it came from her upbringing - from a Vietnamese Mother and a Chinese Father - who both instilled in her the pillars of obedience and duty, values which she was taught to uphold, to the detriment of her own development in a world which valued some protest of autonomy.

Her manager relied on Jan Lam's painful submissions, whilst her white American colleagues breezed through their days without any burdens, at least not the ones she carried, albeit from Jan's own arrested development. Jan Lam was often hard on herself for it, and she would let her feelings boil up under a pressure cooker, before erupting on the phone to her best friends, often for hours at a time. Her friends were very patient. Luckily, Jan had a few sympathetic friends, one of whom decided to save alongside her, for her once-in-a-lifetime trip to Egypt. They had been saving for 2 years and the departure date wasn't too far away.

For now, Jan had to spend another night alone in her tiny apartment in Santa Clara, which was tucked away on the outskirts of the university campus. She had spent time in the 6 years she lived there, since taking a job at the university, to get accustomed to her cramped surroundings, whilst living on a meager administrator's salary. It was a relatively humble life, compared with the students and professors, who lived a lot better than she did. Some did, at least. The only thing that kept her ticking over was the money she slowly accumulated for her trips abroad. Jan took a trip every two years and she relished them because she managed to forget all about her awkward drudgery, back in Santa Clara, for a couple of weeks a year.

Jan sat to try and enjoy her evening in the summer heat, with a thermostat that tried to touch 100 degrees. She frequently repositioned on her sofa, eventually opting to sit on the tiled floor of her cramped kitchenette, as the AC attempted to fight off the heat. The balcony above the veranda of her first floor apartment only provided a little cover in the sun-drenched, south-easternly side, so sitting outside on her veranda didn't help her much. She would have to grit her teeth and bear it. Sweat it out a little. Perhaps take a cold shower before bed.

It was a cycle that would get repeated throughout the summer. Jan fell asleep on the kitchenette floor, as the TV continued to play in front of her, in the living room next to the kitchenette, with a mixture of game shows - Double Jeopardy and The Price is Right drolled on into the night. Jan liked the sound of the male presenters, who flashed a kind smile and cracked dad jokes over fatherly tones.

Monday came and the weekend went. Jan had to get up early to attend a meeting at work, which had been scheduled a month earlier, as part of the recent overhaul of duties that was organized by her ever watchful micro-manager, named Karen. At least Jan got to leave early, which made her happy, even though it meant facing a 30-minute walk home in the begrudging heat. Saving a few pennies by not taking a bus ride would make her trip-of-a-lifetime more fun, and Jan always got by on dimes. Fortunately, the trees cooled the streets that day and Jan stopped off for a nice iced latte on the way home, since her sugar levels permitted the indulgence.

The meeting that morning went by without a glitch and Jan accepted her new duties without negotiation or fuss. The Professor in attendance that morning insisted that he help her out. *"There's no need"*, she answered. Jan would be fine if she was just shown what to do.

Her new tasks mainly involved working with the Professor of the History department, to assemble student information for the new curriculum. It was the dogsbody work that everybody avoided doing and, since it was the Professor's undertaking to overhaul the curriculum, Jan Lam begrudgingly accepted the challenge of sorting out the Professor's administrative mess.

Not everyone in the History department was pleased with the overhaul of the curriculum, and the Professor had made some enemies. Jan Lam took pity on him and hoped for more responsibility in the future, pending the success of the Professor's project, so she accepted the new tasks with vigor. Deep down, Jan resented taking on more tasks than her burdens would allow, and couldn't think of anything more than her imminent trip to Egypt.

Jan wasn't looking forward to her first meeting with the Professor. He was a lanky fella, with short brown curly hair, a square jaw, and green eyes hidden behind large brown frames. Under normal circumstances, Jan Lam's short stature would have complimented his tall frame but his personality, or lack thereof, repulsed her. He spoke to most colleagues as if they were stupid and that's why nobody really wanted to work with him.

It was the main reason Jan was seconded to do the work, not least because she was good at dealing with irritating individuals, with her general, non-reactive demeanor. Jan sat with her new colleague and felt a twinge in the pit of her stomach. The Professor began by listing all the things he would like to get done, along with a timeline of deadlines. As soon as Jan had taken all the details and finished asking the Professor questions, she prepared to leave when he interrupted with:

"Are you okay with all of this?"

Jan responded in her typical manner, by putting her head down and quipping a *"yes"* before scurrying out the door.

As Jan walked the corridor in the university building after her meeting, she winced with regret - at all the words she wished she had spoken - just like all the other times she never spoke up, for fear of losing a promotion or being overlooked for an extra challenge that might tax her intelligence. The only thing that held Jan Lam back in life was a degree and she knew that having one would see her wipe the floor with her colleagues. She pitied them. Instead of allowing herself to feel intimidated by them, though some of them liked to throw their intellectual weight around and treat her as if she was less intelligent, Jan Lam always put her intelligence to better uses - like reading up on ancient civilizations, exploring undiscovered territories and keeping a blog of all her travels.

By the time Jan returned to her office that day, after her meeting with Jonah, the Professor of History, Jan's manager pulled her into her office for a quick chat:

"Hey, Jonah said you were pretty quiet during your meeting with him," said Karen, bullishly, her red hair peaking into a bee-hive.

"I've just returned. He gave me a list of the things he wanted and I took notes and I asked him a couple of questions and that was it. I don't understand what he means?" responded Jan, non-reactively.

"He says he sensed you aren't happy doing this," quipped Karen, with tense lips.

"I don't know what he senses and I can't do anything about that, Karen. I already agreed to it and I've already met with him to cover what needs to be done and how it will be done so I don't know what else to say to you, Karen."

Karen shrugged her shoulders, knowing that she couldn't pursue her line of bullying any further and responded with: "okay, perhaps he's just feeling nervous about the changes he wants to make."

"Yeah, maybe," responded Jan and flashed a nonchalant glance at Karen, whose cheeks appeared to grow red around the edges.

As soon as Karen left the office, Jan put her hands on her face, breathed a deep sigh of air-conditioned Californian air and continued about her day. She felt mad, whenever she had to face all the false projections, all the accusations, that were designed to manipulate her. But she was becoming wise to the gaslighting in her professional life, after spending the majority of her life being guilted into doing things she really didn't want to do, such as working in the family restaurant when she just wanted to hang out with her school friends.

After some soul-searching, Jan always came back to the same conclusion whenever she was thrown off her center - that she was in a work environment that was populated by inadequate idiots and she just needed to leave. Either that, or she just needed a break. And Jan would get that break soon, having saved her vacation time since the last time she took a break, which was two years prior, when she went on a trip to Europe with friends. They explored London, then Paris, then Amsterdam, before a brief trip to Copenhagen ended their tour. Jan was now ready for another adventure - her forthcoming holiday to Egypt.

That night, she rang up her other bestie, for a catch-up. Toni, a near middle-aged gay black man, whom Jan loved as a dear brother, was almost ten years her senior. He was always there on the other side of the phone, to pick her up and guide her, at times whenever she felt unable to cope with life's peculiar unfairness. Jan Lam knew that the way she was treated in life was partly due to her own inability to set boundaries. Nevertheless, she couldn't help but feel that the way she was treated at work had nothing to do with her skills as an employee. It was something she felt after exhausting all other possibilities - and she wasn't just imagining it.

In a moment of pure exhaustion with what she continuously experienced, Jan resigned to tell herself that she was just being bullied so that she would leave. It was only her obstinate nature which kept her stuck in the same situation. It was always at the moment when Jan accepted her fate when Toni added fuel to the fire with his soundbite: *"white people, eh!,"* he would often say.

Jan had some things to iron out with her travel companion Toni, such as accommodation, itinerary and expenditure. Toni had been looking forward to the trip, since he wasn't able to join Jan's previous trip to Europe. It was a combination of a lack of interest in the places they wanted to visit and lack of finances, so Toni started saving as soon as Jan returned from Europe and proposed Egypt as their next destination. After her complaints of the day on the phone ended, Jan and Toni discussed and spoke at length and in detail about everything they wanted to cover.

Jan was a meticulous planner, and Toni was easy-going enough to compliment her controlling nature. They both looked forward to their trip in the coming month. After ending the call, Jan finished some chores before settling into another muggy evening in her cramped apartment, to watch a couple of travel videos on youtube about Egypt. That night, Jan dreamt of Cleopatra and the dynasties of the Ancient Egyptians.

Friday rolled forward and Susan called round with her bottle of white wine. They sat on the veranda, in Ikea rocking chairs and had their usual giggle at their anecdotes about their interactions with the world, since they last saw each other. The way they were spoken to and were treated and the things they had to deal with, in an increasingly hostile and terrible world, provided them with ample material for hours of comic relief.

The fact that Susan shared similar experiences with Jan, made Jan feel a bit better. It was nothing personal, it's just the way their world was, surmised Jan. Susan dealt with the same issues as a receptionist at a doctor's surgery, where she worked. Susan was not immune to assholes, she would say, not even as a white woman. Then they both laughed off their experiences in unison.

That evening, Susan and Jan made a pact - that they would make a trip together somewhere, after Jan's trip with Toni to Egypt ended. Toni would not be able to save for another trip after returning from Egypt, after he moved into his new house, which would leave him house-poor for a couple of years. Susan, on the other hand, lived as frugally as Jan did, also in a one-bed apartment, and she too was yearning for the trip of a lifetime that Toni and Jan were about to experience.

Jan was always grateful for a travel buddy, and Susan would be a welcome partner for a future trip to Cambodia. For now, Susan and Jan enjoyed the balmy Californian Friday evening together, on Jan's veranda and chatted about everything under the sun and laughed at the absurdity of the people they encountered in their world. As they laughed, Jan couldn't help but wonder about the boy on the bike, who randomly appeared on the wrong side of the road when she sat and drank her tea the other day. It began to bug her, but she didn't pay it too much mind. Before Susan left that Friday evening, Jan invited her to have coffee with her and Toni the following week.

The next week rolled on, as expected. Jan got to grips with the new project with her new colleague, Jonah. Jonah irked Jan, but she took refuge in knowing that being an irritating prick was part of his genetic makeup and it wasn't anything personal. The problem was compounded by Jonah's inability to make himself affable towards Jan. Never letting his guard down, Jonah was always on the defensive and spoke to her as if she was his maid.

After the first day with him, Jan returned home and ate herself silly to comfort herself. She made a promise to herself that she would try a different strategy, instead of returning to the same condition and problem every day. So, the next day, Jan took some home-cooked doughnuts to work with her. Jonah took what was offered, ate them slovenly, licked his fingers and made a few chortled grunts and spoke, asking almost out of necessity:

"So.... how are you finding your new department?"

Unsurprised at the lack of gratitude Jonah expressed from receiving the fruits of her labor, Jan shrugged her shoulders and replied: "it's going well so far, as far as I can say about my second day here!" Jan was careful not to sound sarcastic because she was sure she would be hearing about it later from Karen. Using her foresight, Jan quickly followed up her response by saying - "I'm looking forward to working with you, I'm sure it will be quite challenging… " - but then had to check herself again because she became aware of her undertone. Noticing her gaff, she quickly said: "... and I am so looking forward to learning from you." Jan's apparent attempt at charming Jonah fell flat, when he simply responded with:

"Please don't say 'sooooo' looking forward. That's a vulgar American quantifier," before miming *I am looking forward to working with you* to Jan, as if she was in kindergarten.

Jan put her head down and wanted to breathe a deep sigh but was immediately filled with a burning anger instead. She stepped out of the small office that accommodated 6 employees at various stages of hot-desking, and headed towards the lady's down the hall, where she entered and screamed into her blouse in the cubicle. She did not want to spend another moment with Jonah, let alone months. Maybe she could bring it up with Karen, she thought. But then, she thought again. Her appraisal was due soon and that could make it difficult for her to keep her job, since she was always a target for gaslighting. She opted to seek advice from her friends when she returned home, in an attempt to diffuse her growing anxiety.

That night, Jan didn't sleep well. She had another four days of work to endure and she was beginning to fall into the trap she often found herself in - internalizing her experience until she was riddled with anxiety. She tossed and turned that night, thinking about all the things she should have said or the way she should have handled Jonah then beat herself up relentlessly whilst doing so, falling into deeper states of anxiety until she was completely worn out by 4 am.

Jan managed to get a couple of hours' sleep before her alarm whistled her out of bed again. She returned to work that Wednesday, with little anticipation of encountering tension with Jonah - the exhaustion from the restless night stopped Jan from working herself into a frenzy again. Jan aimed to get through the day with as little interaction with Jonah as possible. With any luck, he'd be too tied up in lectures and other meetings to bother her with his own insecurities about what he thought she should be doing.

Jan sat and carried out her work, occasionally glancing out the window, as she sometimes did, when she needed a break away from her screen. The morning sun was threatening to beat strong that day, in early May. Jan enjoyed watching the light penetrate smoothly through the office window, when it travelled through the single panes of glass that were set in archaic window frames. Jan breathed a sigh of relief, in the anticipation of the day ending, when she would be free from the anxiety that working with Jonah already brought.

The other colleagues who sat in the 6-seater office space were a mixture of lecturers and administrators, each of whom kept themselves to themselves. Jan wouldn't have time to build a relationship with them in the short months she would be there, nor did she want to. Although, she was motivated by the idea of getting one of them to open up about Jonah and his behavior, and perhaps offer her some valuable advice on how to deal with him.

Jan's trip to Egypt was due to commence in the following few weeks. She guesstimated that her troubled time with Jonah would dissipate after she returned from Egypt - so, perhaps, she should relax a little. Perhaps Jonah picked up on her tense energy, she kept telling herself, and was simply mirroring Jan, unbeknownst to her, a thought which led her down a deep negative self-talk spiral, before she eventually snapped herself out of it. It was a habit which she had developed since a teenager, and was beginning to read self-help books to try and stop ruminating.

As she slowly awakened from her slow daydream of the light that shone through her office window, Jan noticed something peculiar. Similar to the incident involving the boy on the bike, when she sat on her veranda at home a couple of weeks earlier, Jan noticed something which didn't sit right with her. There appeared a break in the light, a trick of light through the office window. The building opposite appeared different. It no longer had the usual brick-and-mortar construction. Instead, it appeared to be floating, as if it was on a cloud.

There appeared before her, through the window she had fixed her gaze on for the light that sent her into a daydream, another building that floated like an echo on top of the stone building at Santa Clara University:

Jan rubbed her eyes, stood up out of her chair and shouted, pointing out the window: "Do you see that? Do you see that?", she said, to the three colleagues who were in the room with her.

They all gazed out of the office window in amazement, in various stages of curious inspection, cautious to express themselves freely, a moment at which they might have demonstrated some sign of life. After a couple of minutes of heady academic deliberation, a colleague put his glasses on and inspected the scene closely, before picking up the phone in the office. After a couple of minutes of what sounded like considered confirmation, he put the phone down and said:

"Yes, it's Fata Morgana. Our colleague in the physics department confirmed it! He can see it, too, from his window downstairs. It's just a mirage! The heat from the sun has heated the atmosphere above the building so it's created a mirror effect."

Jan slumped into her chair, disappointed that the distraction didn't last more than a couple of minutes, and ended with muted acceptance of the logic behind the mirage. Jan was also annoyed, for feeling shot down after expressing elation at what she saw. Instead of squirming in her seat with pent-up feelings, Jan decided to pity the man who could only interpret the world through logic and rationality. Jan's feelings swung continuously from disappointment to annoyance.

Something which could have been magnificent and splendid for everyone that dreary afternoon in the office was explained away by academics in the most soul-less of fashion. The other two colleagues in the office that day summarily shrugged their shoulders and returned to their computer screens. Jan breathed deeply and reflected on what just had occurred - what she really wanted to say and what stopped her from saying: *"do you see that glitch in the matrix?"* Moment's later, Jan thanked herself for not humiliating herself with such an utterance.

The phone rang. It was Toni. He wanted to remind Jan of their lunch date, which she had completely forgotten about, but welcomed at that moment:

"Oh, just give me an hour. I'll meet you by the Espresso Royale over on Neil Street," she muttered.

They had to meet to finalize the details of their trip - Jan told Toni that Susan would be joining them, after they settled with their hot drinks at the Royale. Toni paused for a moment, but Jan reassured him that Susan would only join them as a listener. Toni and Susan were not close, and that resulted in the usual awkward dynamic of a three-way friendship:

"Okay, see you in a bit," said Toni and ended the call.

Toni took a cursory look at the program which Jan had devised for their holiday, then proceeded to catch up and chat about other things. Jan was not dismayed by Toni's manner. Jan reflected on the good intentions with which she planned for her trip, more than Toni's lack of appreciation for her organizational efforts. Besides, other things appeared to take precedent every time they converged, such as bitching about their jobs and their bosses.

Toni worked as a librarian at the graduate library and was having a hard time with his boss, Steve. Steve, like Toni, were part of the closely-knit gay community in Santa Clara and working together brought its own sets of challenges, since Steve liked to treat Toni as though Toni did not exist when they both were out on the gay scene. Toni complained about it a lot to Jan, to which Jan comforted Toni's adolescent complaints with an appropriate level of guidance:

"Maybe Steve is just trying to keep his work separate from his private life. Does he need to hang out with you socially?" asked Jan, tentatively.

"No, that's not the point, Jan. You're not listening to me. Steve completely blanks me when he sees me at the bar, but I don't. I say hi to him, but he just completely ignores me, and I don't know why. It's really awkward. It makes me feel uncomfortable," answered Toni.

"Yeah, okay. Right, well, the next time just blank him too and see how he responds," said Jan, then sighed.

Toni's adolescent complaints were beginning to wear on her. Jan would sometimes tire of Toni's complaints, complaints which she couldn't understand for a man in his early 50s, but then Jan would always remind herself to understand that Toni's social development was delayed in part due to his sexuality. Well, that was what she told herself anyway. Jan had known other gay men, so she had something to compare Toni with, but then Jan would conclude that Toni was just Toni, given what he had told her about his struggles with being gay. And black in America.

Susan interrupted their exchange, appearing 15 minutes into their 30-minute lunch date. Jan welcomed her arrival, since she was beginning to suffer from Toni's complaints. Jan's sensitivity to others was a burden to her, and that's why she coped better in small groups of twos and threes. The small group of friends that Jan had were equally deficient in some way, a deficiency which stopped them all from fulfilling their true potential.

Susan pulled up a chair, saying cheerfully: "so what are we talking about?"

Toni immediately withdrew from the exchange unfolding before him, slumping into his chair. He knew that Susan would not entertain his needless complaints. Susan was too direct a person to care for Toni's insecure nature, which is why Toni was relieved that Susan would not be joining them on their trip to Egypt.

"Oh, we were just discussing where we wanted to visit first," said Jan.

"I thought you received a schedule from the agency?" asked Susan with a perplexed look.

"Yeah, but we're free to decide when we choose to do what," replied Jan.

"Oh, I see," said Susan and nodded with feigned interest, hoping to keep their brief conversation light.

"You see it's a good idea to plan something but to keep our options open as well. Well, that's what I think," said Toni, attempting to appear rational and diplomatic.

"Yes, that seems a good idea," agreed Jan.

"May I suggest something?" asked Susan with some interest.

"Of course you may," said Toni, inadvertently sounding patronizing. Susan rolled her eyes. Despite his best attempts, Toni could never get away from sounding patronizing with Susan, and that was what annoyed her the most about him.

"Well, how about you just both do whatever you want?" shrugged Susan. She threw her hands up in the air to gesture a sense of apathetic frustration at their apparent problem.

"What do you mean?" asked Jan.

"Jan - you do what you want and Toni does what he wants," asserted Susan.

"Yeah, we could, but it seems a waste of money because we both put the same amount of money into this package deal so …. kinda need to get our money's worth. Besides, we don't want to do things on our own. We wouldn't feel safe," added Toni.

"But you'll be with other people when you're on your excursions, right?" questioned Susan.

"Yeah...but…" said Toni.

"But what?" interrupted Susan: "You guys are too attached to each other. You need to detach from each other. Stop using each other as a crutch. See it as an opportunity to free yourselves up a little."

There was a pause before Susan continued, as she read the room, timing what she was going to say next with measured precision: "What about if either of you wouldn't lose out and you both had someone to go with?", asked Susan surreptitiously.

"What?" said Jan, shocked.

Toni didn't react, unsure of what Susan was trying to say, whilst attempting to stay neutral so he didn't give himself away.

"Yes!" said Susan with a large smile.

Toni looked at Jan with a furrowed brow, who looked at Toni with no expression, before returning her gaze at Susan, who said: "I won at bingo last night. If I can get myself a late deal! I can come with you!"

Toni's mouth opened first, followed by Jan's. Jan leapt up to embrace Susan: "girl, no way, no way….no way….but what about your debts? Don't you just want to pay off your credit card?" Jan began exploding with excitement.

Susan threw her hands up in the air again and said: "Fuck it! I only wanted to pay it off so I could start saving for the trip to Cambodia with you, but I can't wait that long. You only live once, right?"

Jan started laughing at their inside joke - the phrase *'you only live once'*. It was the thing they would say to each other whenever they laughed at all the spendthrifts that they knew, who had thrown their future away for momentary pleasures then had nothing left to show for it. Susan and Jan both looked over at Toni, who was sat with his arms crossed, blinking slowly:

"Oh, come on, Toni. Live a little! Trust me when I say this - that you will thank me for joining you…. in the end! I can't imagine you sitting on your own in a hotel lobby or on a bus, trying to talk to people! At least you'll have me to keep you company! Three weeks is a long time to be stuck with your best friend in a strange land!" said Susan.

Toni's shoulders dropped as he breathed out a smile, which then turned into a smirk. He got up from his chair and hugged Susan, telling her that she would be welcomed on the trip:

"Well, honey, let's pray to Black Jesus that you can get yourself a deal! Let's all meet at mine next weekend for drinks and snacks and go over the final plans because we will need to sort out which hotel you need to book in the area and how to get around because I have been reading up on useful stuff that you both should know about!!!" said an newly enthused Toni, a change of demeanor that took his friends by surprise.

A stranger might have considered him disingenuous - his quick flit in mood was received by some startled glances by patrons sitting next to them, at the Espresso Royale.

Susan turned and kissed Toni on the cheek and said: "... thank you, hon. Thank you for speaking it into existence for me. I'm sure I will be able to join you."

"But do not make yourself broke. Promise me you will not add anything to your credit card," said Jan, concerned.

"Here's the number of a friend at American Airlines. Give him a bell. Tell him that Toni asked you to ring him. I'll text him ahead to let him know - he owes me a major favor and I think it's time to call that favor in!" said Toni.

Jan looked at Toni, in continued surprise. It was not like Toni to be so forthcoming with anyone, unless he really meant it. Jan then hugged him and said: "Thank you, Toni. This is going to be the trip that will change our lives. I can feel it!"

They all returned to their jobs that day in a cheery mood. For the rest of the week, Jan sat in her office and remained unperturbed by Jonah and his gruff manner, having the prospect of a her lifetime-trip to Egypt to enjoy instead. By the end of the first week with Jonah, everything that Jan previously gave attention to about him disappeared. Her attention shifted to her upcoming trip, and Jonah stopped appearing as an asshole to her.

Toni returned to his job that week in the graduate library at Santa Clara University and went out that weekend and bumped into Steve, to whom he paid no mind. It was a first for Toni - Toni came to an understanding, to try and feel at peace with a world he couldn't control. He ended up relaxing in his own skin in the space he shared with Steve, his manager, outside of work.

Susan returned to her job for the rest of the week with a glow about her, radiating in silence at the thought of Egypt. Susan joyfully arranged cover for the time she was going to take off. Her employer, a surly doctor, was not going to stop her - unless he wanted his wife finding out about all his affairs. Whether Susan would have a job to return to, she didn't care. She took the risk joyfully, and her employer joyfully agreed to her proposed plans. In her joyful manner, Susan rang the number Toni suggested and, in her joyful approach and tone with the man she spoke with, she booked a late deal to Cairo. That week, she found a hotel in the area Toni and Jan were going to stay at and booked herself a room.

Along came the end of the week again and Jan took her tea on her veranda again, as she began to wind down for the weekend. She sat and saw the world differently. It vibrated differently. The heat from the May sun eased off at the end of the day and dusk began to settle in, and the heat waves from the ground began to soften their pulsations. Jan had been seeing the world vibrate ever since she was a little girl. It wasn't only the world's energy that she saw vibrate. It was the energy from people too.

From her observations over the years, Jan learned that everyone vibrates differently: some with love, some with hate, some with anger, some with jealousy, some with greed, some with lust, some with pride and some with no desire at all. Those were the people that Jan considered to be dead inside, as if they had no souls, or as she liked to put it, empty vessels. Over the years since her childhood, however, the majority of the population around her began to vibrate from a place of hate, anger, jealousy, greed, lust and fear. That's what made Jan retreat from the world over the years.

Her little respites helped Jan cope in the world, though. Jan's place of work was relatively safe from the level of hate she saw in the world in general. Her place of residence was safe from it, too. Though, she sometimes wondered what life was like down the end of the street where she lived. Because, at the end of the street where Jan lived, the vibrations changed somewhat. It was the place where the university campus ended and the rest of Santa Clara lived.

The residents outside the safe campus bubble ran their daily routine of work, children and home, alongside the stresses that came with it. It wasn't anything unusual but the vibrations were somewhat different at the end of the street where Jan lived. Jan could see the difference, in the atmosphere, the difference in vibrations.

It was at the end of street from where Jan lived where Jan happened to chance upon a strange incident some weeks prior, at the traffic lights, which intersected the safe haven of the university campus borders, with its ivory towers and dusty corridors. Jan sat on her veranda with her cup of tea, and reflected on the incident in the office the previous day. Then, Jan suddenly recalled who had told her new colleagues in the small office that the optical illusion was *Fata Morgana.*

It was the Physics Professor, whose office was directly below hers, in the old university building. Jan recalled having met him at a gathering for international students. She remembered that interaction quite well, as she sipped her tea. Being of an inquiring mind, Jan asked the Professor about the nature of the physical world - specifically, about how the physical world was constructed. She knew it was a Physics 101 question, but she wanted to engage with him regardless. Moreover, given Jan's ability to perceive vibrations, she was curious for an explanation from the Professor. His name was Professor Greene - a near-middle-aged man with a mild eccentric manner, who was happy to indulge her that day, from what Jan remembered:

"Well, you know there is a quantum physics theory of a simulated universe currently being explored at MIT. I think this is what you might be getting at. Basically, the universe is a simulation, a projection if you will, so what we perceive is really a projection," said Professor Greene. Jan recalled what Professor Greene told her at the time, between her sips of tea on her veranda that evening.

Jan sat with her tea on her veranda and reflected on that glitch in the matrix some weeks earlier. She sat sipping, thinking about contacting Professor Greene about the incident - the *Fata Morgana.* She subsequently spent the weekend packing, cleaning and sorting out her apartment. She had coffee with her neighbor, a retired librarian, who told her about the old days in Santa Clara after the second world war, when she was a wife and a mother and her husband brought home the bacon, and she didn't have to work, but she wanted to, so he encouraged her to carve a path for herself - to find her passion - and she found it in learning.

Jan's neighbor-friend kept an eye out on Jan's apartment and watered her plants whenever she was away, which Jan repaid by entertaining her neighbor's stories, dog-sitting and dog-walking for her. Her neighbor's Corgi was terribly demanding and interrupted most of their conversation, whenever they happened to chance upon one. Despite the dog's dominant behavior, Jan managed to build a good rapport with him.

A new week rolled on and Jan began to count down the days to her big trip, in a fortnight. She made a point to contact Professor Greene that Monday morning, emailing him with a request to meet, to discuss the *Fata Morgana* of the previous week.

He replied, quickly and unexpectedly: "sure, I remember you. It was nice chatting with you and I would love to share more with you. When are you free?"

Jan froze a little upon reading his lightning-fast response. She paused, breathed in and continued. She didn't want to analyze the meaning of his fast response - she wanted to desperately let that thought go - she wanted to be released from considering too much in too much detail. Jan wanted to act on instinct instead of overthinking everything, like she normally would - by debating the merits of the action, or putting up resistance, or having an internal dialogue about what the world was presenting her with. At that moment, Jan decided to simply go with the flow, since she already had some reference to what that could mean for her, when she let go of what she thought about Jonah.

Jan was grateful for that release and effect on her experience with Jonah. She was happy with it and wanted more of it, in her life in general, although she knew she lacked the courage and discipline to trust it. Nevertheless, she immediately felt less anxious - which she achieved by allowing herself to let go of unnecessary thoughts, which would lead to emotions which were not in alignment with her goals.

Jan met Professor Greene at Espresso Royale for lunch that Monday. Since she had worked extra hours the previous week with Jonah, Jan made an agreement with her manager Karen to take the afternoon off. Jan banked on her time with the Professor being extended far past lunch, and hoped he too could extend his time with her. Lunch was a slow start, where they exchanged pleasantries and the Professor inquired about her interest in his field of work - Quantum Mechanics:

"It's really nice to be able to talk to someone who either isn't a student or a fellow academic. I don't get any joy from either. It's either a contest with colleagues or tiresome interactions with students that chip away at you and make you forget why you went into education in the first place," he said.

Professor Green's red-tartan bow tie over a crisp white shirt and khaki suit aged him somewhat beyond his 50-something self, thought Jan. His salt and pepper hair and goatee beard rested on his medium-tanned skin, a particular shade of Native American. Perhaps he had Native American blood, thought Jan, a thought which she didn't let linger.

"I'm sure you have so much knowledge that you would love to share, and I would love to learn," said Jan, careful not to appear desperate but to express a genuine interest in Professor Greene's knowledge.

She was also very careful not to give off the wrong signal, so she decided to be very specific about what she wanted to know: "well, you know the other week, we all saw something happen, outside our window and that's why I contacted you - to find out more because I have many questions which I have always pondered on, and I guess the questions lend themselves well to your work. But I'm not too sure about it, and I thought maybe you could tell me," said Jan, carefully treading between exuberance and detachment.

"Oh, I am curious indeed," he said, perking up with wide eyes, his chest out a little.

"That mirage. What was it called?" asked Jan, trying to broach the subject that she desperately wanted clarity on.

"Fata Morgana," quipped the Professor.

"Yes, what if.... I don't know how to say this..." said Jan, hesitantly.

"Go on, you can ask what you want. This is what I am here for," said the Professor in reassuring tones, that were dulcet in nature, and were followed with a friendly smile and a wide grin like a sunflower. "I won't judge you".

"What if what I saw was more than *Fata Morgana*?" asked Jan, pulling the chords on her ease with him.

The Professor, still wide-eyed, relaxed his shoulders and breathed a smile: "That's always a possibility," he said, to encourage Jan to continue speaking and motioned: "What do you think it was?"

"Well, maybe it was something from a different dimension," said Jan. She paused, without looking at the Professor directly, then followed with: "could that be an explanation?", she asked, careful not to sound completely mad.

Professor Greene breathed a sigh of relief and smiled widely. Grabbing her hand, which Jan then withdrew, he said: "Sorry… for touching you, but I'm just overjoyed with what you said. We need to visit my lab. Do you have time next week, so I can go through more of this with you?"

Jan smiled, warmly content. Seizing the moment, she asked: "how about now? I have the afternoon off" and smiled a sense of relief, from feeling good for taking the chance.

The Professor dithered a bit, checked his emails from his phone, then said: "well, I have a few emails to answer from students, but they can wait. To hell with it! Let's go, and I will show you what I've been working on."

They walked to the Arts and Sciences building, in the center of the Santa Clara University campus, which was four blocks down from their lunch rendezvous at Espresso Royale, a straight walk, down to the center. Cappuccino buildings and their flat red roofs began to dot the street-scape as they approached the center, some 20 minutes away from the Royale.

Jan took in the breeze from the trees that lined the streets and smiled in delight, that she was going to spend the afternoon learning something other than how to organize the curriculum into schedules and spreadsheets. Professor Greene flashed an occasional smile as they made small talk, whilst they walked. Jan and Professor Greene learned about each other's backgrounds - Jan had moved from Illinois, where her parents still lived and worked their restaurant, and Professor Greene was born in Oregon and moved down for studies in Sacramento and eventually got a teaching job at Santa Clara University, whilst he studied for his PhD.

They arrived at the building, walked into the stone-cool interiors, down the cream-colored halls with white doors and white door-frames. The Professor passed some occasional nods to his colleagues and answered their quips - *"new colleague?"* and *"had a nice weekend?"* - as they walked down the corridor into the lab. It was noticeably cooler in the lab than in the corridors, which was the first thing that struck Jan.

"Why is it so cold in here?" asked Jan, rubbing the elbows of her crossed arms.

"Sorry, we're conducting an experiment and we need to cool the room for it. Here, put this on," said the Professor. He then handed her a cardigan. After Jan was done putting on her cardigan, the Professor smirked and said: "It looks better on you than on me. Here, put these on!" and proceeded to hand Jan a pair of plastic goggles.

They moved towards a glass box which housed a metal prong. It was a few centimeters in length and had a current of electricity running between the two spikes of the prong.

"What is that?" asked Jan, stepping forward to peer into the glass box.

The Professor took a few readings from the panel on the glass box, then recorded them on his clipboard, then switched off the apparatus in the glass box. He then moved over to the temperature control panel on the wall next to the lab's door, and increased the room temperature back to 22. Turning to Jan, he then answered her question:

"It's a particle - an electron - which we are experimenting with. We need to create a unit of energy to then project it in wave form, to see how it reacts when projected onto a surface," said the Professor.

"Erm, that makes no sense to me," said Jan with her eyebrows raised and her chin lowered. She didn't want to appear ignorant but she couldn't help it.

"In simpler form, we're working on a theory that the universe is a hologram," said the Professor, diligently.

"Professor, you have to stop using difficult concepts around me," said Jan with a comical tone, having relaxed in the Professor's company.

"Let me put it this way, what you think you saw with the *Fata Morgana* the other day, what looked like buildings on top of each other in the sky, was a trick of the light. We know this because the thing that created it was a difference in temperature. It had nothing to do with the distribution of electrons or light. We know this because this phenomenon has been seen many times before. Like a mirage in the desert - what traditionally was considered an oasis in the desert, was really the heat reflecting off the ground, not a pool of water," explained the Professor, with an ease that reflected Jan's interest.

"I will look for that when I'm in Egypt in the next couple of weeks," remarked Jan.

"You're going to Egypt? Wow, that is superb. I wish I could come with you. You must really be looking forward to that?," asked the Professor, enthused and happy for her.

"Yes, I've saved up for it for two years." said Jan, with a broad, bright smile

"Wow, that takes an impressive amount of self-discipline," he said, visibly taken aback.

"Thanks but… about your hologram theory," said Jan, anxious to move the conversation forward.

"Yes, sorry. Back to that. We are working with the idea that the universe is a hologram but we need to understand how particles behave in order for us to prove that theory. The particles need to be able to stick to surfaces but behave independently of the surface, in order for us to truly confirm the theory. Well, at least, that's a part of it. It's mostly explained with equations," he said, with progressive levels of enthusiasm in his voice.

Jan stood, looking confused, feeling too polite to curb her excitement.

"Here, let me show you," continued the Professor.

The Professor got on a stool to reach for a projector which hung from the ceiling, and proceeded to project something onto the whiteboard to illustrate the point he was trying to make:

"Now, you see the dust from the room cutting through the light? Now, imagine that someone from some place in the universe was projecting an image and creating our reality for us. The question is, how can the little bits of dust not interfere with the image which is coming from the projector? Using this example, can we observe the specs of dust as physical matter in the universe? How is it possible that the physical matter in our universe is not affected by what is being projected? If we can get particles to stick to a surface and behave independently of it, we can start to explain how the universe might be a holographic projection."

Jan looked at the Professor with some new level of confusion and curiosity and said: "I follow you, I think…but how does that answer my questions?"

Professor Greene turned to look at Jan from his musings and was immediately struck with a demand he never expected from her: "you know, Professor, my question about *Fata Morgana* and dimensions?" Jan repeated herself with collected patience.

"Oh, that is related to frequency. That's something else entirely," said the Professor, flippantly unaware of his own divergence from Jan's original inquiry.

"What is that related to?" asked Jan, desperate to follow the Professor, for fear of losing him.

"The universe is made up of sound. Factor in atoms and particles, which then create matter. Now, in this universe, at least in this world, we operate on a certain frequency. If the frequency is different, or higher, then the density would change. The particles and atoms would operate on that frequency and that is what we would consider another dimension of physical matter, or world," he said.

"Ah.... by frequency, do you mean vibrations?" continued Jan, with serious intent.

"Yeah, like the Beach Boys song. Good Vibrations," he said, amusingly, completely oblivious to the reception of his tone. Upon seeing Jan's non-plus response, the Professor corrected himself and expanded with: "They're related but separate in Physics. A particle moves around at a certain rate and the frequency is the speed at which it does that."

"So...it's like when I saw the *Fata Morgana* and when I see...." said Jan, trying to ignore the Professor's attempt at humor that caught up with her and made her light up.

"When you see what?" he asked, this time without the comical tone.

"Oh, just the heat rising off the ground on a hot day," shrugged Jan, with a sudden need to end the meeting with the Professor.

"Yes. That's what gives that wavy effect. It's something like that. That's a wave pattern caused by heat which disrupts the light," he said, sensing the end of Jan's query.

"Yes ... and when it's a warm day ... and when I'm at the lake... and when I'm watching the trees .... and the water ... all of which seem to behave differently," said Jan, careful of not opening holes with her choice of words.

"Do you mean they move in the wind or reflect light differently?" asked the Professor with a deep, genuine tone.

The Professor continued to look at Jan, but she hesitated because she was afraid to look and sound stupid, so she didn't continue. He tried to encourage her out of her hesitation.

Eventually, Jan answered: "I see vibrations."

The Professor looked at her and nodded his head and said:

"Ermmmmm……ooookkkaaaaay…… I have to go now but let's pick up this conversation some other time!!!!!"

Jan put her head down, flushed at her mistake. She felt weak at the knees, embarrassed with herself. She grabbed her bag, draped it around her and walked swiftly out of the lab, all the while thanking the Professor profusely for his time and hospitality. Just as soon as Jan was out of the lab, she was at the end of the hallway and out the front door of the building. She put her hands to her face and wiped her brow, as soon as she was outside. A man walked past and looked at her strangely, setting her face aflame in embarrassment and frustration.

Jan walked a few steps outside and a gust of wind cooled her burning face. She grabbed her phone, which she rarely used, except for emergencies, since she was sensitive to the radiofrequency from phones that would often leave the side of her face and ear burning with heat after she used them. She rang Susan who picked up immediately and Jan put the phone on speaker, turning down the volume.

Sitting on the garden wall, Jan proceeded to ask if Susan was free to talk. After confirmation, she started:

"Oh, hon, I just made a fool of myself at work. I feel awful," said Jan.

"Oh, hon, what happened?" asked Susan with reassuring concern.

"It's a long story but I just embarrassed myself with a Professor here. I wanted to get some info on something but I just went in, full-on Jan, you know…." said Jan, deflated with punched holes in her throat.

"Oh, hon. Do you need me to come over tonight?" asked Susan, pressing as a friend would be.

"No, I'm just gonna walk on home and get myself settled tonight and I'll see you tomorrow at Toni's. Hey, did you manage to get everything sorted? Are you still coming to Egypt?" asked Jan, quick to change the subject between short, shallow breaths.

"Yes!" shrieked Susan in shock.

Jan took a deep breath before she heard Susan's answer and shouted, after exhaling: "Oh my gawd. It's gonna be lit!" Jan licked her finger, lifted it in the air, then cocked her head from side to side. Her mood was lifted.

´´Listen, I have a call coming in but let's chat more tomorrow. See you at Toni´s at around 8," said Susan with a pressing tone, from where she rang - her place of work.

´´Okay, hon. See you tomorrow. I can´t wait!´´ said Jan and ended the call.

Jan sighed and dropped her shoulders. She stared down the road, which she had to walk - a long walk of around 40 minutes, to her apartment. The road out from the center of Santa Clara was lined with buses that served the campus but the confines of a bus on a May midday would be too much for Jan, since her anxiety still lingered from her faux pas with the Professor and continued to taunt her. Walking home would also allow her to get her 4,000 steps, for her daily target of 10,000.

As soon as Jan got home, she kicked off her shoes and fell asleep for an hour, to sleep off the curse of diabetes - tiredness. She curled up on her couch and woke up half an hour later, her usual average nap time. After grabbing a cup of Earl Grey, she headed to the porch, to see if the neighbor's dog, Porgy the Corgi, would be sitting in the window as he sometimes would, and bark at her, despite having known her for 6 years. Jan took in the scene and drank her tea on her veranda, silently staring down the street to the traffic lights, just day-dreaming, drifting into her own world, to escape the day and the week.

After a while, after she had taken off the day, Jan sat and saw the sun slowly drip down to the west, from her south-eastern facing veranda. She marveled at the purple and orange hues in the sky, whilst the traffic lights down the street turned from red to amber then green, intermittently. She watched for the boy on the bike, but he didn't appear.

The next day, Jan made her way to the Saturday Farmer´s Market in the center of Santa Clara. She bought an assortment of fruit and vegetables, enough to get her through the final week before they flew out. She also bought a couple of bottles of White Zinfandel from a local winery. It was her favorite drink, which she liked to share with Susan and Toni, even though both of them were beer drinkers. Despite his sensitive nature, Toni had very conventional tastes. Susan, being a no-nonsense type, matched her personality with traditional beers like Coors and Bud and the occasional vodka.

Jan was the first to arrive at Toni's that Saturday evening. Susan was going to be late, as she always was. Toni was always pleased with Jan's punctuality - which suited both their sometimes-tense and often-anxious nature - they both always wanted to know what was happening and when, though Toni was a lot more relaxed about it. The time before Susan's arrival gave them both a head-start to discuss their plans for their vacation, even though they couldn't navigate their discussion past how to get to the airport and whether they were going to spend time in the drinks lounge once they got there.

Susan joined them not long after, with her usual cheery energy. Her blonde hair complimented her personality perfectly, perfect for brushing the world off her shoulders, which she needed to do often, to cope with the multitude of assholes that crossed her path daily. She breathed a sigh of relief, as she opened up the bottle of beer that she brought with her and grabbed a handful of chips, a small portion for her slender frame. After Susan got settled, they all slumped into their seats in Toni's two-bedroom modern apartment, which he lovingly furnished with pop-art pieces and coffee-table picture books on architecture and art. His spartan interiors reflected his somewhat cold and detached personality.

Jan spoke first, ready to unload the events of the previous day, with Professor Greene:

"Oh my god. That was just so embarrassing," said Jan, shaking her head.

"Oh, Jan. You just need to let it go. What happened, exactly? What did you say?" asked Susan, careful not to encourage Jan to dwell too much on the event.

"Well, whatever it was, it couldn't have been that bad!" chirped Toni.

Jan threw her head back and said: "Oh, Toni. Stop. It was embarrassing. Just take it from me!" gesturing with her open palms.

"Go on, Jan," continued Susan, ignoring Toni.

"Well, I didn't have time to tell you but we witnessed a natural phenomenon last week in the office called a *Fata Morgana.* It was a mirage, outside the window. And I just wanted more information about that from the Physics Professor. And then I….." said Jan, before she was interrupted.

"You ended up putting your foot in your mouth!" interrupted Toni, dismissively.

"Oh, Toni, shut up, will you?" blurted Susan.

"There's no need to be like that, Susan," said an indignant Toni.

"Oh, hon, you just worry too much. You're too sensitive… you're that thing...what do you call it? You're an a-path," said Susan.

"Em-path!" corrected Toni and cut Susan a stare, which was reciprocated by her with a squint.

"What's one of them?" asked Jan, ignorantly.

"You take on the world, hon. You take on everything around you. You absorb everyone's energy like a sponge. Whether they're happy, sad or miserable or hateful. You take it all from the other person," explained Susan, with her sisterly comfort.

"Is that why I spend a lot of time with myself?" reflected Jan.

"Yes, hon. You have to find a way to shield yourself. I mean you cope well at work, don't you?" chimed Toni, agreeing with Susan.

"Yes, I just go to work and function but I'm a mess after I leave work,' said Jan.

"You have to imagine that you are still at work. What makes being at work different to being outside of work?" asked Susan.

"I put my shield up and I'm in a role," said Jan, sullenly.

"Well, I guess that's what you have to do. Keep your shield up and play a role," shrugged Susan.

Jan slumped into her chair and rolled her eyes in apparent exhaustion: "I can't do that. It's already heavy to bear."

"I tell you what, I know some excellent techniques which will help but first we need to get to Cairo and start our vacation," said Susan: "In the meantime…"

Susan then stood up before finishing her sentence and began to dance in the center of Toni's living room, grabbing Jan and Toni up from their chairs and engaging in a rickety dance that demonstrated their 40-something years. Susan grabbed her phone, took a few swigs of beer, played Madonna's 'Holiday' and, after a couple of minutes, they all let out a burst of laughter at the ridiculousness of the scene. Toni took several swigs of beer and Jan sunk more White Zinfandel than her diabetes would permit.

It wasn't long before they were all shouting *"I can't wait!"* and *"It's gonna be so lit"* and *"I am going to bleep as many Egyptian men as I can!"* in between chortles of laughter, before slumping into a stupor and returning home, in an Uber, back to their final week of their life in Santa Clara before their trip to Cairo.

They still hadn't gotten round to planning their trip, aside from organizing their Uber to the airport, and arranging for house and plant-sitters. Toni's cat, bird and fish would be fed by his ex and Susan, much like Jan, had already sorted out a house-sitter. Susan's flight was to depart in the evening and Jan and Toni would leave in the morning - meeting each other again at the other end, in Cairo. After their get-together at Toni's, they braced themselves for the trip of their lifetime.

Chapter 2

Cairo

Jan and Toni arrived at Cairo Airport after a full day's travel, which included a change-over in Dubai, after a 3 am taxi ride to San Francisco Airport, from Santa Clara. Depleted from their journey to Cairo, they both stepped into a wave of heat that the interior of Cairo Airport tried to beat, with its modern air conditioning that circulated its interiors. The tall palm trees inside the airport were the first thing that Toni noticed, after leaving customs. Toni smiled past the customs officers relatively unchecked, compared to his experience in European countries and in his own country, where he would be *randomly* pulled aside and interrogated.

Jan, on the other hand, had been searched and her lowering blood-sugar levels did not support her growing levels of discomfort and cranky attitude, when she was searched:

"Oh my God, that lady was so rude and horrible," screamed Jan, cantankerous.

"I'm sorry, hon," said Toni sympathetically, knowing only too well the indignity of being treated that way: "You know what they say - *they're only doing their job*!" he said, trying to lighten the mood, albeit awkwardly, the only way he knew how to be, at that moment.

"Thanks!" said Jan. Fortunately, she understood Toni's sense of humor very well. Jan breathed a deep sigh, shook her head and said: "Look, let's go and take a load off and figure out what we're going to do next. I really need something to eat and drink."

"Sure", said Toni, leading the way to the nearest café with the trolley he found for both their bags and cases.

After some fresh mint tea with honey and an Italian baguette, which they both shared, they perked up swiftly, then Toni said, smiling: "I love it already….I feel at home, amongst a sea of brown and black faces…"

Jan cut Toni a look, then said: "Well, you'll soon see people who look like me and Susan when we get to the hotel!", with a smirk.

Toni shook his head, then checked for Susan's flight on the board and found it was delayed, so they agreed to unload at their hotel, get refreshed and return after several hours:

"Should we take the bus or taxi? I don't mind either way. The bus will be easier. We won't have to deal with haggling, but it's also trickier to get to the hotel. If we take a taxi, we might get ripped off. But a friend said that if you simply quote the guide price from the travel guide, then he'll know what to expect from us. I'll negotiate with him if I need to, though. It seems like the best thing to do. Don't worry, I'll sort it out either way," said a frantic Toni.

"Okay, thanks Toni. You're a lot more equipped than you give yourself credit for!" replied Jan. She was in no mood to deal with Toni's indecisiveness but resigned herself to truly go with the flow, even though it was Toni's flow.

They walked outside, towards the taxi rank. Toni followed the instructions in his travel guide: *agree the price in Egyptian pounds and check that the driver has a meter and that it's running.* Toni knew that he would already be mistaken for a local, until he opened his mouth to speak. It was the only social currency he had, he knew that, but it was currency that freed him, and pushed him forward, to step into his power. And Toni was pleased to see that the taxi driver appeared to momentarily light-up at the sound of Toni's accent.

Toni accepted the fare and they both got in. The taxi driver did not get out of his car - instead, he pulled the lever with a *humph* and Toni dropped the cases into the trunk. Regardless of the driver's surly start, Toni promised a generous tip to the taxi driver. Jan questioned Toni's efforts to avoid being ripped off, if he was then going to tip generously to over-compensate for not wanting to appear as though he was a difficult foreigner. Toni gave Jan a puzzled look, then turned his gaze to the road ahead.

After a relatively easy taxi ride to the hotel, during which Toni persistently tried to engage with the unresponsive taxi driver, they unloaded to recharge their batteries, then returned to Cairo Airport some hours later, to repeat the process back, with Susan in tow. Susan, like Jan and Toni, was completely flat after a tiring journey, which involved grappling with a difficult Uber driver to San Francisco Airport, then dealing with an unpleasant middle-aged married couple on the flight to New York, where Susan changed for her connecting flight to Cairo. Susan needed a much longer nap and more time to herself, after her trip. On top of that, Susan did not fare much better than Jan at Cairo Airport.

The customs lady there gave her the third degree and told her to cover her modesty, which left her seething.

After their first day of recuperations, to settle into their new surroundings, which they absorbed and relished at the excitement of being there, they all arranged to meet for breakfast. They found a spot not too far from their area, in a location which was convenient to their respective hotels. They converged on a café outside the Hanging Church, which was situated in a Christian and Jewish enclave:

"This could be any Southern European city," said Toni, keen to show off his travelling experience.

Not knowing what to order, they chose the easiest items on the picture-menu. Pita with falafel and salad - which nobody apart from Toni found appetizing at 11 in the morning. To top it off, the strong, chicory taste of the coffee took them all by surprise:

"It's almost charred" said Toni, to which Susan laughed and followed with: *"I've tasted detergent less bitter!"*, then Jan added *"I think you're meant to chase it with a cola!"*.

They all sat and laughed for a good while about it, then their laughter continued with different subjects - specifically, the people and incidents that made their journey to Cairo abysmal - all the things that provided a good source for the beginnings of a great adventure. The café owner cut them several stares as he cleaned the tables and chairs, bemused by the comical spectacle.

After the newbie tourists stopped laughing amongst themselves, they exchanged opinions about Cairo. Toni interrupted their embrace of the city with: "okay, girls, do we agree that we are going to try and do our own thing but meet for tours? I mean, we still haven't gotten 'round to discussing what we're going to do while we're here."

"Relax, Toni, we have three weeks and they always say that the best holidays are the ones where you just do what you want and make the best out of it," said Susan.

"What? No they don't. I've never heard that. You just made that up!" replied Toni.

They both laughed and Jan said, eager to share what she was beginning to learn about herself and her friends: "look, this could easily all go pear-shaped if we end up constantly arguing, and I don't think my nerves can take that, so I think we should just all go with the flow but make time to do stuff together. We could do stuff together, or just do it individually, or with two of us together. Whatever!" Jan shrugged her shoulders, drank her chicory coffee and screwed her face at it.

Susan and Toni both smirked at Jan's continued attempts to enjoy the coffee. They then looked at each other, which Jan noticed before interrupting with: "and you two will have to find a way to get along because you might find that you just don't have a choice!"

Tony and Susan made a prompt agreement in return, without contest. Tony would pursue his interest in Ancient Egyptian relics, history and contemporary architecture; Susan would take in the sights and the sounds; and, Jan added to her plans by stating that she would do a mixture of both. After breakfast, they all walked around their hotel's vicinity, to familiarize themselves with the area. They popped in and out of a couple of churches, greeted the local café and business owners, who customarily stood on the pavement, attracting passers-by. They searched for the transport links and looked at a couple of maps, despite having their phones with them.

They then felt ready to explore but, just as soon as they had built up the energy to do that, they returned to their hotels, to escape the midday heat.

They reconvened that night in Jan and Toni's hotel lobby before heading out nearby, where they were welcomed by streets lined with exuberant lights, that flooded out from shops and businesses, under white-sand buildings. They took the bus to downtown Cairo, by paying a one way ticket, which was purchased by sticking one finger in the air and smiling with an unpolished attempt at saying "tadhkirat min fadlik", which Toni had Googled before they ventured out. His incomprehensible attempt at interacting in Arabic was met with a response in English by the bus driver - who appreciated it nevertheless.

Toni, Susan and Jan began their first dance as tourists with the locals - where they slid into their role as tourists who actually made an effort, with natives who appreciated their efforts, versus the ones who arrogantly spoke in English and French without any regard for the local custom. Toni knew what it was like to be continuously disrespected in public, so he made sure he didn't return it in a country where he was a guest. Jan and Susan promptly followed his lead.

They stepped off the bus, directly into downtown Cairo and were immediately struck by its similarity to downtown Paris. Toni was the first to call it, informing his travel companions of the history behind the French architecture in downtown Cairo. Meanwhile, Susan and Jan spotted a shisha-bar which they summarily dove into, primarily to escape Toni's impending lecture. Jan and Susan were out to enjoy the flow of the night with the locals, something they wanted to protect.

To avoid trouble with local men and women, Susan decided to cover her modesty with a long black tunic, with gold embroidery and a white head-dress with Versace print - all items she bought earlier that day from a family-run shop, upon her return to her hotel. Susan had an irresistible charm and a chameleon nature, which allowed her to navigate new environments easily, even as a white blonde woman in Cairo. Susan looked comfortably suited to her new attire. She carefully placed the temples of her black sunglasses under the creases of her head-scarf and reclined in splendor, leaving Jan laughing:

"Susan, you look like an undercover agent! You're worse than Toni, trying to fit in!"

Toni was the second to laugh: "Gurl, just be yourself. Most of the world here is very modern. You are not going to get bothered. You just do here what you would do at home - don't venture out at night on your own and don't wander about on your own too much in the day. Stick with another person… that sort of thing!"

Susan shook her head, unimpressed with Toni and Jan's ignorance. She replied with regal restraint: "Oh dear little lost souls… this is my way of getting more privileges here. Watch me!"

"'Well, anyway, isn't it marvelous?" asked Jan, trying to divert their attention to the wondrous city they had arrived in: "The energy here is just wonderful. It's like we're in Paris but in North Africa."

"Yeah, that's one way of putting it. There's a very special vibe here, now that you mention it," said Toni.

"Well, this is definitely the jewel of the Nile," said Susan.

"Oh my god, Susan. I can't believe you said that! That's exactly what the King wanted for Cairo, at the time!" exclaimed Toni, in a sudden fervor, as if something had brought him back to life.

Jan and Susan both rolled their eyes amidst shaken heads, finished their mint tea, paid the waiter and made their way to the center square, Tahrir Square. Toni was prompt to explain the history of Tahrir Square, a historical site of protest, most recently in the 2011 Egyptian Revolution against the then president. Susan was the first to shoot Toni down, sensing Jan's discomfort with Toni's heavy tour-guide routine:

"Hey, Toni. I know you want to share your information, and you want us to learn as we go along, but us ladies here are more into feeling this moment right now. I'm sorry, hon," said Susan softly, letting him down gently, to prevent an argument from brewing.

"Okay, ladies. Your wish is my command, said Aladdin," said Toni.

"Oh, Toni. That's just so ….. " said Jan, with feigned disregard.

Toni and Jan saw Susan run a little in front of them, with her arm pointing straight out, to her right. She became as giddy as a child, at the sight of something ahead of her:

"Look, over there!" shouted Susan: "Can you see that embankment? That's the Nile! Can you believe that?"

"Yeah," said Jan, with dropped shoulders. Breathing in deeply, she said: "I can feel the breeze!"

"Hey, let's walk over!" said Toni.

They walked down the main road that led away from the giant roundabout around Tahrir Square, to the beginning of a bridge that went over the river:

"Can you believe it?" said a thrilled Susan.

At night, the Nile was illuminated by the multitudes of lights which were emanating from Cairo's promenade, leaving it shimmering in the glow of their embrace. Toni eyed an exit before the bridge:

"Hey, let's walk down there on the promenade, for a better view!" pointed Toni, who walked with a spring in his step.

Jan and Susan picked up their pace on their trail behind Toni, until they came to a restaurant with splendid views of the Nile. As they stopped outside to ponder the restaurant, the maître d' cut them a curt stare. Whilst they all stood to admire the front of the restaurant and its position overlooking the shimmering Nile, the maître d' said:

"Non…Non…non... non réservation!" in a heavy French accent.

Susan looked at a non-plus Jan and Toni, then cut a response back to the ostrich-like waiter:

"But it's just a bar-and-grill... It's not the Radisson!"

"Wow! I'm a nigger here too!" exclaimed Toni.

Susan looked at Toni and said: "don't you start!"

"Look around you, guys. The promenade has dozens of restaurants that go on for miles. Come, let's just move onto the next one!" said Jan.

They continued walking for a few moments and came to a café, opposite a hotel, the Hotel Cleopatra.

Susan rolled her eyes and said: "great, another café! Are we going to end up in cafés throughout this trip?"

"Well, at least we can still see the river!" said Toni: "That view isn't just for fancy restaurants!"

"We're here for three weeks, we can return anytime - we'll all get dressed up and make a *reser-va-shon* and have that splendid evening overlooking the Nile through that fancy restaurant's windows. Don't worry!" said Jan.

Susan cocked her head and sniggered: "Hotel Cleopatra, eh! I wonder how long it took for them to think of that name!"

Jan burst out laughing and said: "Yeah, I wonder how many restaurants and hotels will be named after the ancients!"

"I sense a bingo game throughout this holiday!" added Toni.

Jan and Susan looked at each other, then rolled their eyes at Toni with an acute shake of their heads.

"Oh, Toni!" said Susan: "Stop being a nerd for a second!"

After getting settled into their second-choice for that evening's meal, they began to savor the food and their view of the Nile. Their evening in the café was accompanied by laughter, the only remedy to their recent experience as novice travelers to Egypt. In the spirit of their holiday, they also expressed their gratitude and marveled at Cairo and the modernity of it. They discussed the area across the river, the famous Giza, the haunting place of the pyramids. Toni and Susan planned all the sites they wanted to visit in the coming weeks - the zoos, the botanical gardens, churches, mosques, university buildings and museums. There would be a lot to take in.

They talked about "learning the language" and "blending in with the locals", as far as that was possible. Despite their differences, Toni, Jan and Susan were in agreement with one thing - the best way to experience Egypt was to dive right in. Their original plans ended up as a broad outline of what they eventually decided they wanted to do, as they eased into their holiday. One thing was for certain - until they got familiar with the area, venturing outside a 10 km radius of downtown Cairo was off-limits, which they all firmly agreed upon, that evening by the Nile.

The next day, Toni decided that he was going to trot off to a nearby mosque after breakfast, which was within walking distance of the hotel. He explored the grounds outside and snapped some selfies from his phone when nobody was around, careful not to appear disrespectful. For the first time in his life, Toni admired his milk-chocolate skin - it contrasted beautifully against the cream from the mosque's marbled grounds. In his home country, where every move he made outside his apartment was met with casually-racist suspicion, Egypt gave Toni permission to feel comfortable in his own skin.

A passer-by greeted Toni on the street and asked if he would be joining the man for mid-morning prayers. Toni politely shook his head with a smile and sparkling eyes - and he was met with a hand-shake by the local man, with a bright smile and darting eyes: "It's okay, okay. You come, you come next time!" said the local man and walked away, with a gentle wave.

Toni was taken aback and smiled widely inside, thankful for experiencing the kindness of a stranger for the first time in his life. And, with that, Toni no longer felt a stranger to himself anymore. That feeling, he knew, would change everything about his experience in Egypt. He would feel the connection to the world around him that he so desperately desired. Toni spent some more time in the area and took a bus to downtown Cairo, to appreciate it during the day. He had coffee, met with more friendly owners of the various shops he patronized, where he engaged in smiley small-talk, and surprised himself with his own level of sociability.

Susan's day, on the other hand, was more of a free-spirited affair. She hung out at the Zoo over the bridge in Giza, the area they had all agreed not to venture into alone but to save it for a group excursion. Susan got a taxi-ride after asking for a cab from the receptionist of the 3-star where she was staying. Her effervescent manner allowed her to get to places with ease - though, once she got out of the taxi in Giza, she realized that she would have to repeat the journey back without any solid logistical plan. Susan did not panic, however. Instead, she focused her attention on enjoying her time at the zoo and staying in pure joy, in the moment.

Whilst she continued to enjoy herself at the zoo, Susan met a young English couple, who pleasantly gave her some pointers on how to return to Cairo, by way of the frequent modern buses available from the zoo to her hotel. Susan simply breathed in the news, from their brief encounter, and continued to relish her day and her surroundings in the dry June, mid-afternoon heat, in her safari-hat and tank-top, under a pink-linen shirt. After her jaunt, she returned to her hotel at around 5pm via an effortless bus ride, information for which was gifted to her by the friendly English couple. After washing and resting, Susan got ready to meet the others for dinner.

Jan's first day out alone was a muted affair, void of visits to monuments or buildings or other places of interest. She wasn't in the mood for history or culture. She just wanted to enjoy the energy of the city, so she took a walk around the pedestrian areas. After a couple of bus-rides into downtown Cairo, Jan found a spot on the promenade to admire the Nile, where she had lunch, took some pictures, posted on her social media and returned several hours later. Jan was captivated by the views of both Cairo and the city on the other side of the Nile - Giza.

Jan loved seeing the vibrations of the place, the flow of energy, the buzz of the cars and people around her. Jan sat mesmerized, for most of the hours she spent on the promenade, casually saying hello to passers-by, as the mood suited her. The city was alive and Jan felt every sound and fell into every wave of vibration, smiling as she breathed in the energy of Egypt. She shared her views of the world around her, in the form of snaps on her social media, which were liked by both Toni and Susan throughout the day, just as she had done with Toni, since Susan was not a social media type, preferring real-life interaction.

No doubt they would all share their day over dinner but, for the time being, Jan decided to keep her view of the energetics of Cairo and the Nile to herself.

That evening, they all returned to the restaurant they promised to return to, after their initial rejection led them to the café, this time they came with a reservation and respectable attire. Upon being greeted by the French maître d', they enjoyed an evening by the window, eating their faux-nouvelle-cuisine and relishing the sights over glasses of white cold, crisp wine. They were all in their element, sipping and eating between giggles, as they sat amongst other guests in the slightly air-conditioned restaurant of around 50 covers. They all reflected on their day, starting with Toni:

"I had the most amazing experience this morning, when I visited a mosque nearby the hotel. The locals are just so welcoming. I've never had this treatment in my 40-plus years on Earth. I feel at home here. I could live here so easily. I could return so easily. I feel accepted."

"Honey, you're in North Africa. Of course, you feel at home," said Susan, with a wry smile.

"Susan!" corrected Jan.

"What? Oh, no, you know what I mean!," said Susan, flipping her flippant wrist in the air.

"This is the place of your ancestors. Everyone here looks like you. On top of that, you're an American with a certain amount of privilege above the locals here," explained Susan.

"Yeah, aside from that stuck-up French maître d', I've never felt so welcome anywhere," said Toni.

"I think you just need to step outside of America to feel respected, Toni. God, I think any place outside of America would be great for anyone right now!" said Jan, with measured sarcasm.

"Yeah, what a shitshow it's become, eh!" chimed Susan, between sips of wine and a fork full of food.

"But let's focus on the here and now, shall we? Say, where did you go today, Susan?" asked Jan, with a sharp look in Susan's direction.

"Oh...You know... wandered around a lot... took a bus ride here or there. Took in some sights." said Susan, matter-of-factly.

"You're being cagey....where did you really go?" asked Toni.

"The zoo," said Susan, resting her fork, a pause for a response.

"The zoo?" shouted Jan.

Toni echoed the shock: "But that's on the other side of the river. In Giza!"

"What? So? Look guys, I know we agreed, but it was really easy. I just got myself a cab and I found my way back easily, simply just by asking around. All you have to do is speak English to other tourists, and you'll get all the info you need to get around. I think you should both stop overthinking. Just be free and enjoy every moment," said Susan with her usual care-free manner, a trait which always made her the most attractive of the group.

"Easy for you to say!" said Toni, shaking his head slightly.

"Look, you said it yourself. You feel accepted here, so what are you afraid of? We come from a country filled with violence - violence is so ingrained there that we expect it continuously. I feel a lot more safe here than there, I can tell you that for starters!" said Susan. The seriousness of her tone cut through.

"You're right!" said Jan. After a considered pause, Jan added to the conversation by sharing her day: "I just enjoyed the energy of the city. It is so magnificent. I feel like I'm not on Earth. It feels so other-worldly here. I never imagined it would vibe like it does. Do you guys dig the vibe?" Jan looked on at her friends' bewildered faces: "sorry, silly question. Of course you do. You both sound like you've had a fabulous day. We still have a lot more time to experience it. I just soaked it up all day. A dove came and sat next to me when I was sitting eating my lunch. A few locals said hello. Everything and everyone was pleasant!"

"I'm glad you're enjoying yourself," said Susan, then clocked Toni with a side-eye that was aimed at Jan.

"Yeah, it's hard to imagine this is real! It's so unlike everything I thought it would be! I'm glad we didn't book a resort and just sit on a beach over there in the south of Egypt!

Hey, do you think you guys might be interested in a trip to Alexandria? That looks good," continued Jan.

"Yeah, though aside from the ruins that might make it worth a visit, it looks as though it's very built up. Sort of like the heart of Cairo here. It might be worth a trip, though I'm not too sure if I would like to travel too far out. Maybe after a couple of days, when I've settled in a bit more," answered Susan, with a promising smile: "ask me again then."

"Sure," said Jan, then she put her head down to continue eating her food.

"What's wrong, Jan? Are you not enjoying it so far?" asked Susan, concerned.

"Oh no, it's not that," said Jan, then suddenly perked up: "I love it. There's just something about the energetics. It's so vibrant. I just love the vibes," said Jan. After a pause, she added: "It's just so overwhelming." Jan refrained from saying what she really wanted to say, though she was certain her friends got the gist of it.

Jan began to feel a bit drowsy from her heavy dinner. After paying up, they walked to the center of downtown Cairo to perk themselves up. They didn't opt for a coffee after dinner, instead they took in a nightcap in a tourist-bar, in a random watering hole that served alcoholic drinks. They sat in a colonial white-tan building, with dark-wood interiors and ceiling-fans, with lamps that lit the yucca plants. They sat by the bar, in the cooling evening- breeze and ordered a few Gin cocktails, which they shared and paced between the three. The splendor of the bar allowed them the opportunity to imagine themselves in the 1920s, wearing khaki and safari hats, knocking back Gin, to take the edge off the day.

After a couple of rounds, they flagged a taxi and returned to their hotel. Toni threw caution to the wind and got into the taxi, without haggling. Susan smiled kindly at Toni and Jan praised his efforts.

The next day, bright and refreshed, they all made their much anticipated trip to Giza. Taking a tour bus from the hotel, they spent a leisurely morning, stopping at several different places, before they got to the Pyramid Gardens. It was a slightly breezier morning than usual, making the winds blow from the Sahara. They all came prepared with their desert scarves, sunglasses and hats. Susan had a steady supply of water bottles in her tote bag, which she planned on dispensing to her friends upon request, and Jan catered the trip with sugary substances. Toni's knowledge of the sites and local phrases in the local language completed their tourist arsenal, for their much-anticipated visit to Giza.

By the time they got to the gardens which overlooked the Great Pyramid, it was noon. They hurried to the nearest watering hole, for a bite to eat and to use the restroom - at a café restaurant under a shade of white canopies, an avenue of palm trees that lined the street. As Californians, they were accustomed to the dry heat, but the sand which hung in the air from the winds made them incredibly thirsty - all the time. Susan passed Toni and Jan bottles of water, which they chugged down, in-between the waiter taking their orders and bringing their food. Finally, their lunch was served after the wind stopped blowing.

The weather changed drastically, bringing clouds which hung heavy over the pyramids of Giza, that left them feeling cold all of a sudden - something for which they had not prepared:

"The weather changes rapidly, doesn't it?" commented Susan, to the waiter.

"No, this is not normal. I think a storm is trying to come in from the Sahara - but it usually doesn't make it this far. It will die out, I'm sure. I'm not sure about the clouds. I think it could be because of a change in temperature or pressure," replied the young waiter.

"You must be a student here," interrupted Toni, perceptively.

"Yes, at the University of Cairo. But not sciences. I'm studying physical sciences for sport. I want to become a football coach," replied the young waiter.

"Oh, wow, I love football," said Toni.

"What? Since when?" asked Susan sarcastically.

Jan laughed and said: "Well, he likes watching it!"

"And I can guess why!" chirped Susan.

The waiter laughed along with the banter whilst bringing the food, but left the table without prolonging the exchange, as Jan began to plan which pyramid they should visit first. After being satiated, they all walked outside the garden area that overlooked the pyramids, walking silently together for the first time since they arrived, in their reverie of the famous structures that photos simply could not capture.

Jan let out a scream, raised her hands in the air and said: "Wow, oh my goodness. Can you believe that? It's, it's…. I can't…."

"What? What do you see? Describe it!" said Susan, with giddy laughter.

"No, she can't!" added Toni, in a giddy manner: "It's indescribable!"

In their giddy state, they all held collective honor of what they beheld before them. As they approached a ticket booth to purchase bus tickets to get to the Great Pyramid, a well-dressed tour operator in freshly-pressed khakis, and cropped Egyptian-cotton shirt walked up to them. She was a young woman with a friendly, frozen smile. She said: "oh, they're closed, but we can certainly sell you tickets, and we also do a deal with a camel ride and the tickets for the pyramids all in one. You can have a single or a return."

"Wait a minute, the sign says they're back in a moment!" said Toni, with a rude point to the bus ticket booth.

"Oh, Toni. Let it go! What difference does it make?" said Susan.

"We do the same prices as them," said the young woman.

"Toni, just let it slide. They're not going to kidnap us!" said Susan, then rolled her eyes.

Toni stood, indignantly considering his response: "yeah, you're right. What's the worst that could happen?"

"That's the spirit," said Susan. Susan leaned in next to him and whispered into Toni's ear: "you went with the flow when we had to hitch a cab last night. You can do it again."

The young tour guide smiled at Susan, then priced up their tickets. Toni handed over her Egyptian Pounds: "Oh, sorry, the price is in dollars," said the tour guide.

"Well, their prices are in Egyptian Pounds," said Toni, pointing to the closed bus booth.

Susan interrupted with her hand outstretched: "here, take this. It's everything you asked for in dollars."

Susan then grabbed Toni's arm and led him to the nearest camel-handler but Tony became visibly frustrated: "you shouldn't have. They want dollars cuz it's worth more than double. We've just been ripped off!"

"Yeah, I know, hon. But you gotta ask yourself - how much have we really lost?" replied Susan, soothing Toni by clutching him by the arm.

Jan heard their exchange when she caught with them, to add: "Besides, Toni. We might gain something from this. You never know. Just see it as a gift to the universe. We'll be rewarded. It will come back to us. There's no use in holding back and counting every penny every time," interrupted Jan, before pointedly blowing air through her lips at him: "Just GO with the FLOW."

"Okay, Jan, whatever you say," said Toni, with lips tighter than a bursar's purse.

Susan and Jan both shook their heads at each other, before they all mounted their own camels to make their wobbly journey to the pyramids with laughter that Jan and Susan were quick to resume, and Toni was quick to follow, after his hissy fit. Jan marveled at the way in which the whole of the landscape around her vibrated, something which she absorbed into her energy from the top of the camel. Jan saw the immense strength of the vibrations there - they were stronger than the summers in California, stronger than Lake Tahoe and stronger than the nature that surrounded Santa Clara. Jan was enamored by the vibrations around Giza - they were sharp and strong and they over-powered her.

Taking in the energy, Jan opened up her arms to embrace the air and exclaimed: "oh, my goodness, this is out of this world! Can you feel that?"

Toni, laughing on his camel, said: "I can feel my back cracking!"

To which Susan added: "Enjoy it whilst it lasts, Toni!"

"Cut it out, guys," screamed Jan, from a wobble.

"What's wrong with her now!" chimed Susan.

"It's the energetics of this place. The energy, the energy! It's superb!" screamed Jan, loudly.

"Oh, yeah, the energy. This is your empath thing, isn't it, hon? Well, if it makes you feel great, hon, just soak it all up!" shouted Susan to Jan, alongside her.

The three camels came to a stop after fifteen minutes and were rewarded with apples and buckets of water that were provided for them. After disembarking, their three wild riders entered the Great Pyramid in a daze. Once inside the Great Pyramid, they huddled together as they followed the crowds into the various chambers. The cool interior gave great respite to the dry midday heat outside but the narrow crevices made Jan feel nervous, making her stop for breaths that only got shorter.

"What's wrong, hon?" asked Susan, with a hand on Jan's shoulder.

"I don't feel good. I think I need to sit down," replied Jan.

"Hon, you can't. You have to just keep going," said Susan, who was in front of her, in the single file of people walking down the narrow, enclosed passage.

"We're coming to the King's chamber soon, so you'll be able to catch your breath," said Susan.

When they arrived at the King's chamber, the narrow passage that led all the tourists there appeared to Jan to close in on itself, making her anxiety shoot out of her body like an entity that needed to come up for air. Jan closed her eyes and shuffled through, into the chamber, focusing on her breathing all the while, until her legs gave way, making her lean towards a stone seat at one side of the room. Her head fell into her chest when she sat for respite, continuing the deep-breathing techniques that she learned from therapy, for her high-functioning anxiety disorder, that being an empath gave her. Flanked by her understanding and supportive friends, Jan found some refuge as she worked through her anxiety attack.

After a few moments of sustaining breaths, Jan felt a weight bearing down on her chest, a weight that felt as heavy as the great structure itself:

"I'm sorry. I didn't realize I was going to be affected, in this way. I felt totally different outside. It's almost deathly inside. There's an odd presence. I feel watched, almost," said Jan, with wispy breath.

Susan sprung into action like a nurse: "Don't worry about it, hon. I totally understand. Try to imagine a shield of light around you to protect yourself," said Susan: "This might all just be because it's dark and cramped here. There really should be a warning about that here," continued Susan, with her hand gently placed on the back of Jan's neck.

Jan tapped her temples then massaged the back of her head: "oh, I have a headache!"

In an attempt to solve the problem, Toni suggested escorting Jan out of the pyramid, carefully reassuring his friends that he would be okay to continue exploring on his own there. Jan took him up on the suggestion, but insisted on leaving alone, to avoid breaking Susan's enjoyment of the Great Pyramid.

"I sense this is a lot older than what we think it might be. It might have been ancient even for the Ancient Egyptians," said Jan, whilst trying to gather her strength from where she was sitting, gently rocking back and forth on the stone seat at a wall in the King's Chamber.

Susan and Toni had grown accustomed to Jan's occasional random outbursts during one of her anxiety attacks so they ignored what she said. Jan closed her eyes for a moment, to catch the dozens of thoughts that came swirling through her head, apparently out of nowhere, and tried to organize them so she wouldn't completely lose her cool. A guard noticed her and moved towards her when she was beginning to find her composure - which she did with closed eyes and intense, deep breaths. The guard looked at her in horror and shouted:

"Please do not meditate here. No meditation! No!"

"Who is he talking to?" asked Toni, dismissively.

Susan looked at the guard, then Toni, before resting her concerned gaze on Jan and said: "I think he's talking to you, Jan."

"What? Meditation? What does he mean?" asked a confused Jan, in a blurred state between her deep day-dream of soothing pastures that cooled her and the stifling embrace of millennia-old mysteries.

"I guess they get a lot of cranks doing it here," said Susan, who proceeded to sit with Jan on the stone seat and embrace her.

"Yeah… and they're probably all from California too!" said Toni, who then turned to the guard and said: "No, she is not feeling good. She needs to leave - go out!", pointing to the entrance of the cramped King's Chamber.

The guard swiftly parted the crowd in the King's Chamber with his police-stick, in an egalitarian manner, allowing Jan to weave through to the exit, which Jan paced towards, out through a series of narrow and tall dimly-lit passages, on dodgy wooden platforms, which were placed on metal scaffolds, all the way out of the pyramid. Jan continued towards the pyramid's exit that eventually entered her sight, her anxiety dissipating to the ground as she walked towards it, clutching the rails and ropes tightly as she shuffled through the passageway, pushing through her high levels of anxiety and the sweat that was pouring off her.

Jan was accustomed to the bouts of sweat, when fear rose through her body, that left her shaken, leaving her feeling hopeless for states she never had any explanation for.

Her therapy had helped her get through her social anxiety, which she needed for large groups, where she was prone to absorbing everyone's energy, leaving her unable to breathe and function properly. But the deathly energy of what she felt around her in the King's Chamber was energy which she had never dealt with before. It was dark and low and it suffocated her, even as she continued to focus on her breathing, as if non-human hands had gripped her chest. Breathing in, breathing out, breathing in, breathing out, she walked in pace, to one, two and three seconds, to deepen her breathing, but she couldn't get past one.

She began to hyperventilate, the panacea for which was only the view of the exit.

When Jan put her hands on the exit and felt the dry atmosphere outside the pyramid, her deep breathing returned to two-seconds, finally alternating to one, until she could feel her breath travel down the rest of her body from her chest where it was stuck and she could feel her feet again.

Jan ran down the ramp of the Great Pyramid, barging past the line of people making their way to it from the base. When she touched ground, Jan ran to the side of it, and rested herself against one of the large stones and closed her eyes. Looking up at the overcast sky after a few still moments, Jan breathed a deep, three-second breath for a few rounds, then thanked it for being able to threaten rain. She grabbed a scarf from her bag and proceeded to wipe the sweat off her glistening face, then draped it around her neck to cover the damp patches on the front of her t-shirt.

Jan softened her gaze on the horizon ahead. From experience, she knew not to look at either side of her, just in case someone cut her a stare, which might set off another attack. Jan came to accept her anxiety attacks for what they were - a part of her that she had no explanation for but had developed some coping mechanisms for - such as distracting herself after her come-down, which she did by fixating on the area they had just travelled from - the pyramid gardens on the near-horizon. She breathed deeply one last time, in the hope she would be able to find her center. Then a flood of guilty feelings surfaced, after her post-adrenaline rush, leaving her feeling depressed and hungry.

It was a typical end of a rollercoaster ride, that she soothed with some dextrose and a swig from her bottle of water.

Susan and Toni emerged an hour later, in time to start making headway back to Cairo. They hugged Jan when they met her, promptly brushing off the incident as they both had done many times before, though they hadn't seen her in that state for a while. In any case, they knew it was best not to dwell on it too much. They returned to the pyramid gardens on their camels in a completely different mood to the one they had arrived in. Susan suggested grabbing a drink and perhaps something to eat at the café they were at earlier that afternoon. By the time they arrived at the café, it was lit up in tiki-torches, under dusk.

After they all got settled for an evening at the hotel-café, a breezy Jan ordered herself a Gin cocktail to take the edge off the day, and the others joined her, to relax for their view of the pyramids ahead of them, under a deep-blue sky. After a couple of cocktails, they ordered some small bites and began to relax, with the view of the pyramids ahead of them, with their backs turned on the colonial building behind them. They recreated scenes from Poirot and Indiana Jones, basking regally in their attire of t-shirts, shorts and sandals.

Susan was closest to playing the part right by way of her dress and Toni's manner was sufficiently starchy for the mood, as was Jan's. The young student-waiter kept returning to the familiar faces of that day's afternoon, to take orders, but nobody had worked up an appetite, apart from Jan, who had to eat to take her medication for her diabetes:

"I'll have a wrap. Just an avocado and hummus wrap," said Jan, as she took another swig of pink Gin and sugar-free ginger ale: "What's in your Gin, guys?"

"A tonic," said Toni, sipping reservedly.

Susan continued drinking as her friends sat and watched and waited for a response from her: "Is there supposed to be Gin in this?" asked Susan.

They all burst out laughing spontaneously and synchronistically. Susan's uncanny timing always provided the right relief at the right moments. Jan smiled from the inside - she began to feel good again and tried to hold that feeling. Toni started to relax and began to order some small bites of food, like Jan had, followed by Susan, who did the same, in a constant to and fro-ing with the young waiter, who was happy to humor them with his good nature and patience.

They progressively got drunk on the light relief at the end of a disjointed day, on various Gin cocktails, as they recounted the day and their management of it. Susan's ability to temper both Toni and Jan did not go unnoticed - Toni's bookish approach to the holiday and Jan's curious relationship with *energy* and *vibrations* would tire out the most robust constitutions of any seasoned traveler, but Susan was always there to administer the right type of medicine:

"Well, I'm glad you made it out to the other side," said Susan, jokingly: "It's a good job you didn't have a knife with you, Jan. You might have resorted to using it when you were trying to get out of the pyramid!"

"God, no, we'd all be man-handled and locked up by now!" exclaimed Toni.

Jan was suddenly overcome with fits of laughter, releasing the tension of the afternoon to put the day behind her. The young waiter kept returning with more cocktails until they all buzzed under a wave of intoxication. As they enjoyed their celebratory drinks, the sky turned a deeper dark-blue. In front of them lay the ground-lit road to the Great Pyramid, a few hundred meters away, and the lights turned on, one by one, drawing all of their attention to it, in their tipsy state. The road to the Great Pyramid continued to light up, reaching its base, where bold-spot-lights illuminated each of its sides.

"You know what I'd like to do?" said Jan, continuing before her friends could answer: "return to the Pyramid tonight!"

"Are you on crack, honey?" stated Toni, with a side-eye.

Before Susan could respond, Jan got out of her chair and walked towards the bar behind them on the terrace in front of the palatial, white Art-Deco hotel that was lined with mammoth palm trees that covered red roof-tops over its brilliant white-stone edifice. Jan turned around to see her friends sat drinking at their table and said, comfortably tipsy, to the barman: "is there a way I can hire a cab for the night?"

Jan was ready to throw caution to the wind and move into the flow of potential joyful experiences. She, too, wanted to feel liberated, just as she saw in the moments when Toni could let go of control and move with the energy that Susan successfully could in the world. Jan expected the barman to refuse her, but he replied with: "sure, I can arrange that for you. Where shall I say you want to go?"

"The Great Pyramid!" said Jan, without turning to face him, staggering on her wobbly knees, her gaze fixed on her friends where they were seated.

"Okay. You may be able to see it from the outside because I think the road may be closed, but it's within walking distance, if you are prepared to walk it. But I really would not recommend it because you'll need to get past the guards, or you can just go and see the light show tonight," said the barman, in a curt manner.

Susan walked over to the bar to join the conversation, and Jan relayed to Susan what the barman told her. Like any good friend would, Susan obliged Jan's desire for an adventure, after sensing her friend's need for it. Susan then asked the barman: "how much for a personal escort to the Great Pyramid?". Whilst asking, Susan stuck out her chest and looked at the young man deep into his repressed eyes.

"A hundred dollars. I can take you there in my car after my shift in a couple of hours. You can have a look around, but I will only wait for an hour. If you go missing after an hour, that is up to you. I will drive away. You are then at the mercy of passers-by and the elements, and that is not advisable," said the young barman, with an assertive tone and a heavy French-Arabic accent.

"You've done this before, haven't you?" smiled Susan, in her exchange. She continued to ask the barman, despite his increasingly unfriendly demeanor: "How much for helping us get a room for the night nearby? For all three of us."

"Susan, stop. You can't! I can't! We can't!" interrupted Jan, who was beginning to sober up from her momentary fantasy of experiencing care-free living.

"'Shush," responded Susan.

"That's another 50 dollars plus whatever you pay at the hotel, if they find you one. We're all booked up here, but there is a little inn that my friend runs for guests like you," said the barman.

"Guests like us?" asked a defensive Jan, propping herself up at the bar.

"You know, middle-age foreign tourists in desperate need of some adventure," smirked the young French-Arabic barman, smiling quietly and confidently.

"Honey, we come from California. Every minute in California is an adventure!" quipped Susan.

The barman laughed and said: "touché! Wait a couple of hours. I really wouldn't advise any more drinking. The heat from the day can hit you very hard and it would be a waste if you did not get to enjoy your little adventure."

After the bar closed at 2 am, the barman escorted his guests to his car - his carriage for his second job, as a taxi driver. He drove them down the ground-lit road to the Great Pyramid, past the light show around it, and parked to the one side of the pyramid where there were no spotlights. Jan got out of the car and walked towards the Great Pyramid, turning slowly round to find her friends shaking their heads back at her:

"You have exactly one hour," said the driver, then switched off his car and lights: "after that, I am gone!"

Jan bathed in glow from the spotlights that seeped from the other sides of the pyramid, throwing her arms up to embrace the air as she approached it. Toni looked at Susan and said: "we better watch out for her. Looks like she's on one tonight!"

Turning to Jan's direction, ahead in the distance, Toni shouted: "If you climb that, we will all be arrested!"

"Don't worry. I'm only going to sit here for a bit. Come and join me," said Jan, near the base of the pyramid.

The driver shook his head at the spectacle from his car, as the trio mounted the large stones at the base of the pyramid, to settle into a happy state for their late-night escapade.

"Isn't this the most amazing thing ever!" yelled Jan, with a large smile.

"Yes, it is," sighed Susan in great contemplation then added: "It is spectacular. I can't imagine what they're getting from that light show that they can't by just sitting here and being in the moment!" said Susan.

Toni reclined on the stone, where they all sat, at the base of the pyramid. Looking up at the stars from where he lay, he added: "I'm disappointed with the lack of visibility here. Since this place is more lit up than I expected it to be, we can't really see the stars. I was hoping to see Orion's belt."

"I think that only happens at a certain time of the year, with the procession," said Susan, who rolled her eyes, sighed and shook her head. Then said *"Oh, Toni",* for effect.

Jan did not respond to their little bickering exchange but took a quick scan of the area to see who was around, instead. She stood on the stone at the base of the pyramid and looked up along the side of it, on her right, the line of the side that travelled up into the sky, into the deep blue sky at night, and was taken aback by the vastness of the void that promised her so much more than what she found at the base of the pyramid. It was a mystery that consumed her whole being, a mystery in the ethers that beckoned her to it.

Jan carefully turned her head to the left, carefully balancing herself on the stone, feeling as if she was being lifted somewhere in space, with feet firmly planted on Earth. She asked Toni for the approximate length of the side that she tried to breathe into view. Toni responded quickly: "around 140 meters". Jan stood, thinking to herself for a couple of moments and then looked at Susan, who was also laying on the stone with Toni, both of them looking up at the stars.

Jan waited until her friends got lost in their own conversation again and, after a quick glance to check if the driver was watching, Jan decided to scale the Great Pyramid. She moved swiftly but quietly, like a cheetah. After ten minutes, she managed to scale some distance, despite her short legs and wide frame. Not wanting to turn around, for what she might see or hear that might knock her off her course, Jan continued for another ten minutes until she was near the top. As she approached it, Jan heard Susan's voice first, calling out to her from below: "Jan, I am going to kill you! This is madness". It was followed by the muffled sound of Toni's voice: "Gurl, you are a hot mess! You are going to get us all into trouble! My black ass is going back to the car! I am not going to jail because of you!"

Jan mouthed "sorry" back at them, followed by: "you better keep your voices down if you don't want us all caught!" but it was returned with silence. Jan and her friends were no longer within earshot of each other. Just a few more meters and Jan was at the top of the pyramid. She reached for the final stone and felt the flat surface. Jan pushed her weight to the top, a flat-top square of a few meters squared, that marked the absence of the Great Pyramid's original capstone. Jan smiled deeply, sat down and enjoyed the view, like the Queen of Egypt, adoring the bronze-orange colors that shimmered from the lights on the ground, some tens of meters down on the ground below her.

She surveyed the land and the horizon, under the deep majestic sky with lush navy blues. Jan let out a scream. A joyous, thrilling scream: "Yes!"

Light from the light show, which was still in motion at one side of the pyramid, reached the summit where Jan's leg's dangled atop the Egyptian air. Jan carefully stood up, placing both her hands on the flat surface, to balance herself against any unexpected gust of wind, making her whole body arch into a downward-facing dog position. When she arched herself up, she avoided the beams of light that trickled up the side of the pyramid, and intermittently hit the top where she stood. Jan laughed in exhilaration, at the absurdity of the light show. A green laser beam was fired from a distance, in the direction of the pyramid. It came from another part of some other light show from a neighboring pyramid.

Jan saw the point of the beam travel towards her, making her swing her right arm in the air as it passed by her face, making her whole body tilt back, whilst she planted her feet firmly on the flat top surface.

Jan stood, ten toes down, on feet that were firmly rooted on top of the Great Pyramid. She pulled her chest up into the air to regain control of her core, eventually standing up straight again. She closed her eyes in gratitude, from having regained her stature, and noticed something move under her. It felt like a tremor, as if the Great Pyramid was disturbed by the soles of her feet. There was no noise coming from the ground below her, at least none that Jan could hear. Jan decided to ignore it but the feeling grew, and moved through her, making her feel as though her feet, legs and buttocks were gently being massaged.

Jan's sensitivity to energy, particularly from people, rose through her intensely. It was a sharp feeling that moved through her but it carried a certain warmth, until it hit her lower back, and it started to rise like a serpent, hugging her in a spiral motion, until it reached the top of her head, leaving her feeling bewildered. Her eyes flickered as she tried to shake off the feeling, thinking that perhaps her blood sugar-levels were low. Trying to resist the feeling of sleep, the energy that arose within her overwhelmed her, and Jan fell into a slumber, passing out where she was, on the flat-top surface of the Great Pyramid.

In her sleep, she had a lucid dream. It was the time of Ancient Egypt, and she was in the King's Chamber, standing next to a large device, a sort of telescope-like mechanism. She pressed a button and a ray of light shot through the large shaft in the chamber. Then, suddenly, Jan was standing outside the pyramid, pointing at it, alongside a group of men who appeared to her like priests and astrologists. The Great Pyramid in her dream was a white, smooth structure and marble in appearance. Then it was night, in her dream, and the pyramid shone a light from within, through the top, to the heavens above. Then her dream took her to the Queen's quarters, where she sat with a mirror, combing her jet-black hair, which was cut into a bob.

She took a kohl pencil and drew it around her eyes and the gold and Lapis Lazuli from her necklace glistened in her hand-mirror. Her maidens dressed her and helped her descend the stone staircase. Jan was Cleopatra, Queen of Egypt.

Just as soon as Jan saw herself as the Queen of Egypt, Jan awoke from her dream, feeling uneasy and other-worldly, after returning to her body and waking up. As Jan came to, she saw the vibrations of the earth in a gentle hum, the only thing that gave her a semblance of herself in that moment, on top of the Great Pyramid. Then she heard Susan´s voice, nearby:

Susan's arms rested on the flat top of the pyramid, and Jan heard her say: ´´Come down, Jan. The taxi driver is livid, and he's about to call the police, unless you come back down NOW!"

"Don't come up. Don't come up!" said Jan, alarmed, and she followed with: "I'm coming down. Right this second!"

"Well, hurry because he is not going to wait much longer!" yelled Susan.

As Jan was getting ready for her steep descent, she turned around to take a final look at the panorama of the majestic Egyptian landscape, to admire the deep-blue night-sky which blanketed the orange, bronze and white specks of light that shone from the ground beneath. It was a sight she captured on her phone, gingerly reaching into her bag as she stood up, carefully anchoring her feet to the ground. Whilst trying to get her balance, she snapped a couple of pictures and asked Susan to grab hold of her feet.

Before finishing with her memento, Jan noticed something in the sky. Between the dark sky and the hues from the ground below, there lay a band of bright white light which ran all across the horizon and all around the panorama. Before she turned around to Susan's beckoning call to descend, Jan fixed her gaze for a moment to find that the band of white light between the sky and the horizon also ran adjacent to it, in a criss-cross, grid-like pattern.

Jan shook her head and just before she took her step to descend, she took some more pictures of what looked like a part of a grid in the sky, that was constructed by beams of white light. Jan shook her head in haste, not having time to stop and stare, hurried by Susan's growing and frequent calls to descend, which travelled up from the base in increasing intensity. After returning to the ground, some minutes short of the taxi driver's clock, they all ran to the taxi, where the driver berated them profusely for disrespecting Egyptian laws and customs:

"I'll explain later," said Jan to her livid friends, after apologizing profusely to the driver, who continuously berated them to their destination.

They were taken to the nearest inn where they unloaded for the night in their separate single rooms and the driver sped off, leaving a trail of dust. Jan, berated by Toni, then Susan, in equal measure, and alternating fashion, for several minutes, whilst she stood in a daze, stood and stared at them both from the doorway to her room. Both Toni and Susan continued to express their frustration with Jan, but Jan looked on at them with disregard.

Jan wasn't angry with her friends. She was thrilled and happy with herself, for the first time in her adult life. The intense pleasure of what she had done and what she had experienced consumed her. It didn't matter to her that her friends were upset. She knew they would move on from it. As soon as she got into her room, she threw open the shutters to a splendid view - the pyramids continued to call at her, spoke to her, enticed her - under the brilliant-deep-navy night sky that became soaked with the silver clouds of a half-crescent moon.

The next morning, Jan did her best to appease her friends who had shaken off the previous day's events, just as she knew they would, leaving them all to resume their usual dynamic and jovial relationship. Susan and Toni could not abide the thought of having to rely on each other for company, so they were quick to put Jan's shenanigans behind them. They made some cursory comments over breakfast, about how lucky Jan was to have escaped the consequences of her actions. Susan joked that Toni might have actually enjoyed being man-handled by police officers, had the driver reported them.

They then decided to spend their final day in Giza, walking the rest of the beaten path of the pyramids. Before they left the area via the main road that led out of the area, Jan spotted a nightclub. Outside the venue, there was a local merchant selling runes, stones and necklaces.

Jan stopped by to have a chat with the seller: "can you tell me something about these stones?"

"Yes, certainly," said the old, bearded man in a black tunic that was adorned with all sorts of stones, necklaces, crucifixes and ankhs: "They are different stones that represent different points in your body and serve different functions. Amethyst is a violet stone, which also is the same color as one of the chakras. It's good to wear if you want to keep that particular part of your chakra clean."

"What are chakras?" asked Jan.

"They are energy fields in your body," interrupted Susan. Jan looked at Susan, surprised.

"That is correct," said the old merchant: "Your friend can tell you much more about it, but here is a diagram."

The old man pulled out a chart with a diagram of the human body in the lotus position, pointing at it to show Jan all the chakra points in the body. The diagram illustrated the flow of energy in the shape of a serpent. Jan pointed in return, tapping the sheet of paper in acknowledgement of what she felt on top of the Great Pyramid.

"That is how the energy rises from the body, from the base of the spine through your top, to align your chakras. That is the Kundalini energy. Once your chakras are aligned, you can connect to the divine source of creation - God, the universe … or source, as you may wish to call it," explained the man, comfortably.

The old man then burned some incense and pulled a chair for Jan and said: "come, sit down, I will teach you about it…"

"No, we don't have time," interrupted Toni anxiously apprehensive of having to engage the mystical whims of the old merchant.

Jan turned to her friends and turned back to the old mystic: "I'm sorry, we don't have time but if you don't mind, I would like something to help me deal with negative energy. I feel I take on everyone's energy, and I'm overwhelmed by it. Do you have anything for that?"

"Oh, you're one of them. I have sadly advised a lot of your types over the years and your numbers just keep on increasing," said the old man, comically.

"Well, how long have you been doing this for?" asked Susan.

"30 years, but the last 20 years have been significant, in that regard. The generations that are to come will be especially sensitive," said the man.

"Oh, come on, this is nonsense," said Toni.

"Hush, now," said Susan.

"For your condition, what I would recommend is a lot of meditation and to work on your inner self. You can try

Amethyst or Crystal Quartz when you sleep, and you can take some to wear," said the old man.

"Yes, I'll take a couple, please" said Jan, quickly handing over her cash.

"But you could really benefit from a chakra alignment. That's when you work on balancing all your energy points, but you need to understand what each one represents, first. That requires a lot of teaching and patience. I could leave you my details. I have some literature I could email you," said the man, carefully selecting leaflets from his stand and inserting them into a paper bag, along with the stone necklaces that Jan wanted.

"Okay, thank you," said Jan and she stood up to leave. Before leaving, she said: "One thing….I had an awful experience in the Great Pyramid. I felt something pressing down on my skull and chest. Do you know what they might have been? My friend Toni here thinks it might have been something to do with the air pressure but…"

"Oh," sighed the mystic: "We do not explain things in our world with Western science. We have our own interpretations. That, my dear, is the remnant energy from the Ancients and all the people who have gone before, ever since that pyramid was built. I would say it's largely negative energy from souls that are trapped there. Perhaps their greed led them to die early, so that's why you felt it heavily. Or it could simply be the souls of the Kings and Queens travelling in and out of the astral plane. I myself would never enter that building. All of this land is cursed,´´ continued the man, unfettered at how he might be sounding to his patrons.

"Oh come on, I am going to leave now," interrupted Toni.

Susan said with an impatient tone: "stop it, Toni. Just wait for Jan to finish."

´´What might happen to your chakras if you were on top of the pyramid?" asked Jan.

"Oh, you must never do that," warned the old man.

"Yes, because it's illegal, and you could have killed yourself!" added Toni, adamantly.

The old mystic took a careful glance at what he heard Toni say and shook his head ominously to say: "No, because my dear, especially for you and your condition…that would not have been advisable."

"Yes but what would happen?" pressed Jan.

"Hundreds come here every year looking for some sort of spiritual experience, but it all depends on their soul, to begin with. I have seen many people go crazy after coming down that pyramid because they weren't ready for their awakening. It would awaken your kundalini energy and open your third eye. You will be able to perceive all matter and time simultaneously, as well as see other levels of reality. Like an Ayahuasca experience. But you must be prepared for it. You must be guided through your awakening. It's what the Buddhists called Samadhi and it could go very wrong for you," said the man, sternly, his eyes piercing Jan, as if he was looking through her soul in judgement.

Jan was then swiftly led away by Toni, without protest, followed by Susan. They all walked down the street, to the main road that led back to Cairo. They came to a bus stop and boarded one of the buses that lined the streets and headed back to downtown Cairo. They all spent the rest of the afternoon quietly. Jan spoke very little, Toni spent the time looking up information on his phone, and Susan snapped random photos on her phone. They all felt a definite need to distract themselves, to try and retrieve any sense of enjoyment they could for the rest of their holiday, after recent events. An unspoken agreement swept them - to focus their attention on resuming a regular holiday like regular tourists.

After the fateful events of the previous day, the rest of the two and half weeks were spent with relative order. Jan, Toni and Susan conducted their days in the usual pattern: breakfast either at the hotel or in a café, a trip to the local souk for supplies, then sightseeing in Cairo. In their final week, with very little to do or see, they collectively decided to take a day trip to Alexandria where they explored the Ancient Greek remnants but returned unimpressed. Their hearts lay in Cairo, sipping Gin cocktails in Art Deco buildings, wearing khakis, with linen shirts and straw hats.

Toni began to loosen up with the locals, secure in his advances towards men, who became willing recipients of his flirtatious behavior, for the possibility of purchases from their stores. Susan made herself known at the colonial bar they frequented in downtown Cairo and Jan counted all the names of businesses that were named after the ancients. After a while, nobody took part in a name-bingo, save for the times when it was needed to break the occasional tension that sometimes simmered between them.

Despite the distractions, Jan continuously thought of the dream she had when she was on top of the pyramid. She also thought about contacting the mystic that she met by the side of the road, but she refrained from retracing her steps in favor of keeping the peace with her friends. She already was cursed with the ability to read energy and see vibrations, and she decided that she already had enough of an adventure. As the days progressed since her little adventure, however, Jan began to experience instances of clairvoyance and synchronicity. She was beginning to foresee events occurring before they did. Such as the time when Jan felt Susan wanted to spend an afternoon together, so she expected and received a call from her.

Instead of alarming her friends, however, Jan decided to keep her new gifts to herself. As the days rolled to the end of their holiday, Jan began to think more about contacting the old mystic but she came to a solid conclusion to can it!

The night before they left, Jan was looking through her photos on her phone, the first time she had done whilst on holiday. She came across the photos she took on top of the pyramid after swiping for a few minutes. But she couldn't find the grid of white-light in the sky. Jan switched her phone off and put it away. Maybe the Professor would be able to explain it to her when she returned to Santa Clara, she thought. For the first time since her faux pas with Professor Greene, Jan had forgotten about her embarrassing exchange with him. She just let it be and smiled at the thought of making contact with him again when she returned: "He'll tell me what that was. He'll be able to explain it" she said to herself, out aloud, in her room.

After getting dressed for bed, Jan decided to check her blood sugar levels on her device. It revealed that they were normal. "That's funny", she said to herself: "maybe it's because I've been more active and the food here is a lot healthier" and left it at that. She looked in her suitcase and realized that the supply of her diabetes pills remained untouched. Shrugging her shoulders, Jan turned off the lights to get herself to sleep before their early flight ahead.

A few hours later, Jan awoke for her middle-of-the-night trip to the airport, with Toni and Susan, who managed to get herself booked on the same flight with Toni and Jan, back to San Francisco. On the flight back to California, Jan dreamt of Ancient Egypt again, where she reigned as Cleopatra, under a clear navy sky with the cosmos above her. Then the plane touched down and it was time to wake up.

Chapter 3

Santa Clara

The jet lag from the trip was tiring for all. Jan took copious amounts of melatonin to ward off the heaviness that was beginning to bear down on her, like the heavy air that she had to escape from, in the King's Chamber. Jan eased herself back to work, welcoming questions from her new colleagues, in her new temporary office, for the short-term project with the irritating Jonah - the least inspiring person to face after the holiday of a lifetime.

Jan periodically glanced at her phone during her lunch breaks at her desk in the week following her return to work, to remind herself of the wonderful moments she had in the weeks with Toni and Susan, which still resonated with her and gave her the wonderful feeling she needed to help her through her week. Whilst flicking through the copious amounts of photos, Jan came across the picture she took when she was on top of the pyramid and it made her smile.

"That's the first time you've smiled since you returned from your holiday," said her colleague, a middle-aged secretary.

"Yes, I just found something. It was when I climbed to the top of the Great Pyramid, after an evening of drinking with my friends," smiled Jan.

"Oh, that sounds so wonderful. Can I have a look?" asked the colleague. Jan passed her phone to her colleague: "Oh my goodness, that is so spectacular. Wait. Were you allowed to do that?" asked Jan's colleague.

"No!" said Jan, smugly.

"Oh my goodness. It looks like you had a lot of fun. That must have been an awesome trip. Any plans to return?" asked her colleague.

Jan flashed a wry smile and said: "yes, it was - and no - I don't have any plans just yet. I saved up for 2 years for it, and it will take a lottery win to return anytime soon."

"I can imagine!" said the colleague, who then returned to her desk.

Jan sat at her desk and examined the photo a bit more, quietly reminiscing of that night, when she saw the strange grid-like white stripes in the sky. Jan sat back and thought of Professor Greene and thought of emailing him again but paused for a moment. She checked her inbox again, but there wasn't anything, so she decided to walk off her lunch for fifteen minutes. She walked to the garden wall outside the building, where she sat for a moment, breathing in the midday Californian air, looking up at the white lines that had been created by airplanes. Jan couldn't shake what she had seen, there on top of the Great Pyramid.

She looked at the Californian sky again and a thought occurred to her, something which she was sure Professor Greene would be able to answer. It was a simple question, but it would give her the right reason to approach him.

Upon her return to her desk, Jan fired off a quick email to Professor Greene, inviting him to answer a question related to physics, then she carried on with her work with the same amount of pleasure she had since returning from her holiday. After finishing for the week, she returned home that Friday to begin her home-routine, which always began by sitting on her veranda with a nice cup of tea. Jan sat quietly, watching the world turn, with the neighbor's dog watching her from his window. She stared down the street and continued to drink her tea. Just when Jan was about to get up from her rocking chair and return indoors, the boy appeared again, and Jan's eyes darted open.

The boy crossed the street again, much to Jan's alarm, certain she was experiencing deja vu. Despite a determined attempt to not lose sight of him again, Jan's phone pinged a message, causing her to inspect it. Jan looked back up from her phone and, much to her dismay, the boy had disappeared. She shook her head again, perplexed. With no time to dwell upon what she had witnessed, Jan became preoccupied by the text she received. It was from the Professor, and it read:

Let's meet.

Tomorrow? At the Espresso Royale for lunch? - texted Jan, in swift elevated response, after the disappearance of the apparition.

You're on! - responded the Professor.

They met on a warm early-August day, in the air-conditioned café. The Professor seemed anxious and spoke with haste, diving straight into the topic of Jan's inquiry: "To answer your question about why the sky is blue, that's to do with light waves. The light that travels from the sun hits earth's atmosphere, and it scatters in all directions from the gases in the air. What we perceive as blue is light, simply scattered in a certain way in the spectrum," said the Professor.

"Okay," replied Jan, and decided not to proceed further with her line of questioning.

The Professor leaned over to Jan and said, softly, with a friendly smile: "so, tell me about Egypt. I know you're dying to share."

Jan caught Jim's eyes sparkle and returned a smile. She put his spark down to his curiosity, a burning need to learn about her experience, rather than any physical attraction for her. Besides, Jan was almost always oblivious to the charms of any potential suitors. She clenched her glass of fresh lemonade, in anticipation of relaying her experience to the Professor.

"It was great. We did so many things, drank lots of Gin cocktails and I scaled the Great Pyramid," said Jan.

"No!" said the Professor, aghast: "You are full of surprises, Jan. First your interest in physics, now this!"

Jan wanted to be asked about what she saw on top of the pyramid, so she tried to steer the conversation back to where she wanted it to go. She decided to humor him and turn on some of her hidden charm:

"Oh, there are a lot of things you don't know about me. I'm a bit of a dark horse!" she said, with a wink.

"I'd like to find out more," smiled the Professor, and leaned in across the table in the cafe.

Jan stopped herself from daydreaming herself into a relationship with the Professor. At almost 10 years her senior with a slight paunch, a hipster beard and an eccentric dress sense, Jan wondered if she could abide being with him, without feeling the need to completely control every aspect of his appearance and being. He was cute though, she thought, in his slightly awkward and introverted way and would, she then thought, compliment her 40-something desire for adventure.

Jan reclined in her chair and said: "You might get to learn more."

The Professor continued to smile, chuckling to himself at her response, with shoulders that shrugged with his inner joy.

Jan followed with a smile before leading the conversation back to a sobering topic: "so, about the sky…." she said and cleared her throat.

"Yes, yes, about the sky…." echoed the Professor.

"Is it possible that it could be any other color?" asked Jan.

"Yes, it could be red, from pollution," answered the Professor.

"Could it ever be white? Like white stripes?" continued Jan.

"I've never seen white stripes. Do you mean when planes fly in the sky?" asked the Professor, cautious not to appear condescending.

"No, like a band of light on the horizon. Actually, it was above the horizon. From where I stood, it was in the sky. It was horizontal. That's what I saw first. It was like a tube and it first appeared where the lights from the land met the night sky.

Then when I looked again, I saw more of the band of light run across the sky but it wasn't just a tube of light. It then appeared like a grid. Like a net," said Jan, still clenching her lemonade.

"I don't know what that could have been. Without a picture, I wouldn't be able to tell you further," said the Professor, and put his head down to continue drinking his coffee, without raising an eyebrow.

Jan sensed that she wasn't getting anywhere with the Professor, so she decided to give her curiosity a rest. Doing her best to hide her frustration, she moved the subject back to familiar ground. After a few minutes discussing the antiquities, Jan made preparations to leave and return home.

The Professor eyed Jan with some concern, then said:

"You seem to be in search of something. I'd love to help you out more, but I only know what I know. I'm sorry." The Professor paused for a moment, sensing Jan's disappointment and a sense to please her, he offered a solution: "I do know someone who might be able to help you out more. He's in the History department and a senior researcher. He's not long for retirement. He's really into unexplained phenomena, and I think what you're explaining is not necessarily related to any mainstream subject in schools. Maybe he can help you more. I'm sorry, it's just not my area of expertise," said the Professor, as he extended his hand to Jan.

Jan opened the palm of her hand to accept his offer - a piece of paper with a name and number, which he scribed for her.

Jan took it with a mixture of disappointment and encouragement and left the café. During her walk home in the mid-afternoon sun, shaded by oak and maple trees, she watched the heat rise off the earth and the trees vibrate in their full bloom, and she took a moment to come to the slow acceptance that there wasn't anyone with whom she could share the way she saw the world, let alone try and find an explanation for it. They simply wouldn't understand because everything that Jan understood about the world wasn't taught in schools or universities. Back in her apartment, Jan unstrapped her bag from her shoulders, crumpled the piece of paper with the telephone number that was handed to her and pushed it into the bag. Her phone rang and she grabbed it from her bag. It was Susan:

"Girl, we have not seen each other since we returned. Where have you been? What have you been up to? Are you still alive and kicking?" said Susan in her usual chirpy voice.

"Yeah, I'm good. It's just depressing being back, you know. Post-holiday blues and all that," said Jan.

"Hon, let's go out tonight. There's a singer and a small band playing at the Royale tonight. I don't think they'll be too loud. We'll have pizza and wine and talk some," proposed Susan.

"Okay, I'll see you there at 7pm," said Jan decidedly, then ended the call.

After spending some time catching up with her neighbor, Jan showered and got ready for her evening. Jan took a moment to look outside the glass door, to her veranda, hoping to catch a glimpse of the boy on his bike again, but her efforts yielded no result. She reminded herself to take some time, in the following days, to walk to the end of the street, to see what she could find at the traffic lights. For the time being, an evening with her bestie awaited her.

Later on that evening, Jan and Susan settled into a cozy night at the Royale - the place which changed from a café by-day, into a lounge-bar at night. Susan was still elated from the holiday, a few weeks after they had returned and Jan welcomed her with a hug.

Jan, enjoying Susan's exuberance, said: "oh, it's like we're back there now."

"Oh, I know," said Susan. "I can just feel it now."

"The spotlights against the white walls and the black frames of the windows and the red rooftop of this place kinda remind me of some of the places there ...." reflected Jan.

Susan shot Jan a cynical glance and said: "Oh, Jan, please stop...you're beginning to sound like Toni!"

Jan replied: "okay, it's not the same, but a girl can try!"

They continued laughing, reminisced about their holiday, bitched about how difficult Toni had been and how he eventually loosened up and began to enjoy himself. Susan shared some titbits about her indiscretions with a couple of young men at the hotel and how she indulged in a couple of escapades with the barman-turned-driver, after he took them to the Great Pyramid that night:

"No way," said a shocked Jan, though she was somewhat unsurprised.

"Now you know why you never got arrested for your stunt!" said Susan.

"Stop!" giggled Jan. "No way!"

"Way!" parroted Susan.

"But you enjoyed it, right?" said Jan as they both continued giggling and got progressively drunk.

"So what did you see at the top of the pyramid anyway?" asked Susan.

"Oh, you do not wanna know!" said Jan, under her breath.

"It must have been amazing because ever since that moment, you haven't been the same," commented Susan.

"Oh, can you tell?" asked Jan with some suspicion.

"Yes, of course. Your whole vibe. It just appears different. There's something going on and you're not telling me," said Susan, and sipped her wine.

"Well, I will tell you but you have to promise me you won't tell Toni cuz he will just freak out, and he'll stop speaking to me," said Jan.

"Go on then!" encouraged Susan.

"It's like…you know… when we were talking with that old mystic and he gave me these stones to wear…." said Jan and she flashed Susan the stones she had been wearing religiously ever since she bought them. Jan then said: "Well….I see the world a lot differently now. More so than ever before…."

"Well, how did you see it before?" enquired Susan.

"Through energy and vibrations," said Jan, with as much matter-of-fact as she could muster.

"Well, I know about your problems with people's energy…but vibrations? That's a new one for me!" said Susan.

Jan winced a little but remained unfettered. Comforted by Susan's presence, Jan continued: "Oh…well…I can see things vibrate. It can be a place or building, but it's usually more visible in nature - earth, mountains, trees, water," said Jan, growing in confidence, losing all reticence about the subject.

"Oh, that must be so cool. Can you see it in people?" asked Susan with a tone of inquiry that made Jan feel at ease.

Jan dropped her shoulders and let out a deep sigh, as if she had unpacked a heavy load from the relief of Susan's acceptance: "No, I can only really feel people's energy very strongly. But not now, cuz I'm drunk, and I'm focused on you," answered Jan.

"It must be hard for you too, right?" asked Susan sympathetically.

Jan put her head down and took a swig of her drink. She began to relax immediately upon hearing Susan's understanding response, saying: "Yes, especially when the energy is heavy or negative on a person. And that energy gets converted into vibrations that are often hard for me to handle. It's like when you know not to drive or go near an area because it's creepy. That's because of the energy of the people there," explained Jan.

"Yeah, that's the sense I get but not as strongly as you, I imagine," echoed Susan.

"Toni wouldn't understand this at all," stressed Jan.

"Is that because he's a guy, do you think?" asked Susan.

"Possibly, but I think it's because he's just been taught to see the world in a certain way and that's all he's prepared to see," explained Jan.

"So what do you think happened after you scaled the pyramid? Cuz that old man told us that it wasn't a good idea for someone like you. Is that what's changed with you?" asked Susan.

"The difference is that I see things happening now before they occur. I suppose it's some sort of clairvoyance. Also, things happen a lot more quickly for me than they did before. Coincidences occur a lot more frequently and, if I am looking for someone or something, I am more likely to find it more quickly," stated Jan.

"Synchronicity. That's a sign that you are special. But we know that already. Have you spoken to anyone about it? About what you see?" continued Susan.

"No. You know how people are. I can't even tell one of my best friends in case he freaks out!" said Jan with a sigh.

"What about that physics guy?" asked Susan.

"Oh, don't ask. I tried. He just wants to get laid. Besides, he freaked out the last time I mentioned seeing vibrations, and he can't explain things to me outside what he's been taught. I wanted to know about the glitches I've been seeing lately, but I am not prepared to go anywhere near that subject with him," asserted Jan.

"The glitches?" asked Susan, confused: "you mean, the synchronicities?"

Jan looked up from her glass of wine and said: "oh, yeah… I mean the synchronicities!"

"Honey, don't bother with him. What about that guy, at the side of the road? You know, in Giza?" continued Susan, completely engrossed with Jan's revelations.

"Oh, yeah. Maybe I can contact him. I completely forgot about him. But he can only explain the spiritual stuff, but that's not what I want to know. The Professor put me in touch with someone who could explain the unexplained, but I haven't had time to contact him yet."

"He sounds the right person, hon. Explain the unexplained," laughed Susan, then affirmed: "Ring him up tomorrow!"

The night ended with Jan feeling somewhat more confident with herself, less of a stranger. She returned to her apartment, feeling assured in the knowledge that she did have friends who could help her make sense of the world as she saw it and didn't judge her for it. The next morning, after having her breakfast on her porch, supervised by her neighbor's dog opposite her, Jan got dressed and headed to the end of her street, to the junction where the boy on the bike was often seen by her, hoping to find him in the vicinity again. Jan got to the traffic lights, stood and waited, looking up and down the street. But nothing. She looked up at the sky and, after a brief moment of contemplation, Jan returned, forlorn, to her apartment.

Without any break in momentum, back at her apartment, Jan grabbed her phone and rang the number Professor Greene gave her:

"Hi, this is Jan Lam. I got your number from Professor Greene…" Before Jan could finish, she was interrupted.

"Yes, this is Cornelius West. Professor Greene told me you would be ringing. I was only speaking to him last night. You sound very curious and indeed experienced in the unexplained and mysterious. Is that correct?"

Jan was caught off guard - "Yes, well, erm...." - she responded.

"Would you like to come over today? I don't live too far from you," said Mr. West, in a very calm, warm and welcoming manner.

Before Jan could respond, Mr. West said: "Great. I'll prepare us some lunch. Is a salad okay with you?"

"Yes....great," said Jan, somewhat taken aback.

"I'll text you my address," said Mr. West in a forthright manner.

Jan arrived at Mr. West's house, a short walk later. He lived not too far from the traffic lights at the end of her street, where she had often seen the boy - the place she had just returned from investigating. Mr. West lived a couple of blocks off the main road that ran across the intersection where the traffic lights were. Jan approached the Victorian house and was promptly greeted at the door. She was led through the dark wooden interiors of the entrance hallway, out to the back garden, by his wife, who welcomed Jan as if she was their own child.

Mr. West appeared in the garden and approached Jan with the manner of a doting patriarch. He extended his hand with a broad smile to usher Jan to the white furniture, in the middle of the plush garden tropics of palms, yuccas and eucalyptus, that were lined with cannas, plumerias and birds-of-paradise flowers.

"Come, please, take a seat" said Mr. West. He nodded to his wife. Mrs. West walked indoors, only to return moments later with a large jug of home-made lemonade:

"Thank you so much for seeing me at a moment's notice," said Jan, and breathed herself into the beautiful garden that appeared to vibrate in the same way she felt.

"Before we begin, I have to warn you that I am quite excited about meeting with you. I rarely meet anyone who shares the same fascination with the natural world. I am assuming you share the same misfortune. I don't know much about what you have seen, though I gathered the basics from Professor Greene," said Mr. West, who then poured Jan a glass of lemonade, which she welcomed in the dry Californian air of that late August day.

Mr. West continued to speak with a broad smile: "You know…aside from the work I have published over the years, I would love to publish a book which explores the great mysteries, of which I have a personal interest in. But, I will have to retire first, because all my work is in traditional academia. Then, I'll be able to publish the book I've always wanted to publish," said Mr. West.

"What's it about?" asked Jan, as she bit onto a vinaigrette-laden lettuce, from the salad that was lovingly presented to her by Mr. West's wife.

"Oh, Jan, please don't encourage him. It's the book that's going to destroy his legacy," interrupted Mr. West's wife, whilst popping in and out of the house to the garden table, with various items of food and drink.

"Ignore her, Jan. The only thing that was worthy of my legacy was our only son, who sadly passed in a car accident before he got to live out his life and become the great citizen of the world that he was destined to be," said Mr. West, unflinchingly.

"I'm sorry," said Jan. She put her head down with hunched shoulders and took a bite of a cucumber.

"Oh, that's very sweet of you, but we've left that with God, or whatever the creator of this universe is. It was almost 30 years ago. He was 12 when he passed. I have never since met a child with so much zest for learning," said Mr. West, then paused for a moment before continuing by saying: "So, back to the book. And you."

"Me?" asked Jan, taken aback, at the sudden change in topic.

"Yes, you," said Mr. West with a friendly demeanor, leaning forward on his chair: "What have you seen?"

"I don't know what you mean" answered Jan, reservedly.

"You know exactly when I mean. You are talking to an eccentric old man in his own home. Go on… I welcome the distraction," said Mr. West, reassuringly patting Jan's hand.

Mr. West's passion reminded Jan of Professor Greene. Jan dropped her shoulders, breathed in deeply and exhaled: "I think what I have seen is called a *glitch in the matrix*."

"Ah...that... " said Mr. West, with restrained confirmation: "*Strange occurrences which give credence to the idea that the world we live in is indeed a matrix - a physical and social one.*"

Undeterred by Mr. West's pragmatic response she continued, comfortable in his company: "Yes. I've seen people appear and disappear or appear in places they shouldn't be in, for example."

"That's been known to happen," continued Mr. West, knowingly and nonchalantly, munching on his salad.

Encouraged by Mr. West's response, Jan spilled everything: "Well, I also see vibrations. I can read the energy from people and places, and I see different vibrations in different places. I was in Egypt recently, and I saw something when I scaled the top of the Great Pyramid. I saw bright tubes of light, in a grid-like pattern, and ever since then, the glitches and synchronicities have increased."

Mr. West stopped chewing his food and looked at Jan. Taking a sip of ice-water, he stopped for breath and said: "continue."

"Yeah, well, the grid that I saw... I only saw it momentarily. I was told by a mystic at the roadside there that I may have had something called a Kundalini awakening, but I'm not sure if that explains anything," blurted Jan.

"Did you tell him what you saw?" asked Mr. West with growing intensity.

"No, I never got around to it, but I still have his contact details," stated Jan, in a quick exchange.

"I think he could explain that better than I can...." said Mr. West, careful of not disappointing Jan: "You might want to speak to him about the spiritual aspects. I am not versed in that matter so I can't explain the relationship. But maybe your vibrations have been raised since your Kundalini thing and that's why you are experiencing so many synchronicities."

Jan sat back and let out a deep sigh with her arms folded. Mr. West looked at Jan with some empathy for her frustrations, then tapped his hand on her arm and said: "but I can possibly explain what you saw."

Jan's expression then revealed a slow swing back to her own center. Her eyes lit up and locked Mr. West's, and she said loudly: "You can?"

"Yes," follow me to my study.

Mrs. West turned around from where she stood, plucking the fruits from a Sharon tree and said, knowingly: "I'll make you both some coffee. I have some great Arabica beans. Perfect to toast your project."

Jan followed Mr. West to his study, up the grand staircase, to the second floor of their grand Victorian home. Jan was instantly taken aback at the grandeur of his study. The walls were lined with books, on antique wooden shelves and supported by a rolling ladder. There was little furniture in the room: an antique desk, with a green patent-leather surface and green desk-lamp. There was also a large chestnut-colored Chesterfield sofa:

"We both decided, after our son passed, that we both needed our own space in our home to cope with the loss. I retreated here, and my wife has her garden. It's really saved our marriage. I call it Burnwood. It's where I spend most of my time, outside of work, out of contact with the world, researching and studying what makes this world tick," said Mr. West, lovingly.

Jan stood in grace and acceptance of that moment, having longed to meet someone like Mr. West - an archetypical eccentric academic. She walked over to the Chesterfield sofa and placed herself on it, spreading her palms on it to stroke the cool leather in the lingering warmth of that late August day. Jan then stood up to admire Mr. West's book collection, which lined the walls of his grand study:

"Ah, you're my first customer," he said: "So, where should we begin? Near-death experiences? Dimensions of reality? The paranormal? Consciousness?" said Mr. West, pointing at his books, continuing with growing excitement and a smirk: "Sasquatch?"

"Oh, no, none of that," said Jan, smirking politely: "I would just like to know more about what I saw. I've always seen vibrations, though. Ever since I was a kid. I just thought everyone could. Apparently not."

"Do you see them all the time?" probed Mr. West.

"Yes, but with nature, where I see it clearly. It's usually when summer's in bloom. But hills and mountains and the natural landscape always move in a slow resonant hum," said Jan, at complete ease with the flow of conversation with Mr. West.

"Well, it sounds like that's a gift you've always had, but this Kundalini awakening that you had on top of the Great Pyramid might have enabled you to perceive at much higher frequencies. It's just a hunch. Or maybe your third eye has been opened up a lot wider, so to speak," said Mr. West.

"Yes, my friend Susan affirmed that for me. She's been following yoga on and off over the years. She is kinda into that sort of thing, but doesn't really know that much about it," said Jan, her wry smile returning.

"Well, your perceptions and your own energy are not exclusive. We are all part of the same thing. The esoteric philosophies speak of that," added Mr. West.

"'Esoteric?" asked Jan, perplexed.

"Mystical," said Mr. West, nonchalantly, between sips of the coffee which his wife brought them both. He cleared his throat: "You know, all Ancient civilizations all had a close relationship with God. Only, they didn't call it God, not as such. They had Gods. But they worshipped a source of energy from deep in the universe. And they were deeply connected to it. We all are, in fact, but an overwhelming lot of us don't know that. The Atlanteans tried to harness that universal energy, but they were struck with a cataclysm as punishment for it. And we are sadly heading in that direction. Our spiritual development has not matched our technology, and I'm sure there is more hidden technology which will only be released to us by the controllers of this world, once we have reached that point and are ready for it. If smartphones are a reflection of our spiritual development, then we have not advanced very far," stated Mr. West.

"Wow, you don't know what it feels like to listen to you. It's very isolating, experiencing this everyday and not having anyone to share it with. It makes me feel better to have this conversation with you. You've really made me feel a lot better," said Jan, who then slumped into the Chesterfield sofa with complete ease.

"Well, it seems like you have a problem that you would like solving, and I have the knowledge to help you solve it. It seems a shame to let you suffer in silence, and I'm happy to guide you through your journey. I only ask that you help me document this journey to its end," said Mr. West, with a broad smile and starry eyes: "I really want to publish the results!"

"Sure, not a problem," said Jan, with an uncertain shrug of her shoulders.

After seeing Mr. West's joy in his proposal, Jan became infected by his enthusiasm and reflected his joy with: "yes, that would be great. I would love to deliver the results for your book."

Mr. West proceeded to teach Jan about energy: "There have been many scientists who have tried to harness Earth's natural energy, just like the Atlanteans did. There are two major contributors that I can think of. Their names were Nikola Tesla and Wilhelm Reich. Both of them never got far, of course. The world wasn't ready for them, at the time. I do know that Reich was trying to build a device that could harness Earth's natural energy, but I don't know what happened to that. Nothing much is known about that since Wilhem Reich passed," said Mr. West.

He put his head down and walked over to sit at his desk and looked straight at Jan, still with starry eyes: "Maybe the world is ready for Jan Lam!"

Jan sat and waited for Mr. West to continue, from the sofa opposite him. Mr. West continued: "Since you were standing on top of the world's most potent energy vortices, you might have triggered something in yourself which was already dormant. Maybe your junk DNA was activated," said Mr. West, then swallowed his smooth Arabica coffee.

"Junk DNA… mmmm… possibly… but wait… what do you mean by vortices? There are more than one? How many are there?" retorted Jan.

"Yes, oh sorry. I missed the important part. The Great Pyramid is one great energy vortex but it's a part of some sort of energy grid. They're called leylines - they form a sort of net, or matrix, if you will, around the world, and these structures, usually pyramids and ziggurats, are found on the intersections of this grid. These ley-lines are magnetic in nature and are powerful. When they criss-cross at a point, they form incredibly powerful energy portals. You could say that Earth is covered in a magnetic net." spoke Mr. West, with comfortable authority.

"Grid. Yes, that's what I saw. I saw what looked like a grid. Beams of white light in a criss-cross pattern," mirrored Jan, with vigor.

Mr. West stopped drinking his coffee and his cup made a large clank on his desk. With wide eyes open, he got up and darted out of his chair, standing upright to attention.

Jan stood up too, from the chestnut-Chesterfield sofa, to ask: "has anyone plotted this grid out on a map? Can I find it on the internet?"

"Sure!" said Mr. West, joyously.

Mr. West typed away at his computer and presented Jan with a map of the magnetic net around Earth, within seconds:

"These are the leylines and this is the grid that is formed by them," said Mr. West, pointing excitedly at the monitor, that he twisted round in one swift motion, to show Jan.

"Do you think that I saw these leylines in the state I was in at the time?" asked Jan, without any curb in her enthusiasm.

"If we were to perceive magnetic energy, we might see it as white light. But that's Professor Greene's department. You'd have to ask him," said Mr. West.

Jan gave Mr. West a doubtful glance, and Mr. West responded with: "he's not that bad. The best way to get the information you need out of him is to frame your question from a hard science perspective, then he'll engage. I know that because he does not engage with my whims, so I understand where you're coming from. You just have to ask him in a way in which he doesn't feel he's indulging *crank* notions."

"Okay. I'll try that. I asked him about why the sky was blue, and he couldn't give me an answer which satisfied my curiosity, based on what I know - he just explained it in the way he was taught, but not in the way I see things," added Jan.

"That's my point. It's interesting you mention that because none of the Ancients described the sky as we see it now. Homer, the Ancient Greek poet, described a very different color of sky and sea. It was of a wine-dark sea. Blue didn't enter the language in every single language and culture on Earth until recently," stated Mr. West.

"That is indeed fascinating," responded Jan, in a swift wistful daydream that she broke with: "There is so much to explore. But, for the time being, what are these leylines for?" asked Jan.

"Isn't that the billion-dollar question? Well, for that, we should consider Wilhelm Reich. I suggest you look him up and return to me. I will give you an assignment - your first assignment for your quest. Find out what Wilhelm Reich was developing. It has something to do with leylines. In the meantime, take up contact with that mystic you met because he might be able to give you some more information that might help you with your quest. Every awakened person needs a good shaman or priest. A guide," said Mr. West, in a paternal glow.

After a couple of intensely energizing hours with Mr. West, Jan left for her apartment. As soon as she returned to her apartment, she checked her phone for missed calls and saw Toni's number. Before turning to bed, Jan returned Toni's call, by sending him a message to meet in the week for coffee, at Espresso Royale. She went to sleep happy that night, knowing that she was a step closer to making sense of the world. That night in her dream, she was Cleopatra again, and she was operating the golden telescope-like contraption in the King's Chamber.

The following Wednesday, Toni met a cheery Jan for lunch in their favorite haunt. Toni was taken aback with Jan's upbeat manner, since her previous texts to him conveyed somber undertones, following her return from Egypt. Jan explained her meeting with Mr. West and how it left her feeling upbeat, having someone to talk with about *"things"*. Naturally curious, Toni asked what those *"things"* were and Jan reluctantly told him that it was about the *"unexplained and mysterious"* but opted to spare him the details. Toni was not pleased, advising her to abandon her pursuits for better hobbies. Jan was unabated, though slightly disheartened with Toni, whilst they continued to eat:

"Look, Toni, I don't expect you to understand or be interested, but there are things in this world which science can't explain," said Jan after a while of listening to Toni's biting criticisms.

"Honey, you do you, and I'll do me," said Toni: "but I am not getting involved, gurl. You do what makes you happy, chasing ghouls and getting probed by aliens!"

"Toni, that's what I mean. That's why I didn't want to tell you anything!" said Jan, gurgling at Toni's joke: "I'm not going to say anything more about it so let's talk about your love life. Anything on the horizon?"

"No, sadly. I miss teasing the men in Egypt," responded Toni flippantly, before continuing: "Say, didn't you have any romance when we were out there? I distinctly remember a couple of men giving you the eye over breakfast in the hotel," smirked Toni.

"Honey, they just wanted a tip. Trust a girl when she tells you she knows what a man wants! It's usually written all over his face," said Jan.

After lunch, they parted company. Jan knew that it would be a while before she saw her friend again, not least because an adventure was about to begin for her. Jan hugged Toni, who was taken aback by her spontaneous embrace, and jokingly responded by saying that she would see him again soon. Jan knew different. She saw one chapter of her life beginning to close and another opening before her eyes, starting with the assignment Mr. West had assigned her.

She spent the weekend at the library, researching everything she could find about Wilhelm Reich, and found a Museum in Maine dedicated to him. She decided she wanted to visit the Museum so she filled in a contact form on the website. After that, and without further thought, she finally emailed the roadside mystic from Giza, asking to find out more about Kundalini energy and the energy around the Great Pyramid - to try and understand why she felt it so strongly when she was there. After she was done, Jan was left feeling happy with her first steps towards seeking the answers to the questions which troubled her.

Jan opened up the bag which was strapped across her shoulder, to take out a pocket notebook and pencil. She was about to begin her journey into a deep discovery, and she intended on marking every step. She wrote her first entry: *"end of August - found the Wilhelm Reich Museum in Maine and sent an email and read up about him. Want to visit soon. Emailed the roadside mystic.*"

Jan felt a purpose beginning to form in her, firing a rocket in her that she hadn't felt for over 20 years. She felt she had the right support. In her journal, she scribbled: *"forming a team*" with *"Mr. West"* and *"Professor Greene"* with a question mark alongside the latter.

As Jan left the university library, she bumped into Professor Greene, who was returning some books and her eyes opened at the quick synchronicity. The Professor's eyes lit up too when he saw her, and Jan cheerily returned his greeting with wide eyes and a smile.

"You look happy with yourself" he said.

"How did it go with Mr. West?" asked the Professor.

"Better than expected. He's given me some leads which I was just following," smiled Jan.

"Good, that sounds wonderful. Look, I hope you don't think I was being dismissive during our last meeting. These things are outside my field of expertise, so…." he said gracefully.

Jan interrupted: "You don't have to apologize. I'm glad I bumped into you again though because I was going to contact you to tell you. I might be going to Maine, to the Wilhelm Reich Museum. It might help me with my search."

"Oh," said Professor Green, with some astonishment: "I don't know much about him, but I would love to come along with you, if you need the company."

"That's very kind but if it isn't up your street, it might be a wasted trip for you," responded Jan.

The Professor looked disappointed. He had hoped that Jan's enthusiasm at that moment would turn into the spark that he was hoping for, but he felt somewhat rejected, having grown tired of their dance around each other over the previous weeks, a dance he had very little patience for, and he suspected Jan felt the same. He feared he could be wrong so he gallantly proceeded with: "let me take you out to dinner tonight… to celebrate the start of a very rewarding quest!"

Jan was pleased with the Professor's proposal, and his forthright manner, something she needed at that time - someone else that can take some burden away from a situation that she felt hopelessly lost in. That evening, they sat in a relatively quiet Royale and shared a bottle of White Zinfandel together, during a light dinner. Afterwards, the Professor walked Jan home, down the tree-laden streets in the amber-lit night, through patterns which formed from the soft lights against the leaves, on orange hues on the walls of beige houses with accented red-rooftops.

Jan turned around to thank the Professor at her door, by referring to him as Professor Greene:

"By the way, my first name is Jim," he said, then leaned in to kiss her.

Jan stood still, in wavering surprise. She returned his embrace then said, ever the shrewd: "thank you for dinner, Jim. I would love to do this again."

Professor Greene looked at Jan and, in quiet disposition muttered "sure", then parted company for the evening.

The following day, Jan invited Susan to hang out at her apartment. They sat for lunch on the veranda, laughing like schoolgirls at Jan's spontaneous romantic dinner. Susan invariably asked Jan about the ins and outs of their evening. Jan filled Susan in on the details, stopping short when they bade each other goodnight:

"His name is Jim," said Jan.

"Jim. Really? That it?" responded Susan.

"Jim Greene," said Jan, taking a swig of wine.

"Sounds like Jim Beam," said Susan. Then they both chortled and snorted in deep laughter, and Jan paused in between laughter and sips of White Zinfandel that Susan plied her with.

Jan reflected on what it all meant - she was falling for a man she ordinarily wouldn't think twice about. Perhaps it was the allure of converting someone's rigid thinking and beliefs and opening him to another possibility that attracted Jan to Jim.

The following week, Jan pursued her project with more momentum. She emailed the mystic again, who introduced himself simply as Abbassi in a prompt reply. They subsequently spoke on the phone, recalling that he remembered Jan vividly. She relayed to him what she saw when she climbed the top of the Great Pyramid, but he responded by telling her that he wasn't impressed with the action she took. The mystic warned Jan to take care, telling her that she had awakened in her a power that might be too much for her to handle. Jan listened intently, but didn't heed the warning. Her thoughts lay on the long weekend ahead, which she planned on taking to Maine, for her fact-finding mission.

She anxiously awaited a response from the Reich Museum, as another week passed, during which time she started examining her finances for the trip.

Toni wanted to meet Jan when he found out about her trip to Maine. Though she still hadn't received a response from the Reich Museum, Jan was determined to go nevertheless by the time Toni met Jan for lunch at the Royale:

"Girl, I am worried about you. I've been hearing all sorts of things from Susan, and now you're going to Maine. What is there in Maine that you can't find here? And you're going on your own?" harangued Toni.

"Toni, everything is fine. Don't worry. I just want to do something with my life. I still love you. Nothing's going to change that," responded Jan.

"Yes, but everything is changing. You're suddenly dating, which I had to hear from Susan, and you're doing some sort of investigation with all these new people. Who on earth are you hanging out with, Jan? Who are you becoming?" continued Toni, with growing discontent.

"Toni, you said you didn't want to get involved, and now I am doing what I want, so what's the deal, exactly? Besides, it's just a short trip in America. It's not like I'm going away forever." said Jan.

Their lunch was interrupted by a call from work, which Toni took, ending their date abruptly, leaving Jan somewhat dismayed at the table, unwilling to finish her lunch. She paid and left, with a heavy heart. She had hoped for a better meeting, but she understood that Toni needed time to deal with the changes that were taking place in her life. Jan reflected on her friendship with Toni, as she walked back to work that day, thinking of how they had become a crutch for each other in the past 5 years, brought together from loneliness. Jan felt a sigh of relief, not regret, that her friendship with Toni was reaching its inevitable conclusion.

Toni couldn't understand Jan, and it was easier and perhaps better to just let him go his own way, she thought, instead of fighting for him to truly embrace her. If Toni wanted to return to her as a friend, he would have to do it with more understanding, Jan told herself. Whilst she pondered her friendship with Toni, Jan grew downbeat. Frustrated with Susan for oversharing with Toni about the recent developments of her project, Jan decided to take her distance and not return Susan's calls either. Jan chose to press on regardless, choosing to re-group and re-center herself to her mission.

Jan's eagerly anticipated trip to Maine was fast approaching. She was busy packing her bags on a day close to her departure, when her phone rang. It was Professor Greene:

"Hi, Jan. Do you need a lift to the airport tomorrow?" he asked, kindly.

"Yeah, I wouldn't mind. That's so sweet," responded Jan, to the friendly offer.

"I'm surprised your friends aren't going with you?" he asked, gingerly.

"Yes, not as disappointed as I am. It's a long story. Best left alone," replied Jan, firmly.

"I'll come and collect you at 6 am, seeing as your flight is at 10 am," he said.

"Are you sure? I can always get an Uber," asserted Jan.

"No, not at all. It will be my pleasure," responded Jim, with increasing affection that Jan welcomed.

After ending the call on a high, Jan felt reassured and optimistic that her new endeavor was finally attracting the right type of support, energy and attention. After telling Mr. West about her trip to the Reich Museum, he replied by telling Jan that he would welcome what she found - he also encouraged her to pursue her vision regardless of the outcome - to simply trust in the process. Jan was comforted by Mr. West's words - words that embraced her with a gentle touch and warded off fears that might have otherwise consumed her.

That evening before her flight to Maine, Jan sat and thought for a moment, with a cup of ice tea. She contemplated what she was undertaking, resigning herself to the idea that it was just her nerves that were getting the better of her. Jan focused her gaze at the end of the street again, watched for the young boy who didn't appear, then drifted off into a daydream, as she tried to give her feelings about her fading friendships a place. In her reflective state, watching the cars that passed, she imagined the young boy in his red t-shirt and wondered to which home he might belong. A thought then occurred to her and she promptly rang Mr. West:

"Hi, it's me, Jan. I was just wondering. I'm sorry to ask, but you said that your son died in a car accident. Where was that exactly? I'm sorry for ringing so late. You don't have to tell me…" muttered Jan.

Mr. West answered before Jan could finish her sentence: "Oh, no, it's okay. Close by, really. Just down the street. He was on his bike when he was struck," said Mr. West, bluntly.

Jan paused for a moment, unsure of whether to ask for what was pursing her lips: "I'm sorry to ask, Sir, but I have one more question…"

"Sure, it's fine. I have my peace with it. I've made my peace with the creator. I like to think he's still around. He was wearing a red t-shirt," said Mr. West.

Jan was struck with Mr. West's psyche - which revealed the response she was looking for in lightning synchronicity. With a shaken head, Jan received the confirmation she was looking for and thanked Mr. West, telling him she was just curious. But Mr. West sensed that was not all Jan wanted to tell him, then pressed her to tell him the truth of the matter. So, she did. Mr. West responded with a long pause, followed by "I see."

After ending the call, Jan felt out of sorts. She began to feel the strangeness again - the strangeness that isolated her from her old friends and possibly new ones, the strangeness that continuously haunted her and isolated her from the world around her, ever since she was a child. Jan took a long shower to shake herself off negative thought patterns and watched Double Jeopardy on TV, to lull herself to sleep under the presenter's soothing tones. Jan then got ready to have an early evening. That night, Mr. West's son appeared in her dreams.

Early the following morning, Professor Greene picked up Jan in a punctual manner. She was neatly dressed in fall leggings, a short skirt, camel boots and a shawl, with her bag draped across her shoulder:

"You travel lightly," said the smiley Professor.

"I'm easy like that. I don't need to pack too much makeup," said Jan.

"Naturally beautiful," added Professor Greene, with a smile.

Jan got in the front seat of the car and returned Professor Jim Greene's smile. She filled him in on the previous weeks, carefully omitting the information which would make him feel uncomfortable. He was beginning to open up to her and to soften his guard - he told her that he had been watching some videos on youtube about the paranormal. Though he touched on subjects which fell short of what she was interested in, Jan was happy that Professor Greene was at least opening his mind to new ideas.

Professor Greene dropped off Jan at the airport with a tight hug and a kiss on the cheek. She walked with some glow in her confidence to the airport entrance, then nestled herself in the lounge as she awaited her call to board, careful not to think too much of the energy around her or how it might make her feel. She focused her mind on exactly what she wanted from the trip, or where it might take her, trying not to overthink what she was doing, trying to just go with the flow of a possible adventure that she might enjoy for herself. For the first time in a long time, Jan was happy to ride a wave of feeling which allowed herself to take her to new places. Those feelings grew as she sat and waited in the airport lounge, with both feet on the ground.

Just as Jan waited and pondered, stronger emotions began flowing through her, taking her back to what she experienced in Egypt. She took a drink at a restaurant, to change her energy a bit, where she reminisced of the time she sat with Toni when they landed in Cairo. Jan sat and ate her breakfast, holding pleasant memories of breakfasts with her friends in Cairo, before she had to go through security to get to her gate. Her phone bleeped, and it was a text message from Susan:

"Where are you at, girl?" read the text message.

"At the airport" texted Jan, in quick return.

"But where at the airport?" came the reply.

Jan brought the phone to her face, to examine the messages closely, to try and understand it better:

"What you do you mean?" texted Jan: *"I'm having breakfast at the bar by security."*

''Stay right there, we're coming," replied Susan.

"Whaaaat?" screamed Jan, leaping up from where she sat.

Within minutes, Jan was face to face with Susan, who had managed to track her down, flanked by Toni, and Susan spontaneously told Jan that she would be joining her.

"...how.. what… why?" out came three words from Jan.

"Never mind that for now. Just forget about that and let's get on this plane. Oh, are you going to finish that? I'm starving," said Susan, as she grabbed Jan's half-eaten bacon and cheese bagel, scraping the cream cheese onto the paper plate. Susan then said with a mouthful of bagel: "Here, Toni has something to say"

Toni appeared from behind Susan, and walked over to hug Jan: "Look, I'm sorry, I was acting out of jealousy. You need this for your own self, and I'm right here for ya when you get back. You do whatever you need to. Go and find what it is you're looking for."

Jan cried a tear, which Toni wiped: "don't be silly Jan…tears will bring bad luck. I'll see you soon."

Susan took Jan by the hand and led her to the security gate, where they both hastily waved goodbye to Toni, who looked on with encouragement and admiration. After a few considered moments, Toni kissed his fingers and blew them in their direction. Susan and Jan scarpered to their gate and got settled into their seats on the plane, to Maine. To Wilhelm Reich's Museum.

Chapter 4

Maine

A summer's day in Boston yielded a drinking session in the multitudes of Irish bars that lined the center of the city. Susan enticed Jan out after they checked into their hotel. They sat in a sports bar, surrounded by groups of young men who were shouting and chanting soccer songs at the screen that played World Cup Football. Susan and Jan decided to take their drinks outside, to soak up the presence of fall by the river, in absence of the flexing noises from inadequate men.

"So, why are we here?" asked Susan and Jan burst out laughing: "Cuz it ain't the men," concluded Susan.

"Girl, stop it and cross your legs!" giggled Jan, as she sipped her Guinness, which she wasn't taking to, but hoped for the best.

A particularly unwelcoming bartender came to clean the tables nearby and passed a comment about the bar becoming busy later with a surge of soccer fans. Susan and Jan took the hint without any argument, though Susan wanted to challenge the bartender about his attitude. Jan motioned her to leave it:

"Probably a haunt for gangs here. It's not worth it. Besides, we need to be fresh for our trip tomorrow to the Museum," stated Jan.

"Wait, what Museum?" said a shocked Susan before continuing: "We're going to a Museum? I have officially entered middle-age!" whilst taking another swig from her bottle of beer.

"Yes, it's not far from here. I thought we could head out early. Or you could spend the day on your own, wandering the streets of Boston with all these strange men here….or… you could grin and bear it and come with me," stated Jan bluntly, before giving up on her Guinness.

"You're right about that!'" said Susan, before taking Jan's Guinness and downing it in three.

"Oh, Susan, you are full of tricks!" said Jan: "Come on, let's get some rest. We have a long day ahead!"

The next day, they left early for the Reich Museum, which lay hidden in the countryside, 3 hours north of Boston. Jan was sober so she drove the rental with Susan and her hangover - who had eaten a dodgy hot dog the night before and had been up all night as a consequence. Susan said very little and loudly gulped her cola:

"You know, water and some Imodium might have been better for you," said Jan, unwilling to stir Susan from her upset stomach.

Susan was relatively unresponsive but managed to mutter: "Warm cola is the only thing that settles my stomach if it's upset."

It was 11 am when they arrived at their destination, after a quiet journey. Once there, Jan realized that she did not know what she was expecting to find at the museum, nor what she was supposed to be looking for. The previous weeks in

California and her burgeoning friendship with Mr. West, formed out of her frustration with Professor Greene, was the only thing that brought Jan to where she was, aside from a tenuous link for her quest.

Susan ran to the restroom as soon as they entered the empty building. As soon as Susan disappeared from view, an old lady suddenly appeared to the side of Jan and enquired about their visit:

"Yes, we're here out of curiosity, really, to learn more about this place. I was wondering if I might learn something here related to energy. I sent an email before we left California, but I didn't receive a reply," said Jan.

"Oh, you must be Jan Lam. I'm sorry. This is a very small operation, mostly run by volunteers. I saw your email and I completely forgot about responding. You said you would be coming here on your own?" asked the quiet, smiley old lady.

"No, my plans changed. I came with a friend, who is here somewhere." said Jan.

"Oh, yes, I saw her run to the ladies." said the old lady, with a perma-smile.

"She doesn't feel too good. Erm… I saw there was a workshop or a course on learning more about the contents of this museum. Is that still available?" asked Jan.

"Oh, no, sorry, my dear. You have to pre-book that," said the old lady, warmly. She continued by saying: "But you can leave a deposit today and I will make sure someone contacts you, if you want to participate in one. How long are you staying for?"

"Oh, just a couple of days. We're flying back on Monday," answered Jan.

"Well, why don't you have a look around, and I'll see who I can find. If you give me your number, I will get someone to ring you today," said the old lady, still friendly.

"Sure thing," said Jan, before scribbling her contact details for the lady, who deftly took it from her.

"I'll get on to that for you. Feel free to have a look around," smiled the old lady and glided away.

Jan proceeded to explore the museum, reading the plates against the various objects on display, whilst inside the central room of the museum. Jan saw a cottage through the window that was nestled at the end of a long lawn behind the museum. Jan paused, to ask the old lady about it:

"Oh, that's a rental. You can rent it for your stay here. I believe it's vacant this weekend," said the old lady, with an overly-welcoming tone.

"Oh, no. We're booked in downtown Boston. If I had known, I would have booked it," replied Jan, resigned and resolute.

"Maybe another time then," said the old lady, who smiled and shrugged swiftly.

Jan began to get tired of the small talk, then blurted out: "What is the energy, exactly? I read it on your website. It's called Orga….something," hoping the old lady might oblige.

"Oh, honey, I don't know much about it. I'm just the caretaker here. I barely even see the owners. It's a husband and wife affair. He's the great-grandson of Wilhelm Reich. His name is Billy. We have annual meetings about the direction of the trust but, other than that, it's left to the management or someone else. I was only hired a year ago, to take care of the place. We do get swamped in the summer. If you had come a few weeks earlier, you wouldn't have been able to move around here," stated the old lady, her tone raised after her other patron entered the central room of the museum: "Oh, look, here's your friend!"

Susan joined Jan, then introduced herself to the old lady with a wavering hand. After a short conversation, they visited the museum grounds where they found a harpoon-like structure that was perched on a mount, like a telescope. They were trailed by their impromptu guide for the day, who slowly began to fill-in some more details for her visitors, as they stood to look at the large metallic-object in front of them:

"It's for Cloudbusting. That's all I know," whispered the old lady.

"Cloudbusting?" asked Jan.

"Yes, something to do with making it rain," said the little old lady.

"I wonder how that works!" said Jan, with her mouth ajar.

In a hurried tone, the old lady then said, after checking her phone: "I've managed to get in touch with the manager who will be here shortly. I'm not sure how long you're staying for..."

"Say… Do you know where we can get something to eat?" asked Susan.

"Sure, there's a diner nearby. We'd offer you some lunch, but you would have to ring ahead for that," said the old lady and smiled, then turned around and walked back up the lawn, to the museum.

"God, Jan. Of all the places to spend the weekend, you've picked the right one! So far, we've had a few beers, I've gotten dire-rear from a bad hot dog, and we've driven 3 hours north from anything worth seeing, to stand in a garden next to a bizarre instrument that has no use, guided by an old lady with no personality. Nice one, Jan! Another couple of hours here and my knees will start knocking together in excitement!" said Susan, in between frequent caresses of her stomach and the press of her hand on her clammy forehead.

"Okay, okay. I'm sorry. Are you okay? You don't look so good!" replied Jan, quickly, with her arms outstretched towards Susan.

"No… I think I need to go again!" said Susan, before running up the lawn with a pained expression, back to the museum.

Jan sighed, stood and walked over to the telescope-like object on its mount. She rested her hand on it, sighing deeply, feeling like she possibly had wasted a trip and had no idea how to save a trip that she was beginning to think she made on a whim. She tried to grasp at the feeling she felt when she was back in Santa Clara, fresh from her trip to Egypt, when she still felt the wonderment of everything she had witnessed on her holiday. Jan's quest had now hit a dead end, and she felt at a loss. Her phone rang. It was an unknown number:

"Hi, who is this?" asked Jan.

"It's the owner of the Museum. My name is Billy. Billy Reich," came the answer, with a deep baritone voice.

"What? I wasn't expecting you to ring," replied Jan.

"Yes, it was Deborah who rang me. I think she rang me by accident. She left a voicemail. It sounded urgent. And she left me your number. I believe you wanted to know more about Orgone Energy. The thing is that we do all of this in bookings, but I need to pass through the area this weekend anyway… so I won't mind stopping by for a couple of hours to answer any questions you might have. I'll be there in a couple of hours. If you're hungry…."

"Yes… your caretaker Deborah told me already. We'll take ourselves to the diner nearby, and we'll see you here later," confirmed Jan.

"We?" asked Billy Reich, inquisitively.

"Yes, my friend Susan and I. We're both looking forward to speaking with you," said Jan.

After a quiet lunch at a local diner, haunted by a familiar albeit polite and subdued demographic that appeared to mind their own business, they returned to the museum to meet Billy Reich. It was a lunch where Susan quietly expressed her displeasure with the trip thus far, which Jan tried to ignore whilst they returned to the museum.

By the time they returned, Susan had perked up somewhat and was ready to re-engage with the day and with Jan's mission. Jan was immediately pleased, whilst they sat drinking the tea and coffee that was provided for them by the sweet old caretaker, Deborah, leaving Jan

able to focus again, after Susan's mood also improved. Shortly after they finished their hot beverages, little old

Deborah came back out from the main building to let them know that Billy Reich wouldn't be long:

"How young do you think he is?" asked Susan, in a short fit of giggles.

"Oh, Susan! I know you're feeling better when you talk like that!" echoed Jan.

A tall man walked from the top of the little hill where the museum stood. As he walked towards them at the end of the lawn, at the picnic table by the brook behind it, Susan glanced at his somewhat disheveled appearance. His pants and shirt, in colors that aged him somewhat, made Susan wince. Upon setting her gaze on his appearance, Susan made a dismissive comment, telling Jan *"he's all yours!"*. Jan ignored Susan but smiled politely when she stood, to greet Billy Reich.

Billy Reich extended his hand to greet them both. In his mid-30's, he was of a Germanic frame, with brown-blond hair and blue-green eyes. He wore a pale blue cotton-shirt, with sleeves rolled up on thick forearms, that would suit a farmer or a laborer. His khaki pants rested on broad hips over thick brown Birkenstock boots. He smiled with clean white teeth and a twinkle in his eye. Susan was the first to take his hand and grasp it, with an eager smile and said: "hello, my name is Susan. I'm Jan's friend."

Unfazed by Susan's sudden flirtatious behavior, which Jan was accustomed to, Jan waited her turn patiently until Billy Reich turned his attention towards her. Jan's exuberance was no match for Susan's - it being somewhat differently driven than Susan's. Jan posited a *"I'm so glad to meet you"* and *"this is completely unexpected"* and *"I hope you don't mind spending time with us to teach us what your great-grandfather was building here."* After exchanging pleasantries, they all sat pleasantly at the picnic table, where little old Deborah supplied them with fresh coffee.

"Well, I was heading this way to pick up some paperwork, then Deborah rang, but I don't mind," said Billy, with youthful delight: "I think it might be better to start with what you don't know, then I can fill you in."

Susan's enthusiasm in the moment gave way to a much pressing matter. Realizing she was out of her depth, she looked at Billy intently and nodded: "Jan can explain."

"I was curious about this Orga…," said Jan.

"Organon. That's the name my great-grandfather gave his laboratory. But it's actually Orgone Energy. That's what he had discovered. It's pronounced Org-own," said Billy, with a cautious and rhythmic nod.

"Yeah, Org-own," mirrored Jan, with a loose nod and her gaze fixed on Billy: "Yeah, I just wanted to know more about it because, well, I have a sort of interest in the unexplained. I'll put it that way," said Jan, in a cooperative manner.

"Well, my great-grandfather discovered a biological energy that lies in the body. It's a take on the word orgasm. Similar to an orgasm, there is an energy which is created. You can think of an orgasm as energy," said Billy, bluntly.

"Oh, tell me more!" said Susan, resting her hand under her chin with wide, schoolgirl eyes.

Billy laughed a little, blushed, then stammered a response: "Ermm… yeah...it's the life force of our planet and my great-grandfather was trying to harness it!"

"What was he going to use it for? To make rain?" asked Susan, with a slight grin and a sparkle in her eyes.

"No, no. The Cloudbuster you see here was designed to manipulate the orgone energy in the ether and rain would have been a product of that," said Billy Reich, measuredly, pointing over to the harpoon-like metallic structure that was perched like a telescope on its mount.

Jan sat for a moment, carefully remembering what Mr. West had told her about the energy vortices on Earth: "How was your great-grandfather putting the energy into the machine?"

"He wasn't. He was trying to channel energy into the machine. He began using a chamber to capture it," answered Billy again, methodically.

"Like in the movie Barbarella?" asked Susan, with a giggle and loose shoulders.

"Yes, the Orgasmatron," nodded Billy, with a smirk.

"So… the energy he was beginning to harness in that chamber was Orgone? Is that correct?," asked Jan: "is it possible that Orgone Energy could be harnessed to shoot into the atmosphere?"

"It is possible. Though I don't know what the effects of that would be," replied Billy.

"Well, Orgone Energy might be more powerful than other energies out there," said Jan, in a day-dream.

"It is possible. You would have to consult with a physicist for that. I'm just a farmer and keeper of this estate, desperately trying to maintain my great-grandfather's legacy," said Billy, with a bowed head, over his coffee, on the picnic table.

"What happened with Wilhelm Reich's experiments?" asked Jan.

"He was largely debunked, defunded and discredited as fringe pseudo-science. That's the story my grandfather told, anyway. He spoke bitterly about his father's treatment," said Billy, with a low head.

After their short conversation, they were interrupted by a phone call on Billy's cell. It was Billy's wife asking about when she would expect him home. Susan's energy changed in an instant. She stopped looking at him with starry eyes, upon hearing Billy's wife's voice on his phone:

"Do you have time to give us a demonstration of the chamber? Maybe we could see some devices that your great-grandfather was developing, to harness that energy?" prepped Jan, and continued with: "is it possible that the energy from ley lines could be harnessed?"

Billy put his coffee down and breathed through a slight cough and said: "How do you know about ley lines? That's something I've often wondered whether Wilhelm was trying to achieve, or whether he was aware of. I've never really had the keen interest to find out more, but you've just touched upon something which I've wondered lately, since finding out about ley lines through a program I've been following on TV."

"What are they?" asked Susan, her interest returning in an appropriate manner.

Billy stood up from the picnic table where they all sat, gesturing that he had to leave, then suddenly ran back to the museum. A few moments later, Susan and Jan were informed by the old lady that Billy had been called away on an emergency, but would ring Jan later. Susan and Jan dropped their shoulders, then decided to return to Boston for dinner. On the way to Boston, however, Susan took a phone call on Jan's behalf. It was Billy:

"I'm sorry, ladies, but I was called away for a moment. I understand that you're only here for a couple of nights, so I'd love for you to stay over at the cottage here as guests of mine, if you could tomorrow. We could talk more, and hopefully we can get to the bottom of your questions," said Billy, with a baritone command.

"Oh, this is Susan, Jan's friend, but sure, we would love to. What time tomorrow?" answered Susan, intentionally.

"Oh, I'll be there straight after breakfast at around 10. The museum will be locked, so I'll meet you at the picnic table," said Billy, before ending the call.

Susan slowly placed the phone between her lap in the passenger seat of the rental, then turned to Jan to tell her about the invitation. Jan was ecstatic about the proposal, relishing the thought of learning more from Billy and the items left in his great-grandfather's museum - as well as being able to save some money from their hotel stay in Boston. Susan was equally enthralled to meet Billy again, though Jan tempered Susan's excitement by reminding her that Billy was married and nearly 10 years her junior, upon which Jan commented:

"I don't know why I'm even bothering. That has never stopped you!"

Over an uneventful dinner at another Irish bar, Jan and Susan hatched a plan to try and check-out from their hotel earlier than what was booked, without losing any money. Susan said they should go with the line of not feeling safe or being sexually harassed, but Jan's idea gave way. They simply would complain about the quality of rooms and food. Susan agreed without any further argument, then they both headed back to their hotel for their final night there. Staggering into the lobby after dinner, it didn't take long before Susan came across a surly porter.

Unimpressed and ready for a fight, Susan walked straight up to the receptionist to announce their final night there:

"Whilst you may never understand nor will action my complaint, I would like to make it apparent that we will no longer accept the blatant sexism and surly attitude of your staff, not to mention the dusty rooms which leave us itching. We will check out tomorrow morning. If you prefer, I can take this up with your manager but, because I don't want to turn Karen on your ass, I will assume that you will accept our departure tomorrow morning in good nature!"

Jan turned to Susan, and said: "Wow, do you even know what you just said?"

Susan, turning to Jan, said: "us white women have our uses! There's no way in hell you would be able to get away with that. At least not here!"

The next morning, they checked out with ease, presided over by a burly manager. Susan warned the manager that she would bombard the hotel with negative reviews, if she didn't get her refund. Jan pulled Susan away from her simulated outrage, before it escalated into something ugly, and whispered to Susan: "he's still a white man who can call the cops on us!"

On that cue, Susan left the hotel with Jan in tow. And their refund.

When they returned to the Museum, they were welcomed with a mid-morning picnic which was arranged by Billy, who engaged them with good humor. Susan reciprocated his caring attention, by occasionally flirting with him. After their short brunch, Billy took them both into the museum, where he gave them a tour of the chamber-room:

"So, if I sit in that, can you capture the essence of my being?" asked Susan: "Is that the idea?"

"Yes. That's the idea," replied Billy, with a wide smile.

"But how do you harness it?" asked Jan.

"That's the missing link. I think that's what Wilhelm was working on before he stopped. It's not the same as in the film, where she sits and has an orgasm through external manipulation," said Billy, winking at Susan.

"Well, that's disappointing. Aside from sitting in a closet, I don't see how you might capture my energy. Or anyone else's," said Jan.

Billy smiled a response then walked over to a chamber and opened it. He brought out a mechanical device, which he rolled out on a trolley. The device had an appendage, which he attached to an outlet on the outside of the chamber. After attaching the mechanical device's appendage to the chamber, he asked Susan if she would like to be his first test subject:

"Whaaaaat? Am I supposed to have an orgasm in that?" shrieked Susan.

"No. Ha ha. No. But I've been working on this device to extract and capture the energy from the chamber. But my wife is reluctant. I was wondering if you might like to try," said Billy, nonchalantly.

"Whaaaat? Nooo way! What's going to happen to my energy? Are you going to suck my soul out with that thing?" laughed Susan, with her finger firmly pointed at the chamber and the device attached to it.

"I'll do it!" interrupted Jan, in a decisive manner.

Billy smiled gladly and Jan stepped into the chamber. She sat in the chair, in the middle of the small closet-chamber, then Billy closed the door firmly shut. He told Jan that it would remain unlocked, reassuring her that she could open it at any time. In the darkness, Jan sat and closed her eyes to the colors of the world, to the noise of it, and the energies that lived within it. She felt at peace, for a moment, there in the middle of the chamber she had placed herself in. Jan's energy was no longer restless, at unease with the world around her. She felt a stillness overcome her, in that chamber.

She then thought of the heaviness she felt in the King's chamber in the Great Pyramid - how the negative, heavy, other-worldly energies haunted her there. Jan then remembered what the mystic told her - to tread carefully - then she closed her eyes.

Jan drifted into a slumber as she was quietly transported to another place. She could clearly see the strobes of light above the Great Pyramid, in the sky, through her mind's eye. In her vision, she reached for a ray of light that she saw coming towards her from a distance, and a current of energy penetrated her body. A ripple of sensations heightened her sensual receptors. She felt the energy pass through her strongly, to all the erogenous parts of her body, sharply stimulating her sensory receptors, raising them like antennae to the energy of all the world.

The energy flowed through Jan, exciting her womanhood before passing down her legs and dissipating into the ground. As the energy left her body, Jan could feel its current pass through the walls and into the outlet, through the pipe, flowing into the mechanical contraption that lay in wait outside, which Billy had attached. With her head tilted back in arousal, Jan collapsed in a funk, whilst she became a conduit for Orgone Energy - energy that the chamber was beginning to convert from the ether, using Jan's body as a vessel. It stimulated and relieved Jan of all her emotional baggage, all at the same time.

As Jan fell into a state of blissful paralysis, she heard concerned knocks on the door from Susan. Jan could only answer in a breathless mutter, saying:

"yeah, I'm fine. Don't open the door though!"

Outside the chamber, Susan and Billy watched the mechanical device spark up in lights and a rustic meter pointed towards the middle of the counter:

"What's actually happening?" asked Susan, with heightened concern.

"Oh, I installed a simple Orgone energy meter for measuring purposes, and it's at a good level," said Billy excitedly, as Susan looked on at him in horror.

"But what are those glass tubes on top of that device there? Why are they glowing yellow?" pointed Susan, in continued horror.

"Oh these are simply tubes that are storing the energy that has been converted and passed through the chamber, down the pipe. Jan should be finished soon. It looks like they're filling up pretty quickly," said Billy, oblivious to Susan's horror: "This is amazing!"

"What the actual fuck, Billy?" yelled Susan: "Stop it! Stop it now! I'm getting her out of there, you freak!"

Inside the chamber, Jan relaxed into a splendid serene state of being, where she felt all the energies of the world that had burdened her since childhood were being extracted from her. She felt relieved and energized - as if her soul was being cleansed and replaced again, allowing her to become reborn. Jan felt a million tons lighter, envisioning herself as a young Susan at 21 years old, with the world at her feet, without a care, or thought that anything in the world could harm her. The world was for Jan, in that state. No sooner had the current passed through Jan, there came a knock on the chamber door, the place where she converted Orgone Energy from the ethers, like a machine. Susan prized the door open, to find Jan sitting in an altered state:

"Jan, Jan, are you alright? Come on, we have to get you out of this thing! What have you

done to her?" screamed Susan, as she leaned into the chamber to try and pry Jan out, slapping Jan's cheeks violently.

"What, what, what?" Out came the somber awakening tones from Jan's mouth: "Ermm, I'm okay. I, ermmm…." she said, as she moved her head around in a drowsy state.

"Help me get her off this chair, Billy!" hollered Susan, waving her spare arm at him.

After dragging Jan off the chair and laying her on a desk nearby, Susan looked at Billy and started screaming profanities at him, accusing him of harming Jan, who appeared listless. Billy stood firm, taking the verbal blows that Susan was beginning to deliver. After a few furtive moments, which culminated in Billy wrapping Susan's fists in his strong palms and pushing her close to his chest, they were interrupted by a slight murmur from Jan. Susan collapsed in Billy's arms and started to pant a little, before asking him to release her, so she could attend to Jan:

"I'm okay, I'm okay. I just need a moment to compose myself," said Jan, as she came too and dusted her top.

"Good, good, I'm so glad," said a relieved Susan: "I was so worried. Just rest there. Here, let me get you some water, hon."

Billy pointed Susan to the kitchen, then walked over to attend to Jan: "I'm sorry", he said.

To which Jan responded, kindly: "there's no need to apologize."

By the time Susan returned with a glass of water, Billy had propped Jan up to sit upright on the desk where she was placed - and she was slowly coming round. Billy placed Jan's short black hair away from her glowing face, over her ears. Running her hand across her mouth to take a gulp of water, Jan let out a gasp of breath to say:

"Thank you, guys. I want to do that again!!"

Susan and Billy both stood in a heightened state of anxiety, which abruptly came crashing down, to a relief, when they heard Jan speak - from a swift rollercoaster of emotions that were born out of fear and worry for her, which they were both happy when it ended:

"What do you mean?" asked Susan, in horror.

"Susan, you don't know what that felt like for me! I felt like all the pain and energy that I had taken on from a lifetime was drained away from me! I think that thing just went and sucked all that away from me! Honey, I haven't felt like that since I was a child, before I became cautious of going outside for fear of absorbing the world's negativity. That was possibly the finest moment I've experienced in a long time!!" said Jan, who was beaming and glowing, radiating like a ball of light, where she had been propped up, on the desk.

Susan and Billy looked on at Jan, with their mouths open.

Jan continued talking and pointed at the trolley that was placed outside the chamber:
"What happened with that device there? Did it do anything?", she asked, with reborn naivete.

"The tubes were filled in literally a few minutes, with the energy you converted. I expected it to take longer. In fact, I didn't expect it to work at all!" shrieked Billy.

"How long did you expect it to take?" asked Jan, with fresh curiosity.

"I didn't expect anything… that device measures and stores energy in simple kilo-joules, and I'm not sure about the amount that one person can hold… I didn't even expect anything to be stored. I mean, nothing's ever happened whenever I've tried it with willing volunteers," informed Billy, in haste.

Billy then helped Jan off the desk, dusting her off whilst he helped her step onto a chair, to assist her to ground. Jan gulped the rest of the water from the bottle she had been given. After she grounded her energy and regained her balance, she walked over to the device on the trolley attached to the chamber, to inspect the glowing yellow tubes that were set on top of it: "WOW! … so that's the sum of all the extra energy I've been carrying. And I still feel full of things that I'd love to unload. I bet I could power up those babies and create a real stockpile."

"But the real question is what can they be used for?" asked Billy, with burning intensity.

"Yes, Jan! It seems like there's a lot of power in them," added Susan, with cautious concern, leaning down to inspect the tubes that protruded from the top of the device on the trolley. They glowed a bright fluorescent yellow that pierced Susan's pupils.

"What's the capacity and what can that power be used for?" asked Jan, who was also captivated by the yellow misty glow from the tubes.

"I'm not sure. I would have to get a physicist to check what it is. Wilhelm believed that, with the right devices, it could be used for many purposes, to provide some sort of power," said Billy, distracted by the five yellow tubes.

Jan walked over to inspect the five little tubes that were stacked on top of the device, on the trolley - all the tubes that housed all her power. She carefully opened the glass case, which housed the five tubes on the device, and unscrewed one to inspect it. Jan felt a sense of her own power, being able to see and touch it in her hands. She marveled at the tube and pondered on all the infinite possibilities that her power could bring. Her daydream was cut short, however, by Susan's interruption:

"Jan, I think we should go out to have dinner. You must be exhausted, and I think you need to get yourself refreshed, and it's getting late. Come, let's go to the diner. I'll drive!" said Susan, in a terse tone.

Susan grabbed Jan's hand and marched her out of the Museum, leaving Billy mumbling disagreeably to himself behind them. Before Jan could thank or bid Billy farewell, Susan swooped Jan to the car for their short drive to the diner: "We'll be back soon, I promise. We'll bring you back something!", shouted Susan to Billy, as she stood in the doorway to his great-grandfather's museum.

Susan, who was anxiously alert of the danger that Jan was creating, tried not to cause a scene when they sped off. They sat over a dinner of burgers and fries, but Jan only ate the fries and ordered some salad:

"You're not eating your burger? Are you not hungry? I thought you might be hungry after that!" asked Susan.

"No, I thought I was hungry for it, but I'm suddenly repulsed by meat. Here you can have it," said Jan, pushing her plate of burger to Susan.

"Did you bring your meds?" asked Susan.

"About that...I haven't taken them since Egypt and I don't think I will anymore," said Jan, under her breath.

"What? Are you crazy?" asked Susan.

"That's the thing. My sugars are fine. I think something changed when I was in Egypt. I'm getting healthier. I don't know. It's strange. I don't think about my sugar levels anymore. I did a test at home, and they were fine," said Jan with some measured restraint.

Susan shook her head to refrain from rolling her eyes: "What's strange is that you let a complete stranger run his experiments on you. Are you out of your mind?" asked Susan, who grew irritated.

"I'm fine, Susan. Really, there's no need to worry," said Jan, as she finished her dinner and ordered some dessert.

"I gotta say, Jan. You're really treading on thin ice here. How do we know we're going to be safe there, when we get back? How do we know that he's not planning on keeping you for his experiments when we return? I think we should head back to Boston after this and forget about this whole trip!" asserted Susan, leaning towards a demand.

"Do you honestly think he would risk his family's name and reputation for a couple of lousy experiments? I don't think so! If at any point we don't feel safe, we can leave. Has he made you feel uncomfortable since we met him yesterday? You didn't appear to have been uncomfortable when you were flirting with him!" said Jan, deftly delivering Susan a blow.

Susan promptly left the table and went outside to sit in the car upon hearing that. Jan breathed a deep sigh and took a few spoonfuls of her ice cream before paying her bill and joining Susan in the car:

"Look, I'm sorry. I should have considered your feelings before I volunteered to get into that chamber. If you want, we can head back to Boston," said Jan in a conciliatory and defeated tone.

"No. This is important for you, for whatever quest you are on. I was just afraid. That's all," replied Susan. She turned her head to Jan from the passenger seat of the rental and said: "And I know what you keep telling me about fear…"

They returned to the Museum a short trip later to find Billy sitting by the brook, with his head held down, turning his head up at the distant approach of heels. He began to apologize profusely by saying:

"Look, I'm sorry. I've had so many people sit in that chamber ever since I built that device to store energy that I never expected it to work the way it did. I have never seen this effect on anyone. You have to believe me when I say that," said Billy, nodding intently at them both when he spoke.

Jan was the first to accept his apology, then Susan made a cursory acceptance. Without a second thought, Jan then moved the subject along to inform Billy about how good she felt after coming out of the chamber:

"Do you have any more tubes? I was wondering if I might try it again," said Jan, with a smirk that Billy welcomed.

"No, I don't think that would be a good idea," said Billy, shaking his head in an apparent gesture of discouragement.

"Yes, he's right, Jan!" affirmed Susan.

A silence followed and the summer evening began to draw in. Billy suggested a round of drinks at the cottage at the end of the garden by the brook, to take their mind off the events of the day. Susan was the first to accept and walked with Billy inside, followed by Jan. It was a familiar log cabin of basic means and very little splendor - the type of place that required a feminine touch to counter the type of guests who might have frequented it. After a couple of drinks, Billy offered to retrieve his guests' luggage from their car, so they could settle in for the night. Susan and Jan gladly accepted their drinks, and they began to relax and shake off the day:

"There's another cottage next door, if you need extra room," said Billy.

"No, thank you, we're fine together," replied Jan promptly, looking down.

"Say, isn't your wife wondering where you are?" asked Susan.

"No, I told her I had business to take care of here," said Billy, with a twinkle that returned in his eye when he flashed Susan a familiar pearly-white smile.

Susan and Jan started to sip the whiskey and cola that Billy began serving from the bar in the cottage, that duly fired up a conversation between them, leaving Jan to inspect the surroundings outside. Jan walked towards the brook behind the cottage, and sat by the sound of water. Inside the cottage, Susan and Billy continued to make chit-chat. Jan sat by the brook and thought about the tubes that contained her energy.

Her mind wandered to Professor Greene and how much she would have liked to share with him, about what had occurred and what it could all mean. If only he would be interested, thought Jan, to learn from her and share his thoughts on the subject. She then settled on the fact that it was a dead-end, trying to get him involved, then looked up at the sky. The dusk brought out the mosquitoes and crickets that were beginning to make their sounds, with a chirping of birds that faded into the distance. Jan relaxed for a moment, then headed back to the cottage, thinking about Professor Greene all the while.

By the time she returned to the cottage, Jan caught Billy and Susan in an embrace, then turned back out to sit by the picnic table a few yards away. Settling down to take her phone out of her bag, Jan began checking her messages, to see if there were any. There was a missed call from Toni and one text from Professor Greene that read: *"how are you doing over there?"*

Jan immediately rang Professor Greene, but he didn't pick up so she responded to Toni by text, filling him in on the events of their weekend up to that point, but refrained from providing Toni with too many details. Jan paused for a moment, then thought about the batteries again and that thought dwelled in her. Without too much rumination, Jan texted Professor Greene with: *"Hey, what do you know about orgone energy?"*

Jan immediately received a call from Professor Greene: "Oh, I see Mr. West has been teaching you things," said Professor Greene, with a teasing tone.

"No. It's not him… it's…." said Jan, then stopped for a moment and continued with: "nevermind…What do you know about it?"

"Oh, it's fanciful fringe science. There's a theory that it could be some sort of zero-point energy but that is so far out there, there is actually no evidence based on any reality to support orgone energy theory let alone how it links to zero-point energy," said the Professor.

His dismissive tone did not stop Jan from probing further:

"What is zero-point energy?", asked Jan.

"It's the energy between atoms and particles. Why?", asked the Professor with an alarmed tone: "Why do you want to know that?"

"What can it be used for?" asked Jan, with urgency.

"We don't know just yet because we've only just started to revisit it in physics," said the Professor, who sounded somewhat caught off-guard, perplexed and suddenly hesitant.

"Does it have any application in quantum mechanics?" asked Jan.

"Possibly. But why, Jan? What's all this about?" asked the Professor, with growing concern.

"I'll fill you in when I return. Thank you. We're heading back tomorrow, so maybe we can hook up in the week? I'll call you," said Jan. She tried to mask a spark of enthusiasm with a level of composure, so as not to alarm Professor Greene.

After hanging up the call, Jan walked over from the picnic table at the end of the long lawn to the cottage, back to the Museum to see if she could get into it. She became fixated by the tubes. They burned an image in her mind, calling out to her, making her want to retrieve them. When she got to the blue door at the museum's entrance, she discovered it was locked, so she went around the building, until exhausting all the doors. None would open. Billy had locked all the doors with some clear intention, leaving a pang of dread in the pit of Jan's stomach.

Jan stopped for a moment, to think of her plan. She walked to the cottage and waited anxiously outside for a few minutes, recounting how many minutes Susan and Billy might have had together, to gauge how she might find them when she returned. With any luck, she might find Billy's trousers on the floor in the reception room and the rest of his clothes, along with Susan, in the bedroom. Jan braced herself at the entrance then entered, to a room that bore no resemblance of a frenzied tussle.

After drinking a couple of shots of whiskey for Dutch courage, Jan decided to create a distraction to rouse the lovers, who were both in the bedroom, along with all their belongings, which Jan needed access to, at least Billy's trousers. Jan made a loud noise in the kitchen with some pots and pans, then stood in the kitchen and waited for Susan to appear, which she did in a matter of moments, in a bath-towel. Jan whispered to beckon Susan over and told her of her plan:

"Listen, we need to get those tubes. Jim said they could have some use and hold some power, and I'd like to find out what exactly," whispered Jan, wistfully.

"No! Absolutely not! No way!" whispered a frustrated Susan before continuing: "What are you planning on doing now? You are going to spoil this for me! All for your precious Professor Greene!"

"Since when am I going to have any man look at me the way Billy looks at you? This is my only chance with Professor Greene, Susan. I can't believe you're going to ruin THIS for me!" said Jan, with her trump card - playing the perpetual loser when it came to the game of love.

Susan lost to Jan's emotional blackmail and acquiesced: "okay! Gimme that bottle of Daniels and the cola and a couple of glasses, and I'll see you here in an hour, with the keys. You owe me one for this!"

Jan waited to retrieve the keys from Susan after her evening with Billy, who predictably fell into a deep sleep after their tryst. Susan had plied him with enough whiskey to finish the bottle and made sure her feminine wiles wore him out. Around the stroke of midnight, Jan left the cottage to creep back into the museum. Susan returned to the bedroom to ensure Billy was kept in bed.

Jan approached the museum, hoping that it wasn't alarmed. And it was Billy's only oversight. In Jan crept, in pitch darkness, in a building that was shielded away from any light pollution in the Maine countryside. Fumbling into the chamber-room where Billy's experiment had taken place, Jan managed to retrieve all five tubes and placed them into her bag, before draping it across her shoulders. She then returned for a sleepless and anxious night in the cottage next to Billy and Susan, for a couple of hours' sleep on an uncomfortable and undressed bed, before pacing inside and out, to periodically sit by the brook behind the cottage and gaze at the stars, in the hopes of speeding the night away.

By daybreak, just before six, Jan quietly knocked on the bedroom door at the cottage next door, and out popped a fully-dressed Susan, who immediately took back the keys, and placed them back in Billy's trouser pocket. After waking up Billy, Susan and Jan politely said their goodbyes, whilst he lay in bed with his loins modestly covered saying, with a satisfied smile: *"please come again"*. Susan returned a wave, with a grace that masked her pity for his inexperience.

Jan and Susan proceeded to load up their car with haste, under the pretext that they were going to be late for their flight. Billy, meanwhile, stood by the cottage in his boxer shorts and shirt, smiling still broadly with a coffee in his hand, waving at the ladies, reminding Susan to text him when she was in California, safe. Jan and Susan sped off down the country lanes, to join the freeway in a frantic finale of the weekend they had ended in Maine:

"Oh my god, can you believe that?", screamed Susan.

"What a fucking crazy weekend that was, Susan! I am not taking you anywhere ever again!', said Jan laughing, arched over her tight grip of the steering wheel.

"What do you mean?", asked Susan, laughing hysterically.

"Seducing married men!", cackled Jan, as she put her foot on the pedal, speeding down the highway.

"What about you stealing his secrets?", Susan laughed along.

"Well, *thank you so much for coming*, Susan. I really couldn't have done this without you!", cackled Jan.

They giggled their way to the airport, feeling renewed. It was the mental reset they both needed, since their time together in Egypt and their revival never left them that day. Susan discovered that helping her friend was more important than her need for affection from a man, although Susan accepted that part as something that she truly was and didn't need to hide or feel shame or guilt for. Jan discovered that, in his absence, she felt a fondness for Professor Jim Greene - and Jan was determined to spark his interest when she returned to California, with her findings.

Chapter 5

Burnwood, Santa Clara

Jan and Susan arrived in San Francisco Airport later that evening, still with the joy they both felt since their departure from Maine. The following week, Toni heard from Susan about their mission in Maine. Jan fought back tears of laughter, as she recounted the events to Toni, whilst they all caught up with each other at the Royale:

"Oh, you would have loved him, Toni," sipped Jan: "he was just your type!"

Toni was happy to hear about their adventure, though he made Jan promise that she would take him the next time she decided to take another, but Susan teased Toni continuously, for the action that he missed out on, in an effort to teach him about his own shortcomings.

After doing the rounds with Toni, the next port of call was Professor Greene. Fresh from the thrill of her adventure, Jan rang to tell him she wanted to see him - he jumped at the offer and Jan echoed the sentiment. Jim requested that she address him by his first name and Jan honored his request - she too wanted to get to know Jim a lot better.

They met in a mid-September breeze. With the escapades of summer behind them, they could finally begin to relax in each other's company. Professor Greene met Jan with virile energy, which Jan picked up on, when he took her out for dinner at the Royale that Saturday evening. Jim exuded a vitality which Jan was certain sprung from fresh eyes for him. He appeared to her in eager anticipation. Jan too was eager - eager to please Jim with her new knowledge, a knowledge which she was sure would align with his own appetite for Physics. With their mutual interest firmly established, they were now ready to explore each other's horizons in their usual haunt, starting at the Royale. A new level of intensity soothed the clumsiness of previous encounters.

"So, what do you know about zero-point energy?" asked Jim, as he leaned forward with his bowed shoulders.

Jan blinked slowly at the Professor, unresponsive to his burning question, appreciating the way his curly locks fell on his glistening forehead. The shine of his temples shimmered from the lights above them - his aura glowed under his white, striped shirt, that rested on a plump chest. As Jan continued to admire Jim, he looked up, uneasy from Jan's glaring reticence:

"I'm sorry, this is not the time for that. Let's just enjoy the evening," he said, and proceeded to order a bottle of White Zinfandel.

They both walked off dinner, with Professor Greene leading the charge by opening the door for Jan. The evening whistled a fall breeze, which swooped in from behind them on their quiet, sultry walk to Jan's apartment. Professor Greene smiled at Jan and extended his large forearm, which was uncovered by a folded sleeve - his brown hairs resting on his tanned skin. Jan saw his forearm muscles flex, as she took his hand in hers. His knuckles wrapped around her hand - a large hand with knuckles that belonged to a boxer. They walked under a pink sun, in a violet sky that blanketed the road ahead of them.

The sun dropped through their walk, deepening the sky from the girly pinks that lined the clouds, to the deep crimsons of a promise that was yet to unfold. Jan felt Jim's energy strongly, moving through her arm then down her side, when he clasped her hand tightly.

Jan thought about the moment when Professor Jim Greene would present himself to her as Jim, when he would let go of the mask he wore for the world. When the sun dipped down into the velvet sky, Jim would reveal himself, she thought, and accept him into her being. They came together that evening, over a silent dinner at the Royale that drew them together, where they spoke to each other with tempered silence. The sun beat to the promise of their night, as they moved through crimson violets, in a gentle pace, with a slight summer shower that cooled them like a zephyr that swept down from the sky in a haze, passing by them throughout the night. The next morning, the sun returned and roused them for a Sunday-morning snuggle.

Later that morning, they sat at a bay in the local pancake house where they smiled at each other over breakfast and Jan resisted the temptation to talk about the quest she was on, or about Physics. She sensed Jim's desire to talk about his favorite subject, his crutch, so she let him. Jan did not want to spoil his fun, though she struggled - though Jan and Jim both indulged in small talk, their favorite topics finally gave way.

Jan said: "Go on, you want to ask me, I don't mind, Jim," peering over her coffee, submissively.

He looked up at her from his pancakes, having awakened from his mid-morning mumble to ask Jan about her new-found interest in zero-point energy. He broached the subject carefully and observed Jan's response:

"So what happened there in Maine that made you ring me up?" asked Jim.

Jim sat silently, confused for a moment, until she said: "Oh, it will have to wait until after breakfast," and continued to drink her coffee, eyebrows raised as she took a gulp.

On the way back from brunch, they passed by the center of campus, to the building where Jan worked, and settled on a bench outside and ate ice-cream. The campus was usually quiet for the weekend, nothing out of the ordinary. They made chit-chat, largely instigated by Jim, who had the wherewithal to try and understand Jan a little better by allowing her the space to be herself. After some considered moments, Jim gently drew the conversation to the place where Jan might open up about what she discovered in Maine:

"Okay, so zero-point energy is the matter between atoms and particles. Am I correct in understanding what you said?" asked Jan, pointedly.

"In simple terms, yes," replied Jim, blown away by her level of understanding. He smiled with satisfaction, at having Jan's attention again, on all matters related to his favorite subject - Physics.

Jan sat licking her ice cream on the bench, remembering Mr. West's advice - to make Jim help her on her quest, from a conventional Physics perspective: "So, has it ever been harnessed?" asked Jan, continuing with her ice-cream.

"It hasn't even been discovered! It's just theoretical. Meaning, it might work, but there isn't any hard data to prove it. We know it might exist, from all that we already know in mainstream physics," explained Jim, with a teacher's tone, whilst looking intently at Jan.

"So, let me get this straight, theoretical physics is a thing," slurped Jan: "So, you are able to talk about the possibility of something existing even though nothing has been evidenced. I thought science was about matching theory with evidence?" crunched Jan, on the cone.

"That's part of it. It's a bit like the chicken or the egg. We have evidence that the sky is blue, for example, and we have constructed a theory around it. It can work the other way - we can start with a theory and, after assessing the possibility of it, we can then start to apply the mathematics to start constructing the evidence," added Jim carefully.

"The problem I have is with the word *'theory'* I suppose. I think that's what the problem is with me, to understand the validity of it all," said Jan, then bit further into the ice-cream cone.

"The validity of it all?" asked Jim, somewhat dumbfounded. "We need something to help us explain things. Theories do that. They help us to start enquiry."

"But that's the thing. Doesn't it depend on who has constructed these theories? And don't they get established into generally accepted ways of thinking that make a difference to how they are received and taught? Then it takes decades before they are proven, meanwhile other explanations and theories are overlooked," munched Jan, in between crunches.

"Well, in science, we used data to support theories. And data is evidence," replied Jim calmly.

"Okay, I understand that. But who's to say that there isn't an explanation for everything. There could be an explanation for everything and multiple theories for different things. But who decides which theory is worthy of investigation?" asked Jan, who then licked her fingers clean after finishing her ice-cream.

"Well, no...but…." replied Jim, before he was interrupted again.

"Take the theory of evolution, for example," continued Jan with her chest and chin out: "Charles Darwin didn't have evidence of the missing link, but somehow his theory became taught in schools, and this is what people believe as a reasonable explanation for our existence. But there wasn't any real evidence to prove his theory in and of itself, because the missing link has never been found – but, because there was some data on a part of this theory, it became some sort of generally accepted theory, which was then taught in schools. My point is that he could have created another theory and, depending on how it was received and accepted, that other theory could easily have become the accepted theory. Do you see my point?" asked Jan.

Jim swooned at Jan. He had met his match, someone he could afford a great level of respect - for her thirst for knowledge. It was a quality which he placed in high regard in a person.

Jim pursed his lips to say: "You've got me there, but theories take years to be dissected, argued and evidenced until they get filtered down into our education system. I suppose there might be a question about who is creating the theories and who is supporting them, which is a structural argument more suited to philosophy than physics. In any case, most theories get accepted simply by their popularity."

"Well, what happened with Tesla is a good example of that. We're only just learning about his inventions now, but look how his knowledge and inventions were treated then, leaving him broke. My point is that if he had the right support at the time, this world would look totally different by now!" said Jan, who continued to counter Jim's arguments.

Jim looked at her with some surprise, trying not to shake. Jan continued:

"But what about people who are just way ahead of their time and are written off because they are misunderstood?", as she leaned close to Jim on the bench where they sat, outside her office building - the administrative house of Santa Clara University.

Jan continued, unabated and with an enthusiasm that only continued to grow, much to Jim's exhaustion: "So, let's assume that zero-point energy exists, in whatever form you can find it and let's say that someone has harnessed it. What then? What could it be used for and in which theoretical model? Can it be used to tear holes in space? Can it be used to travel long distances?"

"It can be used for anything that requires powering, mechanically," sounded a despondent Jim: "Well, I suppose there's that…"

"How about storing it? How would it be stored?" probed Jan, cocking her head sideways, with an intensity that Jim was beginning to feel was becoming difficult to break from.

"I have no idea! Since we can't observe it, we can't harness it, but I'm sure there is some secret military experiment that the government has been working on," said Jim, with a hint of sarcasm, before proceeding to divert the subject with: "that's a very specific question and query you have there! How did you manage to get to the core of the problem so quickly?"

"Okay," said Jan and put her head down. She closed her eyes at Jim's sarcasm, then said: "I'm sorry… It's just my mind getting carried away, that's all!" She didn't want to extend her line of inquiry with someone who was becoming sarcastic, because she knew she would just end up feeling frustrated and so would Jim. So she stopped.

For the time being, Jan had what she wanted. She was able to disseminate the information she wanted from Jim, despite Jim's continued sighs. She still needed him, not least because she wanted him as a lover, even though Jan saw Jim as a reluctant participant in an endeavor of her own making. Jan weighed up Jim against her friends and made a decision to continue with her quest in true faith, accepting anything that would come on her path. Before Jan and Jim parted company, they arranged to meet for lunch during the week. They then kissed each other goodbye, after Jan finished her ice-cream outside her work.

That evening, Jan misjudged her instincts and resorted to ringing Toni, to give him an update about her love life and her quest, and she was met with a bitter disdain:

"Oh, girl, what have you gotten yourself into this time? Are you sure you know what you're doing?", said Toni.

Jan was immediately repulsed by Toni's response - it rang deep in the depths of her soul. Her instincts - to which she had become acutely aware since her return from the Great Pyramid - told her to make an excuse to end the call, with a promise to follow-up with arrangements for lunch, at some point in the future. Jan knew that it would be a while before she would see Toni again. Perhaps it was time to move on, she thought, since she was beginning to constantly feel let down by his attitude. After pausing for a moment, Jan decided to pay Mr. West a visit.

As Jan walked to the intersection, which crossed at the end of her street and led away from it, to Mr. West's home, Jan reflected on the deflation and disappointment once again, and her mind focused back to the boy on the bike in a red t-shirt. Jan wrestled for a moment, to check if she should return to the subject about Mr. West's departed son, when she appeared before him, in the distance. But Jan's experience taught her to always practice restraint when in doubt, even though the reality she experienced was somewhat different. Jan breathed a breath of gratitude - that Mr. West was pretty open-minded and at peace with the passing of his child. Jan knocked on their door.

Mrs. West opened it, with her welcoming smile and beckoned Jan in, promptly offering her favorite tea, before leading her Mr. West's studio Burnwood, where he sat by his desk, reading his newspapers after dinner:

"Oh, the prodigal son returns!" exclaimed an enthused Mr. West. He greeted Jan with a European peck on the cheek, clasping both her hands in his, tightening them slightly. Then Mr. West said: "Tell me everything that happened in Maine. Don't spare any details!"

"Oh, I don't know where to start, but it was mind-blowing. Quite literally!" said Jan, quickly proceeding to recount the events to a stunned Mr. West, who sat like an eager student, listening to an enchanting story.

"Why, Jan! That is absolutely splendid," shouted Mr. West, standing momentarily up from his chair: "Do you think Billy Reich will find out that you've taken the tubes?" asked Mr. West, leaning forward from his chair: "But, more importantly, what do you think he'll do when he finds out?"

Suddenly, the enormity of what Jan had done dawned upon her, making her draw silence, trying to beat any thought of the consequences of her actions. After noticing her worried expression, Mr. West brushed the notion aside and said: "Come, have some cake and forget about it. Besides, he doesn't know where you live!"

There was a pause, then Mr. West laughed: "Oh, by the sounds of it, he doesn't even know what day it is!"

Jan was not concerned with Mr. West's suggestion, but comforted by his wisdom. She joyfully ate her cake, and proceeded to tell Mr. West how she managed to disseminate information from Professor Jim Greene, choosing to refer to

Jim as Professor Greene in Mr. West's company, to avoid arousing suspicion of their burgeoning relationship:

"So, I think that this orgone energy which Billy Reich managed to harness from me is what Professor Greene calls zero-point energy. Professor Greene told me it could be used to power anything," said Jan.

"But not to tear a hole in the ionosphere, to break through dimensions, I suspect!" added Mr. West.

"No, I don't think it's that powerful," said Jan. She shook her head in good humor, at Mr. West's suggestion of tearing the fabric of Earth's atmosphere, to reveal other dimensions of reality, a matter of Jim's beloved Quantum Mechanics Theory. She then asked Mr. West: "why would you want to do that?"

"Oh, no reason. It's just a thought. If this orgone energy is a type of universal energy then we might be able to see if it could be used to tear a hole in our atmosphere. You never know what we might see on the other side of this reality," said Mr. West, then continued to sip his tea: "Though it would be great to see what else is out there, the things we know are there but can't really see at this time, on Earth."

Mr. West's eyes continued to glow, with the thought he was holding, of all the possibilities which their quest could take them. He stood, looking through his wooden shutters in Burnwood, at the orange-red glow of a Santa Claran autumnal dusk, in silent reverie of the divine.

Jan looked on at Mr. West with kindness and her brow fell: "Well, let me find out from Professor Greene if he can test what's in those tubes," said Jan.

"So, how do you intend on getting Professor Greene to help you with that?" asked Mr. West, turning around from his quiet contemplation.

"Well, he does have a lab with several different types of equipment in there. Maybe one of them might work. I could easily visit him again to find out more. Maybe he might be able to help me put something together," said Jan, to add momentum.

"Like what?" asked Mr. West, with vigor.

"Dunno…Maybe something to help me test the energy in those tubes… ," said Jan.

Mr. West placed his cup of tea down on the table and said: "Be careful. Professor Greene is a precarious fellow. You could end up alienating him for good. Despite his desire to help you, Physics is who he is," he smiled kindly and concluded, with kind eyes: "Just be careful, is all!"

"I will," smiled Jan and said: "Don't worry. I will be very careful. I haven't shown him the tubes nor told him anything about Maine. We only discussed zero-point energy a little, and that's the angle I'm working. But I feel something could happen… something good… I don't know what exactly, just something…."

"Yes, I have no doubt you will create what you need!" said Mr. West, nodding a knowing smile.

Sensing Mr. West's growing ease, Jan decided to broach another subject - his family - most notably, his son. Mr. West began by telling Jan that it was just him and his wife that was left in their world. They didn't have much extended family and spent most of their days together, which suited them both fine.

Then, without another prompt, Mr. West steered himself smoothly back to the subject that Jan originally had brought up at his home - the world of the paranormal - the world of ghosts, ghouls and lost souls. At a certain point, Mr. West confessed to Jan that he sometimes felt his son's presence in their home and Jan listened on, without batting an eyelid, proceeding with some caution at what she wanted to ask him.

Whilst deep in speech, Jan interrupted Mr. West with a declaration: "You told me some weeks ago, before I left for Maine, what your son was wearing when he was hit."

Mr. West's eyes focused on Jan, with some alarm: "Yes, that's right," said Mr. West, stirred in perplexity.

"Oh, I hope you don't mind me bringing you back to that subject," said Jan, tentatively.

"Oh, of course not. I told you, I'm at peace with it all," said Mr. West, then reclined in his chair, by which time Jan finished Mrs. West's Arabica coffee.

Jan broke through her reticence abruptly, her right finger pointing in the air above Mr. West's shoulder, from where he stood, at the shutters to the window of his studio Burnwood, that overlooked the main road, ahead of which lay the intersection to her street: "I've seen your son on his bike. Right there by the traffic lights, right there over at the end of the road to your home, at the intersection there, by the traffic lights…."

Mr. West looked at Jan as if his soul was punched, causing him to sit down on the chair by his desk. He sat for a while and simply stared at Jan from his chair, with both his hands clasped between his legs, as Jan stood away, not knowing what to say, with both hands drawn together in prayer, pointing down to the ground:

"I didn't want to believe it when you described him to me. He appeared then disappeared again. I couldn't understand what I had seen, but it wasn't until you told me what he was wearing... That's when it all made sense to me," said Jan, with truth and ease.

Mr. West looked at Jan, then placed his hands on his desk. He reached for his empty cup, which he lifted to look into, then placed it back down. Mr. West called his wife, whose footsteps could be heard stirring downstairs in the same way they always were - dependable, patient and comforting:

"What is it, honey?" asked Mrs. West.

"Jan here has something to share with us. I think you ought to sit down," said Mr. West.

Mrs. West came to join them, sitting down cautiously on the Chesterfield in anticipation of the news. Mrs. West began to shed silent tears, which Mr. West stumbled over from his desk, to wipe from her cheek:

"My wife. Please don't be upset. We should be honored. Jan is truly gifted. Truly. I always knew she was. From when I first met her," said Mr. West.

Upon the exchange, Jan made her excuses to leave, promising to keep Mr. West abreast of future developments. During her walk home, Jan thought of Mr. & Mrs. West's son, as she passed by the traffic lights, before pacing back to her apartment. As the sun set, Jan became enthralled by Mr. West's idea of tearing a hole in Earth's magnetic field, the magnetic ionosphere of the net - the matrix - into another dimension.

Jan's instincts grew and were sparked by something she was certain she knew - Mr. & Mrs. West's son was out there, still riding his bike, in his red t-shirt, just waiting to be seen by them again.

Chapter 6

The grid

The following week, Jan moved with cautious certainty, occasionally speaking on the phone with Susan, who asked about Jim. Susan was warmed by the prospect that her best friend was no longer going to spend her weekends alone, even though Susan may encounter the occasional disappointment when trying to arrange a girly night with Jan - though it was something Susan prepared for, with love and gratitude.

Susan imparted some wise tones on the phone to her bestie: "if he shows you who he really is, believe him the first time. Don't wait for him to change. You're too good like that. Let him come to you. Let him do the work," - to which Jan responded with quiet agreement. She knew, deep down, that Susan was right, that she indeed was too good a person. Always running around people for their company, something she had to learn to stop doing - and trust that everyone and everything she ever wanted would just come to her, at the right time, when she was in alignment with her vision.

Jan checked her personal inbox for signs of Abbassi, after ending her weekly catch up with Susan, but it was empty of messages. She then retrieved the business card Abbassi had slipped her, by the roadside in Giza. Breathing a sigh of relief, finding it after a search, Jan put her feelings about needing to talk to Abbassi aside. For the time being, Jan decided to get Jim to take her back to his lab, so he could talk her through some of the machinery that may help her realize Mr. West's vision of using the energy that was stored in the tubes, to tear holes in the clouds, into new dimensions.

Jan was certain about one thing - that, despite the intense feeling of relief that being in the chamber had given her, Jan was burning with new curiosities about her own abilities. The intense amount of power that ran through her was not for the weak-hearted, she knew that. Nor for someone of a fragile mind. Or a body riddled with ailments. Whatever had passed through her and filled up those tubes, did something to her, which inadvertently made her feel normal - but limited her ability to perceive vibrations to the same extent as before.

Jan was beginning to see the world for what it was - a 3D-reality, a form of a world which only presented a surface meaning - a world where she wasn't riddled with all the information that came along with the surface meaning of each item that presented itself to her. It offered Jan some glimpse into the 3D-nature that everyone around her perceived, completely devoid of anything other than the surface meaning.

It was a world that was completely devoid of energy, and all the information that Jan usually skimmed from it, which left her feeling terrible - not having access to the information that helped her make sense of the world, left her falling into low moods. Jan couldn't face the prospect of not being able to see the world in the way she saw it, before her trip to Maine. It was as if she was losing her identity, her state of consciousness, dissipating her gifts and her being. It would be a curse to lose the gifts that Jan used to carry as a burden, throughout her life - and she wanted them back.

Jan's thoughts turned to Abbassi again - thoughts which began to feature more prominently in her mind's eye. History told her to expect a call from the person she often thought about, for her thoughts were not merely thoughts - they were messengers which came as clear images, like a hologram. A clear image that she would be communicating with Abbassi stuck with her all week, interspersed with colors that irked her anxieties like alarm buttons. By the end of that week, Jan checked her private email before logging off at work. Before doing so, she breathed a satisfied sigh, to the sight of an email headed *Catch up.* From Abbassi.

Jan opened the email, to an explanation from Abbassi - he had taken ill and was recovering from a bout of sickness, but stated that he was feeling fine and offered his apologies. Abbassi then followed with a brief answer to her previous communication to him about chakras: *"chakras are energy fields in the body. I think that you experienced an alignment of those energies when you were on top of the Great Pyramid. This is what is called a chakra alignment."*

Jan responded, telling Abbassi of her experience in Maine, adding: *"is it possible that the energy that flowed through me and was captured in the closet-chamber is the same energy that flowed through me, when I was on top of the pyramid?"*

She received an immediate response from Abbassi: *"Yes, the energies that you speak of and the energies of these ley lines are the same. I am very curious to see what will happen with what you can do with the energy in those tubes, that you say was captured. The Great Pyramid is a greatly powerful energy vortex, because it is placed at the crossings of powerful ley lines. It is extremely potent. If it was able to run through you, who knows what ran through you when you were in the chamber. Who knows what is in these tubes you speak of."*

After her email exchange, a renewed sense of mission flowed through Jan again, that brought a relief and a laser-sharp focus that she needed, to shift her attention in the right direction. That week, Jan didn't return calls from Toni, choosing to only reply to Susan, who relayed Toni's attempts to contact her. Jan became doggedly focused on getting Jim to demonstrate which devices could project energy from the tubes that she took.

Jan became sure that every moment was giving way to a path that was beginning to unfold in front of her, which required a gentle undertaking that only she was in control of and could master. Jan was resigned to walk her own path, to wherever that was and only she was responsible for allowing whatever or whomever came on that path. Jan took a breath and looked back, on the short distance she had travelled and progressed through her own choices and actions and, in that reflection, Jan gained the momentum she needed for goals which were becoming all the more clear to her.

Jan arranged to meet Jim one weekend in late September. Jan paid close attention at the sight of the new moon, on her veranda one evening with her tea, staring down the street at the traffic lights. School was in full swing again and Jim, of a solitary persuasion, was inclined to spend time at the lab in-between his scheduled classes. Jan expected to get busy again, as an administrator at the university, having to deal with students and staff in predictable fashion. She had enjoyed the quiet lull of the summer, before the onset of students and staff took her away from herself.

For the time being, Jan savored her freedom and felt relaxed. The project in the department to which she was seconded was coming to an end, and she was glad to be able to see the back of the overbearing and obnoxious Jonah. Jan had a month to decide if she wanted to return or to stay with Jonah. For the time being, she enjoyed the offer, for her perseverance with the greatly irritating Jonah was a quiet foregone conclusion. She didn't want to dwell on him too much, choosing to pace herself with the immediate and daily tasks that confronted her.

Jan met Jim outside her office building, and they walked the quad to his lab. He had just finished lunch and had brought with him an ice-cream for Jan to enjoy:

"Have you had a word with your doctor about your diabetes?" asked Jim, to which Jan simply shrugged her shoulders.

Jan and Jim had come to a mutual understanding - whenever Jan didn't respond to Jim's questions, he knew not to pursue it. Jim was always full of too much acquired knowledge to let things go or to leave them be. He needed an answer to almost anything from books and established thought, especially if the questions were related to his field of work. Though his thirst for knowledge mirrored Jan's, he was learning to temper his way of thinking with Jan's quest for something that defied conventional explanations.

Whilst at the lab, Jan did not waste any more time in getting the information she needed, to move forward:

"So which one of these devices might be able to fire a laser?" she pressed, ready to devour Jim's brains again.

"Well, it depends on the source. All of them, really," replied Jim.

"What about one that might fire zero-point energy?" asked Jan, with muted emotions.

"Well, since we don't know the nature of it, I'm guessing none because we need to understand zero-point energy first," replied Jim.

"Let's imagine zero-point energy is invisible energy, because it exists between atoms and particles, couldn't it be used with a standard device that projects any laser?" continued Jan.

"Jan, I love your sense of imagination and logic, but I can't talk in hypotheticals like that. I need data before I can answer that!" stated Jim, whilst locking one of the glass cages.

Jan rolled her eyes, something she didn't approve of in others, then took a glance at a glass cage that housed a torch-like device with a needle-like front and broad base, resembling the point of a sword: "How about this?" jumped Jan, when she saw it: "what's this one used for?"

"That is a standard laser projector for firing particles onto a surface," replied Jim.

"Could it be modified to accommodate a different source of energy to fire through it? Could you direct any type of energy through it?" repeated Jan.

Jim breathed a deep sigh. Jan looked at him, confused.

After a short pause, Jim took Jan by the hand and said with all seriousness: "Tell me something, Jan. What exactly are you getting at here? What exactly do you want to happen? I can't help but suspect that this has something to do with what you found in Maine and you seem to be on a mission to do something with zero-point energy. Whatever happened, you can tell me, Jan. I promise I won't freak out or tell you that you're crazy."

Jan turned around, taking Jim's hand in hers: "Jim…stop it, you idiot! Just tell me! I'll tell you what I need it for after…."

"After what?" asked Jim, slightly impatient.

"After you help me build a device which can project a source of energy, maybe zero-point energy," said Jan, shrugging her shoulders: "I'm just curious!"

Jim laughed off Jan's persistence: "Jan, you're asking too much of me and I don't really know what it is you're asking of me. Like I told you, it's not possible, and I think we should leave it there."

Jan backed off a little, still reluctant to tell Jim everything, leaving Jim standing there in his lab, wistfully wishing on an answer from her. Before Jan left, she dropped a little gem for Jim - she told him about her frustrations with him, for being unwilling to entertain her desire for knowledge. She accused him of failing in his capacity as a teacher; then accused him of not being a man because he was too afraid to broaden his horizons; lastly, she accused him of being limited in thinking, since he was unable to use his imagination.

Jan's parting shots cut Jim deeply: she said she felt sorry for him, claiming he would have gone farther in his career, if only he had a propensity for real inquiry and imagination. Jan threw everything she knew about Jim at Jim, to attack his ego - the only thing that she knew would work, to break him down and get him to work with her. She walked away from his lab in her shrewd gamble, never once looking back as she walked on, with her chin and chest out.

That evening, her phone rang constantly, but Jan did not answer. Jan wanted so desperately for Jim to work with her, but she wanted Jim to go further than a simple phone call, so she waited for Jim to knock on her door. Jan waited. Patiently. A week went by without a knock - the ticking of the clock signaling the end of their relationship.

Jan was back on her veranda, on a Sunday, gazing at the traffic lights, above it, into the ether, which she hoped one day to tear, to reveal the true reality behind the matrix, to one day return Mr. & Mrs. West's son to them. She drank her tea to brace herself for another week at work, unsure of what it might bring, mindful of not thinking too negatively of the previous week's events with Jim. Then came the knock at the door. It was her neighbor – who wanted to drop off her dog for Jan to look after, for an evening of dog-sitting, since Jan was going to stay in, predictably so. Just as Jan was closing the door, a hand wedged itself in. It was Jim:

"It was foolish of me to react like that …" said Jim, sullenly, then in an assertive but conciliatory tone: "...but, you have to tell me what happened in Maine. Otherwise, I don't know what I'm getting involved with here."

Jan looked at Jim as he spoke, who softened the tension in his throat as he did so:

"Okay, I think you better sit down," said Jan. Before Jim could sit, Jan told Jim everything that happened in Maine.

"Really, Jan?", shouted Jim, enraged.

"This is what I was afraid of, Jim!", replied Jan, with her head down.

"Jan, Wilhelm Reich was a crank. Fringe science, Jan. It means pseudo-science. I can't believe it! And his great-grandson hoodwinked you. Only you would believe that…", said Jim.

"Only I would believe that? Because I'm an idiot?", said Jan.

"Oh, Jan, don't start that. Anyone can see you're as smart as hell. Hell, even smarter than me, but please don't waste your time with this. This is not worth it. It's not worth your time or my energy. Come on, let's just let it go," bartered Jim.

"Jim, I'm not sure if it is zero-point energy! But I just want to eliminate the possibility. Isn't that what science is all about? Besides, you might call it pseudo-science, but that's what they thought about Tesla 100 years ago, but look at how Tesla is being considered nowadays," countered Jan.

"Jan, you can't compare Wilhelm Reich to Tesla. You just can't!" said Jim, shaking his head.

Jan slumped into the sofa, next to Jim, who looked hopelessly forlorn. Jan then said: "I never knew this would cause so much fuss. I don't see what the problem is. I call it enquiry, but you call it crank science. Maybe the problem is there - we just see things differently," said Jan, as she began to straighten Jim's collar.

"Okay, okay," said Jim, who succumbed to Jan's siren ways.

He kissed Jan, then said: "Okay, I'll help you with your investigation. I don't see what harm it would do, since nobody, not even Reich, was able to harness zero-point energy, and I doubt his great-grandson knows how to. The best I can do is built a prototype for you, but I'll need to know what the energy source is, so it's compatible with the device."

"The energy is stored in tubes. I have them!" said Jan.

"Oh, Jan, what are you doing to me?" said Jim and proceeded to kiss her more, leaning back on the sofa.

"Don't worry," replied Jan, in between their embrace: "I would never put you at risk of anything, and you can pull out anytime."

"I don't intend on pulling out. I'm in this with you. All the way," added Jim, suddenly consumed by Jan.

They breathed an effortless kiss, and swooned into the night. Sleeping with Jim in the fall night, Jan woke up with the sunlight bursting straight into her bedroom. Monday morning was welcomed with a lover's embrace, as Jan turned to Jim and held his head in her bosom, and she kissed his forehead. Jan was thankful for Jim's presence in her life. She kissed his forehead again in gratitude, with sweet remorse in what she was asking of him, an accomplished man - to compromise his identity and possibly his career. She knew he was completely enthralled with her and it no longer scared him. Or her. Her experiences, as an undervalued being in the worlds she moved in, left her with scars that she was only too aware of. Jan had to face new waves of feelings for someone from a world that ordinarily threatened her peace. She kissed his eyes as he slept, waking him:

"I have to leave for work," she said. "I'll leave you a key to let yourself out."

Jim uttered some words, in between snores. Jan crept out of bed to get ready, leaving a note, before heading out on a crisp morning - opting to take the bus instead of walking, which she did with a smile on her face. A gentle warmth fell on her, whilst she looked on out at the pink morning sky - a sky that seemed to be changing, a light that seemed to be changing. It was no longer the blurry haze that she usually saw. Three birds ascended above her, in the rhythm of Santa Claran life. Jan was overwhelmed with a feeling that everything was going to be alright, everything would work out - that was the vibration she wanted to hold, like a chalice full of abundance.

The lights in the sky were changing for a new season when Jan stepped off the bus with a smile on her face, to face the light of a world she knew she would soon break.

Jim called Jan for lunch. He brought with him a packed lunch he had prepared especially for her - a lunch that included fresh, cool satsumas from the farmer's market - which Jan peeled with flush fingers. The cool, succulent flesh of the satsumas pressed her lips, reminding her of how much she had missed eating fruit since her diabetes diagnosis some years prior:

"When do you want to start?" asked Jim, looking intently at Jan, where they sat, on the bench outside her office building, on Santa Clara's university campus.

Jan almost choked on her segment, then said: "What? Are you serious?" Putting her arms around Jim, she kissed his cheek and said: "I promise I won't ever disappoint you!"

"Okay, okay, enough of that. I'll come over tonight to draw up plans with you. I'm going to need to know what you're looking for. But you're cooking," said Jim, seizing the moment to become unusually assertive.

"Sure, sure... yes, of course," said Jan. She kissed Jim on the cheek and, after finishing their lunch, they parted in an embrace, which drew the attention of passers-by, mostly colleagues who were returning to their building after their break.

That evening, Jan cooked the only types of dishes she knew, for the best outcome. She patiently labored over dumplings, wantons, soups and mains that took hours to prepare and minutes to scoff down. Jim sat eating, watched lovingly by Jan - she enjoyed watching him enjoy all the recipes her mother used to woo her father with. In the years since her parent's marriage, Jan's mother's kitchen exploded with culinary delights whenever she needed something from her husband. The chicken soup calmed the nerves, Jan's mother would say, and the braised pork would have a man eating out of the palm of Jan's hands. Jan was happy knowing that Jim wouldn't need much convincing, and relaxed herself into receiving the fruits of Jim's labour.

Immediately after dinner, Jim opened a large folder and unfolded a large sheet of paper with a drawing of a prototype model. It was the hand-held device that Jan had in mind - the size of her hand, a cylinder wand, with an aperture at the top, presumably where the energy would be emitted from, when pointed in the right direction:

"It's called a directed energy device," said Jim: ""The military are trying to perfect it."

"Military? What? Seriously? How did you get your hands on this?" asked Jan, shocked at the turn of events.

"Oh…This is something I sketched myself. It's just to show you what it would look like, but I need to understand the source of energy. Do you have the tubes?" asked Jim.

Without a second thought, Jan went to retrieve the tubes from her bag and returned smiling. Jim took them to inspect them closely, inspecting one carefully, bringing the bright yellow tube close to his eye:

"Careful," said Jan.

"It looks like some sort of liquified gas," said Jim, whilst inspecting them.

"They haven't been opened, and I am scared too!" said Jan.

"I'll have to test them first, to see what type of charge they hold, before I fire it up there in that device," said Jim.

"Okay," nodded Jan, in gentle trust of him.

"I doubt it's zero-point energy, though. I reckon this Billy Reich character is just as much of a crank as his great-grandfather was and built his contraption to draw in the crowds for his freak-show museum," muttered Jim, under buried breath.

Jan remained relaxed at Jim's opinion, exhaling a shrug and a chortle. In a way, she was glad that Jim wasn't taking it all too seriously - at least he was finally prepared to entertain Jan's notions, and was prepared to build the device that she wanted. Though Jim perceived it as a folly, it was clearly something different for Jan and she didn't allow herself to be blown off her course by Jim's opinion, which was quite a development for her and gave her the balance she was desperately seeking. Jim was confident in his belief that the tubes held nothing more than an innocuous charge, and Billy Reich had duped Jan by inserting some sort of gaseous element to make it look believable to her, like a cheap magician's trick. Deep down, Jim felt the need to make Jan see sense with her notions. Jan kept to her resolve, undeterred by his masked skepticism.

The following week, an excited Jan called Susan to arrange lunch and to keep her informed of the progress of her secret project, taking the time to express her disappointment with Toni:

"Oh, he'll come around, he normally does, when he sees how much of a jerk he's being. He's insecure about everything. You just have to give him time," said Susan.

Jan responded by saying: "I don't think I can deal with his negativity anymore. Ever since we returned from Egypt, he's been different. I mean, I get it. He doesn't have to support me with my interests, but at least he can still be a friend! Or am I expecting too much?" said Jan with curt lips. Susan looked at Jan with raised eyebrows:

"Hey. Maybe we could all go away on a trip again to regroup. Just the three of us," proposed Susan: "It doesn't have to be far, and it doesn't have to be expensive."

"I'm not too sure about that," replied Jan, with her head down over her coffee at the Royale: "Someone needs to tell him the truth about himself. He's never gonna change!"

They both parted ways that day and Jan resumed with her week, anxiously awaiting news from Jim, whom she didn't want to push, and refrained from contacting Mr. West, until she had further news from him. Jan spent the rest of her week pondering her friendship with Toni, relying on her instincts to allow her to make her own decision or to let him go his own way, at least for the time being, until he made a conscious effort to invest in their friendship. To wile away the rest of her week whilst she heard from Jim, Jan contacted Abbassi again to ask more about the energies of the world, so she could make more sense of where her investigation was leading her. They spoke on the phone, after a few fumbled attempts at making arrangements:

"You told me that the ley lines are a grid, but these vortices that you speak of, in places like the Great Pyramid where I had my experience - how many more are there in the world? Do you have a map?" asked Jan.

"Yes, I'll send you a map," replied Abbassi and quickly filled her inbox with an attachment whilst speaking on the phone.

Jan checked her inbox, which was quickly filled with an empty email that came with an attachment. Jan opened the image and waited for Abbassi to continue:

"There are significant areas, some big, some small. They all vary in strength, but the map I sent you shows you the 6 significant energy portals, and they loosely link with 7 energy portals of the body. The 7 chakras. Each place represents a different chakra. The Great Pyramid is the 5th chakra, the throat chakra, which relates to communication. The chakra about communication that has been awakened in you relates to your desire and your ability to speak your truth and to express yourself."

Jan examined the map on her computer monitor with great intent. She then said: "I see Mount Shasta is the root chakra, the base chakra for survival. What's that all about?" asked Jan.

"The root chakra is red. It has to do with survival and your basic needs as a human being. If your basic needs are not being met, then that chakra is out of balance," said Abbassi, with a tone that only a teacher could best impart.

"Oh, wow, but what about the rest?" asked Jan, feverishly, "What about the rest of the chakras? What does it mean if they are not in balance?"

"Well, then we have the sacral chakra. That's to do with pleasure and sexuality. You have to balance your needs with your wants. The solar plexus is above that, under your heart and near your base. It's the navel. That's what you Westerners love to call navel-gazing. It means your own feelings of self-worth and self-esteem are crushed, if you are out of balance."

"Oh, that is beginning to make sense to me, Abbassi," said Jan, with increasing wonderment: "Please continue."

"Now, moving up from the navel, to the heart. Of course, that chakra is about love and joy and it is green. Not red - that's a common misconception. Red is the root chakra. There's a reason why nature on Earth is green. Mother Earth - Gaia - is green. She is loving but she is suffering from human activity and that is why she is out of balance," quipped Abbassi.

Jan listened quietly, as Abbassi continued: "Moving up from the heart, as I mentioned before, is the throat chakra - blue - and that is to be found at the Great Pyramid. Then moving up, to the third-eye chakra, you might have heard about the third-eye before… that is related to your awareness, intuition and wisdom - and it's purple. Always listen to your intuition. If you don't, it may lead you to dangerous places. It's all about responsibility, Jan. Just do everything from your inner voice."

"Ah….." echoed Jan, in resounding agreement.

"Finally, the crown chakra is at the top of your head and that is the highest white light. It is divine light. Some say it is yellow, or golden," concluded Abbassi, with the deep relief of having ended the lesson he started when Jan met him, at the roadside opposite the pyramids of Giza.

"Wow, Abbassi. Have you seen all these colors? How do I get to the highest white light, Abbassi? Is that what I saw up there, in Giza?" asked Jan, consumed by Abbassi's kaleidoscope of hidden knowledge.

"Jan, let me warn you now… this quest you are on, it comes with a lot of responsibility," said Abbassi, his tone changing in a breath.

"What type of responsibility?" asked Jan, unfazed.

"It's your individual responsibility. That's what makes it difficult. It's about you. Not about the world around you. Once you master that, you can change the world around you by combining your thought with your emotion and turning that into an action for the outcome you desire."

"So, what you are saying is that, I have to stay mindful of my thoughts and deeds and never blame anyone or anything else for my circumstances. Ever," mirrored Jan like a dutiful student.

"Precisely," added Abbassi.

"Then I can connect to the highest white light?" asked Jan.

"Then you are your own source," echoed Abbassi.

"But what do I need to do to become my own source?" begged Jan.

Abbassi paused and did not respond, whilst Jan listened attentively and patiently, drawing a deep breath from every cell in her body, from the ground below her, up through the full capacity of her lungs, into her nostrils, holding it until Abbassi spoke:

"You need to clean your chakras, then they will become aligned … But you must never forget to find your balance with your power, once you attain it. Otherwise, it could go very wrong for you. The dark forces - the demons, the jinns and the Devil himself will come and feast off your energy and drive you into your ego. Then you will forget all about the source - God - and all your gifts will be lost to the material world, along with your true self."

It was a warning that penetrated Jan's entirety. She took a gulp of air, exhaled the tension and looked at the map that lay before her: "It's crazy that Mount Shasta is on the map….

That's actually not so far away from where I live here in California.... I could think of someone who could really benefit from a renewal of passion, someone who could do with being fearless, someone who could benefit from connecting with others....," said Jan between measured pauses, her imagination running wild: "...but what if these seven energy portals in the world were unleashed on the world? What would that mean for everyone in the world?"

"Oh, like that? ... Who knows..... It would be similar to what you experienced on top of the Great Pyramid. Well everyone would have an alignment, like you may have had. It would mean that everyone would have their third eye opened and everything would be revealed to them in the way you see it, perhaps as the ancients saw the world, allowing everyone to connect with the divine," responded Abbassi.

"But can this happen to everyone?" asked Jan.

"Oh, yes, everyone can align their chakras. You are not special, in that regard," replied Abbassi.

"Well, I'm not too sure if the world is ready for that!" said Jan: "It took me a long time to accept myself. I've always felt like an alien on this planet but I do think I've had something other people can't see, from a very young age."

"But maybe it's the world that is crazy. Not you! The reason you struggle in life is because you know more about the true nature of this world than most people. You live on a higher vibration than most people. You are highly sensitive to low vibrations, and this world is just getting darker by the day. Something is lowering the vibrations of this planet. Your vibrations are just not a match for this world. That's why you feel like an alien. Wouldn't it feel a lot better for you if everyone rose to your frequency?", soothed Abbassi.

"Yes, I suppose so," replied Jan, somewhat solemnly: "What do you think is lowering the vibrations of the planet?"

Abbassi made an excuse to end the call before Jan could open new avenues. She knew in her heart the answer to that - and bade Abbassi farewell. After their phone call ended, Jan immediately thought of Toni, her heart rising with hope for their strained friendship. She promptly contacted Toni and invited him to a trip with Susan for the weekend. Toni responded warmly to Jan's unsolicited phone call, with mild acceptance of Jan's proposal:

"Hey, are you free this weekend?", chirped Jan, as she used to with Toni.

"No, why?", came the hesitant response.

"What do you think about coming with me to Mount Shasta this weekend, for a hike and an overnight stay? Susan's coming too! Have you ever been? It's meant to be quite a mystical place. It's meant to hold great value for the Natives," proposed Jan.

"Well, seeing as I didn't get to go with you to Maine, why not?", responded a non-committal Toni.

Jan tried not to become irritated by Toni's bitterness and closed her eyes, to focus on her inner strength. She then rang Susan for a conference call, which she patiently directed for all three participants:

"Is this going to be another Maine? Or is this going to be another version of Egypt? Are you going to places you shouldn't and am I going to end up having to call search and rescue?", asked Susan jokingly, trying to break the tension that she picked between Jan and Toni, during the call.

"Guurl, stop. You know you loved it. What do you say, Toni?", said Jan: "Are you still in?"

Jan breathed in and tried to not let out a sigh when Toni confirmed his attendance. After she ended the conference call, Jan's shoulders dropped, and she began to feel a wave of nerves pulsing through her, from the momentum that she gained for her quest, from her friends.

Jan then received a call from Jim, who spoke with some haste: "Jan, how soon can you be at the lab?"

Jan arrived at Jim's lab within half-an-hour, to a stunned-looking Jim, who stood with arms outstretched in his white coat, in his lab, at Santa Clara's university buildings:

"What is it? What's the matter?" asked Jan, as she hastened into the lab.

"There's no electrical charge in these tubes, but I can't rule out that it's not zero-point energy!" exclaimed Jim.

"What are you saying?" asked Jan.

"It might or might not be. Since there is no electrical charge, what might be in there is anyone's guess," said Jim.

"But is it zero-point energy, or not?", asked Jan.

Jim really wanted it to be what Jan was looking for. He didn't want to disappoint her, but felt obliged to state what he knew. He said, with some level of unease:

"I hazard a guess that it's not zero-point energy. But that could be because I don't have a way to detect it with my equipment. I'm sorry," said Jim, with a tinge of pity for Jan.

Jan felt deflated, but was comforted with Jim's proposal that he would be done with the device that she requested in a few more days. Jim told her that he would let her know when it was ready, patting her on her shoulder in sympathy. Jan returned to her apartment, disappointed with what she had been told. She felt at odds with the world again, this time of her own making. Regardless, Jan accepted responsibility for her feelings and carried on with her mission.

Jim called round to see her that Friday and, after a dinner she spent the afternoon preparing, they enjoyed a glass of wine together on her veranda. The neighbor's dog sat and observed them, from his window opposite. Jan asked about Jim's childhood, his family background, and she shared her childhood as an immigrant from Vietnam, having arrived as a refugee with her parents in Illinois, and she described to Jim how her parents slowly built a business over the next 30 years:

"Do you think that's why you see the world differently to most?" asked Jim.

Jan responded, wryly: "yeah, that could be it!"

After a couple of glasses, they went indoors. Jan walked over to the sofa to sit and, after a cuddle, Jan withdrew slightly. Reading her body language, Jim leaned over the side of the sofa to grab his bag. Jan looked on in anticipation and, before she could say anything, Jim unzipped the bag and her eyes lit up. After seeing the change in her appearance, Jim smiled at the prospect of pleasing Jan. He reached into the bag, and pulled out a silver rod. Jan took the cold metal into her warm hands with her mouth open:

Jim said: "here it is, your very own cloud-buster!"

Jan glowed when she held it in both hands, gently laying it on her lap. Then Jim leaned in for a kiss.

Jan then said: "thank you, Jim. You don't know what this means to me. Even if it's just a load of nonsense to you. I can't thank you enough for trying."

"I'll show you how it works after," said Jim. He then kissed Jan's lips, softly biting them, before falling on top of her, with the cloud-buster between them.

Jan reached down to take the metal rod and placed it on the side table as they swooned in embrace. Jan felt herself letting go for the first time in a long while. No longer did she feel the guilt of thinking she had manipulated Jim, resigning herself to the idea that it was indeed Jim who wanted to indulge Jan. After what he had constructed for her, Jan found herself aroused with him for brushing his ego aside and being able to think outside what he had been taught. Jan fell deeply in love on that sofa that evening, in a longing lust for what Jim was able to demonstrate for her.

That evening, Jim took Jan out to the end of her street, the first place she wanted to visit, by the traffic lights. Jim pointed the metal rod at the sky, above the traffic lights and pressed the button at the base of it:

"Why can't I see anything? Why can't I see a laser? I was expecting to see at least a beam of light" asked Jan, before adding: "is this thing working?", tapping the device that Jim held.

"I told you, Jan. There's nothing in the tubes. All you're doing at the moment is just pointing and pressing something which contains something we know nothing about," said Jim.

Jan remained undeterred and said: "but you said zero-point energy can't be observed!"

"We mean by the laws of physics and mathematics, not necessarily plain sight," said Jim, with a smirk: "Come, let's head back. That's enough for tonight."

They walked back together to her apartment with a mixture of uncertainty and dread. Jan began to feel a sense of humiliation, though she was grateful for what Jim had built for her. She was comforted by Jim that night, who held her tightly in bed to reassure her that her quest had been noble in its endeavor - but it was something she just had to learn from:

"Sometimes, the evidence doesn't support the theory and that is fine," said Jim, hugging Jan tightly in bed.

That night, as they slept, the night sky above the traffic lights at the end of her street began to break into different hues. From deep navy, to a purple in a little patch, where Jan had pointed her cloud-buster. As morning crept, Mr. West took out the trash - he looked down the road from where he stood, where he too often gazed, as Jan did, from his road, adjacent to Jan's, where his gaze often met the point where Jan focused hers.

Mr. West saw what looked like a boy on a bike with a red t-shirt. Rubbing his eyes, the boy faded away before Mr. West could lay eyes on him again. Mr. West went indoors, shaking his head in disbelief, and wondered whether he should share what he saw with his wife. Once inside his home, Mr. West looked back behind him, at his front door. And stood in silence.

Chapter 7

Mount Shasta

Jan announced that she was going to take her friends with her to Mount Shasta and she extended an invitation to Jim, who declined because his parents were due to visit that weekend. Jan suggested a trip to his parent's when she returned from Mount Shasta, which he welcomed. On the night before she was due to leave with her friends for their weekend get-away, Jan happened to glance upon the bag that Jim had brought with him to her apartment.

Jan stopped for a moment, before taking out the cloud-buster from the bag. She looked over her shoulder and saw Jim lying in bed, looking happy with himself - prompting her to collect her thoughts before putting the cloud-buster back into the bag. Then she took it out again and thought for a few more moments. She then placed the cloud-buster in her own bag, zipped up Jim's bag tightly and placed it back beside the sofa, where he had dropped it when he arrived.

"It's a pity it didn't work," shouted Jan, in an attempt to arouse Jim from his mid-morning slumber.

"Hey...whey.... what ...?" said Jim, awakening from his sleep: "what's that?"

Jan walked into the bedroom where Jim fought off a snooze and repeated what she said: "I am really grateful that you tried though."

"Yes," said Jim and proceeded to snore, back to deep sleep.

"I've left it in the bag by the side of the sofa," said Jan, then moved towards the bed to drag Jim out of his sleep.

"Yes, okay, I'll see what more I can do with it at the lab," said Jim, then breathed in deep snores, which grew louder.

After getting ready for bed, Jim slipped under the covers with him. As they both slept, a warm glow filled her apartment, a light which shone from the end of the street, directly to her bedroom that faced south-east. That night, Mr. West's son appeared to her in her dream, riding his bike in his red t-shirt, circling the end of her street, near the traffic lights. The next morning, Jan left her apartment early with a note for Jim, reminding him to lock the front door with his own key when he left.

After collecting her friends in her seldom-used Toyota, Jan, Susan and Toni arrived at Mount Shasta by midday, calling for a spot of lunch with the locals. They then visited the Native American Center at the base of Mount Shasta. Jan asked the clerk about any events and activities during the weekend and the clerk pointed to several pamphlets which Jan then collected. All three of them headed promptly towards their cabin.

Shortly after checking into their cabin, all three friends took time to regroup and reflect on the events of the previous months. Jan took time to repair her friendship with Toni, by telling him how she had been acting out of selfishness. She diligently explained to him how the call within her to undertake her quest left her blinkered to the important parts of her life. Though sympathetic to Jan, Toni took a somewhat skeptical stance, which left her feeling non-plus again. Jan knew that Toni's skepticism was born out of a general malaise, and she wanted Toni to feel the same passion for life as she had become awakened to. She just wanted Toni, more than anyone, to simply embrace life.

The night outside the cabin offered a blanket of still mist and the stars were somewhat absent from view. A group of tourists passed by them and said *hello*, as the three left the cabin-park where they stayed that night. Jan walked with Toni and Susan into the night at the base of the mountain, straddling her bag, which Susan and Toni both took an interest in:

"What's in that thing? Why do you need it?" asked Susan: "It makes you look like a hopeless student!"

"Oh, just my valuables, my phone battery and water. I thought it's best to be safe than sorry," quipped Jan.

"Sweetie…we love you but try a purse. It might be more appropriate for you," said Susan, and Jan laughed.

They came to the entrance to the cable car ride to the top of the mountain, but it was closed. A young man, in his early 30s, with a hipster beard and a beanie stood outside his car from a distance, outside the entrance to the cable car ride. He looked at Susan first, then nodded at Jan and Toni - greeting them all with a casual nod and a friendly smile. Susan looked at Jan, and smirked.

Jan immediately said: "no way! DO NOT even think about it! Whatever is going on in that mind of yours."

Susan looked at Jan with raised eyebrows and said: "You have a very low opinion of me!"

"Whatever either of you are planning, do not count me in. I want to return home alive!" said Toni, in his usual way.

Before either Jan or Susan could respond, the young fella shouted by the side of his car:

"Hey, guys, we're all cool here, if you are. If you want, I can have the local sheriff drop by, cuz he's in the area, and he can take you up if you prefer. Just saying, we're not all crazy inbreds here. I come from San Francisco. I moved here for an easier life. I work at the Buddhist center, not too far from here. It's up to you," said the young fella with a friendly demeanor.

"Hey, what do you know about the energy portal here?" asked Jan, stepping forward.

Toni turned to Susan and said: "Oh no! Here we go! Guurl gone lost her mind already! She acting crazier than a white girl!"

"Oh, I don't know much about no energy portals, but I do know it's an important spiritual site. The natives here have a history going a long way. There's a legend about a being who came from the mountain to fight the bad spirits, and the being in question has a connection to Lumeria."

"Lumeria?" asked Jan.

"You know, the lost island, like Atlantis, but in the Pacific," said the hipster with a broad, silent smile.

Jan shook her head somewhat dismissive, then turned to the rest of her party with puppy eyes. Toni and Susan both reacted without too much resistance, and agreed to take a taxi ride up the side of the mountain. The driver was very knowledgeable about the area, despite having been there for only six months. As soon as he started to share his knowledge, Jan became completely engaged in conversation with him, asking a plethora of questions related to the mysterious and the unexplained, which the driver shared with enthusiasm. Toni interrupted Jan, in his abrupt manner, to ask her not to distract the driver whilst he was driving:

"Where's your passion, man?" retorted the driver, then flashed a smile in the rearview mirror at Toni, who was immediately disarmed by it.

The driver reached a spot where his passengers could take in a breathtaking view of the night, near the top of Mount Shasta. Toni and Susan decided to stay in the vehicle, but Jan stepped out for a moment, to explore the area. She found a viewing spot with a telescope, and put in a couple of coins, after she scrambled for them in her trouser pocket, in the dark, whilst her friends watched on in the car. The night was shy of stars, for the time of the year, said the driver. The light pollution from the valley below dotted the landscape and left an artificial residue that blocked the natural beauty that a naked human eye could otherwise absorb.

Jan walked to the back of the taxi before getting in. She reached into her bag and grabbed the cloud-buster, and pointed it to the highest point in the sky, to the peak by the side of the mountain. She pressed her finger for a few seconds, on the button, at the base of the silver rod. The cloud-buster warmed up in her hand, delivering a peculiar buzz, which disarmed her. Jan then retracted her finger off the button and put her device back into her bag. Certain that she had not been noticed by the occupants of the car, she walked to the side of it and got in:

"Had enough?" asked Susan, as Jan got in, to sit next to her.

"Yes. I think so. Let's head back," replied Jan, whilst surveying the area through the car window, nervously.

The driver turned the car to head back down the road. Jan continued to look out the window, up at the side of the mountain, to the top, to the night sky:

"Oh, we're just in time. I think we're going to get some thunder and rain," said Susan.

Jan looked through the window, with bated breath, which she held, as she gained view of the side of the mountain, the peak of which was beginning to come into clearer view, as the car sped down the winding tracks. Just as the peak became visible, Jan saw the sky above it turn from a deep navy to a deep purple.

Jan looked up, quietly admiring the colors that were turning at the top of the mountain, where clouds were now beginning to form. A red mist suddenly billowed up from the side of the mountain, to mask the deep purple in the sky above the mountain, leaving Jan feeling very peculiar.

Susan noticed the change in Jan, causing her to turn and peek out the back window and say with calm alarm: "wow, that's totally weird, how the colors are changing like that! I think we need to get out of here as soon as possible. It looks like the weather is going to turn real quick, and I'm afraid of thunder!"

"Say no more!'" said the driver, before putting his foot on the pedal.

He sped down the narrow mountain road. No sooner than a few minutes of speed, which both Susan and Toni began to feel uncomfortable with, a large shadow appeared in the middle of the road ahead. It had a large human-like frame, the silhouette of which faced the car that was speeding towards it.

Jan leaned in from where she was, to peep through the car's front window. Just as soon as the words left her mouth, she was echoed by her fellow passengers, who collectively gasped:

"What the fuck is that?"

The driver took his foot off the accelerator but the car sped forward, regardless, whilst the young driver tried to gain control of the vehicle. The car's headlights then met the figure in the road, to reveal a tall and large furry creature, around 8 feet tall, that covered its eyes as the headlights met the creature's face. Sitting in the middle of the back seat, Toni got a good view of the beast in the road:

"Oh, good god. I think that's a Sasquatch!" hollered the taxi driver.

The car continued to speed forward, too fast to slow down the winding mountain descent. Toni continued screaming, fastening his seat belt as fast he could. His screams were accompanied by Susan's, who began to kick the driver's seat, using all the profanities at her disposal, profanities which were not going to save any of them, in the seconds that followed. The car hit the beast with full force - sure to send them all crashing down the side of the mountain, with the car tumbling, in the middle of the night, down the side of Mount Shasta. The car continued to speed, colliding within inches of the beast, before passing through it.

Toni's screams continued, but Susan was the first to stop shrieking. Aside from the driver, Susan was the only one who managed to keep her eyes open. She saw the car pass through the beast and continue on its path, straight down the winding road, with the steely driver remaining at the helm. Jan crouched down, ready to brace herself for the end of her life. She looked up to find Susan's expression first, her mouth wide open with one hand clasped over it, as the car continued to speed down the narrow road, down Mount Shasta.

Jan then heard Toni's cosseted passion being unleashed, with gargling screams that were previously unheard of. Toni stopped, when the taxi came to a stop, at the base of Mount Shasta, where they all started their adventure. Toni was the first to step out of the car. Without saying anything, he headed straight to the cabin in audible silence. Susan followed Toni in a stilted, silent walk. No sooner had Jan turned to pay the driver, he sped off, leaving Jan to take a solitary walk back to join her friends at the cabin park, to face their wrath.

A quiet night at the cabin, with all parties not speaking to each other, was interrupted with festivities that were beginning to take place outside, in the cabin-park. Jan went out to investigate and was met by a crowd that was gathering a makeshift fire in a metal trash-can, which was being strewn with skewers of marshmallows:

"Come and join us, don't you miss how we used to live?" said one man and his wife followed with: "come, don't be so shy!"

Jan stood outside the cabin, then looked back at the entrance to it, to find Susan and Toni peering out tentatively, from inside. Jan turned back around, to see other people coming out of their cabins, carrying beverages and food items, meeting others with smiles. Toni stepped out first, to join Jan, where she stood, in the center of the cabin-park. The area became illuminated by small fires and the sounds of beer-bottle tops popping and marshmallows crackling. Toni began to dance spontaneously, vivaciously, holding a woman's hand in his, to twirl her around, in joyous leaps, leaving behind everything that previously held him back from embracing life.

A park warden suddenly appeared and stepped out of his truck with a penetrating frown. As soon as he smelled the air and as soon as the air touched his face, his frown turned, and he relaxed, bringing out a beam of laughter and smile that was kept within him. Walking over to the guests of that park, he too began to feel the passion that coursed through everyone, taking Toni's hand, raising it in the air and twirling Toni under his arm.

Jan stood and watched and saw something she hadn't in a long while. Jan could see the colors in the atmosphere again - the colors of the people - the colors of people that she used to see when she was a child. A red fire burned that night, in the center of the cabin park. It was the fire that burned all over all the visitors that danced and enjoyed being together. They danced into the night, until the fires died out in the metal trash cans and the forgotten marshmallows added the scent from their embers. When the fires died out, the people added their fire, dancing with strangers until the sun rose. Their inextinguishable dance and laughter was carried in peaceful silence, in tune with each other - in love, passion and the joy of being.

Meanwhile, on the other side of the country, in Maine, Billy Reich was preparing to meet the authorities. He had called them after discovering that the tubes were no longer in their glass cage, which he did some weeks after Jan and Susan left the museum. Billy was at a loss as to who may have removed the tubes from the glass box in the chamber-room. Billy battled with himself. He waited weeks before he plucked up the courage to contact the police. Requesting to see the visitor log books, the sheriff took a cursory glance and dismissed the case, saying that there wasn't much to go on, aside from names and comments:

"Until you get me a real lead, I can't really do much, and you don't have any camera footage. Maybe you should upgrade your security," stated the burly, surly chief.

Billy took one look at the sheriff and said: "gee, thanks. I'll get onto that," sarcastically.

"Hey, I can only work on what you've given me. Don't shoot the messenger!" clapped the sheriff, as Billy left the sheriff's office.

Frustrated, Billy returned to his great-grandfather's museum. Together with the caretaker, they tried to pinpoint who might have taken the tubes or might have had a desire to take them. After getting nowhere with the caretaker, Billy decided to summon the manager for a brainstorming meeting:

"Look, we have no leads to follow, so we need more than the visitor's book to go on," said Billy.

"Well, we could look back into the query forms online to see who might have contacted us in that period. Let me quickly check this for you now," said the manager before adding: "I have a list of around 6 people - all with e-mail addresses and telephone numbers."

Billy scrawled through the names on the list and became triggered as soon as he saw the name Jan Lam, alongside her email address and phone number. Billy took the information to the sheriff, who took a cursory glance and agreed to make inquiries. The sheriff slovenly rang all the numbers which were made available to him by Billy and relayed the cursory information back to Billy, who waited in dumbfounded anticipation:

"I'm sorry, but I don't have any more leads for you. Half of these numbers don't work, and I can't get through the other half," said the sheriff, before dropping his papers on his desk.

After the dead-end with the sheriff, Billy decided to register the missing items with the state police, opting to describe the tubes as *'batteries'*. The state police pressed Billy for a description of the *'batteries'*. Billy navigated the futility of the question by embellishing the description. Instead of calling them *'batteries'*, Billy described them as *"zero point energy batteries"*, in the hope the state police would take him seriously. A week later, Billy was visited by the Feds, who wanted to know more about what he had described, having been alerted through a shared database, which left Billy shaken.

Billy was suddenly faced with the challenge of having to describe exactly what he had been experimenting with. The Feds departed after making cursory notes, leaving Billy hanging on by a thread. A day later, two men visited him at the museum. They were dressed in black attire, with pale skin and darting eyes. They sent a chill through Billy, by passively asking him steely questions about the nature of his experiments at the museum. Whilst Billy tried to focus on his complaint - the stolen tubes - the two men glared at him, as if they were looking, rather peering, into Billy's soul. Then they demanded to inspect the apparatus in the chamber-room.

Billy felt compelled to lead them both to it, almost without any of his own free will, as if he had been hypnotized into opening the room where the experiments with Jan took place. Upon inspection of the chambers, the two men, in ill-fitting suits and black ties, took a copy of Billy's list of possible suspects and said in a strange, mechanical voice:

"Thank you, You'll be hearing from us."

As they departed the museum, towards their black car, Billy called out to them from afar:

"When will you let me know?"

Billy was met with silence. The two men in black suits walked in a stilted and synchronized manner, back to their sedan, with their backs firmly turned on Billy.

Billy clamped his fists and banged them on his desk, when he got back to the museum, the first moment he was released from the terror of his two visitors. He took a look at the copy of the list that was made for him and was supportively handed by little old Deborah at the museum, who pointed her manicured and bejeweled fingers at a couple of specific names. Billy breathed a tense breath and raged at the name at the end of Deborah's fingernail - Jan Lam.

Jan's phone rang constantly as she drove back to Santa Clara with Toni and Susan, which she didn't pick up since it was on silent mode. The festivities from the previous night infected them all with a spirit that hung around them, and didn't appear to leave them. Jan checked her phone, to dozens of missed calls and messages on her phone, when she returned home to her empty apartment. A note from Jim telling her he would see her as soon as his parents left lifted her spirits up further. Just as she was getting settled, Jan accessed her voicemail and her heart beat to a curl:

"Susan and Jan, you fucking bitches. I'm coming to get you!" raged Billy - his anger spilling through Jan's phone, into her apartment.

Billy warned Jan of the Feds and the two strange men, raging in a blind promise that they'd soon be knocking on her door and, no sooner had Jan finished listening to Billy's tantrum, she heard a car pull up outside her home - a large black sedan pulled up outside her apartment building. In a heartbeat, Jan grabbed her bag and escaped through the veranda, scurrying behind the neighbor's house, peering from behind it, to watch the occupants leave the black sedan.

Two tall men in dark suits, black ties and fedoras, with very pale skin approached her apartment building, walking synchronized towards it. Jan watched them from a distance, hiding behind the neighbor's trash can. The neighbor's dog barked wildly inside, from the window that overlooked Jan's veranda, causing one of the men to menacingly gaze in the direction of the neighbor's dog. As he turned his head, Jan peeped the pale skin on a face with no eyebrows and what looked like painted lips. As well as the acute strangeness of the men, Jan noticed something that she had never witnessed with any person on Earth - they left no energetic trace, no vibration and definitely no aura - as if they had no soul.

Jan's skin quivered at what she saw - then she ran, running as fast as she could, thinking only of the destination ahead of her - Mr. West's house a few blocks away.

Stopping short of the road before she crossed it to Mr. West's home, to check behind her for the ominous looking men and their car, Jan ran to the back of Mr. West's large Victorian house, to find him where she knew she might - in their garden. She scrambled through the back door to their garden, which was lined on either side with dense shrubs, running into it panting, where she found Mr. and Mrs. West quietly enjoying their dinner. When they both looked up at her, they both had spoonfuls of food poised at their mouths:

"What's wrong?" asked Mr. West.

Jan responded by insisting that she needed to speak with Mr. West immediately.

Mr. West led Jan calmly to his study, conscious of her urgency. Mr. West sat Jan on his Chesterfield sofa, where she divulged what had occurred, omitting the part which would cause him the most alarm - Billy's threatening call then the strange men at her home - focusing her attention on the events surrounding the device that Jim had constructed for her. Jan took out the cloud-buster from her bag and showed it to Mr. West, whilst keeping her eye on the road outside Mr. West's home, for any sight of a 1950s black sedan, closing her eyes to take a pause - and wished for the best:

"I think it's best to store it here. I'm not comfortable with the idea of leaving it in my apartment," said Jan.

"Have you used it?" asked Mr. West.

"Aside from Mount Shasta, no. Actually.... no, that's not right. Jim took it with me to test it here, at the traffic lights. I completely forgot about that," said Jan, hurriedly, shaking her head with her hand on her forehead.

"He did?" said Mr. West, with a deep pause. He then went and sat on his desk-chair, spinning it around to face the large round Victorian window in his study: "Oh my!"

"What?" asked Jan, getting up from the Chesterfield sofa.

"I saw our son at the end of the road, by the traffic lights, in his red t-shirt. He stood and waved at me," said Mr. West, turning back around to Jan, with both hands clasped together.

""What? When did this happen?", said Jan, surprised. She then approached the desk to press her hands squarely on them.

"It was a week ago," said Mr. West, before adding: "...well, that's when it started. I didn't want to believe it at first, then I told my wife, and it became a regular sighting. We've been seeing him almost every night since then. We just stand outside our house and wave and cry. We cry from happiness and relief."

"Have you ever walked towards him? To talk to him?" asked Jan, intensely.

"No, we haven't thought about that," replied Mr. West.

"Why? Don't you think he might want to talk to you?" asked Jan, listlessly.

"Jan, come on, now. We haven't seen our son in decades, and he suddenly appears - we've never dealt with this before. What are we supposed to do? What are we supposed to say?", said Mr. West. He then began to choke up.

"Look, I think this thing has caused enough damage. I think we should destroy it," suggested Jan, shaking her head, in response to Mr. West.

"NO! We mustn't! Think of all the good it could bring us all. You've already seen the impact it's had on us," asserted Mr. West: "We should investigate more before we make a decision."

"Let me remove the tubes - the batteries - and leave the device with you. It's useless without the batteries," said Jan, hastily taking the tubes out and carefully placing them in her bag.

"Fine," said Mr. West, resigned to Jan's decision: "let's move with caution."

Shortly after, Jan made her excuses to leave, opting to go to Jim's apartment where she stayed the night, under the pretext that she missed him, which she did. Jim provided Jan with much-needed comfort - and she chose to omit the details of Mount Shasta, Billy's threatening phone call and the strange men that arrived at her home and caused her to flee to Mr. West, then Jim. That night, Jan felt the passion for life grow through her again, as she made love to Jim, forgetting the danger she had placed herself in, not least those around her, whilst silently holding a power that only she knew of. A power had been unleashed on the people who were at Mount Shasta, the effects of which only time would tell.

The next morning, Jan took the tubes from her bag and carefully placed them under her clothing, in the bottom drawer of the chest that Jim made space for. Jan hid the tubes under layers of her clothing, then she took herself off to work that day, anxiously working a day until she was done with it, to continue on her quest. She made a fearful bus ride to her apartment, stopping a healthy distance away to see if a 1950s black sedan was parked outside. Breathing a sigh of relief with the clear coast, Jan turned the key to her door with eyes shut, which opened after a slow blink, to an untouched apartment. As soon as Jan was inside, she locked her apartment door and laughed in elation.

When Jan walked towards her kitchen, she heard a knock on the door, which stopped her dead in her tracks. Her heart, that pounded out of her chest, was stopped by a familiar growl and bark. She breathed out a smile and opened the door to her neighbor and her dog:

"Where have you been, Jan? You were supposed to be looking after Porgy last night and I had to make alternative arrangements for my Bingo night!" said the short, portly neighbor, with her Corgi clutched clumsily under her arm, like a tote purse.

"I'm so sorry, Maggie. I've completely been tied up with something else. Do you need me to sit for you tonight? I can do that!" said Jan, eager and helpful.

"Yes, if you don't mind. Just for a couple of hours," said her neighbor, promptly leaving Porgy the Corgi, who promptly walked straight into Jan's apartment, nestling himself on Jan's armchair.

Jan shut the door before answering it again, thinking it was her neighbor being her forgetful self. Only, it wasn't her neighbor. Jan froze at their appearance. The sight of the two men cut her breath. She held it tight, close to her chest, after a sharp inhale. Noticing, one of them said:

"it's okay, Jan Lam. We are only here to ask you a couple of questions about your visit to the Wilhelm Reich Museum."

Jan's eyes did not lie, with what she saw the first time, when she first laid eyes on them. She was again confronted with the soul-less, machine-like tall beings. This time, they stood before her, arching into her doorway. Jan became frozen, almost emptied of thought and felt compelled to say: "yes, come in."

They walked towards the sofa and sat down in unison. Jan walked over to Porgy, who immediately started to bark at them - she tried to calm him with various methods that broke the spell that Jan was under, making her thankful for the interruption from a being that was less threatening than the two that were sat silently glaring at her from her sofa.

Jan gathered herself, to look at the men, and said: "you'll have to make it quick. I don't think he's very comfortable with you both being here, and I think you should ask what you want then leave."

The men sat, almost motionless, as Jan's inner resolve grew, finding her courage and comfort from Porgy, the only other being with a soul in her apartment, that afternoon:

"What were you doing at the museum?" asked the men, in a low, monotone voice. They spoke together, mechanical.

"I went to visit, with a friend," responded Jan, jaw clenched.

"Did you meet Billy Reich?", uttered the men.

"Yes," replied Jan, in a flat tone that mimicked her interrogators.

"Did Billy Reich take you to a chamber?" continued the men, with black darting eyes, that didn't appear to have any pupils.

"Chamber? Which chamber?", asked Jan, quizzically.

"The chamber you must have seen in the observatory," quipped the men, together, in a flat tone that matched the angular lines of their impeccably square jaws.

"No, we weren't there long. Billy ended up being more interested in my friend than showing us around the museum. Hey… what's this all about?" asked Jan, trying to throw their line of questioning aside, in favor of topics she was prepared to handle.

After she stopped barking, Porgy strolled up to the tall dark-suited beings and began to bark at them, then she nipped and pulled at their trousers. Bizarrely, the men did not respond and sat motionless, as if Porgy did not exist at all.

Jan noticed their odd reaction and asked: "hey, aren't you even going to shoo Porgy away?"

The two men looked at each other, then returned their gaze towards Jan, amidst the commotion that Porgy was making, and said: "This is all we need. Thank you."

"Okay, well, I'm glad I was of help," said Jan, in some confusion. Jan stopped short of what she wanted to do - which was to give them a hard time for their intrusion.

As the two strange men were leaving, one of them turned around and said:

"We are sorry for having intruded. You won't hear from us again."

Jan tilted her head back in astonishment, then hurriedly shut the door after they left. She stood by her front window, to watch them depart in their 1950s black sedan that matched their black 1950s suits. As she watched, Jan shrieked at how close she came to spilling her secrets, whilst she clutched Porgy and kissed him in gratitude for his assistance. Jan was left with a distinct impression that the two strange men had read parts of her mind that even she didn't know existed. Telling herself that she was crazy for thinking that, Jan kissed Porgy one more time before placing him on the ground.

Jan's next immediate thought was to contact Susan, to tell her what Billy had done:

"What? That son-of-a-bitch. I wonder if his wife would like to know what happened that night!" shouted Susan, on the phone: "Hey, do you want me to sort this out?"

"No, that's not the worst of it. I don't know what Billy's got cooking up there, but they sent the men in black," said Jan, exasperated.

"What do you mean?" asked Susan.

"Yeah. Two creepoids. Just like from the movies… only, they were much worse. Much much worse!" said Jan: "I think I would rather have met the ghouls than those two!"

"That is some scary shit!" exclaimed Susan: "Come and stay here."

"No, I'm not going to be scared by them. I'll be fine here," said Jan, resolutely.

Before ending the conversation, Susan gave Jan an update about Toni - that he had started to write again, often spending hours after work, at the library. Susan also mentioned that she had begun to paint again, something she hadn't done in twenty years. Susan didn't mention what they had all experienced that night at Mount Shasta. Instead, she played dumb. Something greater had followed Toni and Susan since their evening of drinking and dancing at Mount Shasta. It was a feeling which they were unable to shake off, and it imbued everyone they had come in contact with since.

"Wow," sounded Jan: "That's wonderful. That's what I've wanted for you both, for years. To follow your passions. I'm so happy you have both found a zest for it. It's brilliant. Thank you for sharing, Susan. It's really what I need to hear right now!"

After their call ended, Jan decided to pay Mr. West a visit, who spoke more about his son and his longing to see him again. Jan suggested she accompany the Wests to the traffic lights at dusk, when they would sometimes see their son. Mr. & Mrs. West gladly accepted the suggestion - the thought of having Jan as their guide comforted them. They stood and waited for their son to appear and the traffic lights flickered on and off, like a coded message. Mr. West grabbed Jan by the arm, both looking on, at the traffic lights some distance away, ahead of them, on the road. The lights continued to flicker, then he appeared - in and out of sight, in motion with the flickering of the traffic lights. They all made their slow walk towards him, as he continued to blink in- and out of view at the traffic lights, on his bike, in his red t-shirt:

"What's his name?" asked Jan.

"Finn," said Mr. West, with tears running down his cheek: "After Huckleberry."

"Hey, Finn, can you see us?" shouted Jan, waving at him from afar.

Finn sat on his bike, not moving further than the traffic lights, barely a couple of yards away from his parents and Jan. He smiled broadly, staring ahead, through them, at the end of the road that led through to his home:

"I'm Jan, your parent's friend", she said.

Mrs. West stopped walking, so did her husband. She let out a deep, painful cry and rested her head on her husband's chest, who said: "that's enough, Jan. We know now. He can't hear or see us. But we have closure now. We can see that he's happy, just like how he was before he left us. This is how we want to remember him. Seeing him every day will give us closure, in time. This is comforting, Jan. It truly is. We want to thank you."

Mrs. West added, between controlled sobs: "It's okay, Jan. We have a sense he will only be here until we get closure, and we are both ready to move on."

Mrs. West then turned back to head home, followed by her husband. Jan stood for a while before she joined them, back in their home.

Back in Burnwood, his study, Mr. West said, drying his tears: "Jan, I want everyone to be able to see what we've seen. If everything you're saying is true, with what's happening with your friends who seem to be living their joy, this can only be a good thing. The past couple of weeks have been immensely healing for us. You cannot imagine. And it sounds like the events at Mount Shasta are a sign of things to come. Who knows how many people will be changed by this. Countless. In less than a year, we could be looking at a whole new world. A world without violence, pain, needless suffering. That can only be a good thing, can't it?"

"Yes, I suppose…." said Jan, then thought for a moment before continuing. She looked at Mr. West with some consideration, then said: "but the Feds are involved now. They paid me a visit about the tubes I stole from Billy Reich," said Jan, softly.

Mr. West finished wiping the tears from his eyes. He looked at Jan with a furrowed brow, then said after a few moments: "Even more reason to pursue this!"" He then pulled out a large world map and laid it on the desk before them.

"Is this the map that Abbassi sent you?", asked Mr. West.

"Yes!" exclaimed Jan, somewhat bewildered.

Jan looked at the map that Mr. West laid out before her, with circles already marked around six places in the world. The circles crossed at various places in the grid-like pattern over the world. The six energy vortices:

"Let's see …." said Mr. West, then ran his finger on the map: "You have already broken the portal over Mount Shasta," commented Mr. West.

"I suppose so," said Jan: "I'm not sure if I truly have but…"

"What is next?", asked Mr. West, tilting his head up to look up at Jan, with eyes that sparkled under his tears.

"Next?", asked Jan, confused.

"Next is Lake Titicaca, then Uluru in Australia, followed by Mount Kailash, then the Great Pyramids of Giza in Egypt - but you've already been there - leaving Glastonbury Hill in England," said Mr. West methodically and cryptically.

Jan become flustered, whilst Mr. West read out the list, with a grin: "You are going to be a busy girl!"

"Mister West, this is madness, I can't possibly," said Jan, shaking her head with her palms outstretched in the air.

Mr. West began pacing the length and breadth of Burnwood, pushing through to speak, with shortening breath: "No, my dear, it seems to me that the only madness is accepting this reality as the only thing there is. The only madness is not accepting that we are all different and that some people are just more different than the rest of us. We are not all destined to our fate in a world that has us all trapped like caged animals, where we are all waiting for our bodies to wither and die - and we never get off a wheel that has our souls trapped on Earth in an endless loop from cradle to grave. No, my dear, THAT is the real madness!"

Jan attempted to interject but couldn't, as Mr. West became pumped: "And you must listen and listen very carefully. I have been working since I was 13 years old. I am just a couple of years away from my retirement. Seeing Finn again has reminded me of our own mortality - something raising your own children does to you, every day that you see them. Seeing him again reminded me just how lost in the matrix we have all become. What you have given us is hope. So, this is what we are going to do. We are going on a world trip together. I have some savings, more than enough, and I've secured some funding for a final project for my career. You will help me finish my book on the mysteries of the world. I can put in a request for an assistant. A job will be posted, and you are to apply for it, internally. The project will last a month, maybe two, maybe three," said Mr. West, with re-ignited rigor: "When we return, you can walk straight back to your life, to your old job, after your project with me ends."

Jan struggled to put a sentence together. She looked at Mr. West, wide-eyed, still with her shoulders hunched:

"You have to make a choice to join the rest of humanity or make the rest of humanity join you!" exclaimed Mr. West: "...and you are too good to wait for humanity. You will have to drag them kicking and screaming to your level, Jan."

Jan stood still, pausing, stopping from reacting, since she did not know how to. Then she threw her hands in the air and said, surrendering: "Okay!"

The following month, Jan applied for the post as Mr. West's assistant then made arrangements to continue her quest, together with Mr. West, on his final project at the university. She was glad to see the back of Jonah and the colleagues in the small staff room in the university building, swapping the dusty rooms for Mr. West's splendid archaic home study Burnwood, to prepare for their world trip together. She left Jonah's department quietly, opting to not go out for drinks with them.

Jan met Toni and Susan, for an impromptu farewell meal at the Royale: "Oh my god, Jan, if I can get some money and time off work, I'll come and join you in Lake Titicaca. I hear it's magical. I've had some interest in my paintings, so you never know. I might end up selling a few and join you!"

"Wow, so soon?" asked Jan with delightful surprise.

"Yeah, I put them up on the internet. You know, the miracle of social media," laughed Susan.

"Well, I've been writing like crazy so, as soon as I've found an agent, and I've been picked by a publisher… and sold a couple of copies…. I won't be joining you!" said Toni, typically sarcastic, this time aided with exuberant joy. Toni seemed to be finally comfortable in his own skin, something which made Jan get up from her chair to hug him.

The whole of the evening at the Royale was ablaze with a joyous crowd, mostly locals. It was the first time Jan saw and appreciated the atmosphere of the place, an atmosphere which was markedly different to the way she remembered it, since she started to visit with her friends. Jubilation exuded the air, which Jan watched glow from everyone, like little green shoots of pulsating desires, leaving Jan reclining in her chair with a sense of fulfilment.

Jim joined Jan and her friends that evening, where he was introduced to them for the first time and Susan and Toni both embraced him, openly. They shared stories about Jan and Jan shared stories about Susan and Toni and Jim shared stories about his work as a Physics Professor, after which Jan led Jim away from her friends, too imbued with the air in the Royale that evening to want to talk - she danced for Jim, who looked at her with a deep love that hid a sullen embarrassment for his own feelings. He would miss her terribly and couldn't stand the thought of being without her. It was a strong feeling that Jim kept to himself behind glistening eyes. Jan kissed him, to soften the twinge of bitterness she felt from him. That night, they packed together in his apartment, and Jan slipped the tubes into her bag, when Jim's back was turned. The next morning, Jan returned to her own apartment, to finish the rest of her packing. She made arrangements with her neighbor, for the months she would be away, kissing Porgy the Corgi goodbye after a few moments with him. Jan then stopped by Mr. West's home, to remind him to pack the cloud-buster into his suitcase. The tubes were carefully packed into hers.

They said goodbye at the airport, flanked by friends, Jim and Mrs. West. As they both turned to wave goodbye at the gate, Jan clocked a man, a familiarly strange man, in a long, black trench-coat, which was worn rather awkwardly, over a black suit and black tie and grey fedora hat. He sat, peering over a large newspaper at a café, stiltedly. Jan's attention dropped from her friends and boyfriend, and rested on the man behind them, leaving Jan somewhat despondent:

"What's the matter? Don't look so glum!" shouted Susan, over to Jan: "...you'll be fine. Look after each other!"

Jan was ushered to walk onwards, towards their gate, by Mr. West: "We'll call you all when we land," said Jan, as she walked with Mr. West, to their gate.

"Come," said Mr. West: "...we must go!"

As they continued to walk, Jan looked back and waved at Jim, who smiled surreptitiously at her. Jan blew kisses at him in return, before running back to kiss him for a moment. When she did, she saw his aura unfold in green petals:

"Come and visit me if you can," she said.

"I'll try, Jan, but you know how it is with school," said Jim, who forced a smile, under a furrowed brow.

"We'll video call every night. You'll get tired of hearing from me soon enough," added Jan.

"Come on, Jan, this is the final call" shouted Mr. West from afar, near the gate, in their line for their flight.

After their embrace, Jan looked to see if the man was still sitting in the café behind her friends - and, true to form, he was still there, reading a newspaper, with eyes that locked Jan's in an unguarded moment that left Jan with the intense, penetrating feeling that the strange man had invaded the deep recesses of her mind, to reveal her plans for her trip. The spell was broken by Jim, who shooed her to board, and Jan turned, to run, to catch up with Mr. West, before boarding the plane together, for Peru.

Chapter 8

Lake Titicaca

The richness of Peru became apparent after Jan and Mr. West got into the taxi to their destination, the center of Puno, the city that lay on the shores of Lake Titicaca, which was accessed through the winding roads from the airport. Mr. West impressed Jan with his fluent Spanish, peppered with the occasional Peruvian phrases, that caught the ear of their driver:

"You have to make an effort. It makes a massive difference, Jan. Especially since you're a wealthy tourist here. So, it's imperative that you make an effort. Humble yourself, to their level. It will really help you," said Mr. West then patted Jan on her knee, saying as he got out of the cab: "come on, we must get checked in…I have lots to show you around here."

"You've been here before?" asked Jan, nodding to try and sway her compliance away from feeling out of sorts.

"Once or twice," said Mr. West, in his usual eccentric manner.

They checked-in, had dinner in the center of the small city, then walked to the great Lake Titicaca, which was presided by a quaint red and white-lighthouse at the small harbor, that jutted out cautiously against the expanse of the Great Lake. The center of Puno surprised Jan with its non-descript manner

- appearing to her as a small fishing village by the lakeside - mainly occupied by locals and tourists from other parts of Peru and its neighboring country, Bolivia. Jan and Mr. West appeared to be the only foreigners around, but Jan liked it that way. So did Mr. West, who admitted to being relieved at not coming across fellow countrymen while there:

"They don't travel well" said Mr. West: "Very loud and obnoxious. As if they're shouting into space, trying to make themselves heard. I never understood it."

"It's very offensive," added Jan.

"My thoughts exactly," agreed Mr. West.

They took a short walk after dinner, to get acclimatized to the area, then settled back at their rudimentary lodgings - a family-run 2-star, with a small bar-cafe of a few wooden tables and stools, to facilitate a transitory custom, downstairs:

"I have to ask, Jan, since we are here together, in a new environment, do you take any drugs? Weed, ecstasy, perhaps?" asked Mr. West, with surreptitious inquiry that masked his vicariousness.

"No, sir, no. Not at all. Never. I've seen enough in my life to not want to," said Jan, somewhat defensively.

"Don't be offended, Jan. I've seen a lot in my life too… a lot of which would leave you quite shocked… but, before we go any further with our adventure, I have to warn you that you'll be seeing a lot more of who I really am. This is why I don't fit in at the university and never have. I don't wear a mask, at least not around the people I like. I'm a child of the 1960s, let's put it that way…. There is nothing I haven't seen or done, so please don't be shocked if you see me partaking in a little bit of elixirs during our trip. No pun intended," said Mr. West, before knocking back his Pisco Sour, then making preparations to retire for the evening.

"Oh, no… don't worry, Mr. West. I'm not like that… but…well….It's just that I have a lot of respect for you and I can't imagine seeing you any other way. You are like a fountain of knowledge to me," said Jan.

"I know no more than you do but a little more than the next man. We sadly measure intelligence in a very warped way, so please… and besides….knowledge only comes from inquiry, not from sitting behind a dusty desk espousing things you've read elsewhere," said Mr. West in a tipsy manner: "and you're the smartest person I've met in decades. You are very bright. If only you saw that." He then stood up with a slight stagger: "oh, I've been in touch with the local shaman, and he's arranged to meet us tomorrow."

"Shaman?" asked Jan, with a slight shake of her head.

"Yes. It's my treat for you," he replied, with slurred words: "Right, I'm off to bed and I shall see you here tomorrow morning for breakfast bright and early." He then left the bar by the exit on the right of the small room, to walk up the short flight of stairs.

Jan continued with her drink and tried to connect to the internet with the password that was provided, but gave up after a few tiresome attempts. Her eyes felt heavy, making her leave for her room, which she did after finishing her shot of a local hot drink. When she got up from her chair, she felt she was being watched. She turned to look for the source of the stare. In the corner of the bar, at a solitary table, sat a man, somewhere in between her age and Mr. West's. He was a sturdy-looking Latin, with a brown hat and an open shirt, that sprouted dark and silver hair. He flashed a smile at Jan, that left lines on his face, wrinkles that curved into a smile. It was a beguiling smile, a smile that deceived his weathered face.

The handsome Latino man tipped his hat at Jan, who recoiled slightly and hastily made her exit, flashing an awkward smile before leaving through the same exit that Mr. West had done moments earlier. Jan made her way to her room with a measured pace, up the short flight of stairs. She wasn't alarmed by the man, just slightly taken aback by his friendliness. Once inside her room, Jan was struck by the baren decor of naked wooden floors, a sink and a bed.

Jan washed her face in the bedside sink then opted to sleep on top of the sheets - the hot drink she had earlier helped her doze off into a dreamless night. Her eyes blinked close, fading the din of the day over terracotta, cracked-plaster walls. The next morning, Jan went through a routine of shaking down the bed covers for any incidental insects that might have made their way through the night, and she was glad that she didn't find anything. Then came a knock on her door, along with Mr. West's morning croak:

"Come on, we have a full day ahead, my dear," bellowed Mr. West with an invasive knock.

Jan promptly joined Mr. West outside the hotel, on the terrace under an awning, for a modest breakfast of coffee and Peruvian staples. They then set out to take a boat trip to the floating islands of the Uros people on the Great Lake Titicaca:

"You'll meet some wonderful people," assured Mr. West.

During their rough-and-ready boat trip, Jan passed some comments about the locals, then mentioned the man at the bar the night before.

Mr. West dismissed Jan's concerns, telling her: "stop acting so cut off from the world. There is only one thing here on this Earth. And that's us. It's us who make it difficult for us. It doesn't have to be that hard, Jan. Every stranger is a potential friend. I say potential because you still have to use your discernment but, you know what I mean. Just let people in a bit, once in a while. It will serve you in so many ways," said Mr. West, before beckoning a stranger in Spanish, on one of the floating islands: "hey, it's so nice to see you again!"

Jan reclined for a moment before stepping off the boat, onto the small floating islands which were built entirely out of reeds, where they met the Uros people - the women of whom were busily cutting their reeds to form bundles for the islands:

"Come, we're going to sit and help them with their work," said Mr. West, who examined Jan's apprehension and commented: "at some point, you will have to stop being an observer and become a participant in this world."

Jan shrugged off the different side to Mr. West that she was beginning to experience - but told herself that he had indeed warned her of it. She tried to accept his guidance as part of her own growth and swallowed her pride at being told how to be, constantly. Jan proceeded to sit next to Mr. West, who sat on a low stool with his portly body, and began to engage with the Uros women. Jan took a breath and decided to accept this break from the familiar as part of something that she would have to get used to, on her world tour with Mr. West. Jan mustered some foolishness with Spanish:

"Comme estas?" said Jan. She silently prayed that her question would not elicit any deeper response from her listener, a middle-aged lady of short stature and a peculiar elongated bowler hat, who sat on the stool next to Mr. West and smiled at her frivolous attempt at socializing with the locals:

"Si, si," smiled the lady, then continued weaving the reeds, wisely.

Jan felt relief, that she was able to not overthink a simple interaction. She wanted to be like Mr. West, whose immersion with the world left her feeling somewhat displaced. The familiar unease continued to creep over her, which she tried to break with frequent exchanges of pleasantries with the generally unresponsive Uros women. Regaling against the futility of forcing herself, Jan instead chose to walk to another part of the island, to the sight of reed huts with bulbous roofs, for a little tour. Moments later, Jan's restlessness was broken by Mr. West, who followed her into the huts, with hastened concern:

"What's wrong, Jan?" he asked.

"Oh. I'm sorry, I felt out of place sitting there, so I thought I'd explore a bit," replied Jan, with a grimace.

"Come, sit down," said Mr. West, ushering her to a bench.

Jan stifled a pause and said: "I feel overwhelmed. Maybe I'm tired. I'm not sure what I'm doing here, especially after what I unleashed at Mount Shasta. I'm afraid of what else I'm about to unleash upon the world, especially since I've never really felt a part of it."

"What are you afraid of exactly?" asked Mr. West, with his hand carefully resting on hers.

"Well, it's the sense that perhaps I'm doing this all for selfish reasons. Who am I to decide this for humanity?" asked Jan.

"The problem you have is reconciling the isolation that you have gotten so used to with the unity that this will bring. You know as well as I do that there is no division on Earth. We create it ourselves. If there's one thing that I've learned in my sixty-some years on Earth is that, no matter who you speak to, you can always find at least one thing that connects you to that person. That one thing can be something simple like a shared joke or even a smile or even mutual appreciation of something. But we have been conditioned to only think of our own selves. We've all become conditioned to see the world only through our own ego, and that's what is preventing us from connecting with each other." said Mr. West, with a paternal patter.

A brow-beaten Jan looked at Mr. West and said: "yeah, I suppose so."

"Oh dear, come here," he said, hugging Jan and said: "you have a gift, a power to change the world. Just look at what you changed in California, after your visit to Mount Shasta, in a matter of days. News reports are being filled with items about people quitting their jobs to do what they love. It's catching on. That's the energy you have awakened. It trickled down from Mount Shasta in a matter of days. And has it destroyed anybody? I don't think so…", said Mr. West, pressing his arm around Jan's shoulder.

Jan looked at him and said: "Do you really think that was because of me?"

Mr. West shook his head in disbelief, pressed his arm tight around Jan's shoulder and said: "I think there's something which I think will help you. After dinner tonight, I want you to meet someone."

"Who? The shaman?" asked Jan.

"Yes…He will help you with things I can't," said Mr. West, nodding patiently whilst getting up to resume his activities outside the hut.

Later that evening, Jan and Mr. West quietly shared a paella and Mr. West made continuous reference to his watch. Before Jan could ask Mr. West about his clock-watching, they were joined by a man who pulled up a chair by the side of their table. Jan looked up from her plate and saw that it was the man from the night before - the man who sat in the corner of the bar and watched and smiled at her:

Jan put down the spoonful of rice that she momentarily held in mid-air. She extended her hand and said: "Hello, I'm…."

"You're Jan. I know," spoke the man, in a warm Latin accent that was peppered with odd, long vowel sounds.

"I am Salvador Hernandez. Not a terribly original name, I'm afraid. But, it's easy to remember, at least," said the man with a laugh, who then signaled to the waitress.

Salvador Hernandez struck Jan as a jovial man. His affable manner made her feel at ease instantly, and he continued the evening in the same manner - engaging in banter with Mr. West, whilst trying to bring Jan into the conversation. Salvador and Mr. West caught up with each other and Jan learned the nature of their relationship, as they chatted. In a former life, Mr. West was a hippy young Phd student who taught Salvador and introduced him to esoteric philosophies and forgotten ancient wisdom. As Jan listened to them both, she silently thought of her friends and Jim, back in Santa Clara. As the evening progressed at the table in the little corner of that bar of that hotel, Salvador ordered more glasses of brandy at regular intervals and tried to encourage Jan to drink more:

"So, you're a Shaman," said Jan: "What do you do as a Shaman? What does it involve?"

"Oh, this and that, but mostly I guide lost souls to the purpose of their life here, on this plane of existence," smirked Salvador: "and, from what I gather, you sound like you could do with such guidance."

"Well, I'm not sure about that," said Jan, dismissively.

"Have you ever had an extra-dimensional experience, Jan?" asked Salvador, with a certain nonchalance that didn't fit the topic.

"What type of extra-dimensional experience? Are you talking about psychedelics? Then the answer is no" replied Jan, and then began to withdraw from the exchange. She then motioned to the barman, for the bill.

"Well, you are welcome to experience one with us," said Salvador with a disarming smile.

Jan looked at Salvador, then Mr. West, then left the table without saying more. She approached the barman, who presented her with her bill for the night which Jan paid quickly, refraining from small talk with the barman. She then turned to Mr. West and Salvador and gave them both a quick wave, then proceeded to leave the bar downstairs for her bedroom upstairs, in the little 2-star.

The next morning, Mr. West was absent from breakfast, having excused himself by text for his hang-over. Jan welcomed the break and took a stroll around the city square, after her breakfast. Whilst out, she took pictures of the colorful houses, under a morning canopy of azures and pinks. Jan sat on the bench outside the hotel, after her return from her short excursion and was tapped on her shoulder. It was Mr. West:

"You see that man over there painting?" he said, pointing to a man opposite by the harbor: "He deserves to be rewarded."

"Why?" asked Jan.

"Because he is a rarity. Someone who can connect with the world around him. There's something to be learned from him," said Mr. West, and proceeded to walk over to the man who was painting.

"Have you been painting long?" asked Mr. West, to the man.

"Ever since I was a child," replied the old man.

"You must have sold countless over the years," said Mr. West.

"Yes, I can paint the same thing over and over again, but I still see something different every time," replied the old man.

"'Oh, marvelous. I'd like to buy this one," said Mr. West, before picking out a painting and exchanging coins.

Mr. West handed the painting to Jan when he walked back to where Jan was sitting.

"I don't know … I…." said Jan.

"What? You don't know what you're going to do with it? Take it to remind yourself of the time you really started to connect with the world. It's a gift for your lesson today," said Mr. West.

"Yes, thank you," said a meek Jan and took it from Mr. West: "But, what lesson? Am I here for lessons?"

"Yes, my dear Jan. You are here to learn and I am here to help you learn about yourself," sighed Mr. West: "come, let's continue exploring this wonderful village."

They walked to a café near the Lake and Mr. West took a cigar out of his shirt pocket and began to smoke it. He then said:

"The trouble is that your gift has made you cut yourself off from this world. Because of what you are able to see, the energies and vibrations and so on and so forth, you've become a passive observer. But, you need to be able to see exactly why you are here. I don't mean here, in Lake Titicaca, but why are you here on this Earth at this particular time. Why are you here? I introduced you to Salvador last night for that reason. I apologize for his raucous nature last night but, I can assure you, that he is a very good guide. He guided me through my

Ayahuasca experience after Finn died, and that's how I got peace with his death. Don't worry, I will be there with you, if you decide to do it. But the clarity you are looking for, especially with the isolation you've built up over the years, the isolation you've become used to as a sort of armor against the world will all disappear. But, of course, it's up to you to do it. Participate or observe," said Mr. West, shrugging his shoulders between puffs from his cigar and gulps of coffee: "But I realize it's a tall order for you. Perhaps taking this guided trip with Salvador will help you put into perspective who you are and why you are the way you are. I know he can help you see yourself and what you can create for this world, if you just let it all go!"

"Let what go, Mr. West?" demanded Jan, irritated.

"CONTROL, Jan!" he responded, regaining his composure to repeat himself: "Let go of control. Nobody here has control. You are extremely special to us on Earth but you think you can control it all. You can't. Nobody here in this life, on this rock, under this sky, under this dome has control. You need to release control, Jan. For your sake. And ours."

Mr. West finished his coffee and made his excuse to leave, to spend the rest of the morning alone, walking away from the cafe at the harbor, towards the city square behind them. Jan spent the rest of the late morning and early afternoon on a tourist boat, rowed by locals with broad smiles. She made friendly chit-chat with other tourists and enjoyed the view of the lake and the surrounding mountains as much as she could, soaking in the mysticism of Lake Titicaca. Jan let the breeze flow over her and pondered on the peacefulness of the lake, if she was to bathe in it under moonlight.

After a quiet afternoon by herself, Jan considered her options to break free from the curse of her gift, to break the wall that held onto her like a shield against the world around her, to help her connect to it:

"I'm ready for that experience," said Jan, to Mr. West and Salvador, who were sitting drinking together when she met them at the hotel bar.

Mr. West and Salvador both looked on at Jan, aghast, prompting Salvador to ask: "Have you eaten or had any alcohol?"

"No. I could do with something to eat now, though," answered Jan.

"Okay, but nothing more than a sandwich. You might be sick. When you're ready, we'll go to my home," said Salvador: "It's across the street."

Jan carefully considered her future as she finished her sandwich and juice at the bar, turning to Mr. West and Salvador with a grimace, who waited calmly for her. Salvador tilted his hat and led both Mr. West and Jan across the town square, to a red door sandwiched between an old, large apartment block. Above the doors that lined the street were balconies that supported closed wooden windows. Inside Salvador's home, orange walls and dark tan furniture were accompanied by various rugs and textiles, draped over chairs and benches. A white woman entered the reception room and was introduced briefly by Salvador, his American wife.

After a short exchange with Jan and Mr. West, Salvador's wife swiftly returned to the back room, which was separated by a doorway with a beaded curtain, to attend to their children:

"You're in good hands," smiled Salvador's wife, then said: "if you need anything, I am just here" before leaving, ceremoniously.

Jan sat on freshly rolled rugs and copious amounts of cushions. Salvador closed the shutters to the gated windows, then said: "okay, let's begin. It is important that you only pay attention to my voice. Since this is your first time, I will start you off slowly by placing you under a light hypnotic state. To get you to relax, I will ask you to drink a little of this mix."

Jan sat back after taking a sip from a wooden bowl and began to focus - in the way it was prescribed by Salvador - deep counts of 3, in and out deeply held on each count, until she faded away into a light meditative sleep, somewhere in between a dream and waking up, breathing out and dreaming in. After around twenty minutes, Jan was propped up by Mr. West, who offered her more of the bitter solution, which was carefully dispensed under Salvador's supervision.

Jan lay back with rapid eye movements. After a period of some minutes, Salvador asked her what she could see, asking her to focus on his voice whilst describing the images. "Colors, colors mostly," she said, almost chant-like, then Jan fell into a deeper state and stopped responding to Salvador, at which point she had to be nudged gently to provide a response.

"Good", said Salvador: "I can administer a little more at a time, after the initial effects kick in. I'll give her as much as she needs, no more, no less. It all depends on her responses."

Mr. West nodded, then helped Salvador lay Jan back down on the ground, after she took another sip, before moving to the corner of the room to light some incense, in anticipation of Jan's journey to the outer-worlds.

A deep, burnt-rose scent began to fill the room as Jan swooned into her altered state, muttering random words under her breath. Salvador's voice carried through the room and Jan followed it, responding to Salvador's repeated calls to do so. After a period, Jan's mutterings faded and her eyes moved, in rapid eye movements underneath her eyelids. In her vision, Jan saw colors fill the room, which formed in deep layers and layers around the two figures that were still fresh in her mind - Salvador and Mr. West.

Jan drifted deeper into her trance until a new figure formed in her mind's eye. This time, it was a tall figure, with noticeable divine feminine energy. The energy arched over Jan with open arms, leaving Jan comforted by it. Jan looked up at the figure and tried to reach for her, lifting her arms in the air. Mr. West and Salvador watched on, in the room, occasionally nodding in mutual agreement at Jan's deep hypnotic state. Jan continued to reach for the tall divine feminine being in her vision, but the being that arched over her withdrew its arms and folded them.

Silhouettes of trees, mountains, plants and flowers grew around the shape of the tall being. After the shapes sprouted around the tall being, the being placed its hands on its face, shaking it in apparent distress. The shape of the tall being's head then turned into a ball, a globe and Earth was presented to Jan, and the tall being disappeared. Earth remained, but it began to crumble, fragmenting into pieces. Jan then felt an immense loss at the vision - the despair at the destruction of Earth, which Jan was unable to stop as a passive observer - and it brought her vibrations tumbling down to the core of Earth, bringing a wave of death that brushed over her.

A new shape then rose from the ground. It moved slowly towards Jan - it was Jim's energy because she could sense it. He moved towards her and placed his hand on her stomach, which warmed her in that area of her body. Moving her hand to meet his, Jan felt a glow that made her whole body vibrate with love. Moving towards her side, smiling by her, Jan saw Jim's familiar fresh face clearly, as it came clearly into view. His energy told her it would be okay, leaving Jan with a strong sense of safety that eased the dread that accompanied her visions only moments prior. Moments later, Jim looked up, to a being who appeared to the other side of Jan, making his energy turn to fear, disgust and regret, before fading away. Jan tried to keep Jim with her, but her grip on him faded - before he disappeared.

Jan turned to her left, to face the outline of the other being that appeared. It was tall and wore a hat, bore no color in its aura - unlike the others that pulsated bright sparks - in place of which Jan felt intense malevolence. It leaned into her, and another tall being appeared, on Jan's right. The energy of the two tall beings left her quivering with vulnerability. Jan's body began to shake, as her astral body tried to fight off the heavy feelings that wrapped around her like a dark blanket. The two men in trench coats and awkwardly-placed hats began to inspect potentially intrusive medical equipment that appeared by the end of her feet.

Jan stirred her feet, in an attempt to break free, eventually breaking her vision for the sound of Salvador's voice, which hovered in the air around her ears, which Jan followed, to be returned back to Salvador's front living room.

Jan awoke, with her t-shirt drenched with the lingering effects of Ayahuasca. Mr. West dabbed her forehead with a fresh towel, and Salvador's wife brought refreshments to ease Jan's return to reality:

"Here, it's strong, so just take a sip. It will help you find your balance again," said Salvador's wife.

Mr. West took the cup, to gently move it to Jan's mouth:

"Oh, I'm exhausted. I feel I could sleep for a week," said Jan, as she came round.

"It's okay, you just rest here. You can stay the night here or walk over to the hotel," said Mr. West: "It's only across the town square."

"Yes. I'd rather go back to the hotel," said Jan, staggering to stand.

Jan eventually made careful steps outside, assisted by Salvador and Mr. West. Before they walked to the hotel, a gust of wind swept Jan from the valley and hit her face. Jan looked in the direction of the Great Lake, which called her. She said, with starry eyes:

"Take me to the lake! I want to bathe in it."

"Well, it's ice-cold, and you'll need Salvador to help you," said Mr. West, somewhat alarmed by Jan's suggestion: "And I'm not sure Salvador would like to do that!"

Salvador nodded in deliberate agreement and walked with them, a few yard's distance to the lakefront from his house, down the steps to the still, dark lake which was covered with a dazzling sky, with ice-capped mountains on the Peruvian horizon:

"You can walk down the steps but, before you go any further, put this on," said Salvador, pointing to the ring buoy which was attached to the rail, moving swiftly to grab it.

Jan took the ring and stepped into the center of it, pulling it to her waist. She then walked down the slippery steps, into the cooling water that struck her spine, leaving her eyes wide open, letting out a gasp of cold fright that finally awakened her after her experience, to join the land of the living. She lay afloat on the tranquil Lake, bathing under the moonlight for several minutes before returning to the steps where her friends stood, looking slightly exasperated with her.

Later that evening, Jan got herself ready for bed in her hotel room by taking a long shower, then drying herself off in the arid Peruvian air. That night, she dreamt of a life as an Incan King, who was trying to fight off an evil that had infiltrated his kingdom, an energy that wanted to trade his people for power. Decked in turquoise, gold and feathers, the King stood atop of a stone edifice and made deals with strange creatures with crocodile skin. That night, Jan was awakened several times from nightmares where she was forced to kill people as an Incan King, at the instruction of fierce-looking creatures with crocodile skin that possessed a great evil within them.

Over breakfast, Mr. West asked Jan about what she saw during her guided Ayahuasca experience with Salvador the previous night:

"Did you see an Earth-like figure?" asked Mr. West.

"Not really that.... I saw the globe, but it was like an entity. A living being," answered Jan.

"Oh. That might have been Gaia," commented Mr. West, taking a spoonful of corn-cereal.

"Gaia?" asked Jan.

"Yes, Earth's spirit. She often appears. It seems she has been appearing a lot lately in many people's experiences with Ayahuasca. It seems she has a message for us. Some say she is desperately calling for us to help her," said Mr. West.

"That would explain what I saw then. She seemed tragic. As if nothing could be done to save her," said Jan without another thought.

Mr. West suddenly grew irritated. He put his spoon down and said: "Jan, this is where you come in. This rotten stinking filthy world filled with the plague of locusts that is humanity - you - You - only YOU can change it! We've forgotten that Earth is our only home, and we are destroying it. What for?"

Jan slumped into her chair and apologized with some deference: "I'm sorry, I just never thought of it that way. I guess I've just been a passive observer after all. I don't know how to solve a problem like this."

Mr. West breathed in deeply, then took another mouthful of cereal. After a few calm moments, he said: "Well, I was once like you, I suppose. Somewhat indifferent and clueless. But, then again, I have the added advantage of having nearly 30 years' life experience over you. I just hope you begin to see in yourself what I see in you," said Mr. West softly, then patted Jan on her arm.

Jan shook her head in apathy to Mr. West's judgement, opting to steer the conversation in another direction: "I was wondering though, about the King of the Incas. What do you know about them?" asked Jan somewhat apprehensively.

"Well, there are many civilizations that overlap here throughout history, the Incas are one of the most recent. Did you see him last night in your visions?" asked Mr. West, with interest.

"No. Not during my visions with Ayahuasca. It was in my dreams at night. It was similar to what I had when I was in Egypt. Dreams of the Ancients. Then, I was Cleopatra, and now I dreamt I was a King doing deals with malevolent entities for power," replied Jan.

"Well, I don't mean to alarm you, my dear, but it sounds like you're having dreams from previous lives. And I suspect you've lived many lives, and you're here to fulfil your soul's purpose before you leave this Earth for good," added Mr. West, who bit into his toast without batting an eyelid.

"Wouldn't that be a fine thing…not having to live on Earth!" said Jan, sullen and serene.

"This could finally be your chance to get off the karmic wheel," responded Mr. West, with tight lips.

After having finally established her wifi connection at the hotel, Jan made a couple of phone calls to her friends. During light-hearted phone calls, Susan and Toni told Jan of the unfolding changes in California since Mount Shasta - a new movement was firmly sweeping throughout America, originating in California that was reminiscent of the Hippy movement of the 1960s. News reports began to locate the source of it and the media began to inflate it, trying to settle on a name for the revolution which made people turn away from the regular order of their lives of work like caged animals, opting to follow their passion. Young and old, nobody was immune to it.

Some media outlets narrowed down the origins of the movement, to a night of festivities at a cabin-park at Mount Shasta. Jan ended both calls to her friends gobsmacked, which left her shaking with what she heard. In just a matter of weeks after her cloud-bust at Mount Shasta, a change was beginning to unfold that only she was responsible for. Jan paused for a moment before ringing Jim:

Jim answered with rapid, alternating breaths: "Jan, where are you?"

"I'm here in Peru, you know that," said Jan.

"Look, we can't talk here. Switch off your phone and I will email you with details of how we can connect. Do not ring me back," said Jim with haste, then ended the call.

Jan checked her emails on her phone, after it pinged immediately with a link for an encrypt chat that Jan immediately logged into and saw the first message "turn off your location" and "use this VPN" and "make up a name for your chat", which Jan promptly did to join the chat conversation:

JimJones: What the fuck did you take from Maine?

J-Lo: From Maine? What do you mean?

JimJones: Whatever you took, Jan, you pissed off the wrong people. And they are coming for you. Whatever you took, they want it!

J-Lo: Fuck. What did you tell them?

JimJones: Nothing. But I don't think they bought it. They were creepy as fuck, Jan. Who are they?

J-Lo: Shit. I can't tell you. I don't know. They came to interview me too. Jim, I'm freaking out here now. I saw one at the airport. What should I do? Shall I destroy them?

JimJones: No way, that might do untold damage. We don't know what's in them. You can sit it out and wait for them to catch up with you, or go on the run.

J-Lo: I gotta go. I don't feel comfortable staying on this thing for too long.

JimJones: Before you go, I'm going to send you a link with an app I've managed to construct for us. Nobody else has access to it. Download it and I'll be in touch there.

J-Lo: Okay, thanks.

JimJones: J-Lo though? ;-)

J-Lo: Jim Jones? Don't drink the Kool Aid! ;-)

JimJones: I already have!

J-Lo: :-)

Jan ended the conversation to find Mr. West looking at her with deep concern. She hesitated, debating with herself whether she should say anything to Mr. West, but then decided against it, making an excuse to visit the bathroom, which she did, since she did not feel well, and proceeded to vomit out her breakfast. The enormity of what she was now involved with had sunk in, upon returning to the table where Mr. West was waiting for her. Jan excused her sickness and Mr. West raised his eyebrows:

"Perhaps it was the effects of the Ayahuasca," added Mr. West, to which Jan nodded in agreement, between sips of water.

It wasn't long before Salvador joined them, pulling a chair to join them in his usual, joyful exuberance to ask Jan, who sat slumped into her chair opposite a concerned-looking Mr. West.

Salvador looked at them both, oblivious to what was unfolding before them, then paused for a moment before speaking:

"I have just the solution for you. Since my friend Mr. West mentioned the Incas on the phone this morning, I think it would be a good idea for you both to visit Isla del Sol. It is a tiny island with ancient Incan ruins," he said, his Peruvian accent growing heavier with the intensity of his suggestion: "I have a friend that runs a little hotel there. It's not much, but it will give you a chance to experience the splendor of the lake, especially at night, it is divine. Why don't we go for a day trip first to see if you like it before you decide to stay there the night?"

"Yes, that's fine," nodded Jan. She then excused herself, to go to her room and rest for an hour, looking very pale, leaving her companions on the terrace outside the hotel where they were to express concern.

As they were chatting, a man in a khaki suit took a seat at a table further down the terrace, where Mr. West and Salvador were sitting, facing Puno's city square. The man in the khaki suit sat facing the same direction as Mr. West and Salvador, as if he was mirroring them, leaving him looking odd and out of place. His peculiar attire was reminiscent of a man in a television advert, from some tropical fruit product that was sold in the 1980s, complete with a straw hat with a black ribbon. The man caught Mr. West's eye for his remarkable peculiarity, as if he was an avatar, imitating being a tourist, rather than being himself.

The rest of the tourists, mainly from South America, immediately took notice of the way his smart and shifty appearance contrasted with the everyday attire of everyone around Puno that day. The strange man placed an order for tea and drank it awkwardly, stiffly.

Salvador spoke to Mr. West, to outline the itinerary for the afternoon: "When Jan returns, I think we should head in my boat. There shouldn't be any guards on the Bolivian side. I know of a safe route to avoid being spotted."

The vacant eyes of Mr. West that didn't flinch caught Salvador: "hey, what are you looking at?", he asked.

"Oh, nothing," said Mr. West, then shook his head.

The strange man then paid his bills and left the terrace abruptly, all the while watched on by the tourists in the vicinity. Jan appeared shortly after, breaking the gaze that held the tourists on the strange man. As soon as Jan entered the terrace, the usual hustle and commotion resumed amongst the tourists. Jan and her two friends then swiftly made their way to the harbor, where an assortment of small boats were anchored.

Salvador hopped on a small cabin cruiser and ushered the rest of the party with open hands and helped them hop on.

Salvador drove the boat past the canoes that trailed the floating islands on the right, at the banks of the Peruvian side of the lake, before cutting through the pristine blue of it, until the lake widened, leaving Jan to remark on the beauty of the blues that fused together, from the waters and the hills, seeping up to the sky.

The hasty boat trip made Jan's stomach hurt, leaving her reaching for the guard rails, before projecting a line of vomit into the water:

"Oh, Jan," sighed Mr. West, whilst holding Jan.

"I'm okay. I'll be okay, as soon as I'm on land," said Jan, wiping her mouth.

"There's some bottled water in the cabin!" shouted Salvador, driving the boat along.

They reached the island in the middle of the lake by its side, where there was a steep side, a small shingle beach and no pier. Salvador threw a dinghy into the water, to make it to the shallow parts, precariously dodging slippery rocks to make it to the shingle beach:

"Why are we doing this again?" asked Jan.

"It's a shortcut. Otherwise, it's a lot of work getting to the island through the Bolivian border on land, like we're supposed to," shouted Salvador.

Salvador led them to a beaten track, which they had to crawl, finding any twig or stone for support, until they reached a narrow pathway that led all the way up the side of the island.

"Wait, I'm not going to make it to the top," shrieked Jan, breathless.

"Relax," said Salvador: "there are ropes that hang off the cliff to help you. I'm right behind you and there's no wind on this side ever and the path is wide enough."

Jan took her steps on the path that was just under a meter wide and started to walk up, holding onto the ropes for security and answering Salvador's incessant questions about her life at home in California, which he persisted on asking to help her retain focus. Before long, they reached the first plateau to a sigh of relief, the loudest from Jan, when she examined the island's landscape that was embraced by cascading farmland from the mountain tops to the plateau which they were on. Jan spotted a causeway less than a mile away, with some ancient ruins:

"Shall we walk there?" asked Jan, pointing in the distance.

Between sips of bottled water and bites of a protein bar, Jan and her comrades walked the distance to the stoned ruins half a mile away, which were being inspected by a handful of slightly disappointed-looking tourists, who meandered through the views over the lake and the two countries on either side of it. Jan and her companions walked to the ruins, which were nothing more than a rubble of stones arranged in squares, forming an underwhelming atmosphere.

An underwhelmed Jan turned to her friends and said: "well, there's nothing mysterious about this place."

An American traveler in the vicinity looked at Jan and shouted over at her: "you'll have to go to Bolivia for that!"

"Say what?" asked Jan.

"If you're looking for a special place, you might want to try Tiwanaku. Here, take this pamphlet. I don't need it. There's a bus that leaves from Copacabana, which is not too far off from here. Though it's best to go via Peru. There's a checkpoint, but you won't have to worry if you have nothing to hide," said the young American woman.

After their brief visit to the ruins, Salvador led his guests towards the B&B, which was sunk into the hilltop some distance away, then left to return to Puno, leaving them safe in the company of their host in the B&B. Jan's stomach churned like a slow drill into her abdomen that night, making her sweat a pool in her bed. She awoke several times in the night to vomit, then decided to leave her room, which was on the front side of the homestay they were in, to stand outside of the small Peruvian cottage for fresh air.

Between wiping her face with a towel and her t-shirt, Jan saw in the distance a shadow of a man, standing on the hill near the ruins they had walked from a few hours earlier. She peered closely in glazed vision, in an attempt to get a clear view and, when she did, the shadow turned from its side into a tall slender figure, emitting a wave of fear that travelled towards her. Under a breath which she had trouble forming, Jan gathered all her strength to purse her lips to form words which wouldn't form, as if something had control of her jaw, locking her into fear.

Jan exhaled and mouthed the words into the ether: *"I ...am ...not ...afraid of you."* But she stood frozen, watching as the shadow continued to move in her direction, in a manner which was not human. It protracted one leg, which appeared to extend some yards in front of it, to move within Jan's reach. It then protracted another to gain distance, moving forward in Jan's direction, in alternating motion.

Jan froze in the air, paralyzed where she stood, under the apparent lock from the shadow in the distance ahead of her. She turned her head, the only thing that moved, back at the cottage behind her, to gauge the distance to the front door. Closing her eyes, chanting: *"I am not afraid of you. You are not real"*, Jan felt movement in her hand and broke the spell temporarily, to stretch out her arm in the direction of the doorway some feet behind her, to attempt the rest of her body to break free from the hold she was under.

She turned back around, as quick as she could, to check on the shadow. It lurched forward, one long leg extending before the other, in spider-like spatial swings. In a thrust from her soul, Jan's legs moved, and she lunged to the front door of the cottage, which opened to a thud. She clasped it and bolted it tight inside. By the time she pushed the small bolt which really offered no security, Jan heard footsteps outside, on the shingle path that led to the cottage. The figure outside cast a shadow through the shutters, moving Jan to slide the bedside cabinet in front of the door, all the while aware of the futility of doing so.

Jan yelled threats through the door, stopping the footsteps outside but awakening the other guest and their host inside, to a knock on Jan's bedroom door, with Mr. West's mumbled voice prying the thick door open. Soon after the commotion from the roused occupants, another sound was heard. The sound of footsteps moved onto the roof, tapping its way to the center, to a consistent slow tap. Mr. West, the host and Jan all looked up at the ceiling. The portly land-lady grabbed a shotgun then went outside, through the back door of her guest home, yelling obscenities in English and Spanish.

A couple of shots later, the landlady returned with her mouth agape and said: "son of a bitch disappeared. It must have been a dog or a raccoon", she said between labored breaths, "or chupacabra," then laughed and turned to return to her bedroom, with her shotgun.

Mr. West and Jan looked at each other in the hallway with silent confusion. Mr. West raised his arms in the air in incredulity at Jan, then turned to return to his bedroom for the night, in the same direction as their host, shaking his head in incredulity before opening the door to their host's bedroom. Jan looked on with her mouth open and mirrored Mr. West, in equal measure of incredulity. After returning to bed and trying to sleep, Jan fell into a slumber for an hour before waking up to a wrenching pain in her stomach, which she relieved by vomiting in the red-velvet-colored bathroom that was adorned with mirrors and native decor.

The landlady gave Jan a knowing nod over breakfast the following morning, but Jan didn't think much of it, especially since her mind was on going to Tiwanaku. Salvador met them with a familiar warm smile and twinkly eyes, then led them back down the side of the island and back on the boat, back to Puno, where Salvador packed his guests, along with their belongings, into his Corolla then drove straight them through the three-hour journey to Copacabana, through Bolivia, to Tiwanaku:

"You look excited!" said Jan.

"Prepare to be amazed," said Salvador. He swung his palm in the air, then looked around at his two passengers, in the back of his Toyota.

Jan and Mr. West did not speak of the previous night's events, with good reason. They made their way through their destination in relative silence, apart from Salvador informing them that he would be joining them for their night's stay. In a moment of panic, Jan motioned Salvador to stop the car, which he did, by the side of the freeway, and Jan ran to check her bags for the tubes and the device, which was in Mr. West's luggage. Her worries were allayed when she found them:

"Don't worry, Jan. I'm constantly checking," assured Mr. West, when Jan returned to the car.

After arriving in Copacabana, they checked into the hotel nearby Pre-Columbian sites of Tiwanaku - a square mile of assorted ruins, sculptors and buildings. As soon as Jan got out of the car and took a look around the area, she instantly felt it. The ground vibrated below her, moving through her legs, warming her pelvis, causing Jan to holler:

"This is it!" she beamed and repeated: *"This is it!"*, with her arms open in the air.

Mr. West and Salvador looked at her and said, in unison: "that's women for ya!"

After unloading their bags in the homestay and removing the valuable items from their bags, they walked to the historical site, passing by Salvador's parked car.

Jan noticed that the trunk was opened: "hey, I swear I closed that," said Jan.

"I'm sure of it too," said Salvador.

Jan looked at Mr. West, who shrugged his shoulders with indifference.

Jan's concern was interrupted when Salvador said: "come on, we haven't got much time before it gets busy, and I'm sure Mr. West has a lot to show us."

They visited the first site of the ruins and walked into its basin, and a dark cloud began to form over the area. Above the basin of the ruins, were layers of stone plateaus and an archway in the distance. Behind the archway, further away, stood an ancient stone sculpture of an Incan god that, from a distance, appeared to be sitting in the stone archway.

Jan marveled at the majesty of the design and its simplicity and uttered: "It looks as though it's a doorway to another world."

"Well, that pretty much sums up their belief system at the time, Jan," added Mr. West.

"Why has all of this knowledge been eroded?" ask Jan with renewed passion.

"Christianity, mostly. At least in this part of the world. In other parts, it would be whatever the dominant religion is. Islam in Egypt, for example," added Mr. West.

"That archway, can we get to it?" asked Jan, eager.

"Yes, but it's fenced off," said Salvador.

"That's okay, Salvador. I just would like to be near it," said Jan, masking her plan: "that's all."

After stepping up the plateaus of the sacred Incan site, with the ground beneath her carrying her vibrations, Jan felt the pulse of the Ancient worlds draw her silently towards the archway. She was taken by the mystery of the archway that promised the lure of a world that could only be accessed by a connection with the universe:

"I sense a definite other presence here. Don't you?" said Jan, careful not to alarm her companions.

"Well, this is all we know here, so I suppose I don't see it, unlike you," said Salvador, before side-eyeing Jan, to say: "Well, I guess you see things differently."

And Salvador was right. Only Jan saw what she saw and felt what she felt: "that's me, hombre!" she said and stepped closer to the vicinity of the archway: "There is something here. There's a reason why this was built here. But it's different to Giza or Shasta or Lake Titicaca. The presence of another world here is very strong. I think we should return at night, to see what it's like."

"Good idea," said Mr. West abruptly, then walked away from the site and headed back to the car.

"Wait!" beckoned Jan.

"I'm hungry, let's get some lunch!" shouted Mr. West as he walked away irritated, his elbows knocking the air.

"Come, let's return later. It's always going to be here," said Salvador, extending his hand for Jan to grab it, which she did, to aid her step down from the ledge of the plateau.

That night, over dinner, they sat and talked about the ancient cultures. Jan began to finally enjoy herself, loosening up and joining in the raucous laughter as her company drank more and more brandy. They tried to encourage Jan to drink, but she resisted. Mr. West approached the subject of the previous night, asking Jan what she thought it might have been that had caused a ruckus on the roof of the B&B:

"Oh, something or nothing, probably just an animal, like the landlady said," responded Jan.

"Why, what happened?" asked Salvador.

Mr. West filled-in Salvador with the details. Jan sat listening, contemplating whether to tell them what or who was after them and she chose not to draw Salvador into her secret project. Jan shrugged off the conversation and continued with her dinner. Jan observed the waiters shuffle between the tables on the terrace - movements which were accompanied by the clatter of utensils and the low hum of tourists that were gathering to be seated on the street-side. After finishing dinner, they got up to leave and Mr. West spotted the strange tall man again, dressed in the same attire, with the same strangeness:

"There he is again," said Mr. West, with a quiet nod to Salvador.

Jan didn't hear Mr. West. She was otherwise engaged with the pregnant waitress, who came to clear the table, with whom Jan exchanged chitchat on the details of the waitress's pregnancy.

"Oh, do you know if it's a boy or a girl?" asked Jan, followed by a series of other questions such as "is it your first?". Jan became fully engaged with her short conversation with the waitress because it was the first time Jan felt any deep connection to anyone during her visit to Peru.

After Jan's conversation with the waitress ended, she looked at her two friends, to break their discussion, adding: "come on, let's go and explore more."

As they continued to walk, Jan commented: "You both looked very alarmed at something!"

"No. It was a strange fellow that I noticed earlier at the hotel, and I saw him again just now," replied Mr. West.

A strong bolt ran through Jan's body, freezing her on the spot. She turned to check, from a distance of several feet, if the man in question was still there. A tall man walking away, with a familiar frame and gait, made Jan's stomach ring an alarm. A gasp of air filled her lungs and she opened her mouth to try and say something:

"Jan, are you okay? You look in shock," asked Mr. West, who walked back a few steps to where Jan stood, frozen solid.

"What did he look like?" asked Jan, turning steely slowly to face Mr. West.

"Oh, strange. Very strange. He had a very peculiar presence," replied Mr. West, shaking his head rapidly.

"Sort of human but not?" she asked.

"Well, I suppose you could say that. Very stiff and strange. Just strange," added Salvador: "it was the first time I've seen him and I could only say that he was strange. He looked like he wasn't from here."

Salvador's response rang through Jan's ears and she continued to ask, in hurried disbelief: "You mean from Peru?"

"No, here," replied Salvador, with a finger darting to the ground: "Not from here," he said, pointing to the sky.

"Jan… Is there something you should be telling us?" asked Mr. West, eyeing Jan with a certain level of concern.

"No, it's just that you said about him being peculiar and strange, but Salvador answered my question," said Jan with skillful deflection, with blood that ran cold.

They ended the rest of the afternoon with visits to tourist shops to feed their curiosity, then to a small art gallery before resting at the hotel then returning to their previously chosen restaurant for dinner. All activities which did not allay Jan's crushing sense of alarm, which ate at her, deep inside, all the more impacted by the fact that she could not bring herself to share her fears and worries with her companions.

As the sun set and the stars began to intrude into the night sky, Jan decided to take some photos of the Bolivian night sky: "just imagine what else is out there? Just imagine what untold worlds there are, possibly next to us, interacting with us right now, that we don't know of and are waiting to be discovered," she reflected.

Salvador leaned back in his chair and took a sip of brandy to say: "oh, here in these parts, we interact with some of them every day!"

"Oh!" quipped Jan, with feigned surprise.

"Well, our myths and legends are rooted in a real belief, and we just believe that whatever was here before is just simply hidden from view. The lake, the mountains and the forests here are all holding those secrets," replied Salvador.

"But wouldn't it be amazing to see the beings from these different worlds? I mean, the Incan God-like sculpture over there through the stone archway could be that type of being. Just stepping in and out of two different worlds," said Jan.

"Yes, and we will never know," said Salvador, with quiet acquiescence.

"Hey, are you feeling any better, Jan? You look like you've recovered a bit from whatever it was that was troubling you," said Mr. West.

"Oh, I am?" said Jan, who was taken by surprise by the comment: "I suppose I am. I feel better. When I was at the ruins, I felt good."

"Talking about the ruins, let's head up there since now is a good time - after dusk," said Salvador.

They walked the short distance back to the site whilst Jan texted Jim on his special app, about the sighting and the disturbance on the island and the sighting of the strange man since then. She wanted Jim's guidance:

J-Lo: What do I do?

JimJones: Stay calm. It sounds like they're just trying to scare you. If they wanted to, they would have got you by now.

J-Lo: Thanks. I've gotta go, I'll chat to you later.

Jan's fears were allayed by Jim's support, though she was alert and alarmed at the real darkness that faced her, a darkness that she wanted so desperately to bring to the light. As Jan and her friends walked to the archway of the Gods, Jan thought of Susan and Toni and the change that was sweeping her country - she knew it would soon sweep through other countries in waves, at the right time. Jan's heart began to beat a slow hum of joy at the thought of what would unfold before her, on her path.

They got to the top of the ancient ruins, at the top of Copacabana, and Jan circled the archway, looking up at the starry sky that promised so much but showed so little. The stoned area was spot-lit at night, similar to the sites in Giza. Turning around to her friends, Jan saw the silhouette of a tall man appear behind them:

Jan looked aghast, and whispered: *"he's here!"*

"So he is," said Mr. West, exasperated. Pointing behind Jan, he said: "and he's not alone!"

Through the archway, stood another man, next to the stone sculptor of the Incan deity:

"Walk slowly this way and if they follow we'll start to run," said Salvador.

Walking furtively out of the area, Jan and her companions kept pace ahead, whilst looking back at the two tall men that were standing in the archway, that did not appear to move. Jan urged her friends to keep walking and, after several dozen feet, Jan stopped and shouted at the tall men, behind them, in the distance:

"What do you want?"

Salvador and Mr. West urged Jan to keep moving, but she stood her ground. Jan then reached for her bag, reaching around, deep - she took out the cloud-buster and pointed it in the direction of the two unwelcome men. She pressed and fired a couple of shots above the stone archway, pressing down hard until a thunder was heard above the stone edifice, landing bright yellow beams that lit up the night sky, in the vicinity, causing the two tall men to run:

"Run, just run!" yelled Mr. West, as they witnessed explosions in the sky, above the Tiwanakun hills above Copacabana.

The tall men ran in Jan's direction - Jan passed the cloud-buster to Mr. West, who then passed it to Salvador, who ran faster than them all, circling around the site, out of sight - leaving Mr. West and Jan to get caught up by them. By the time Salvador returned around to the site, he was accosted by an ancient Incan King, who appeared from the stone archway, out from thin air, holding a shaft, covered in turquoise feathers and adorned with gold, on his broad shoulders.

Salvador stopped dead in his tracks: "Oh my god!"

The two tall men stopped their scuffle, leaving Jan and Mr. West to push themselves free from them. Salvador came out of the shock at the sight of the angry Incan King, to defend himself from him, who approached him to fight with the spear at the end of his staff, thrusting it at Salvador like a bayonet, to impale him. Salvador fell unguarded to the ground, screaming out in agony at being wounded in his shoulder. With his free hand, Salvador took aim at the King and pressed the button on the cloud-buster and the King evaporated into the ether.

The two tall men walked towards the scene, but their efforts were thwarted by Mr. West, who hit them both on the head with a large stone, dropping like heavy stones on the ground, without a stir. Jan walked over the two men on the ground and Mr. West ran to inspect Salvador's wound, removing the King's implement from Salvador's shoulder with painful precision.

Mr. West lifted Salvador up from the ground, and they staggered a few feet away, holding the golden Incan rod from the eviscerated King as support. The two men lay still on the ground, with their fedoras next to them, revealing bald heads with peculiar skin that looked pale - pinkish powder, over gray skin. Jan poked their faces to find a flap of skin that moved in her hand and seemed to curl away from the surface. With both her hands, Jan curled the rubbery flesh that formed in a fold over one of their faces - and began to peel it back. It pulled back neatly, to her horror and *"Stop"* from Mr. West.

Jan continued to peel the flesh back over the face like a rubber mask - to reveal a creature with a pear-shaped head and a pointed chin, with large black eyes that formed most of its face, that hovered over tiny nostrils, under an apparent absent nose, over a horizontal slit that formed a mouthpiece:

"What the hell?" said Salvador, resting himself on the ground: "I think you guys have some explaining to do!"

"Well, we can't leave them here," said Mr. West: "we'll have to get rid of them."

"Yeah, but how?" asked Jan, who saw Salvador holding the device.

"Like this," said Salvador, and pointed the cloud-buster at the men on the ground, then pressed it.

With one press, the strange men disappeared from sight, leaving the ground shaking with a tremor:

"Oh, I don't think you're meant to hit the earth with it," yelled Jan, before getting up from the ground, after the tremor stumbled her towards it.

Jan picked up the cloud-buster, after it fell from Sal's hands, and put it safely back in her bag: "Come, we'll explain later, now's not the time," she shouted.

She grabbed Salvador, rested his body on her shoulder like a crutch and marched forward, together with Mr. West on the other side of Sal. They walked their precarious steps away from the ancient ruins, as the ground continued to shake. After some tense minutes on shaken ground, they returned to the entrance of the site, where a mist, a dull-orange mist, began to form, from the top of the archway, before it trickled down the plateaus of the site of Pre-Columbian ruins, at Tiwanaku:

"It must be the dust from the site," said Salvador, shrugging the orange cloud of dust from his shoulders.

Before anyone could answer, a rumble formed in the distance, in the direction of the ruins as the ground appeared to rise up and the plateaus on the causeway were no longer separated by a short height. More plateaus became visible, that grew out, and stacked upon each other, until they were no longer plateaus but levels of a pyramid that continued to rise and grow from the ground up. A crowd gathered around the site - Jan hastily took the golden King's shaft that Salvador held as a crutch and ran to the car, and placed it in the back seat, covering it with blankets to keep it safe. When she returned to the site, a crowd began cheering and chanting.

Jan, looked at Salvador with a wink and said: "you can keep it. It's a reward for your help and for keeping quiet!"

It wasn't long before local media appeared, to film a burgeoning pyramid structure from the ground, which was now surrounded in an orange cloud from its rubble. The orange mist descended down the plateaus, down at least a hundred feet of plateaus, stopping short of the base of where a pyramid formed. Shortly after, the entire area was populated by several hundred locals and tourists who came out in the middle of the night to witness the natural phenomenon. Among them, a camera crew and reporter were present. They accosted Jan and her company of men to ask them about it:

"I see you were one of the first to be here. What can you tell us about what happened?" asked the young female reporter with a strong Spanish accent.

"We were visiting the pyramid, and it was very late and then all of a sudden the ground started to shake, so we came down to see what was going on, and my friend here was hurt when the ground shook," said Jan.

"Oh, that looks bad. I think you should go to the hospital right away," commented the reporter, without inspection.

"Yes, you are right" interrupted Mr. West abruptly, before grabbing his friends briskly and leading his friends away from the cameras.

Jan, surprised by Mr. West's action, asked him why he did that: "I'll tell you later, but it should be obvious to you," said Mr. West in a cranky but muted tone.

After Salvador was stitched up at the nearby hospital, they returned to the hotel, where he arranged to drive them the next day, but nobody slept that night. A couple of thousands of spectators began to gather and celebrate that night, and the hotel began to fill with amorous couples seeking shelter for passionate encounters.

Jan walked back out of the hotel, followed by Mr. West and a bandaged Salvador, to see the newly formed pyramid from a distance. The crowd around swayed in a trance-like motion with their hands in the air and lovers held hands. Men and women, men and men, women and women. Jan placed her hands on her belly and felt the energy from the crowd, the deep sexual energy that pervaded the crowd as it fluttered through her, moving in her. That's when she realized something about her sickness over the previous days.

As the energy from the orange mist flowed down the pyramid and worked its way through the crowd, Jan sensed it straight away, telling her friends: "guys, I don't think I'm sick. I think it's something else!"

Turning to Mr. West, she said with her mouth agape: "I think I'm pregnant!"

Chapter 9

Uluru, Australia

Jan took her phone from the bag and began to text Susan, but received no immediate response. She then walked to the baggage claim area and waited anxiously for their baggage in Brisbane Airport, where they arrived following a hasty exit from Peru, after the events at the Ancient Incan ruins in Bolivia began to unfold in the media. The long flight was tiring on Jan, forcing to rest whilst on the trolley, whilst the conveyor belt ground slowly and her heart pulsed in a continuous state of anxiety.

Mr. West returned from the restroom looking exhausted. With a deep sigh, he said: "I think we're going to need a couple of day's rest before we do anything," he said, furtively. "Sure" said Jan, with a sigh of relief that mirrored Mr. West's, leaving her to breathe herself back to life again.

Just as they began to ground themselves, two customs officers approached them, after Mr. West and Jan entered the passageway to the exit. The two extended their arms, to usher Jan and Mr. West aside. After initial confusion, both Jan and Mr. West complied with the request - any refusal was not worth considering and they didn't have the energy to protest. As with everyone else there in the airport, passengers were expected to follow the set routine - open their suitcases and stand aside for them to be inspected.

The piercing gaze of the two customs officers tore through Jan, leaving her with an uneasy feeling that passed by her momentarily, before it returned. The pang of anxiety came, then went, then returned again a while after. After searching through their luggage, the customs officer looked at Jan piercingly and asked her to close the suitcases. Not long after breathing a sigh of relief, the customs officer ushered them to a side door to a side room, which they both followed, with perplexity.

Upon entering the room, Mr. West immediately asked: "what is this about?"

After being seated, a man entered the room, dressed in a sharp suit, and proceeded to sit at a makeshift desk. He was a young man in his early 30s, and he sat with an air of authority which would have only been possible because it was supported by his position, outside which he would be rather unremarkable. The young man sat with his back upright and his shoulders relaxed. He projected a poised voice from the depth of his lungs: "I'll be with you in just one second, after I've logged in," he shuddered.

Mr. West felt compelled to protest the imposition, since the customs officers couldn't find anything in their luggage, but he stopped short of doing so, gesturing to Jan to also keep quiet. The young man stopped tapping on his keyboard to engage with the travelers:

"So, we're just going to go through the nature of your business here in Australia."

A confused Jan looked at Mr. West, who said: "sure. I'm a researcher for a university in California, and we're here to look at some historical sites and then move onto Tibet."

"Okay, so we just need to ascertain your stay, your money and whether you are here for any other activities," said the bold young man, brash and bold.

"Such as?" asked Jan.

"Well, are you going to be undertaking any work which would result in some payment?" asked the young officer.

"Not that we know of," responded Mr. West, before turning to Jan and asking her: "are you aware of any paid work?"

"Absolutely not," added Jan.

"Can I ask where you will be staying and for how long?" continued the officer.

"Yes, we have arranged to stay near Uluru. We'll be there for a week before we travel to Tibet," responded Mr. West glumly, through his post-flight fatigue.

"A couple of nights?" asked the man, who looked at them intently.

"No, a week," said Jan.

The man looked at Jan with a certain penetrating gaze that ran deep through her, leaving her with a feeling she had felt before, deeply uncomfortable. She had only known that level of contempt from a white man before, during her frequent encounters in rural America, where she was made painfully aware of her place through countless micro-aggressions. The officer's gaze triggered Jan's unease, and she tried to maintain her composure, when the young immigration officer barked at her:

"NO, you will NOT be here for a week. You will be here for 3 nights and our immigration officer will accompany you to the airport, to make sure you leave."

"What?" said Mr. West with a raised voice that made him stand up, to get ready to leave the room: "This is an outrage!"

"'Sit down, Sir, if you still want to stay here for three nights. We have information that you are both high-risk travelers, and it is only with the grace of our legal system that you are allowed three nights because, trust me when I say this, you are lucky you are not on a list," said the officer, with a measured drop in his hard demeanor.

Jan and Mr. West were left sitting in a daze, as the shock sank in. The attention they had attracted overwhelmed them both, in equal measure. After accepting their fate in a conciliatory manner with the officious officer, Mr. West and Jan both got out of their seats and left the room, to the exit hall of the airport, where they stood to plan their next steps. The original plan to have Salvador bring the cloud-buster with the tubes separately would have to be scrapped:

"The bastards are onto us," said Mr. West with measured exasperation.

"Well, that's one way to look at it! But, whoever it is, they know a lot about us," said Jan, her mouth drying at the suggestion.

"Well, if that was an attempt to scare us, I don't feel pretty scared right now! Quite the opposite, in fact," said Mr. West, with pumped breath. He turned to Jan and flashed a reassuring smile, after sensing her anxiety.

After biting the bullet and paying the extra to change the dates of their forwarding flight to Tibet, Jan and Mr. West fell into a bar in the airport and began to drink away their sorrows whilst trying to plan their revised stay. Salvador was due to arrive in a couple of days - his flight would have landed on the day they were now forced to leave Australia, for Tibet. They contacted Salvador to inform him of the change of plans and to await further instructions, then they boarded their connecting flight from Brisbane to Uluru:

"The only thing we can do is evade the authorities, but that won't end well for us," said Jan, on the flight to Uluru.

During their flight, they both dwelled on their predicament and its possible solutions, eventually resigning themselves to their fate, before arranging for Salvador to meet them in Tibet, when they got there. At least they managed to stop Salvador from travelling to his fate with the cloud-buster at the Australian border:

"There's no way he would be able to get here with all that stuff," said Jan.

"I don't think sending it by courier is going to help either," added Mr. West.

After their short discussion, they both fell asleep in an unspoken agreement to give up the ghost, after the futility of their conversation overwhelmed them into a slumber. They would have to continue the rest of their tour under their assumed ruse - sightseeing, with archaeological fact-finding, for the purposes of Mr. West's final book before his retirement. After a couple of hours, the plane landed hard, shaking them awake.

After landing, a taxi took them to their accommodation several miles away from their original destination - the sacred mountain Uluru. They stepped out onto the bronze landscape, the mud-earth humming the beat of their feet, cushioning and absorbing all their emotions of fear and grief, and supporting their walk towards the hotel - Mr. West and Jan both felt a warm glow of Mother Earth, under the soles of their feet.

Upon reaching the entrance to the hotel, they heard an Aboriginal woman mutter something to them. Mr. West stopped for a moment, before they were greeted at the entrance by the concierge who motioned to the woman on the bench to go away, shooing her away like a fly:

"Go away, before I call the police!" demanded the concierge. Shaking his head, the concierge said, to his newly arrived guests: "I'm sorry, she's such a nuisance! She's been warned several times!"

"Oh, it's okay," responded Mr. West, before being interrupted by the woman on the bench.

"Fuck you all, ya fucking bogans. Get off my land, ya fucking bogans. Suck my dick and pay me, bitch. You're on my land, ya fucking bogans. This is my land, bitch," said the woman on the bench.

Just before Mr. West walked any further, he turned around to Jan and said: "she does have a point!"

Jan and Mr. West walked into the hotel grounds with their luggage, attended by the concierge. A sea of darting faces made Mr. West feel uneasy, and Jan instantly felt an intense and hostile glare from the other tourists, who were sitting on the terrace, overlooking Uluru. Just as they were about to enter the hotel, Mr. West turned to look at Jan, who looked forlorn from the glares. Mr. West extended his hand to Jan and led her back to the entrance to the hotel's grounds. The concierge's face and shoulders dropped with frustration at his new departing guests, as he stood waiting for them to check into the hotel. Mr. West led Jan to the Aboriginal woman, on the bench outside the hotel:

"Hey, if you have a place where we can stay that's reasonably comfortable… we'll take it for the same price we would have paid for here," said Mr. West, directly.

"Yeah," said the woman, monosyllabically: "...wait here!"

As they waited for the woman, Jan and Mr. West cancelled their booking at the hotel with the chagrined concierge, who insisted they pay a cancellation fee. By the time they had finished dealing with the inconvenienced hotel staff, Jan and Mr. West were ready for their new accommodation. A young man of mixed complexion appeared where they waited outside the hotel, and pointed in the direction of the Aboriginal Cultural Center in the distance:

"I have a friend who runs a B&B for tourists like you. It's clean and safe and a lot friendlier than these pretentious bogans here. If you'll just follow me," he said.

As they walked to the nearby cultural center, Jan and Mr. West made themselves acquainted with the Aboriginal people and their culture and lifestyle:

"The problem we have is with the white man trying to tell us how to live our lives," said the young guide, as they walked towards the center: "They just can't accept that this is how we want to live it. So they see us as a problem. But it's only a problem for them. Not to us. We don't see a problem - they are the problem… it makes us laugh, the way they carry on!"

When they got to the cultural center, they were met by their host, who led his guests to his abode, a few yards away. After Jan and Mr. West unloaded and washed, they were invited for a meal, followed by an event with a local tribe, to discuss events and issues related to the Aboriginal community.

Jan and Mr. West ate the freshest items on their plate - rice - and picked at the chunks of processed meats and canned veg. Placing the meat to the side of her plate, Jan slathered the veg and rice with various bottled sauces, whilst Mr. West looked on at her aghast, gulping down sugary drinks. They then took their trays to the trolley in the corner of the canteen in orderly custom, and walked out to meet their host in the communal meeting room next door. At the meeting, an Aboriginal doctor attended to discuss diets and health:

"But a lot of the food our ancestors ate is no longer grown, and we have to eat the white man's diet, and it's killing us," said one old woman, on a cushion on the floor. Her comment was met with sounds of approval from the congregation of around thirty members, mostly families from the local Aboriginal community.

"Maybe they should pay us rent, so we can buy better food. Maybe we can get one of them, what you call it, personal cooks!" said one community member and the room erupted with laughter, leaving the Aboriginal doctor looking overwhelmed and out of her depth.

At dusk, with the sunset over Uluru, the local tribe gathered around a fire and said a few prayers, to the creator of the universe and to all the elements. Jan and Mr. West felt taken-in by the community, simultaneously eating marshmallows and joking about the poison of the white man's food. Behind them stood the hotel where they would have stayed, where guests sat and watched the Aboriginal community and their guests enjoy their fire, under white canopies and electric parasols to keep them warm, for their view of Uluru. Jan and Mr. West were handed blankets with kind smiles, into their night with their hosts next to the fire, on the sacred grounds of Uluru. After general exchanges about their origins and the purpose of their visit, Jan and Mr. West started making their way to their home-stay for the first of their three nights.

The next morning, they ate with their host-family whilst expressing their desire to learn more about Uluru and its significance to Aboriginal life. They were educated about the Anangu people, the original protectors of Uluru, and how their priests communicated with it, passing down its secrets throughout the centuries:

"Modern-day explanations have tried to wash the true meaning of Uluru", said their host. Their guests probed further, but were met with a stiff: "we'll tell you later."

Mr. West explained to Jan that closely guarded secrets were not easily shared with strangers - Jan replied by expressing gratitude to their host family for sharing what they did. After breakfast, Jan contacted Salvador in Peru using the secret app to which she added him, and Salvador expressed his frustration at trying to arrange a flight in time. He tried to assure Jan that he was doing everything he could, to try and make sure he could get the cloud-buster to Tibet, even if it meant he would have to fly over with it himself:

"It's okay. maybe it's not meant to be," replied Jan, though she struggled with the sunken feeling it gave her.

Soon after, Jan and Mr. West got ready for their excursion to the base of the great red mountain that slept like a bloated giant on the landscape, waiting to be roused from her golden slumber on Earth. They were taken in a Toyota cruiser, by the park ranger. Getting out, Jan took off her shoe and placed her bare feet on the red Earth, leaving her completely at ease. She took a mound of dirt and blew it into the air with a prayer, and a blessing for Mother Earth. Mr. West looked at Jan and rolled his eyes. The guide looked at Jan then continued walking, and talking, to tell them what to watch out for on the ground:

"This terrain is hostile for tourists. Spiders are the main problem, though dehydration will probably kill you before the critters will. Since climbing is now banned, Uluru has peace," proclaimed the park ranger, before taking them to the base of the mountain, where it formed a ridge to the top of it, like the stealthy arch of a dingo:

"I can imagine. It must have been very hurtful to see her disrespected like that," said Jan.

"Man's arrogance makes him blind," said the ranger.

"Yeah, blind to the spiritual, but sadly not to the material," said Jan.

"Ya got that right!", nodded the ranger.

After catching up with Jan and the ranger, Mr. West asked about the possibility of scaling Uluru and was given a short response.

Jan made a comment, to appease the offense that was caused: "you probably get asked that all the time. It's very majestic. I can understand why people feel they need to climb it to appreciate it. But, I don't understand why people just can't leave things alone to appreciate them. I mean, I could see and feel her majesty from where we were sitting last night."

"Sorry, my sincere apologies. I suppose it's human nature," said Mr. West, after feeling the ranger's offence to his impertinence.

After kissing the hill and saying goodbye, they were driven back to their accommodation. Since there wasn't much else to see around Uluru, they decided to book a table at the restaurant of the hotel where they cancelled their stay previously, to enjoy the view of Uluru with some resplendence. They waited for their table and made their order, after being seated by a young smiley waitress.

At the table next to them, sat a bunch of young tourists from cities, who were beginning to get raucous with their beers. One of the young lads turned to Jan, to ask her where she was from, but Mr. West responded to avoid Jan having to answer. The young lad proceeded to squint his eyes at Jan, which led Mr. West to request another table. After a sustained period of jeering at Jan and Mr. West, the young group were asked to leave the restaurant, exiting with exclamations *"you're going to end up like that Ching Chong over there if you're not careful"* and *"stay any longer at Ahuluru and you're end up speaking*

Abungobungo" to a ripple of laughter from the group of ten adult men and women.

A kind-hearted young couple next to Jan and Mr. West offered their apologies, dismissing the group's behavior as a combination of drink and heat. Jan accepted their support with kindness and Mr. West added: "The saddest part of it all is that we somehow expect it to get better with the next generation."

The kind-hearted young couple replied: "sadly, they're still learning it from their peers and parents."

A local elder approached the gate of the hotel restaurant terrace and appeared to wait to be seated, but was customarily ignored by the head waiter, until Mr. West reminded the young waitress, who was clearing the tables, that the elder was waiting to be seated. The young waitress turned fidgety and walked agitated, towards the elder at the restaurant gate, to ask:

"How can I help you?"

Mr. West's countenance changed from his simmering patience, after witnessing the micro-aggression. Standing up from his chair, with a red face, Mr. West blurted out to the young waitress:

"That's no way to talk to our guest!"

The head waiter froze from where he stood at the door, with eyes that widened like an ostrich above a neck that appeared to enlarge with tension at the very tense exchange between Mr. West and the waitress. The elder was never going to be welcomed at the plush restaurant and the ostrich came clucking, after Mr. West exposed their hostile behavior:

"I'm so sorry," said the flustered head waiter, as he swooped towards their table, hurriedly ushering the elder to join Jan and Mr. West, frantically covering the indiscretion whilst trying to hurry the elder out of the gaze of the other patrons.

The elder took a seat at the table with Jan and Mr. West and the first thing she said was: "Thank you but don't worry…let's leave it in the past…"

"But, how can you say that? Look at how you were just treated. Is this normal?" asked Mr. West, bewildered.

As soon as Mr. West asked the elder that question, something appeared to have changed for her, as if she had been awoken to an injustice, but her face then turned, to express stress and worry, as though admitting what she was so used to experiencing was like adding another layer of injustice, which distressed her more than the treatment she was accustomed to:

"I guess we are just used to it. But since we closed Uluru, the tourist industry here has been affected. Maybe that's what it is," said the elder, who introduced herself with her Anglicized name, Alison.

"But still, I'm sorry you have to experience that," said Jan.

"Well, it's about boundaries too. We don't hold grudges. It's the way it is. Why fight something like that? There are restrictions in our lives, and we've just grown used to accepting them. They could have completely ignored me like they normally do, but I get it, I'm entering their space," said Alison.

"Oh, the irony!" exclaimed Mr. West, leaning back in his chair with frustration.

"Oh, I know. But here we are. Let's focus on this drink and the present," said Alison and took a gulp of the ice-cold beer. After a few gulps, Alison said: "Besides, our boundaries are what we've been trying to teach people here ever since the Europeans came. That's why we had to close Uluru. Because we couldn't continue to let people disrespect our sacred spaces."

"How is it guarded at night?" asked Jan.

"Well, for a start, the access to the park at night is restricted which protects it and the desert here at night is a suicide mission for the untrained," said Alison: "Uluru herself is her own guardian."

"I bet she holds magical secrets," said Jan.

"Unlike any you can ever imagine," said Alison, her drink nearly empty: "here, let me get another."

The young waitress took her order and promptly left, without any pleasantries:

"Before the settlers came, of course, our stories were completely different, and we lived in a different world. We revered the ancient beings when the creator sent them, and we were left to protect Uluru."

"Well, I'm glad you managed to find a way to protect her again," said Jan.

"Can you tell us more about the mystical beings?" asked Mr. West.

"There were ten ancestors that the creator sent to help create our world and Uluru is part of that story," said Alison.

"Sort of like the archangels?" asked Mr. West: "When the angels fell on Earth, they were covered in mud and clay and became immobilized and immortalized."

"I suppose you could say that," said Alison, clinking her bottles with her visitors: "They were the ones who carved out our world for us."

"Were they spirit beings or were they made of flesh and blood like us?" asked Mr. West.

"No - they were spirit beings. Uluru was carved by them and that's why it's a special place," said Alison.

"It's funny you say that because it feels very spiritual, and it's important because it's on a grid…." said Jan.

"Yeah, the ley lines. Uluru is one of those nexus points," said Alison before Jan could finish her sentence.

Mr. West nodded at them both. Jan looked at him in return, and nodded: "Vortices!"

Jan's eyes lit up for the first time since they landed in Australia, with the engaging Alison, who resumed their discovery of energy portals around the world, leaving them both relieved to be back on course. Whilst Mr. West headed inside the restaurant to use the restroom, Jan and Alison continued:

"What do you think it will take to change the world for you here? I mean, what's wrong with it and what needs to change?" asked Jan.

"Well, let's start with the fact that we don't even get a say in our own governance," said Alison.

"Don't you have any representation in government?" asked Jan.

"No. That's the problem and all the policies are decided for us" said Alison: "a vicious circle of non-representation and disempowerment. On top of that, the elites of the Aboriginal industry have hijacked it, pretending to speak on behalf of every tribe."

"That's unfortunate," said Jan: "Is there any way of organizing?"

"We say we're at where the blacks in America were, after slavery first ended there," said Alison with her head down, on her beer.

"Maybe a mass gathering, or an event, especially for the Aborigines," suggested Jan.

"Indigenous or First Nations, never Aborigines," corrected Alison.

After continued talks about the issues surrounding the indigenous people of the world, Jan and Mr. West were invited to join another community meeting that evening. Copious amounts of soda and other fatty and unhealthy food items were being dispensed in the kitchen of the local community center, when Jan arrived with Alison, to find Mr. West mingling with the members:

"It's a never-ending cycle," said Alison, pointing at the congregation, who were each carrying drinks and stacks of junk food to their chairs.

Alison stood to meet the community as the elder, to address the issues that the council had set on their agenda. The first item was the absence of representation in government. The crowd expressed their discontent, amid mumbles and groans that were washed down with sugary drinks and snacks:

"It's just so difficult" groaned a member of the community: "we're all still feeling the effects of the white man and their system doesn't fit our system."

"No, that's not it. They just don't care. Nobody cares," echoed another.

"We gotta all stop caring about the white man and get our own lives together, but we all need to come together," said another.

"We'll stop caring about the white man as soon as they stop deciding shit for us," shouted another, at the back.

Alison appealed for calm and focus before she continued, surprising Jan and Mr. West by introducing them to the crowd. Alison asked them to speak, to let them know about their experiences with indigenous issues. After getting over their shock, Jan stood up and walked forward to address the members:

"Just tell them what you see," said Alison.

"Well, I've only been here a little over 24 hours and I can't say I know everything about the subject. I don't know what I can say in terms of what I have seen, aside from the beauty of Uluru," said Jan, looking over at Alison, who nodded her head and gestured for her to keep talking.

"Well… let me see. I actually don't know much about indigenous issues but, just from what I've seen, I can say that you are the most visible invisible people I have ever met. Our indigenous in America are also on the sidelines, but their voices are heard, at least I think so… but I see an invisibility here," said Jan with some hesitation, seeking approval from Alison, who nodded in confirmation: "I don't know how I would feel if I was in your shoes and I can see the suffering, but it doesn't have to be like this. I mean, you can reclaim who you are. I've seen it happen where I'm from," continued Jan.

"Yeah, but this isn't America," heckled a member of the community.

"Let her finish," interrupted Alison.

"I mean, I've seen the game played, and I've seen the devastation, but nothing is won by forgetting who you are, and you will never win by not coming together. I've seen that's how they've won in my country - by keeping black Americans fighting each other over money and material things," said Jan, before ending abruptly: "that's all I have to say!"

Jan returned to her seat, then Mr. West stood up, walked to the front and prepared to speak. He looked at Alison, who granted him approval to speak, clearing his throat, he spoke:

"I just wanted to say sorry for everything that's gone wrong. I know it might sound trite but, as a white American, it's easy to forget how my existence doesn't impinge on others, and the truth is that my existence was built on the blood of others. That's all I wanted to say."

Mr. West walked back to the crowd to sit with Jan and Alison concluded the meeting by repeating the need for all the tribes to come together for the purpose of determining their own destiny. Shortly after, the crowd dispersed and Jan and Mr. West were left mingling with the scattered members. Jan felt the hopelessness in the air that lingered after the meeting ended when nothing had been gained, but everything had been spilled. The heaviness of ravaged lives filled the meeting room and refused to leave. Jan and Mr. West returned to their accommodation that night with heavy hearts.

The next morning, Mr. West and Jan were awakened by a commotion at the front door of their host family. It was Alison. She was invited in like a royal by the host family - she humbly sat by the dining table as the host fussed around her:

"I'm here to ask something of your guests," she said.

Mr. West and Jan were summoned to the living room, and Alison asked them both if they would like to accompany her to Uluru for the day. Something had occurred during the night after the meeting the previous evening, and Alison wanted both Jan and Mr. West to experience it. Alison led them to her car and drove quickly to the mountain.

When they got to Uluru and stepped out of the car, they saw a crowd of different tribes gathering around Uluru, taking their place on the ground surrounding it. Another dozen or so indigenous people joined from a bus and proceeded to sit on the ground and chant a prayer, asking their ancestor spirits for forgiveness. They began to cry, in between their call to prayer. Jan looked up at the yellow sun over the red mound, which vibrated magnanimously, as if it was calling out to the universe. Mr. West pointed with *"look"* and several other tribe members came walking down the park road, to the side of the mountain where the rest were sitting. They sat and began to pray, to pray for forgiveness from Uluru.

Alison joined them not too long after, to inform them that the neighboring tribe had been informed the previous night of the plans for the following morning. A busload was soon to be expected to join in their pilgrimage to Uluru. Jan and Mr. West asked if they could join in the prayers, but Alison shook her head, saying: "no, this is theirs". A crowd of tourists began to watch at the sidelines, unaware of the power that the indigenous peoples of the Earth were about to unleash for themselves and from sacred Uluru.

As the day progressed, more tribes joined and the line of pilgrims around the base of Uluru began to get longer, forming a barrier around it. They then held hands in prayer and the prayers got louder, and their voices became stronger. Alison, Jan and Mr. West assisted the faithful by scrawling a line in the ground, telling the spectators to keep their distance and to respect the people, asking some to not sit on the ground. The chants of the indigenous got louder and their cries created a thunder.

More tribes people gathered throughout the day, growing in a steady stream, as the word began to spread through the communities of the state, to join the worship, to ask for forgiveness from sacred Uluru. It wasn't long before word spread and spectators became helpers, helping the prayers to stay protected and the line to never be crossed. Word went out and journalists arrived, to document the events, in typical fashion.

Alison conversed with the park ranger, to shut the park. The media weren't permitted and the spectators that were left by the end of the night were permitted to stay, to observe and protect the human chain around Uluru, to break her from her bondage. A change was afoot, and it wouldn't be long before the rest of the states would gather, to draw a line in the sand, in unity amongst all the tribes of the indigenous nations, against the state that controlled their lives. And all through the night, a human chain formed around Uluru to circumnavigate it fully and, with each chant, Uluru awoke from her slumber.

Later that night, Jan and Mr. West were joined by the immigration officials, who kept their promise to escort them back to the airport the next morning, back to Brisbane, via a flight from Uluru. As the airplane flew over, Jan watched the line begin to grow under a yellow sun and the vibrations of the mountain move through the atmosphere, dissipating the clouds around it. Jan sat back and smiled at the immigration officials who growled at her, on the small plane to Brisbane. She was no longer afraid of them or what might come.

Mr. West nodded to Jan, in assurance. Everything was going to be alright. They looked forward to their trip to Tibet, despite being deported from Australia, knowing that their presence in Tibet would unfold as it had been destined to. They were also going to enjoy seeing Salvador again. He was going to meet them in Tibet, just as he promised.

Jan sat back to gaze at the immigration officials, who continued to look at her. As Jan smiled at them, they continued to penetrate her eyes, with a darting darkness around the whites of their eyes. Jan did not flinch, even when their eyes turned again, from black to green, with a slit in the middle. Jan faced the officials and peered back into their eyes, as their eyes shifted shape. Jan sat unafraid, unblinking, whilst the indigenous people of Earth below them, shook the ground with their own power, to break free from their prison, to bring forth their own destiny. Jan was no longer afraid of what she was dealing with.

Jan and Mr. West were shuttled out and placed on their flight to their forwarding destination before being told to never return. Jan smiled at them, which aggravated them further, prompting them to warn her of what awaited them on the other side.

It was a warning that Jan was not prepared for, but didn't pay much heed. Jan saw first-hand the power she held and just how much positive change she could bring from it. She felt invincible - the power that was being unleashed on Earth made her feel like a goddess, unafraid of the world and welcomed by it. Jan was needed. She felt it. She witnessed it. She held her own power in her own hands - to carve a new reality for herself and for Earth. The veil that kept her and the people of Earth trapped was beginning to lift.

Chapter 10

Tibet

Up there, in the air, are worlds that are waiting to be discovered. These worlds move faster than they do here. In these other worlds, there is no such thing as the real dead. It's just energy that is transformed. Transitioned from one form to another. In this life, a life that we spend moving between jobs, family and careers, we forget the reason why we are here, because we are limited by what we can see. What we can see, from a narrow band of light, is what we respond to and are stimulated by, in an endless loop.

Jan was beginning to become more aware of other worlds as her quest progressed - her quest to break the grid and unveil what was truly behind it. The world which she and everyone around her once knew was beginning to change and the news reported each day about it. Violence was being replaced with love - passion for life was supported with connection - the oppression of the powerless gave way to a new voice that shook off controlling strings. Governments were becoming afraid. Jan knew that, when governments become afraid, they begin to plan. Jan braced herself.

As they passed through the Nepalese mountains in the small bus that was crammed with Chinese tourists, Jan looked out the window to set her sights on what lay before them. She turned to Mr. West, who looked pale, and asked if he was feeling okay:

"Yes, it's been an exhausting few weeks. I underestimated the toll on my body," said Mr. West, who grabbed his bottled water before turning his head away, to rest.

Jan checked her phone for messages, but she had no connection, so she decided to wait until they checked into their hotel. From the back of the bus where they were both sitting, Jan glanced at the passengers ahead - who were mostly tuned into their phones, completely oblivious to the wonders of the Himalayas around them. Perhaps they were all waiting to get out and take pictures, to appreciate the beauty of the landscape, thought Jan.

When they got off the bus at their stop in Kathmandu, Jan and Mr. West breathed in the crisp mountain air, and some color returned to Mr. West's cheeks. A boy came out to collect their luggage - Jan and Mr. West followed him into the small yellow and red-colored house at the foothills of the Himalayas. The bright ultraviolet light from the height of the mountainous region gave everything a shimmering silver-shine, leaving Jan feeling optimistic for their stay. Jan scrambled into their luggage to retrieve extra layers of clothing, to shield them both from the biting white mountainous chill, a drop in temperature that chilled their bones.

Inside the small lodgings which couldn't house more than half a dozen visitors, Jan immediately noticed guests sitting in the corner, reading a map, after which they walked out, pointing to a direction outside, before heading off towards it. Jan turned around to the smiling young boy at the desk, who checked them in with fluent English. After checking in and resting for a few hours, Jan left the hotel to explore the foothills of the Himalayas without Mr. West, who decided he needed to rest a lot more.

Jan's first afternoon in Kathmandu involved the usual beaten path of temples, buildings and cafés - a habitual orientation to central places - to find her bearings. After walking a square mile or two, around the center of Kathmandu, Jan walked her way back to their lodgings, armed with bags of groceries for Mr. West, for a makeshift dinner for two. As Jan walked her way back through the small streets on the outskirts of the city, overlooked by the mountains in the north, Jan began to get a sinking feeling in the pit of her stomach. She had known that foreboding feeling before, but this time chose to explain it to a combination of hunger and thirst.

Mr. West appeared to perk up after dinner, setting his sights on their onward destination - Mount Kailash in Tibet - over copious cups of Nepalese tea and sweets. Jan created an itinerary, in agreement with Mr. West. They would spend a couple of days in Kathmandu to rest and recharge, which would give them enough time to arrange transport for their visit to Mount Kailash in Tibet. Mr. West returned to his bedroom but since it was early, still 8pm, Jan decided to stay in the hotel lobby and catch up with her friends after getting access to wifi.

Jim pinged Jan on their secret app with a VPN, just as she was guided by him to do so, at all times. Upon reading her messages about the events in her country, Jan became elated. The population was pursuing their passions, violence reduced significantly, and other forms of anti-social behavior were disappearing. Jan was confronted with the need to disclose her pregnancy, but she stopped herself once again, not being able to trust that she would still be wanted by Jim, choosing to distance herself from him. She kept him informed of recent events, choosing to exchange pleasantries in surface conversations in text form. Jan was glad to hear that her world at home was beginning to change, and its people were beginning to see what she had always seen, although not to the same extent, at least.

The next day, Jan and Mr. West took a tour of several Hindu and Buddhist temples in Kathmandu, both shaking off their tiredness for fresh vigor and a renewed sense of purpose. There, amongst the silent sway of spiritual seekers in the city, a robed monk approached them to say hello. He seemed intrigued with Jan, who took his hand and bowed slightly:

"Do you speak Cantonese or Mandarin?" asked the kind-faced monk, softly.

"Oh, a little Cantonese," said Jan: "but I really need to be at home with my mom to really speak it," chirped Jan, with a broad smile on her face.

"Oh, I understand. I understand," nodded the monk with an accepting smile

The monk walked away to the imposing Buddha statue in the center of the open temple, to light some incense before sitting in prayer. Jan took a look at Mr. West, in amazement at the monk's apparent disregard for much else in the way of conversation from Jan, a detached manner which left her curious to learn more from him, drawing her to sit beside the monk, closing her eyes to sit in silence with him. Mr. West rolled his eyes, walked back outside, and sat on a bench, to feed the pigeons:

The monk broke his silence with a couple of sentences, the first being: "You have amazing potential!"

"I do?" asked a stunned Jan.

"You are a warrior, but you are holding back. It seems that you have not truly accepted who you are. You haven't fully embraced your calling. There is something keeping you back," whispered the monk, in graceful tones.

"Oh, I don't know what you mean," said Jan, respectfully.

"I think you do," said the monk, with a smirk and eyes that lit up like the candles around them in the temple.

"Come here later tonight, when the temple is empty, and I will help you unleash it. You will need it for your battles," said the monk, paternally.

"My battles?" asked Jan with her head cocked, in surprise.

"Yes. I meant that figuratively," replied the monk, still with a smile.

"Oh, okay," replied a stunned Jan, shocked by the monk's heightened sense of it.

Jan left the temple soon after and walked over to Mr. West, who was chatting to an old woman in broken English outside:

"Come, we need to go," said a hasty Jan, short-of-breath.

After sharing her experience with Mr. West, who shrugged off any significance to Jan's interaction with the Monk, they went back to their lodgings to rest. Jan could see that Mr. West's energy was beginning to shrink. He wasn't able to light up the room as much as he used to, which Jan saw him losing, for the first time since knowing him, and began to worry. After eating in a restaurant with Jan, across from their little lodgings, Mr. West insisted he take a nap, which Jan excused to exhaustion from previous weeks. Jan was beginning to feel that there was something wrong, but she couldn't put her finger on it.

After a while of silent debate, she made her way back out to the center of the city, which was a 30-minute walk, instead of checking up on Mr. West.

During her walk through the backstreets from the hotel towards the city, Jan began to get a sense that she was being watched again, causing her to periodically look behind her. She found nothing suspicious - just people from all shapes and sizes, who appeared to be going about their business. So, she decided to pick up her pace, running, in her chosen direction, to her destination. Jan began to move and pick up her pace when a sound of footsteps behind her began to encroach upon her and grow louder. Jan stopped, turned around slowly, to see what it might be. When she turned around, the side street she had travelled down was empty.

She gathered her pace, turning around constantly, to the sound of invisible footsteps that were gathering, footsteps that gained distance on her. Turning around one last time, she saw a silhouette of a man, a scaramouche on the street, with his legs apart and hands on his hips. He began to run from where he stood, in an odd gliding-manner, unlike anything Jan recognized in humans. Within a blink of an eye, the man appeared not too far from her. Jan ran into the first store she saw, and dove into it, to a confused look of locals, who appeared as alarmed as much as she was out of breath.

Jan went to grab a bottle of water, then paid for it, before walking out of the shop, tentatively peering out, out of the doorway and back on the street again.

Jan rushed to her haven, only moments away, at the other end of the small street, arriving at the shut doors of the temple, for her appointment with the mysterious monk. Jan knocked, frantically. The monk opened at Jan's third, hard knock and welcomed her in with a candle that was lit with embers, to light the reds and golds and greens of the temple's dark interiors. She apologized for her hurried appearance, to which the monk summoned her to sit with him and clear their minds, at the feet of the statue of the Buddha.

After a few moments of calming breath, the monk asked about Jan's troubles, to which she responded, with deep measured breaths:

"Do you know that you vibrate differently than most people?" asked the monk.

"Oh, you see that?" asked Jan.

"Yes. You are the first I have seen in many years," he replied.

"Who was the last?" asked Jan before realizing the irrelevance of her question.

"Someone who was passing by like you. From another part of the world. Like you," answered the monk, cryptically.

"Well, I don't know what to do with what I have. Mostly, it causes so many complications in my life," said Jan.

"I can understand. Especially given the way of the world that has been created for us," said the monk, perceptively reflective.

"I really wish I didn't have it. It's opened up so many cans of worms," said Jan with her head down.

Jan's tears began to flow, and she cupped her hands over her face: "I'm sorry," she said: "it's just been so hard for me over the years. I thought I had discovered a way to make everyone else see it too, but it looks as though I only had selfish intentions… you know…so I wouldn't feel alone… I wanted to make everyone see it too. But I guess I've unleashed something that I shouldn't have."

"You are suffering from your attachment to this world," said the Monk, wryly.

"I know. But, I've never really felt a part of this world even though I'm from it," said Jan and a tear ran down her eye.

"Nobody here in this world is! We're all just visiting from one place to the next, from one corner of the universe to the next. Don't be so hard on yourself," he said, compassionately.

"Perhaps you could teach me something to help me with this," asked Jan, refraining from desperation.

"Yes, I am glad you said that because that is why I invited you here. There's a lot you can do with your abilities. I'm going to teach you something," he said, with a mouth trying to catch up with his breath, before he rolled his eyes: "It will help you deal with your anxieties … especially when you feel your energy is being pulled down. It's called Qi Qong. It's done in many forms. The one I am going to teach you will help you raise your vibrations whenever you feel attacked. It will protect you," he said, confidently.

"The vibrations of the planet are already changing. I can feel it. Isn't that enough to help me?" asked Jan, hopelessly.

"No. You will need this now more so than ever. There are darker forces that exist that nobody can see… they will push down against any changes in Earth's energy. If the energy on Earth is being raised, the darker forces will push down harder against it," said the monk.

"Who are They? Do you mean the people who have been following me? Because I think they've followed me tonight, and I'm worried, for myself and for Mr. West, my friend," asked Jan.

"Rest your mind and I will guide you. Nothing will harm you here. You are safe in this temple. Even demons dare not enter," said the monk, and tapped his hand gently on Jan's arm.

Jan nodded in acceptance, after reclining as instructed on the cushions in the corner of the temple, and sank into her deep state of meditation very quickly, guided by the monk, with her mind's eye opening slowly, to bring the energy up through her body from the base of her spine. A ball of intense golden light grew in size, as it floated up through her body to her throat, to the top of her head. Repeating herself in deep breaths, Jan began to pulsate her chest with her breaths, as the ball of energy in her mind's eye kept growing, until the ball of energy from the base of her spine began to feel like it was lifting her off the ground.

This time her trance, unlike her time in Peru with Salvador, was immersed in an energy that she was able to control, and now Jan was able to tap into it , that ball of highest white light whenever she needed it, as she was guided to it, above her, in her mind's eye, to the source of creation - to God and the universe.

Jan felt at one with all that ever was. She felt herself melting into an ever-expanding sea of everything. With her eyes firmly closed, Jan saw swirls of light appearing, around her, to the side of her, in spheres of light, with geometric structures that bubbled on the surface for her to see. Within the geometric structures, that were tiny globular craft, there appeared beings of tiny white light, that were carried within them, in human form.

Jan concentrated her mind's eye on some of the craft, as they travelled past her, and she saw their inhabitants closely, that moved around until she focused her gaze on them, in their light, as she was, with them, on their frequency, on their light codes, with the heavenly angels, the gods of the ancients and the Almighty. And just as she became one with everything, Jan disappeared out of the monk's sight.

Meanwhile, in the center of Kathmandu, Mr. West was roused by a message from Salvador, who sent several messages on their private app. Salvador's arrival in Tibet was imminent so Mr. West sent the details of their stay, then placed his phone on the side table after responding to it. Mr. West then felt a sharp sudden movement, a shooting pain that swung his arm to move it towards his chest - a searing pain squeezed his chest cavity hard, in a tight hard clench, a grasp that removed the air from his lungs to the ethers, until he fell to the floor, with a cry that joined his soul.

Chapter 11

Mount Kailash

Salvador arrived past midnight at their lodgings, standing outside for a moment to catch the yellow and red colors of the abode contrast under moonlight. In the stillness of the night, he saw the lanterns in the small hotel sway in the wind, with chimes that chattered, breaking the stillness. After checking in, Salvador inquired about his friends and was shown Mr. West's room. After a knock and no response, the owner's son walked Salvador outside, to see if they could get a view from Mr. West's room from the outside. They looked and noticed Mr. West's bedroom window was open, with the light on, and the shutters fluttered in the wind. The protracted rattle made Salvador stop in his tracks and look at the boy:

"Something is wrong," said Salvador, and his heart sank like the violet-light over the hills.

Salvador and the boy stormed through the reception, in the direction of Mr. West's bedroom, that was filled with the deathly presence of something that lingered above the echo of midnight, the air of which echoed the thickness of night. Salvador took slow steps up the staircase, followed by the boy, to Mr. West's door and knocked on, with a heavy heart. He knocked. Then again. And again. Continuing until he turned the handle, the door opened away from his hands, to reveal Mr. West's listless body laying on the floor, next to his bed. Salvador put his hand on his mouth and sobbed from his still heart, for the death of his old friend.

Mr. West was pronounced dead on arrival at Kathmandu Hospital. Salvador was only able to process the news hours after formalizing himself with the police, an investigation for which opened immediately. After several hours, it began to sink in. At that time, he was told that a postmortem would need to be carried out, which could take several days. Whilst talking with hospital officials and the police, Salvador was waylaid by a message on Mr. West's phone, which Salvador took out from Mr. West's pocket to read. It was a message from Jan, informing Mr. West of her whereabouts for the evening.

Salvador read the message and replied to it promptly, arriving at the temple not so long after, stepping out of the taxi to scope the area. Before him, he beheld a majestic temple, under dark-night violet-clouds that hovered over a short, breathless Peruvian man, up the steps, to the front door. The stillness of the town square that surrounded the temple sent a shiver through Salvador and, before he could knock again, it opened to reveal the monk where he was last sat:

"Excuse me, I was wondering if you have seen a little American lady here?" asked Salvador with some trepidation.

"Come in, I've been expecting your arrival," said the monk somberly.

Salvador stepped into the temple, to find a cloud hanging in the air - residual energy from where Jan had departed, in her craft. Salvador turned to the monk, who looked at Salvador with familiar acknowledgment, and pronounced his knowledge of Qi Qong:

"Chee - Kong?"

The monk walked to the center of the temple and lit some incense, then proceeded to sit and meditate. Salvador threw his hands up in the air before walking out to get some fresh air and, when he did, saw in the distance the same menacing-looking man that Jan saw not too long before she found refuge in the temple. When Salvador returned to the temple, the monk said:

"Don't worry about him. He cannot come in, nor harm you. He is from another dimension. He is not a vibrational match for our plane. Not yet. They're coming in more and more frequently now."

"Why now?" asked Salvador with his mouth agape.

"Well, Earth's energy is shifting rapidly. Jan has ascended. It won't be long now, before she descends to a place of chaos around her, which she won't know nothing of," said the monk, who was still sitting with his eyes closed, leaning forward in silent prayer.

Salvador's face dropped with the consequences and possibilities of everything they had undertaken. His mind raced with a multitude of questions:

What will come through this world from other dimensions? What will happen to everyone on Earth? Who will ascend with the planet and who will be left behind? What will happen to the world?

The monk spoke where he sat, still silently on the floor, this time with his eyes open: "don't you worry. All will be revealed. There will be no death. Only rebirth. Come and sit with me. We will try and contact her, to bring her back."

Jan had disappeared into a higher dimension, that was not too dissimilar to the one she had imagined - she was still on Earth, but the world around her wasn't as she was born into. In this new world, the New Earth, beings interacted with her - they swooped down from the sky and departed again.

There was no sky, though there was an atmosphere which housed the life forms within the world - they went around their daily lives, freely interacting with other beings that descended into New Earth, in their craft. The sky during the day was clear, without clouds, but there was a dome over it, which turned crystal clear at night, to reveal all the other nearby planets which the day concealed, under the dome.

The moon appeared much larger, and all the different craft that landed on it and departed from it were visible directly to the naked eye. The sun, on the other hand, was not directly visible - it appeared through the atmosphere in cascading vibrations that made it pulsate and glow instead of shine, to light the peculiar pink day-sky that turned baby-blue at night.

Jan watched to view the world around her in the fifth dimension, when suddenly she heard a voice call to her, telling her to turn around and walk towards the tower that suddenly appeared in the town square, where she stood in the fifth dimensional-Kathmandu. She walked away from the temple, towards the tower, opening the door carefully. Inside the tower, books were stacked up on shelves, with ladders on each side of the tower walls. Jan looked up, to follow the ladder, up to an infinite sky.

The amount of books on the shelves was limitless - an infinity of knowledge that Jan was able to instantly access. She took her steps on the ladder, walked up and the ground below her disappeared. She continued to walk up, guided by a voice that was beginning to become familiar with each step up the ladder. Jan recognized the voice more clearly - until it resembled Mr. West's baritone voice.

The sound of Mr. West's voice prompted Jan to follow the ladder down, until she returned to the ground, kicking at the dense energy that was tugging at her feet, down to the ground. On her way down, Jan took a black-sleeved book with a gold spine, before she hit the ground to the exit of the tower. By the time she landed back on the ground, she had learned everything from the book, as if she had just absorbed its contents through the ether, into her being, holographically.

When Jan left the tower, with the book in her hand, she turned to close the door, and the tower disappeared into the baby-blue sky with golden rays around the corner of her eye. With the book in her hand, she walked towards the temple, up the steps towards the door, which then opened.

The temple was empty. And dark. Red and yellow mandalas swayed inside, in the absence of any apparent wind. Jan stood in the doorway apprehensively, with eyes fixated on the moving sheets of paper. Her eyes blinked slowly to the pace of their movements. Focusing on the letters on the printed flags, she noticed something in the shadows behind them, some form of silhouette of some sort of being that stood in front of Buddha, in the middle of the temple, that was covered by the mandalas.

Before Jan took another step, she heard Mr. West's call, that called out to her in the ethers, to open the book and place her hand on the first page - when she did, she received all the instructions she needed to help her deal with the entity unveiled before her. As soon as she stepped forward, Jan was overcome with a wave of emotions that informed her of Mr. West, that he had died in a heart-attack, after which a voice carried towards her, like a song from a spring canary, that taunted her in the temple with the beast.

Jan tried to keep her vibrations high but her heart sank, knowing that Mr. West had departed Earth. Just as she tried to regain control of her emotions, Jan's heart began to feel troubled by the beast in the darkness. After taking a step forward where she stood in the temple, Jan's chest was enveloped with acute sadness and that sadness manifested into pure hatred and it exuded from the beast that stood before her in the temple, behind the mandalas, feeding off her energy.

The presence in the room asked Jan about the reason for her visit, but she couldn't answer with the pressure that bore down on her chest, pressing Jan to answer, taunting her to speak, with a desperation that weakened her at her knees. Jan choked at a breath and thought of Mr. West and, no sooner had she done, she felt Mr. West's breath:

"I'm here to ask to be returned," came Mr. West's voice, through Jan's mouth.

"You will be," said the entity.

"NOOO … you will be!" billowed Mr. West's voice, from Jan, with the cloud-buster raised in the air.

"NOOOOOOOoooooooooo!" hallowed the creature.

Yellow beams shot from the cloud-buster and hit the creature, a blast which threw Jan out the temple, landing at the steps outside. Jan tried to find her center in order to get up, but found herself sinking into the ground beneath her. Above her, the sky howled:

"Get up, get up….. get back in there and fight!"

Jan closed her eyes and focused her energies up through her body to pull her vibrations up, with the strength of every cell of her being. Her body started to shake from the power of her soul, the ground began to shake, when she opened her eyes, she was back inside the temple, standing behind the entity. With her arms outstretched, she hurtled forward, bringing the large-green-scaly-dragon-like-demon to the ground, and the ground gave way to swallow it up. Jan trembled in her power. She heard a voice and looked up at the sky, outside the doorway to the temple. It was Mr. West - his voice carried through the sky, to remind Jan to always follow her inner light:

"Jan. I'm so sorry," he said, in a faint voice, his transparent soul-body appearing after.

"Mr. West. What happened? How are you here?" asked Jan.

"It was a heart attack. I knew it was coming. It's okay. I'm okay with it. I'm ready to move on," said Mr. West.

"But what about returning to Earth?" asked Jan: "That's what you wanted…. to unveil the New Earth!"

"I thought it's what I wanted too… but I see everything from here. Everything will be fine, Jan. My wife will be fine. I'll always be with her. I'm here with my son. We are good. But you…you have a lot of work to do. Your helpers are waiting for you. It's your turn to return to Earth. Leave this place. It is your destiny. My soul belongs to the universe now," said Mr. West - his astral-soul-body flashing in and out in the sky, like a flickering switch.

The tears that ran down Jan's cheeks pleaded with Mr. West, and the ground opened up beneath her, and she began to slip into the world she knew, back into the third dimension. As she travelled between planes, everything around her turned into place, like stars and nebulae. In that place, Jan was met by a group of various different beings that flew by her in their craft, introducing themselves telepathically by their name, their race, their planet of origin in the galaxy.

There were Nordic beings from the Pleiades, some beings from the Andromeda galaxy, and Lyran races from different solar systems throughout the Milky Way Galaxy. They were all exquisitely pleasant, some were beautiful and some were beings of light. After introducing themselves in passing, they collectively told Jan they were going to protect and look after her. Before she could ask them more, she felt the ground beneath her begin to pull her down, down, down to… to Earth …. in the third dimension, and an overwhelming sinking feeling washed over her, as if each cell in her physical body was gaining a pound in weight.

Jan looked down at her feet and the atmosphere began to change, becoming solid in mass - her feet began to feel like iron, from the weight that was pushing around and upon her, heavy, like an iron-blanket. Her arms swelled with the mass, making her gain weight in a matter of seconds, down with the gravity that her soul jumped now to, down a cascade of bodies, into the bodysuit that she was born into… onto… onto…. on Earth. In that moment, in that time, in that place, on Earth. On Earth. On Earth. One Earth.

She lifted one leg up, then pushed another down, then up, then another down, and up, and down, until she was not struggling, she was moving through what felt like a 100-pound weight, pressing down hard on her. As her earthly body took shape again, she looked up at Earth's sky, and it resumed the earthly blue that we all knew. Jan was back in the third dimension, back in the temple, back with the monk, who took her heavy body and laid it down on the ground, covering her with blankets.

Salvador watched in horror as Jan's body suddenly appeared from the ether in the temple. He walked over to her and knelt on the ground beside her, gently pushing her hair to the side. He looked at the monk, who said:

"She will need to rest for a day. It's okay. She's safe here," nodded the monk.

A solemn Jan and Salvador visited the hospital after she had recovered for a day, to arrange for Mr. West's body to be released for the funeral. After returning to retrieve Mr. West and Jan's belongings from the hotel, Sal suggested they continue with their journey to Mount Kailash in Tibet, after the cremation. Jan was non-responsive, leaving it to Salvador to deal with the bureaucracy before the cremation took place. Jan spent the days before the cremation in pensive and painful reflection of her loss. As they waited for the body to be released, Salvador came and sat by Jan:

"He trusted you with his work. That's something to be proud of. He wanted you to do it," said Salvador, reverentially.

Jan nodded and tears poured down her cheeks. The cremation service took place in the evening at a local funeral home, attended only by one other guest - the monk. After receiving the ashes the next day, Jan and Salvador bade farewell to the monk and packed their belongings into the taxi that was waiting for them, speeding off into the night, a journey of around 6 hours that took them straight north, through the Himalayas to their original destination, Mount Kailash. It was a solitary, rude awakening that Jan was left mumbling in the back seat of a lonely taxi, through hills in a strange land, with no friend nearby to warm her.

The Himalayas imposed themselves on the landscape, as the passengers weaved through with their monosyllabic taxi driver. As the car drove through the narrow and somewhat gravelly paths, the Himalayas appeared like dark giants that knowingly followed them, with the whites of their peaky eyes. Salvador proceeded to weave his navigation skills through the foothills for the taxi driver.

In doing so, they beat down their chasers, after going through deep, into the heart of the mountainous region, where a line of cars appeared on the other side of the dual carriageway, as the glow of the line began to subside, until no other car was to be seen on the other side of the dual carriageway. So, when a car began to follow them, through the dirt tracks to Mount Kailash, it became apparent.

Salvador motioned the driver to stop, which he did, at the nearest passing place. Salvador took a look in the rear-view mirror and saw that the car that had been following them had stopped in the distance. He then looked back at Jan, who was sleeping in the back seat. He reached into his pocket and pulled out his wallet, which was filled with wads of cash. After gesturing at the steering wheel in exchange for the cash, the driver and Salvador quickly got out of the car and returned to switch seats. Salvador needed to weave through the foothills quicker than navigating it for the driver.

With their chasers cut, Salvador drove to an area not too far from their destination, towards a concave, a flat plateau under the hill, which was converged by a view to Nepal in the south and Tibet in the north. Salvador stepped out of the car and Jan woke up, to the door slamming. The Tibetan driver lit up a cigarette in the passenger's seat and shook his head in surreptitious intolerance.

Jan stepped out of the car for a moment before she saw, in the distance, headlights of the car, the car that had been following them. It was snaking through the winding road, heading towards them, with the lights of its headlights flashing a glare in the distance as it came towards Jan's direction. Salvador, without addressing anyone, or Jan directly, said:

"Come… we … need to get out and walk up!"

"It is forbidden to climb the mountain!" said the driver, through the window.

"Oh, you speak English now!" said Salvador: "Wait for us, here! I have the keys to the car! We'll be back in an hour!"

The indifferent Tibetan driver shrugged his shoulders, but Jan ignored the driver's reluctant manner, who reclined his seat and waved with a wry smile, then disappeared out of view. Jan and Salvador then pushed forward, walking towards the two hills that parted, gaining ground when the sun began to light the sky behind the hills ahead, until they both stood, at the bottom of the mountain, with their stumped knees, walking the winding path, before the sun began to rise and rays of light penetrated the sky from behind Mount Kailash, to the east above them.

Meanwhile, on the ground, the car that had followed them came to a slow crawl, eventually stopping to a crawl, then two men got out, and walked past Jan and Salvador's taxi. They walked with a fixated gaze, looking at the base of Mount Kailash, as they approached it. Then, they stopped and looked swiftly up, their stony pale and lifeless faces shining in the remnants of the moonlight, making their faces change color into greys then greens. The taxi driver took his headphones out when their shadows passed his vehicle, and he clocked their tall and broad backs in beige trench coats and black bowler hats, as they shadowed past his vehicle, leaving him feeling uneasy and wide-eyed. He stayed in his position, still reclined in his seat.

As soon as the two men were at the base of Mount Kailash, they picked up their pace and disappeared up the hill. The driver had already lost sight of Jan and Salvador, who jaunted to the side of the hill. After losing sight of them all, he debated whether to leave the safety of his car, but he was soon overwhelmed with anxiety that enveloped him and pinned him down, after he caught sight of the men.

Jan and Salvador hid behind a giant rock at the side of Mount Kailash, where they could see the plateau below and the arrival of their pursuers. They quickly assembled the cloud-buster, which they retrieved from Salvador's bag, to aim it to the top of Mount Kailash. Jan fired a shot at the top, but missed it. She tried again, but the cloud-buster slipped from her hands, rolling down the side of the mountain, onto a flat area, some 10 feet below, to its base. Jan and Salvador kept their breaths tight, as the two tall men calmly and non-reactively walked towards the cloud-buster, their feet and eyes fixed on the ground for it.

Looking below, at the flat area below them, Jan and Salvador saw the silhouettes of the tall men, approaching from a distance, on the landscape. They looked at each other in silent motion and became acutely aware that the cloud-buster did not fall from their hands by accident:

"Let's get to the top of the mountain… " suggested Jan, calmly still.

"Yeah… let's go up this side… and find somewhere to hide… then make our way down… back down the other side," responded Salvador, softly.

"No, I have a better idea…" said Jan, pointing up: "let's go this way…."

They then climbed up a sharp side, with only thin cracks to edge them forward in their mount, or crawl and push themselves to the top.

The two men gained speed and approached Salvador before he could follow Jan's ascent, who appeared to them, to crawl up the side of mount Kailash, before disappearing out of view. Salvador stood alone facing the two tall men, on the small pathway in front of the rockside, at the side of the mountain.

The two tall men in beige raincoats stared at Salvador, who tried to open his mouth to yell a warning to Jan, but couldn't because he was in a trance, which was held together by the two tall men.

Jan threw a rock at one of them from above, causing one of them to fall flat and dead, breaking the trance that they held on Salvador, who too fell to the ground. The other tall man took the cloud-buster out from the side of his raincoat and pointed it up, in the direction of the falling rock that Jan had thrown in a static stance. This time, the cloud-buster hit the mountain, making it shake and Jan lost her grip at the side of Mount Kailash, causing her to fall, and stumble all the way down the rugged terrain, of blood stains and tears.

A ripple formed in the air around Mount Kailash. The sky above it began to crack, under billowing clouds, that sped to deep purple majestic colors. The tall man fired another shot in Jan's direction, and it hit the air around her. Salvador called out to Jan, but she could not respond. Just as the tall man aimed the cloud-buster for another shot, out came a rumble. A bright craft appeared above them all and moved to the side of the mountain. Inside the winged craft, sitting in it, inside it, comfortably watching, was the patient observer of the world - Jan.

A cloud formed where the tall man in a beige trenchcoat stood, together with his captive, Salvador. From the bulbous cloud above the mountain, Jan's craft appeared again and she grabbed the controls inside her craft, to shine two beams of light on top of Mount Kailash, to break the penultimate vortex of Earth's magnetic energy grid, the crown chakra of wisdom.

A purple mist fell down the sides of the mountain, lighting it in effervescent purple-blue and red-hues, as dawn began to break. The tall man below looked up and ran away, as soon as he saw the mist descend, and Salvador looked up, as the dawn hit the side of the mountain, to reveal an iridescent violet glow.

As soon as Salvador was bathed in the colors of purples and violets, he was hit with an immense feeling of expansion. The sudden realization that he was a part of it all - all that stemmed from the point of creation in the universe, all the atoms and particles that travelled through the cosmos to form his very being, up from the soles of his feet, up through his body, to the whole of Sal's consciousness.

Salvador was overcome with the *isness* - the tools to access the storehouse of information from the ethers. He became aware that he was on Earth to live out the consciousness of the source of creation, and in doing so, he was able to see into the depths of the universe, through time and space, to understand his own significance. The truth was laid before him and the truth would be laid out, for everyone like him on the planet, and soon. Salvador stood, bathing in the deep purple haze, a mist of which appeared to be brought to him from the deep depths of the universe, where only stars, planets and the divine creator know what they represent and for what purpose.

Above Salvador, in the cloud that had formed above the mountain, other beings appeared in their craft similar to Jan's, in their own bright bubbling craft. Among them were beings of the same energy that Jan had seen on her descent between the different Earthly and non-Earthly realms - each one of them in their craft, swooping down and around the mountain, then back up again, in a dance-like motion with Jan, who sat smiling at the prospect of delivering a New Earth to the world. Salvador stood with his mouth open, as Jan swooped down, in her bright orb, to take him away, to safety.

Chapter 12

Glastonbury Hill, England.

The winds blew cold in Glastonbury in winter when Jan and Salvador arrived, to end their quest for Mr. West. Jan and Sal walked the center of Glastonbury with Mr. West's ashes before they got to Glastonbury Hill, on the outskirts of the center. They stopped for drinks at several old-fashioned pubs, whilst they chit chat and girl-talked, or attempted to, before Salvador faded off. As Jan sat with Salvador in one of their pit stops, she received a text message from Susan for an update of her whereabouts. After responding, Susan swiftly rang Jan:

"Where are you?", shouted Susan, with fiery enquiry.

"I'm in Glastonbury, England," responded Jan, without drawing breath.

"What? How did you get there? The last I heard, you were heading to Nepal. What happened?" shouted Susan, careful not to overpower Jan.

"Well, I can't really explain that to you now, but the short of it is that Mr. West died. I had to cremate him. I brought his ashes with me," answered Jan, despondent.

"What? What the hell, Jan? How can you be so calm about that?"" muttered Susan.

"Honey, it is what it is. I tried my best" said Jan, before bursting into tears, effortlessly.

"Just give me your directions, and I'm coming for you," shouted Susan.

"No. This is madness. I have caused too much. I can't be responsible for making you lose your job as well," responded Jan without too much thought.

"Don't worry about that, Jan. I don't have a job anymore," responded Susan, gleefully.

"What do you mean, you don't have a job?" asked Jan, concerned.

"That's the thing. Ever since Mount Shasta and what was unleashed I - like Toni and millions of others - here have given up our jobs for our passion, and I've just recently sold a painting to get this - Mick Jagger and, before that, Joni Mitchell and Bono. I can't believe it. They all love what I've produced. They want to show my work at the Guggenheim!"

"What the hell, Susan?" said Jan, surprised.

"Yeah. And it's all because of what you did!" responded Susan.

"What about Toni?" asked Jan, still hopeful.

"He started his own boutique from his savings, and he's currently developing his own fashion line. He has a couple of investors lined up," said Susan, with a warm, confident smile, through the phone at Jan.

"Oh my god, that's brilliant," said Jan, exuberant: "I never knew he was so talented!"

"I know. So, I'm a free agent. So tell me how to find you, and I'll be on the next flight out or thereabouts. I'll see to it that Toni comes too," confirmed Susan.

Jan was exhilarated with the news, which came as a welcome relief, after previous months, so she drank a happy pint of traditional beer with Salvador, who comforted her with his presence. If only she received a message from her lover Jim, whom she greatly missed, she thought.

After finishing their drinks, Jan and Sal nudged through the crowds which were beginning to assemble in the center of Glastonbury, to take a bus to their destination, which was on the outskirts, in the farmland which held the music festivals. In her tipsy state, Jan pushed past a middle-aged hippy woman. Jan then stumbled upon her first ever aggression in a country which she always pictured as being full of polite and mild-mannered people:

"Hey, watch where you're going there," screeched the woman, with short pink-hair.

Sal stepped in, to say: "she didn't mean it!"

The gruff woman with a pink-terrier-haircut bit back, to say: "well, I'm sure she has eyes, even though I can't see them!"

Sal leaned forward in anger, poised to cause harm, but Jan stepped in: "come, let's get outta here. This isn't worth it," said Jan.

But when they left to board the bus, to take them to the music festival, on the outskirts, in the countryside, an uneasy and uncomfortable feeling swept the air when they boarded. The bus driver did not say anything as a rowdy rabble of teenagers boarded, led by the troubled and angry woman, who shuffled to the back of the bus, after Jan and Salvador. Jan and Salvador walked to sit at the front of the bus and tried to keep a low profile.

The madwoman began to make loud outrageous comments about the foreigners, who didn't want to look back, in fear of stoking the day. Sal and Jan switched seats so that Jan was outside the view of the madwoman, away from the aisle and tucked neatly next to the window. The madwoman mouthed something at Sal, and the teenagers with her continued to snigger. Sal decided that the best thing would be to ignore her in the hope that she would stop.

Sal closed, not rolled, his eyes and said: "I can't wait to get off at the campsite and start pitching up. That's if there aren't any more assholes like her there."

Jan just looked at Sal then turned at the window to remember her good friend Mr. West, wiping the tear which ran down her cheek: "I'm not afraid of them. I've met those types and much worse before. They'll get lost into a bigger crowd, after we step off. Hopefully, the crowd will help take the attention away from us by ignoring her. You can't deal with crazies like her. She just wants to get off by intimidating us. That's all entities like her feed on. But not on our fears. Because we don't have any."

Whilst Jan and Sal tried to ignore the group of juveniles and their leader, the bus moved through the countryside to its final destination. Sal and Jan waited until the bus was empty to disembark, after the driver motioned with his hand for them to leave. Upon leaving, Sal and Jan both spoke to the bus driver about the intimidating woman, with a wish to leave and be free from her menacing crew. They were both told by him to ignore her because she was still grieving the loss of her husband:

"Well, how long has it been?" asked Jan.

"A little over a year," replied the bus driver.

"But we're not to blame for her tragedy," added Salvador.

"Yeah, it's sad, but her bark is worse than her bite. Besides, once you get her away from her kids, she's normally okay," said the portly, bloated bus driver.

"I'm not sure, we want to find out. We just want to be able to get off with relative safety!" said Jan.

"Otherwise we'll have to call the police on her," added Salvador.

"Okay. Wait here until she disappears into the crowd, then you can get off the bus," said the driver.

The group dispersed into the crowds before Jan and Sal did. They walked to the nearest stand and got some refreshments before proceeding through the huddle of festival-goers. The music began to play in the background and the crowds began to move to the stages. As the crowds dispersed, Jan and Sal saw ahead of them what they dreaded all the while… the woman and her gang.

The mad woman clocked Jan and Sal, who both began to pick up their pace in the opposite direction. The woman followed them until she grabbed Jan by the shoulder to make her turn around. Cautious of what was about to come her way, Jan prepared herself for a showdown with the madwoman, but something clicked in her head and she remembered what she was taught. To carry on regardless, to keep on her path, no matter how hard the world was, irrespective of the amount of stones it throws at her. She must never sink to their level:

"Oh, I'm so sorry. I'm sorry. I'm so sorry," said the madwoman, whose countenance and appearance altered, upon touching Jan.

"It's okay," said Jan politely and mild-mannered, as she always was.

"No. No… ," said the madwoman. She looked at her hands and rubbed them, then looked back at Jan and said, without anger, with every regret: "You see, I was mistaken."

"Some mistakes are hard to rectify," interrupted Sal.

"What do you mean?" asked the madwoman, innocently, as if she wasn't aware of her own behavior.

"I mean the impact of your behavior on those around you. Look at them," said Sal, pointing at the teenagers around her: "How are they supposed to learn?"

"Well, from school and everyone else," said the madwoman, whose countenance began to drop.

"And what is your role then?" asked Jan.

"I give them what they want. That's more than enough," said the woman, still rather defensive.

"But not what they need?" asked Jan, without provocation.

"Hey, don't judge me. You don't know what it's like!" said the woman with pink hair, her arms crossed in the air.

"Well they didn't ask to be born I suppose," said Jan, before checking her tone, then closing her eyes at the sound of what she had just said.

"Look here, you bitch," said the woman, who reached her arm out to grab Jan.

Jan's eyes opened wide at the woman's strong grip, the touch of whom made Jan feel shills, and chills all over her. Jan continued to break free from the woman's deathly energy on her wrist, as the woman's resolve continued, falling again, to dissipate against Jan's strong vibrations, that pulled her up into the sky, away from the woman's shaky, snaky hands that grabbed on Jan's being.

The woman stopped and said: "you're right", then looked at the teenagers around her and began crying. Jan and Salvador then parted the huddle quietly that formed around them, walking away into the fields of spectators, whilst the woman and her gaggle of teenagers stayed behind, looking on at them, in confusion.

Jan and Sal then walked to Glastonbury Hill, some 3 miles away from the music spectators, to their final destination. The world they knew of would forever change, but they needed some time to rest before they decided to do anything. The people were beginning to change over the previous months, and Jan now held the power to reveal the true nature of the world, for the world to see past the matrix. Salvador looked on at her, with quiet regard for the enormity of what she was about to undertake. But, first, Mr. West's ashes had to be scattered, in a traditional Native-American ceremony, in honor of his ancestors.

Sal and Jan pitched a tent for the night at their chosen sandspit, on the hill - the low hums of the late-evening concert drums drew to a close. The stars appeared, lighting the Milky

Way, and Jan and Sal lit a camp stove, and started to cook a meal. They rolled out their sleeping bags and lay back, to look at the stars, marveling at their glory and wondering about life on other planets and humanity's place in the universe:

´´Do you think they are watching us?" asked Salvador.

"They are already here, and they've been watching us for aeons," answered Jan.

Salvador didn't respond, but looked at her, in quiet contemplation.

"Relax. If they wanted us dead by now, they would have killed us off millennia ago. They are only concerned for our development and how we're looking after the planet. Or not," said Jan.

Salvador relaxed a little with a sigh and smiled, then said: "I wonder what the other side will look like!"

"The other side?" asked Jan, gently laughing: "We're not all going to die!" before topping with: "Oh, it's just incredible. Utterly incredible. Unlike anything you can ever imagine with the sights, sounds and colors from Earth - it is beyond our understanding."

"Oh, ha ha. I meant the other side of the matrix, Jan!" shouted Salvador, under a hum of a craft, that was beginning to buzz above them, in the night sky: "I mean, when you break through the final portal, Jan, through the whole of the magnetic field over Earth, when you break through the matrix, Jan…" he shouted, into the ethers, as the hum of the craft in the sky above them attracted the sound of helicopters, that spun in from a great distance, jettisoning from the sides of the skies, carrying a thunder out of nowhere:

"Do you think the world is ready for that?" shouted Salvador.

"I think we underestimate humanity. Look at how quickly that troubled woman with pink hair changed," said Jan. She then looked at Salvador solemnly and said: "besides, I made a promise to Mr. West!"

"To change the world?" asked Salvador facetiously.

"NO!," shouted Jan under the echoes of booms from the ethers above them - she then looked down at the grass, between her legs: "to finish his book!"

Salvador looked at Jan intently, then shook his head. Ignoring what she said, he continued:

"Yeah. I suppose humanity's readiness depends on where they are in the world, what they believe in and the culture they subscribe to. Where I come from, with what we believe in, we interact with the supernatural all the time, and we've always done so!" echoed Salvador.

"Yeah, that's the same in my parent's culture, in Asia," beat Jan.

"I think it used to be a lot like that here in Europe too!" bounced Salvador.

"Yeah, before religion was spread, with the sword!" said Jan, throwing a response to Sal.

"Yeah, it's a shame it's turned out that way.... But hey... I got to tell you something... Muslims still believe in them. They're the Djinn. The demons," peppered Salvador: "maybe they're all those scaly Reptilian races!"

"Possibly… I think we're all part of the cosmos but this world is just an illusion and the truth will be soon revealed!" contemplated Jan, her enthusiasm shining through her veneer again.

"We'll wait for the rest to show up before you do that, though, right?" asked Salvador, boyishly.

"I reckon we just get on with it, as soon as we can!" confirmed Jan: "I don't trust that we are not going to be sabotaged, like the last time. Even though we have our allies, they are no match for the more powerful forces that are in control of this planet at this time."

"But you have a lot of power now. You don't even need a cloudbuster," shouted Salvador: "You are the cloud-buster!", he shrieked. He paused for a moment: "Jan, just how did you do that?"

"What do you mean?" asked Jan, looking Salvador straight in his eye, a brow that was furrowed at the same level Jan held, when she first saw him.

"The craft. Did they give you it? I don't understand how you got in one - you rode it!" said Salvador: "Did they swoop down to grab you off the cliff, when you fell?"

"Oh, that! That happened when we were in Mount Kailash in Tibet!" replied Jan indifferently, and looked away from Salvador, to the crowd beneath the hill, where they had pitched their tents.

"You don't have to tell me…" said Salvador, aware of Jan's discomfort.

"No. It's okay. The monk taught me Qi-Qong which is an ancient martial art. I was able to raise my frequencies and ascend to a higher dimension with it," said Jan: "I am my own craft!"

"What?", asked Salvador, jumping out of his position: "Can you teach me that?"

"Yeah, but it's a kind of continual practice. I can teach you it, but I can't guarantee it will work immediately. You have to practice raising your vibrations first," said Jan unenthusiastically, with the hope of tempering Salvador's enthusiasm.

"What makes you different do you think?" asked Salvador, careful to sound without judgement.

"I don't know. I think I was born this way. I've seen vibrations since I was a young child," responded Jan. She looked at the grass beneath her legs, plucked a few daisies and began making a chain out of them, in the night.

"Oh…" said Salvador, with raised eyebrows and wide eyes.

"But anyone can do it with continuous practice. It starts by not having any attachment to this world and by being mindful of thought and intention. When I started, I realized my diet also changed. I ate better. Nothing processed. Very little meat. More water. It's a mind-body-soul thing. It's constant work, but it's not impossible, once you start it," said Jan, like a sage.

"Do you think that's what Buddhism was trying to teach us?" asked Salvador and leaned over to help Jan cut holes in the stems of the daisies, then said with a smile: "I suppose you shouldn't have plucked them. Mother Earth is suffering enough already."

"God knows. Only the avatars throughout history know what they were trying to teach us. The nature of their original teachings has been lost over the years. The rest is conjecture, I suppose," said Jan, without responding to Salvador's sarcasm.

Jan finished making her bracelet then reclined to sleep, before Mr. West's funeral the following day. The next morning after breakfast, Jan and Sal conducted a small ceremony, that was led by prayers from Sal, for Mr. West's journey through to his next incarnation. They let Mr. West's ashes get blown by the wind, on Glastonbury Hill, where they came to camp. Down the hill, various tents had been pitched, and the campers were rousing from their sleep under the chill English morning sun that brought a promise to people that received it, like a dose of drugs. People were smiling, and the morning commotion was unintrusive, remarkably relaxing.

After the funeral ceremony, Jan and Sal returned to settle in their tent, as they awaited further news from Susan, Toni and hopefully Jim. It wouldn't be long before they would be joined by their friends, but Jan's work had already begun. Just as they were organizing their belongings inside the large tent, menacing large and imposing legs in black jeans appeared at the entrance. Jan moved her arm to alert Salvador:

´´Hey, morning," came the voice.

´´What do you want?" asked Salvador, promptly and sharply.

"I came to say thanks and I brought some of my friends, who I think you can help. That's if you want to," came the response.

Jan looked up at Sal from where she was sitting, and Sal held out his palm, to motion to Jan to remain seated:

"Here, I've brought my friend along, who could really do with your help. She can't see. I'd like you to help her see," shouted the woman, politely.

"Oh, come on now," said Salvador, throwing his hands up in the air, in frustration.

"I mean, she can see. I don't mean she's blind. She can perceive. But she can't see. She can't see what she needs to see to sail the seas of her life," said the woman with the pink hair.

"Okay, okay." said Jan, then continued: "But I need to rest first. It takes up a lot of my energy. Come back in an hour, and I'll be ready!"

"What? What? What? What are you doing?" asked Sal, when the pink-haired woman left with her friend, down the hill.

"Why not? It's just one person. It will impact her life, then the world around her through her. Just from one person. That's all it takes!" said Jan, tired. She stretched out her hand.

"But what about detachment? You're getting too involved. How is this being detached?" interrogated Sal.

"That's not what I meant, Sal!" said Jan.

"Well, we have work to do here! And where are you friends? Aren't they coming?" asked Sal, changing the subject.

"I haven't heard from them," said Jan.

"Maybe we should prepare to meet them first, instead!" Sal insisted.

Jan ignored Sal and went into her bag, to grab items and began to freshen up, pouring a bottle of water to wash her face and brush her teeth. Jan's phone then beeped with a message from Susan:

"She's just landed," said Salvador, after pulling Jan's phone off the ground and reading it: "Susan's just landed!" he said, in excitement.

"Who else is with her?" asked Jan, drying her face with her towel.

"Toni!" replied Salvador.

"Anyone else?" asked Jan, with a deep, disappointed sighing embrace.

Before Jan had time to dwell, the woman returned and Jan got herself prepared, to cure the woman who walked up to her, and sit next to her. Jan put her hand on the woman's friend's head and closed her eyes. Within a moment, the woman's friend opened her eyes and stood up and said:

"Thank you," before walking off, in a daze.

"What did you do?" said Salvador.

"I just opened her Third Eye. Depending on who she is, that might go in either one of two ways - either she freaks out or she just accepts what she sees," said Jan, with forced disclosure, as she got up from the entrance of the tent.

They saw their first converts, the two women, one with pink hair and the other her friend, walk down the hill with their arms in the air, embracing the sky. At the bottom of the hill, people were waking up, from their tents. After beholding the sight before them, one of the festival goers said:

"What happened? Are you okay? Can we help you with anything"

"Yes," said the woman. "That woman on the hill has cured me," she cried, off and away.

"Oh, no Jan. I don't think that was a good idea," said Sal, looking down at the commotion down the hill and Jan's first disciples, who were pointing up at Jan, with majestic resonance.

Jan and Salvador went back into the tent to contact Susan, but a group of people came and stood outside the tent, to inquire about what had gone on. Sal spoke on Jan's behalf, by claiming ignorance of the two women, dismissing them as cranks, but the small group did not believe him, and pressed further, until Jan came out of the tent, to face them. One of the members of the group stepped forward and extended her hand and said:

"I saw the look in her eyes. I want to see what she saw too!"

Without hesitation, Jan placed her hand on the bowed head of the person that came to her and began to perform her miracle, to open the third eye. With each new person that Jan helped see, they walked away in a daze, some elated, some confused, some bewildered, some angry, all the while Salvador watched on, in continuous incredulity. As Jan proceeded to touch the people, who were lining up for her, she began to feel sick:

"I need to rest now," said Jan, glim.

The line of people now appeared to stretch down below them on the hill, and onto the fields.

Sal was taken aback, and said: "That's it. No more. Turn away. Go home. There's nothing more. Nothing for you, here. Go back. Go home. Go and carry on. Go and carry on with your own lives!"

"Who are you to tell us?" said one of the members, waiting to be awakened from their sleep.

Sal rolled his eyes, turned around to create space between them and the crowd, but not before one of them in line grabbed him by his arm, and said: "Tell us, you're our friend!"

"Look, there's nothing here for you. It's all in your head!" echoed Jan, to block the demand.

"What you're searching for isn't going to come from her. It is already in you! It comes from You! YOU just need to find it!" shouted Salvador.

Salvador threw his fists in the air, in Jan's direction and stopped himself from saying:

"God, will you just shut up!"

"Show us. Show us!" said a man, as he grew in desperation. The crowd around him began to chant the same song.

As the crowd began to bay and tug at Salvador, the pink-haired woman appeared again: "YOU have to do the work. She can help you, but you need to be in the right frame of mind. If she helps to make you see, and you are driven by the wrong motives, then it could go wrong for you. Are you ready for that?"

"I lost my son last year and I just need to know that moving on and trying to live a normal life is the right thing to do!" said a man.

"Well, what do you think?" asked Jan's former patient, the pink-haired woman.

"I don't know. I'm confused, and my marriage is falling apart." said the man.

"Okay, I'll see if she can see you," said the woman with pink hair.

The man sat in the tent and Jan worked her magic on him. This time, the man ran out wailing, claiming that Jan's work was of the Devil. The crowd went wild and began to lunge forward towards Salvador, who was waiting outside. All of a sudden, clouds began to form over them, causing the crowd to shout at Sal and Jan at their own dispersal, calling them evil.

"Stop! Just stop!" yelled the woman with pink hair, who introduced herself to Jan and Salvador as Lisa: "You were warned. Believe me, when I tell you! She's helped me see, but you need to be prepared to accept what you see. This man here has worked his deceit on Jan, and now he is paying for it. His intentions were not honest. You need to work with pure intentions!"

After the rabble died down, in and around them, Lisa asked: "Who here can honestly tell me why you want to be able to see?"

"Because we are tired of being told lies by our government!" shouted one person.

"Because I am sick of being told I'm a nobody!" shouted another.

"Because I am frustrated of nothing working for me!" shouted another person.

"Because I hate living the way I do!" added another.

"You see, all of your motives are not good. You are only serving your selves! You need to think of why you want to be awakened.... but for the benefit of others. NOT just for yourself. It's not about YOURself!" shouted Lisa, with both palms cupped around her mouth.

The crowd dispersed to the roar of thunder that came from the ground, underneath the tent, on top of the hill. Jan's tent rose off the ground and placed itself back again, with a baying crowd at the sight of it, causing them to disperse - whilst calling out *the work of the Devil* they saw before them. Fear swept the crowd, but a handful stayed, to witness the commotion, eventually running forward, towards Jan, Sal and Lisa, to ask them if they could be of assistance:

"There's trouble brewing. We need you to help stop the forces that are about to be unleashed!" said Sal.

""What are you talking about?" said a member of the crowd.

Lisa pointed to the sky and said: "Look up there! It looks like hell is going to be unleashed!"

A large cloud appeared above Glastonbury Hill, which appeared to double up in size and change shape, turning into a disc like-object, which appeared as the sky at first sight, eventually revealing itself to be silvery-metal in nature, with its own form that moved in its own manner, under a shiny, reflective disguise. The crowd gasped at the sight and started to run away, in panic down the hill - the rest of the festival-goers were already out of their tents, and gathering their belongings to run:

"Run!" came the cry, and the large disc-shaped craft started to project a beam, on Glastonbury Hill.

Jan, Salvador and Lisa made it to the bottom of the hill and looked up: "Do you know what that is?" yelled Salvador.

"No, but I don't think we should stay here. We need to leave. It feels the same as the dark energy in the temple!" said Jan, to Sal.

"Oh my goodness," said Lisa and pointed to the beam of light that emanated from the craft on top of the hill, where some members of the crowd were walking towards it, calling *take me, take me,* after having dispersed away from it, only moments prior.

A moment later, Jan's phone started to ring. Sal grabbed it from Jan's hand and answered it. It was Susan:

"Hey, where are you?" demanded Susan: "We're here by the entrance, but thousands are running towards us. What is happening?"

"We're over by the hill, to the left of the entrance, about half a mile away from the main stage on your right!"

"Holy shit! What is that?" demanded Susan.

Susan and Toni stood silently still, as people came running towards them at the entrance. Toni took Susan by the hand, and said:

"Come, I have a better idea!"

Toni ran back to the country road, where they had been dropped off by their taxi - the country road was already jammed-packed with cars, trying to escape the vicinity. Toni found the taxi again, amongst the cars in traffic, that chooed to a grid-lock pace, and both Susan and Toni jumped back in:

"Here, take the money. There's a road that cuts to the right, about a mile away. That's as far as we need to go!" shouted Toni: "I saw it on the way here. Here… take the money! Come on…. ! Let's go!"

"Hey man, what's going on? Why is everyone running away?" asked the taxi driver.

Toni looked at Susan, who shook her head: "Nothing, just take us there. Please," said Toni, and threw more money at the driver.

The driver sped down a narrow track, off the main country road. When he came to it, Toni and Susan looked on, along with him, but couldn't see the hill in the distance, pushing their heads back of the cab together, to get a clearer view of the track ahead - what was on Glastonbury Hill that day: "what the fuck is that?" pointed the driver, at the hill, through a thick of drooping trees on the track ahead, that had a clear view to it.

The driver slammed the breaks, and yelled at his passengers to get out. Susan and Toni ran the rest of their course towards the hill, with Susan on the phone to Jan, who ran with Salvador and Lisa, to the fence that lined the farmland, where Toni and Susan had arrived at, a quarter of a mile-away, from Glastonbury Hill:

"What is going on? What is that thing?" yelled Susan, as she and Toni climbed over the fence, to be reunited with their friends.

"They're here to put a stop to it all!" hollered Jan, in the gusts of wind.

"Who are they?" yelled Toni.

"The beings that don't want us to break the grid! They are the controllers of Planet Earth!" said Jan.

"What? What are you talking about?" said Lisa, her incomprehension echoed by the rest of the group.

Jan and her friends quickly regrouped, to think of a plan. Lisa stood away from everyone, looking towards the entrance, a mile away. Jan looked at Lisa and Lisa returned a glance, then joined the rest of the group in their huddle on the ground under a large tree, to try and finalize their quest. Whatever they would have to decide, they would have to do it fast. Jan looked on at Glastonbury Hill, where more people were walking towards it, to the beam of light, from the craft above Glastonbury Hill, before it disappeared into the night:

"What do you think is going to happen to them?" asked Susan, shaking.

"You do not want to know!" said Toni sarcastically: "I have a feeling it's going to be more than an anal probe!"

Jan looked at Toni, then the rest of the group, then told a terrible truth:

"The craft works on consciousness. That beam of light is attracting a specific group of beings. Whatever is in there, needs the souls to survive. It's protecting Glastonbury Hill from being exploded. They won't let us cloud-bust here, though they might. They don't want us to reveal the true reality behind the matrix, without a fight. It will grow stronger as it takes in more souls and feeds on their consciousness."

Toni squinted at Jan and sighed: "What? Girl? Are you out of your mind?"

"It's not in a hurry to move, or do anything. We have time! We could get close, to try and destroy it in the meantime!" shrugged Jan with a grunt and sigh.

"Right!" said Lisa, in astonishment: "And how do you know all of this?"

Susan, Toni and Salvador all looked at Lisa with disbelief, then turned their gaze back at Jan. Without a word, in anticipation of Jan's response, she looked on, in hopelessness, at her friend's faces - without thinking too much - saying:

"I think we need to leave. I need to get away from here, and we need to hatch a proper plan. I can't think, here. It's all too powerful. The pull is too strong. I can't think straight. I can't tap into anything. I can't tap into my instincts. I need to follow my instincts. That craft its…it's messing with my frequencies!"

They sprinted out of the field, down the dirt track, over the main country road that was full of chaos and abandoned cars, down a narrow line of traffic, amidst people fleeing. As they were running down the country road, they came across a B&B and knocked frantically for several minutes, before entering without any force at the back of the property, onlooked by the young cook in the kitchen, who met his incoming party, after all his other guests suddenly packed their belongings and left.

The news on the small screen in the lounge began to circulate of some sort of *event* at Glastonbury Hill, which had people fleeing, calling it *a suspected terrorist attack:*

"It's a media black out!" said Susan.

"It's early days. They'll report on it sooner or later. They won't be able to hide it!" said Toni.

"That's the thing, Toni! Whatever frequency that craft is operating on, it won't be able to be picked up on phones or cameras. Anyone who tries will risk losing their lives by getting too close to it, for a picture. It will be a lot worse than just jamming their TV-equipment!" said Jan.

"We need to try and save them!" said Toni, and Susan returned him a stare.

"We can't!" said Lisa: "Maybe it's all part of the process. Maybe all these old hopeless souls on Earth are meant to leave, to make way for change. Maybe this is it! Maybe this is our Armageddon! Maybe they're here to help Earth clean up!" said Lisa, drifting into a daydream as she spoke.

"What do you mean, we can't save them? Of course, we can! We can try to warn them somehow," said Salvador.

"No, she's right" said Jan in a state of acceptance: "It's like what happened at the hill when they wanted my help. It's too late for a good portion of them. That beam and that craft is like a magnet to those with bad intentions. They would never be able to be saved."

"You mean, it's taking up all the bad people," said Toni, with a smirk, before adding: "that doesn't seem like a bad idea to me!"

"That's the problem, Toni!" interrupted Salvador.

"Why is that?" asked Lisa.

"Haven't you been listening?" said Susan: "That thing is feeding on consciousness and will grow in power. The more bad people get swallowed up, the stronger it will grow. We can only hope that there are some good people left that get swallowed up!"

"Otherwise, it's game over!" said Jan fatalistically, a deep sigh which she guessed might be her last.

The news reports began to dominate every channel, but the narrative didn't change. The TV was muted by the young barman, who left his new patrons to drink and eat and plan alone in the bar's lounge, and shrugged his shoulders as he left the B&B by the front door, before crossing the road, in the direction of the field ahead, in a trance-like state, towards the light that hovered from the craft, directly towards it, that shone from under the craft, that was fixed in position over Glastonbury Hill, for all the souls that were being drawn to it.

Toni sat with Salvador, to fill him in on his own life over the previous months, since Jan embarked on a journey to change the world for everyone. Meanwhile, Jan sat in the other corner of the bar-lounge, where Susan and Lisa made tense-talk over several drinks, at the vacant bar, where they helped themselves to anything, to toast in the end of their world:

"We've been followed and chased ever since Jan and Mr. West came to visit me. They wanted to stop her!" said Salvador, between gulps of brandy.

"Where's Mr. West?" asked Toni, sipping his Gin and adding Tonic from a glass bottle, to taste.

"He died," said Salvador, with another shot.

"Oh shit. What about his wife?" asked Toni, placing his glass carefully down on the coaster, careful not to leave a ring.

"She doesn't know yet. Mr. West made Jan promise to only tell it to her face, back in California," said Salvador, with a deep exhale.

"That's deep," said Toni, then looked away.

"Look! There's a crowd outside the fields, with candles. It seems they are camped there in a vigil," said Susan, pointing out the B&B's bay window.

"This is bloody ridiculous! This is why they think they can easily control us! Just look at them! Pathetic!" said Lisa, facing the window, hands on both hips.

"If they get swallowed up, I won't have any sympathy!" exclaimed Susan.

A sullen Jan got up from her corner of the bar-room and walked out of the pub, through the empty kitchen at the back, to the door they ran through earlier, for shelter. The small car park that was lined with trees was empty and Jan took a seat at the steps of the building, putting her hands on her face and her head down, sobbing an empty blob of regret. The journey she had been on was coming to an end. And Jan was out of her depth. She couldn't save everyone, nor change people, nor save the planet.

Her stomach hurt, she leaned forward in pain. Then Jan remembered that she was pregnant. Three months pregnant, in fact. Something she had overlooked during her mission, neglecting the fact that she needed to look after herself. She curled up in agony, on the ground, looking up at the night sky and the stars that tried to shine through it. The hustle of the traffic on the road at the front of the house began to die down, as Jan slowly blinked her eyes to their final painful flutter.

Meanwhile, her friends inside the B&B made good use of their talk, whilst they watched the little TV, set up high in the corner, for the news. After a while, they talked about being hungry and made their way to the kitchen. Whilst eating their slapdash meal of breads and vegetables, they realized that the most important member of their party, the whole reason they were all together, in that place, at that time, under those circumstances, was missing - prompting them to search the property, from top to bottom. After their search, they found their leader - Jan Lam - had gone missing.

Back in the kitchen, a bright light shone through the window, shielding their eyes to hide from it, until Salvador noticed the familiar flashes that had accompanied Jan when she disappeared in Tibet, and hopped into her own craft. A globular sphere of energy hung over the tree in the car park, bulbing out and shrinking down, as if it was a ball of energy that was bubbling in the ethers, detached from the world but a part of it.

Salvador looked out the kitchen window, into the car park and recognized the ball of light that was descending. He ran out to the car park, to find Jan being carried up in the craft, the globular sphere craft that had also turned her into a sphere being of several inter-changing colors - reds, oranges, yellows, greens, blues, purples and silvers.

Jan woke up inside the craft on a table, and gone was the pain she had felt just moments earlier. When she got up to look around her, Jan was struck by the familiarity of the interior, as if she had been there before. A tall being with pale blue-skin and big, friendly eyes entered the chamber, in the craft. After a medical check with an apparatus, the tall blue- being then handed Jan a silver cylindrical object, with a pointed tip:

"Take this and save your planet," said the blue being, who smiled at Jan with big, black, bulbous eyes.

Jan took the cloud-buster from the being's long hands and delicate fingers, and held it close to her chest. Jan looked down at her stomach, then back at the being:

"We could only save you," telepathed the being, with kind eyes that told Jan everything she needed to know about her unborn child.

Jan held the weapon close to her chest, to comfort her, as tears ran down her cheeks at the news. Her destiny was to change the world. She knew it and accepted it. Accepted everything she already did but didn't want to accept. A life of domesticity with Jim would have to wait. She was told it, as she was handed her weapon, which she placed in a holder, on the strap of her bag, around her chest, down to her waist. With the cloud-buster close to her chest, the life Jan imagined with Jim slipped away in an instant, and she was returned within a blink of an eye, back to the car park, to her friends, who were waiting for her, when she fell back out, out of her craft again.

After Jan appeared out of thin-air on the ground, she was helped up by friends, who dusted her off, saying:

"Come on, we have work to do!"

Jan led them all to the base of Glastonbury Hill, past the crowds who were standing in vigil with incense and candles. Jan looked up at the craft, then at her friends, and screamed out to the universe:

"ARE YOU READY FOR A NEW EARTH?"

Jan's friends formed a circle, with eyes closed, holding hands to match their vibrations, which they collectively did, to raise their frequencies, which created a bubble of protection around them, a bubble that soon turned into a sphere of bright light that glowed bright, brighter than the beam from the craft over Glastonbury Hill. When they were all in Jan's spherical craft, Jan moved to the bow inside it and fired her first shot, at the craft that was projecting a beam above Glastonbury Hill.

The craft fired a shot in return, in their direction, which missed Jan and her friends, but left a hole in the black night sky behind them, as if it had punched a hole in Earth's ionosphere. Earth's sky began to illuminate, in different colors, rapidly shifting from reds, to murky yellows, to greens, then blues, and purples. The moon offered a slither of silver clouds around it, under it, above it, behind it, in a halo around it. The moon stood round proud, solitary, in the sky, above Glastonbury Hill, that night.

The world looked on that night. Outside the purview of those that never look up at the night, a cosmic battle unfolded. When the moon appeared in fullness at night, it was surrounded by the ringed energy of an invisible planet. The roundness of the absent shape behind the moon was accented by silver clouds that formed a bright rim, like an aperture in the sky, behind the bright full moon, with the invisible planet behind it.

The crowds on the ground at Glastonbury Hill looked on, at the new dimensions of the true world being unveiled. Numerous unidentified aerial phenomena appeared from the sides of the visible invisible planet, then entered Earth's atmosphere. Jan's craft was joined by others - some spherical, some oblong, some winged - like hers - that danced a merry dance with hers, in the ethers of Planet Earth.

Mr. West's book was complete, the grid was broken, and a New Earth was unveiled.

THE END

About the Author

Enn Kae is a seer, a visionary. He writes to free humanity from their shackles. His writings resonate with the struggle between the human spirit and the fabrications of this world, and technology.

Acknowledgements

I would like to thank Kate Bush, for inspiring this work, who was in turn inspired by Peter Reich, the son of Wilhelm Reich. I would also like to thank Nikola Tesla, for having graced his presence on Earth. We have a lot to learn from our human ancestors. Aside from my friends from Illinois, whom I met nearly 30 years ago, some of whom inspired the characters in this book, all other characters are fictional.